Benita Brown was born and brought up in Newcastle by her English mother, who was the youngest of thirteen children, and her Indian father, who came to Newcastle to study medicine, and fell in love with the place and the people. Even at drama school, in London, Benita felt the pull of the north-east, as she married a man from Newcastle who worked at the BBC. Not long after, the couple returned to their home town and, after working as a teacher and broadcaster and bringing up four children, Benita became a full-time writer. Her previous novels, A DREAM OF HER OWN, ALL OUR TOMORROWS, HER RIGHTFUL INHERITANCE and IN LOVE AND FRIENDSHIP, are also available from Headline.

Also by Benita Brown

A Dream of Her Own
All Our Tomorrows
Her Rightful Inheritance
In Love and Friendship

The Captain's Daughters

Benita Brown

headline

First published in 2004
by HEADLINE BOOK PUBLISHING

First published in paperback in 2005
by HEADLINE BOOK PUBLISHING

3

ISBN 978-0-755-30167-6

Typeset in Times by Avon DataSet Ltd,
Bidford-on-Avon, Warwickshire

Printed and bound in the UK by
CPI Group (UK) Ltd, Croydon, CR0 4YY

Headline's policy is to use papers that are natural, renewable and
recyclable products and made from wood grown in sustainable
forests. The logging and manufacturing processes are expected to
conform to the environmental regulations of the country of origin.

HEADLINE BOOK PUBLISHING
A division of Hodder Headline
338 Euston Road
London NW1 3BH

www.headline.co.uk
www.hodderheadline.com

To Norman, as always,
and to my two new grandchildren,
Mae and Gabriel

Part One

As is the mother, so is her daughter . . .

Ezekiel, Chapter 16 verse 44

Chapter One

Northumberland, April 1864

'Please let me stay – just a day or two longer!'

Effie Walton rose from her seat at the kitchen table and crossed to where her mother sat in the fireside chair. She kneeled down and grasped Hannah's work-roughened hands in her own. 'Don't make me go back – not yet.'

Hannah looked at her daughter and she knew she'd find it hard to refuse her. Effie was so bonny, with shining golden hair and huge blue eyes. And the way she could look at you, just like a bairn did, made her appear vulnerable. Dressed in a simple grey skirt and plain white blouse with no adornments, she looked like a schoolgirl. You would never think that she was nineteen years old, and the mother of that great lump of a child sitting on the hearthrug, crooning wordlessly to her rag doll and holding it as tenderly as if it were a real baby.

Where on earth did Josie come from? She was not a bit like her graceful mother. The child was solid and clumsy; not exactly ugly, but only her soft baby features and her large brown eyes saved her from being downright plain. She was dark-skinned and long-limbed like her father. As well as his eyes she had his dark wavy hair. Hannah could only hope that, as she grew, she would also prove to have Samuel Walton's keen intelligence. She already had his forbearing nature.

'Ma, say something,' Effie said. 'Don't you want me to stay with you?'

Hannah looked down into her daughter's face. The warmth of the fire had brought a slight flush to her cheeks and the light

3

of the dancing flames gleamed in her hair. 'Of course I'd like you to stay with me a while longer. You and the bairn,' she added pointedly, 'but Samuel will be home soon from the sea and he has every right to expect his wife to be waiting for him.'

Effie snatched her hands away and, dropping her head, she covered her face with them. 'Samuel!' she muttered through spread fingers.

Hannah caught the barely suppressed anguish and frowned uneasily. 'Whisht, lass.' She lowered her voice although there was no one apart from two-year-old Josie to hear them. 'Tell me . . . he doesn't . . . he's not . . . I mean he treats you right, doesn't he?'

Effie lowered her hands and looked up. Hannah was dismayed to see tears glistening in her daughter's eyes. Instinctively she moved forward but Effie rocked back on her heels and raised her chin.

'And if I said that Samuel Walton is a wife beater? What would you do?'

Hannah stared at her, taking in the defiant stare. Then, 'I don't believe it,' she said quietly. 'And divven't talk like that in front of Josie.'

Effie shrugged impatiently. 'For goodness' sake, she can't understand a word of this; she's just a baby.'

'She's not a baby; she's two years old, and just because she never says nowt you'd be mistaken to think she doesn't understand what folk are talking about. She's got a very knowing look.'

Unwillingly, it seemed, Effie turned her head to look at her daughter. The child had fallen back amongst the cushions Hannah had placed on the floor and, still clutching her doll, she had fallen asleep.

'I know she has.' Effie seemed to shudder. 'Sometimes just looking at her unnerves me. She . . . she seems so wise.'

'Don't you . . .?' Hannah hesitated. 'Don't you love your daughter?'

'Of course I do!' Effie sounded genuinely indignant. 'It's just . . . it's just that she's so like her father,' she finished bleakly.

The two women looked at each other. The only sounds in the family kitchen of the old village inn were the crackling of

4

the coals in the hearth and the wind keening down from the hills and buffeting against the windows.

'You don't love your husband,' Hannah said at last. 'That's it, isn't it?'

Effie didn't answer her.

'Why?' her mother asked. 'I don't understand. I can't believe that Samuel would treat a woman badly. He would never do anything to hurt you. He worships the very ground you walk on. Why, he even shaved off his fine black beard just to please you.'

'I know, I know!' Effie's cry was anguished. 'But, Ma, I just don't love him. He's so . . . old.'

'He's thirty-two!'

'That's old!'

'And he's a good, hard-working and kindly man.'

'And so boring!'

Hannah was surprised. 'How can you say he's boring? His letters to you are full of the places he's been and the wonders he's seen. And when he comes home he brings you such bonny fine presents.'

'And all he can talk about are his plans for the future.'

'What's wrong with that?'

'Don't you understand? When he's away at sea I'm left alone with a small child for months on end. When he comes home I want to go out, have some fun. We can afford it. But Samuel says we've got to save for the future, and, anyway, he's had enough travelling for the moment and all he wants to do is stay at home with his wife.'

'That's natural. Any man would be the same.'

'And just like any man there's only one thing he wants to do.' She paused and slanted a look up at Hannah as if making sure that the older woman had caught her meaning. Then she declared, 'Oh, Ma, I can't bear it!'

Hannah stared at her daughter in consternation. 'I can't help you, Effie,' she said, shaking her head, 'if it's that side of things that's upsetting you. I can only remind you that it's your duty to – to please him.'

'Duty!' Effie glared at her mother with outraged eyes.

'Aye, duty, and it's a small price you have to pay for a good husband.'

Effie suddenly dropped her head on to her mother's lap and broke into a storm of weeping. Helplessly Hannah began to stroke her daughter's bright hair. 'Whisht, me bairn,' she said. 'It can't be as bad as that. Samuel Walton strikes me as a man that would be gentle with a woman.'

Effie's shoulders convulsed and she said, 'He is.'

'Then what's the matter?' Hannah was beginning to lose patience.

'I told you. He's boring.'

Hannah sensed what her daughter was hinting at and shied away from it. 'But you were so keen to marry him,' she said. 'You seemed to find him . . . attractive.'

'Oh, he's handsome enough – in a sober sort of way. And, yes, I did want to marry him – very much. But that was because I was flattered that such a man was paying me attention when . . . well, you know . . . Oh, Ma, I had my head turned. Who wouldn't have? But I was so young – only sixteen. Why didn't you try and stop me?'

'I did try.'

'Not very hard.'

'Have I ever been able to stop you doing anything you wanted to do, Effie?'

Suddenly Effie dropped her head. She couldn't meet her mother's eyes. 'Well, why didn't my father stop me? He could have done if he'd wanted to.'

Hannah sighed. 'Yes, you always took more notice of your da. But why should he have refused to let you marry the man? He thought Captain Walton would be a grand match for you.'

'I was just a child.'

'So you keep saying, but you were old enough to marry and now the deed's done. There's no going back, Effie. You must pack your belongings tonight and return to your own house tomorrow. You've already delayed too long.'

Hannah expected another outburst, but instead her daughter rose swiftly to her feet and, snatching her shawl from the back of a chair, she wrapped it round her shoulders and made for the door that led into the inn yard.

'Where are you going?' Hannah asked.

'Out!'

The door opened briefly and a swirl of dust and chaff from the inn's stables blew in across the stone-flagged floor before it slammed shut again. Josie stirred amongst the nest of cushions and opened her eyes. She saw her grandmother looking at her and she rubbed her eyes and then smiled. Impulsively Hannah rose from her chair and stooped to gather the bairn up in her arms.

Effie had gone without a glance at her own child. Oh, she would know that Josie would be safe enough, that her grandmother would mind her until she got back. But it disturbed Hannah how casual her daughter's attitude towards motherhood was. And yet the bairn seemed to be no worse for it. Josie was not neglected in any material way. She was well fed, clean and well dressed – but then Effie had always been particular about her own appearance. Hannah couldn't imagine that, however dissatisfied with her life she might be, she would let her house or her child go dirty.

And she would never be deliberately cruel. But after everything had been done properly there was never anything extra given: no special smile, no cuddles, no time stolen to sit and rock by the fire before she was put to bed at night. Strange, then, that already Josie seemed to be such a loving and motherly little creature. She didn't torment the kittens as some bairns do; she let them climb up on her knee in their own time and stroked them gently. And she'd just about loved her rag doll to pieces, singing to it, cradling it in her chubby arms and talking to it endlessly with half-formed words.

'Hawway, pet,' Hannah said to her granddaughter, 'it's a bit soon after dinner but you and me's going to hev a dish of tea and a slice of bread and jam. I made the jam meself afore Christmas with the last of the plums and the apples.'

She smiled to herself when she realized she was talking to Effie's daughter as if she were a grown-up, but the way the child looked at her with big brown eyes, and listened so intently, it was hard not to believe that she understood every single thing that was said to her.

Hannah sat Josie at the kitchen table, the biggest cushion squashed into her husband's wooden armchair, and now the bairn watched her with solemn dark eyes as she spooned tea into the old brown pot and carried it to where the kettle steamed gently on the hearth.

'Babba,' Josie said, and Hannah turned to find her pointing towards the cushions on the hearth rug.

'What's that? Oh, you want your doll. What do you call her? Susan, isn't it?'

Hannah carried the doll back to the table and Josie clutched it contentedly as she watched her grandmother slice the bread and spread it thick with butter and jam.

The room was quiet with just the two of them. Hannah's husband, Jack Dixon, was through in the main room of the inn looking after his customers and that's where she should have been if Effie hadn't run off the way she had. Hannah glanced at the window and wondered where her daughter had gone. She could guess.

She would be off to the ruined cottage where she'd played as a child. Where she and Ralph Lowther had played for hours when they were bairns. What bonny bairns they'd been – more like brother and sister than distant cousins – both so fair and lithe and full of devilment.

Hannah couldn't help smiling when she remembered the pair of them. Ralph had loved coming here to the inn to sit at this very table and share Effie's meal. Hannah had suspected that the attraction was the wholesome food as much as wanting to be with Effie. When he'd been a little lad Ralph had almost lived at the old inn and many a time Jack had had to carry him home, over the hilltop to that draughty mansion, Four Winds Hall, only to find that his parents had barely missed him; hadn't even known that he'd been gone.

But when he'd got a little older he'd been sent off to boarding school. Effie had gone to the village school. She'd proved a good scholar and she'd worked hard, but she lived for the holidays when Ralph would come home and they could run wild across the hills again.

Hannah hadn't known until it was almost too late that the childhood friendship had changed into something deeper. At least on Effie's part. She had failed as a mother. If she'd been more observant perhaps she could have saved Effie the heart-ache of that summer . . . the summer she had turned sixteen.

Effie hadn't told her much, of course – too much pride. But Hannah had soon guessed that her daughter's stormy moods and bouts of angry weeping had something to do with the guests at Four Winds Hall. The prosperous London merchant Nicholas Richardson and his wife with their daughter, Caroline.

And then Samuel Walton had come to stay at the inn in the village of Moorburn. A seafaring man from Newcastle, he had taken a fancy to walking the highways and byways of his own countryside when he was home from his travels. He had arrived at the Bluebell Inn with his haversack and his boots and maps, and announced his intention of making it his headquarters while he explored the surrounding hills.

Captain Walton had been a considerate guest. No trouble at all, in fact. He'd enjoyed Hannah's generous country fare and encouraged Jack to tell him the local tales and legends. He'd taken it in good part when the village menfolk had mocked him gently about his expensive walking clothes and his compass.

'Now divven't you get lost, Captain, hinny,' they would tease when they saw him setting out. 'We shouldn't like to think of a man who's sailed all around the world and back going astray in the Cheviots where there's nowt but sheep to tell you the way!'

At first Effie hadn't even noticed him. Or so she'd pretended. And as for the way the captain looked at her – well, he was like a man who has seen an angel. That's the only way Hannah could think to describe it. After a while he began to try to talk to her, with little success.

Then one morning after breakfast he had spread his maps out on the table in the inn parlour and seemed to take longer than usual to mark out his route for the day. Every now and then he would look up and frown and then pore over the map again, tracing a way with his fingers. If it was an act it had worked. Effie went up to the table curiously and asked if he needed help.

Hannah said afterwards that she could almost hear the poor man's heart beating when he looked up at Effie and smiled. They sat together for a while and Hannah watched as Effie bent over the map and seemed to be showing him the way. He kept shaking his head and pretending he didn't understand. By now Hannah was sure that it was pretence and she wasn't at all surprised when Effie announced a little while later that she was going to show Captain Walton the way to the waterfall.

'Shall I pack up some bait for you?' her mother had asked.

'No, I'm only going as far as the old cottage, then I can point out the way and come back.'

Effie had kept her word. But when she returned to the inn the lines of misery had eased from her face and she was even smiling. Then, gradually, Effie's mood had changed. Instead of moping about or sulking in her room she had offered to help her mother, especially when looking after their guest, who started taking shorter and shorter walks and spending more time with his feet under the table. Eventually, even Jack had noticed that the handsome stranger was paying court to their daughter.

Hannah sighed when she remembered how pleased she and Jack had been when Effie and Captain Walton had come to them one evening after the pots were washed and asked their permission to marry. Jack had done the right thing – he'd said that Effie needed time to think and that the captain should come back after his next voyage and see if the lass felt the same way. Effie had sulked but Samuel, bless him, had taken her aside and told her that her father was quite right.

The next few months were spent in a fever of preparation. It seemed as though Effie didn't want to allow herself time to think. They married the next time Samuel came home from sea.

Now, the coals shifted and settled in the hearth as a gust of wind rattled the window and blew soot down the chimney. Hannah shook her head as she thought of her headstrong daughter running wild on the hillside as she'd done when she was a child. When would Effie accept that now she was a grown woman with a bairn of her own? Hannah saw that the little one was watching her and she summoned a smile. Poor Josie, how on earth did she manage to be so happy and good-natured when the father who doted on her was away at sea for months on end and her mother barely acknowledged her existence?

* * *

Halfway up the hill Effie stopped and turned to look down. The pale spring sunshine cast a watery glow on the grey slate roofs of the village below. Smoke rose from every chimney, to be caught by the wind and tossed up to join the clouds racing across the sky. But at least the smoke was dispersed. She couldn't smell it – it didn't fill her nostrils as it did at home in Wallsend.

Home? Was that really her home now? Her tidily comfortable house was in a fine square at the top of the hill. But below the square row upon row of cobbled streets lurched down towards the River Tyne. Narrow terraced dwellings housed large families of tired-looking people, many of them dirty and ragged.

The working day began before daylight. The air rang with the hammering and clanging from the many shipyards. The evil odours from the rope works and the tannery pressed down upon the huddled dwellings and even the rain was black with greasy soot.

Effie raised her face towards the sky and closed her eyes as she breathed in the sweet country air. The only sounds were the rustling of the wind through the grass and the bleating of the sheep on the hillsides. She felt faint drops of moisture on her face. It was trying to rain. Good! She hoped the heavens would open and she would get soaked and catch a chill. Then, surely her mother wouldn't send her back to Samuel Walton!

And then another sound made her open her eyes and look down. The whistle of a train. Far below she could see the white steam rising as the train made its way along the valley bottom next to the river. It was the same river that ran past the bottom of the street where she lived with Samuel but, here, the waters were clean and sweet and sparkling as they rushed and gurgled over the stony bed, whereas by the time it had reached Wallsend it was murky and putrid, filled with human and industrial waste before it spilled its turgid contents into the North Sea.

Effie watched for a moment as three small children and a dog raced along the road that led through the village and to the station half a mile beyond. The children were waving to the passengers on the train while the dog leaped up and down, its feathered tail circling with furious joy. Someone on the train was waving back to them. Effie could see something white, a handkerchief perhaps, at one of the windows.

And then, remembering how, if her mother had her way, she and Josie would have to board a train tomorrow at that very same station, Effie turned and fled further up the steep path towards the ruined cottage.

The earth floor of the main room was fouled with sheep and rabbit droppings. Birds nesting in the decaying rafters had left their mark on the rough stone walls. It had been like this for years. No one could remember the last time the cottage had been habitable, although Effie's mother had told her that, when she was a girl, the village children had believed a witch had taken shelter there; and they had tormented her.

Hannah told Effie how they would gather outside and scream abuse, yelling things like, 'Old granny witch, couldn't catch a stitch!' And then, when the poor old thing emerged, shaking her broom at them, they would flee, helter-skelter down the hillside, laughing fit to bust.

Then, one wintry day, it turned nasty. The old woman managed to swing her broom and catch one of the smaller lads across his backside. He slipped and fell on the rough frosty grass, catching his shins on the sharp edge of a boulder. Bawling and furious, he scrambled up and yelled, 'I hope the devil takes you and I hope you burn in hell! That's what happens to witches!'

A few nights later the folk in the village looked up the hillside to see a fierce red glow against the cold black sky. Unwilling at first, eventually some of the men, urged by their wives, went to see if the old beggar-wife needed help. By the time they arrived it was too late. They buried the remains of the old woman in an unmarked grave at the expense of the parish, and the soot-blackened hulk of the cottage was left to rot even further.

In all probability the old woman had caused the fire herself, perhaps heaping too many logs on her hearth in an effort to keep warm. But there were those who believed that some lads from the village had set the fire in petty revenge. Whatever the truth of it, after that no one went near the place. Until Effie and Ralph made it their own secret den as children.

There was a smaller room at the back almost untouched by the fire. They had cleared some of the rubble and brought bits and pieces from their respective homes. It had been easier for Ralph. Many of the rooms at Four Winds Hall were unused for most of the year and the furniture lay covered in dust sheets. A footstool, a folding card table, an old tapestry, a Persian rug – none of them had been missed.

Ralph had smuggled them out at night, lugging them across the moor top and down the hillside by moonlight to surprise Effie the next morning. Sometimes Effie wondered about the strange life he led and wondered whether he, like the household goods he'd made off with, would ever be missed if he didn't return.

Effie had brought more mundane offerings to their pretend house: bowls, plates, cups and an old blanket that she'd found at the bottom of the linen press. She also brought food. Once Hannah realized what was going on and was convinced that it was harmless enough, she had allowed Effie to take bread and cheese and homemade cakes and a container of milk. Ralph, always hungry, it seemed, in spite of his parents' supposed wealth, could contribute nothing to their feasts.

All these years later Effie could still remember how happy they'd been doing not much at all – simply talking and eating like two healthy little animals in their own lair, and sometimes, when they were replete, falling asleep curled up together on the old blanket.

How innocent they'd been. They had imagined that it would go on like this for ever, that they would always be friends. Perhaps Effie, as she began to leave childhood behind, began to dream of something more. There might be another home that they would share one day . . .

But she was only just starting to consider that wonderful possibility when Ralph – or rather his parents – had spoiled it all.

So she'd married Samuel Walton.

The rain that had been threatening began to fall. Effie went into the cottage and entered the small back room. Some of the furniture she and Ralph had smuggled there as children had gone – taken, no doubt, by passing vagrants.

13

But the rug was still there, and Effie crouched down and removed the cloth she had placed over a small wooden chest. Inside the chest was a cake wrapped in a cloth, and a bottle of brandy-wine. She'd brought them here days ago, certain that, as Ralph knew she was staying at the inn, he would come here to see her.

Why hadn't he come?

She knew he was at Four Winds Hall. He'd been there a week now. The gossip in the village was that he'd quarrelled with his parents and he was there alone, apart from the servants. His parents were at their house in London. They spent more and more time there and, considering the state of the Hall, who could blame them? So there was no one to restrict his move-ments – not that they ever had done. So why hadn't he come to this old childhood haunt? He must have known that she'd be there waiting for him.

Effie crouched down by the hearth. Now that the sky had clouded over the day had grown cold. Did she dare light a fire? The smoke from the chimney would be seen from the village. But did that matter? Now and then a tinker or two would make their home here – strangers, people who didn't know that the place was supposed to be haunted by the ghost of a poor old woman. Local people kept away.

She kneeled down and began to clean out the hearth with the battered old fire irons that had lain there since she and Ralph were children. They'd never bothered to hide them and, if any passing stranger had made good use of them, they'd been welcome.

She'd known she was going to do this, of course. Why else had she brought old paper, orange peel and bundles of sticks? Why else over the past few weeks had she brought in logs, one at a time, and hidden them under a pile of stones? She had lain awake at nights in her old childhood room at the inn, praying that Ralph would come home from London while she was here. They would meet at the cottage as they had when they were children and they would eat and talk by the fire and they would . . .

What would they do?

Burning with shame at her imaginings Effie had suppressed

the sound of her weeping lest she awaken Josie . . . Samuel Walton's child.

Why hadn't Ralph come? Perhaps he thought that now she was a married woman she wouldn't want to see her old friend. No . . . even that day when he had told her that his parents wanted him to make a grand marriage, he had said they would always be friends. That nothing would make him forget her.

She took a match from the box and set fire to the kindling. Ralph would see the smoke. He would realize she was waiting. Surely he would come to her.

As the fire sparked and slowly came to life Effie sat back and took an envelope from her pocket. Samuel's letter had arrived the very day that Ralph Lowther had returned to Four Winds Hall. She'd waited all these months hoping that he would come home, and when he had, this hateful letter had arrived at the same time. Even without knowing its contents her mother had told her that she had lingered long enough; and that she must go back to her husband's home. But how could she without seeing Ralph?

Perhaps it was a sense of guilt that made her torture herself by taking out the letter and reading it again.

My dearest wife,

I send this from Bristol to tell you that I will be home with you and little Josie very soon. I have been away so long this time that I fear the child will think me a stranger. I hope you have been talking to her about me, showing her the portrait, telling her that the solemn-looking man in uniform is the father who loves her and who thinks of her every day that God sends. As I do you.

As you know, our cargo of earthenware, bottles and fine Newcastle glass was destined for New York. We had a rough crossing with mountainous seas. Even the most seaworthy of my crew, the experienced old hands, were glad when we made safe harbour.

How sad I was to be away from you and my little daughter at Christmastide. The Johansen family of New York made me welcome, as always. I believe I've told you about them. Mr Johansen is a ship's chandler, an honest one. No weak barrels or poor wine that turns to vinegar to be had from his store. Over the years I have become a friend as well as a valued customer.

Well, there I was, warm and snug, an honoured guest in his fine dwelling. He and his wife looked after me well in spite of their worries about their eldest son, Ethan, who was wounded at the battle of Chickamauga. But at least they have him home now, a hero who fought for the Union. And let us pray to God that the war that is dividing this great country will soon be over.

In spite of the luxury to be had at the Johansens' home, I found myself thinking constantly of my own modest house and how I would rather be there with my two angels.

After leaving New York we sailed north for Boston to take on our return cargo of wheat and best American cured bacon and cheese, which was to be discharged at Bristol.

Where I am now!

How I long to see the mouth of the Tyne again. God willing, that will be in just one week. And this time, my darling, I have some good news for you.

Give little Josie a hug and a kiss from her loving father, and much love to you, my dear wife, from,

Your own Samuel

Effie frowned as she raised her eyes to stare into the fire. What could the good news be? Command of a larger vessel, which would mean more money to put in the bank? That was what good news meant to Samuel.

She glanced back at the letter and chewed on her lip anxiously. She had read out the interesting parts to her mother and father but she had not read all of it. She had told her mother that Samuel would be home before long, that was all. But if he had set sail from Bristol soon after posting the letter, Effie knew he could already be waiting in the house in Wallsend and wondering why she had not returned there. She ought to have packed up and left as soon as receiving it, but how could she have gone once she knew that Ralph Lowther had come home?

Effie began to put the letter back in the envelope and then stopped and gazed at it. Impulsively she screwed it up and threw it on the fire. She watched it burn.

Ralph Lowther stood in the shadows and watched as Effie crouched by the fire, reading something. A lock of hair had escaped from its pins and a smudge of soot marked her cheek where she must have pushed it back impatiently. She was a married woman now, she'd had a child, but her figure was as slender and graceful as it had always been.

He held his breath. She hadn't changed – and neither had his feelings for her. He'd known she was visiting her parents and he'd tried to stay away. But just now, when he'd looked out and seen the thin curl of smoke rising from the chimney of the ruined cottage, a host of memories had overwhelmed him. He'd had to come.

Suddenly Effie screwed up the papers she was holding and threw them in the fire. The paper caught alight and flared and, as it did, he moved forward, half stumbling on a loose stone. Startled, she turned to look. Her eyes widened and she began to rise. Her hands went to her breast as if she was having difficulty breathing. She swayed, and, frightened that she would fall on to the fire, he closed the distance between them.

'I knew you'd come,' she breathed softly before he clasped her in his arms.

He held her close, closer than he'd ever held her before. In fact he couldn't remember a time in the past when they had stood like this, like a man and a woman, straining towards each other, melting against each other with the heat of desire.

Neither spoke. Then, she was the first to move away.

'You took your time!' she said.

'I shouldn't have come.'

'Don't say that! What harm is there? Why shouldn't we meet? We're old friends, aren't we?'

'Friends? We were just bairns . . . playmates.'

Bairns, Effie thought. We're no longer bairns. She looked at Ralph. A bonny lad had grown into a handsome young man.

17

But he was not *her* man. She looked up into his eyes, as blue as her own, and tried to see what he was thinking, but she couldn't.

'We were so close,' she sighed. 'Why did you have to spoil it all?'

'I didn't . . . I mean I didn't mean to.'

'Why did you have to tell me about her? About Caroline?'

'I didn't say I liked her. I just said that my parents were hoping that something would come of it, that in a few years' time we would make a match of it. That's all.'

'That's all! Didn't you know that I was beginning to hope that . . . I mean, that we . . .? Oh, you know what I mean!'

She dropped her head and covered her face with her hands, and he stared at her helplessly. The fire crackled in the grate, sending shadows leaping up the walls into the burned rafters. Outside the wind rose and the rain began in earnest. Instinctively Ralph edged nearer the warmth of the fire. Effie sensed rather than saw his movement and a small sob escaped her. He reached forward to take her hands and pull them away from her face. Her cheeks were wet with tears.

'Yes, I know what you mean,' he said softly. 'But I never thought of you that way.'

She jerked back and pulled her hands away.

'No, listen, you were just a bairn.'

'Only two years younger than you!'

'I know. But remember what a tomboy you were? How we ran and swam and climbed together? You were more like a little sister.'

'Stop. I won't listen.' Now Effie covered her ears with her hands.

'You must.' Ralph captured her hands again and pulled them down. This time he held on to them tightly. 'But that day – that day I told you that my parents hoped to make a match for me with Caroline, I thought we would laugh about it together. Laugh at the very idea of my marrying some spoiled young society lady.'

'You said it would be a good idea!'

'I didn't!'

'Yes you did. You said that when your uncle died you would be a baronet – a baronet without two farthings to rub together

18

and that Caroline's money and your title would go well together!'

'But I was joking!'

'Were you?' She stared at him challengingly.

'Yes ... well ... I mean I had no thought of marrying Caroline – or anyone. I was just repeating what my parents said. The idea of marrying anyone hadn't crossed my mind.'

'Hadn't it?'

'Not until it was too late. When I saw the look in your eyes – the hurt – I realized straight away that your feelings for me had changed from simple friendship. And then, when you ran off, and wouldn't come back when I called, and wouldn't come to the door when I went to the inn, I realized something else – that my feelings had changed too. But it was too late.

'My parents woke up to the fact that I might have made my own choice and they carried me off to London. The next time we came to Four Winds Hall I discovered that you were married. So I agreed to become engaged to Caroline Richardson.'

'But you're not married yet?'

'No. Caroline's father wants to make sure I work hard in the job he's given me. Safeguard his daughter's inheritance.'

'And you and I haven't seen each other since that summer.'

'No.'

'Have you thought about me?'

'All the time. And you? Have you thought about me when you're tucked up in bed with the good captain?'

'Don't speak like that! You have no right!'

'No, I don't suppose I have.' Ralph half turned away from her. His expression was bleak as she gazed into the fire. 'Effie,' he said, 'why did you come to the cottage?'

'Why did *you* come?'

They were still holding hands and he felt her gentle tug as she sat down on the blanket, pulling him down beside her. Then she let go of his hands and opened the old wooden chest that had been there since they were children.

'Perhaps I wanted to go back in time,' she said. 'Go back to the days when this old cottage was all the world to us.' She took out two plates and a knife, unwrapped the cake and cut two generous slices. Then she opened the bottle of brandy-wine and poured it into two pewter mugs. 'Here,' she said. 'Let's eat together like we used to.'

'I don't remember us having brandy to drink,' Ralph said. He took one of the mugs and sniffed the contents before taking a sip. He grinned appreciatively. 'Good stuff. Does your father know you've got it?'

'Of course not,' she admitted, and she laughed. 'Remember when I brought us a bottle of Madeira? We drank it as if it was cordial. I felt wonderful for a while – and then I was sick!'

'Disgusting child.'

As they sipped the brandy and ate the raisin cake together in companionable silence they began to relax. Ralph noticed that her features softened. How beautiful she was, he thought, and how young and innocent she looked. But then she glanced up at him and all semblance of innocence was vanquished by the seductive challenge in her eyes.

He watched transfixed as she caught a stray crumb from the corner of her mouth with the pointed tip of her tongue and he felt his loins quicken. 'No . . .' he breathed. 'We mustn't . . .'

'Mustn't what?' she whispered, and she moved towards him so that he could smell the brandy on her breath.

She took the cup from his hand and placed it on the floor with her own and then, instead of moving even nearer to him as he was expecting, she lay back on the rug and closed her eyes.

She didn't speak and he watched the firelight play on her golden hair. He had difficulty breathing when, still without opening her eyes, Effie raised a graceful hand and began to open the buttons of her simple white blouse, revealing the creamy flesh at the hollow of her neck and the gentle swell of her breasts.

Then she stopped and he raised his eyes to see that she had half opened hers. Looking at him aslant through long lashes, she raised both her arms towards him. It was more than he could bear. Wordlessly he moved forward and covered her body with his own.

Hannah set the plates and the dish of stew before the men at the table and went over to check Josie, who had fallen asleep on the cushions again. The child's face was flushed with happiness and her doll lay forgotten for once on the rug nearby. Hannah stooped to pick it up and tuck it beside her granddaughter, then she straightened and crossed over to the window.

Where was the girl for heaven's sake? What could she be thinking of staying out so long?

She was about to turn and take her place at the kitchen table when a flicker of a movement on the darkening hillside caught her eye. Someone was running down towards the inn. Hannah leaned forward and screwed up her eyes. The figure came nearer. It was Effie. Thank goodness.

And then Hannah noticed, even at this distance, that there was something about her daughter, something not right, a certain disorder, her hair flying wildly behind her. Hannah mumbled an excuse in the direction of the table and went out into the yard as if going to the privy. She closed the door behind her.

The air was cold, and damp from the recent rain. Hannah pulled her shawl across her body and waited silently as Effie drew nearer. She was standing in the shadows of the overhanging roof and she realized that her daughter could not see her. She stepped forward and Effie stopped her headlong flight, gasping with shock.

They stared at each other, and even in the gathering dusk Hannah could see the heightened colour of her daughter's face and the unnatural brightness of her eyes.

'Where hev you been?'

Effie raised her chin. 'Walking.'

'All this time?'

'It rained. I took shelter in the old cottage.'

'Aye. I saw the smoke from the chimney. Just had some kindling and matches handy, did you?'

Effie didn't reply. She dropped her head and, raising one hand, started to fiddle with a strand of hair. Hannah moved towards her and Effie looked up quickly.

'Here, you can't go in like that. Let me tidy your hair for you.' Hannah reined in her emotion as she pulled her daughter's hair back and tried to tame it with the remaining hairpins. She could guess where the others were – and why they had fallen out.

'Let me see.' She stepped back and looked at Effie; then, she couldn't help it, she raised her hand and brought it down across the girl's face.

'Why did you do that?' Effie stepped back; her eyes were wide with shock and pain.

'You know why.'

'No!'

'Divven't lie to me, lass. I know Ralph Lowther's home and I can tell he's been with you in the cottage. And I can guess fine what you've been up to!'

'But how . . . ?'

'Just one look at you. That's how. Now for God's sake do up that button on your blouse and come inside. I've telt him already that you must have been caught by the rain and taken shelter. And a fine job I had to stop him from going to look for you. I telt him I'd be offended if he didn't sit and talk to Josie and hev some of my good mutton stew after his train journey.'

'Telt him? Train journey? Who are you talking about?' Effie's face had drained of colour.

'Samuel Walton, of course. Your lawfully wedded husband.'

Chapter Two

January 1865

When the screaming began Samuel thrust the order book across the wooden counter towards his nephew and ran through the door that led from the shop into the house. Philip watched him go. His eyes widened for a moment, but then he shrugged and reached for the book. He turned it round to face him, took the pencil from behind his ear and carried on working.

The chandler's shop was on the ground floor of the tall, double-fronted, terraced building on the quayside; the family lived on the upper floors. Samuel bounded up two flights of stairs to the bedroom he shared with his wife. The bedroom that he'd been banished from hours ago when the women had gathered to help Effie through her confinement.

By the time he reached the door the dreadful sounds had stopped. He paused, gripped the door handle and prayed with all his might that Effie was all right. When the screams started again he was both grateful and terrified. Grateful that the wife he loved beyond reason was still alive, and terrified that something had gone dreadfully wrong.

Samuel realized that he had been holding his breath and, letting it out in a low groan, he wrenched open the door and charged in. He would have crossed to the bed and taken Effie in his arms, but he was met by the formidable black-clad figure of his elder sister.

'For heaven's sake, Samuel, what are you doing? You are out of place here!' she exclaimed in shocked tones.

Tall and spare, with unforgiving features, Charlotte Bertram gripped his arms and with an icy stare defied him to venture further. On the tumbled bed his young wife stopped screaming and turned her head to stare at him wildly. Her mouth remained open and he could see how her breast rose and fell as she laboured for breath. Samuel's heart lurched as he took in her distress.

Effie's face was pale, her eyes huge and haunted, and her glorious golden hair hung in greasy madwoman's locks. He took a step towards her, almost breaking free from his sister's restraining hands, but Effie shook her head and, taking a breath between each word, she groaned, 'Go – away – Samuel – leave – me – be.'

He remained there, unwilling to leave but not wanting to distress her further. He watched as Annie, their housemaid, mopped his wife's brow with a clean linen towel. Then the midwife filled a cup with something from a flask and gave it to Effie to drink. When he saw Effie's grimace Samuel clenched his fists and strained forward.

His sister pushed him back towards the door, whispering, 'It's all right, Samuel, it's something to dull her pain.'

His emotions in turmoil, Samuel allowed himself to be ushered out of the room and down the stairs. But only as far as the first floor, to the sitting room, which was directly above the shop. Charlotte went with him.

She guided him to the wing-backed armchair near the hearth. 'Sit there until you've pulled yourself together,' she said. 'You can't serve customers looking like a wild man.'

She crossed to the tall windows, which looked out over the river, and drew the curtains against the darkening sky. The wind rattled the windowpanes and the red brocade curtains, which fell from ceiling height to the polished wooden floor, seemed to shiver away from the cold glass.

Samuel did as he was told but he shuddered as he gripped the arms of the chair.

'Are you cold?' Charlotte asked, deliberately ignoring the cause of the anguish pulling at her brother's features. 'Shall I build up the fire?'

Samuel nodded, but his eyes glazed over as he stared into the flames. He was trying to ignore the pitiful moans echoing down the stairwell. Normally he would not have allowed his sister to risk her creaking joints like this, but he was hardly aware of what Charlotte was doing as she kneeled stiffly by the hearth and busied herself with the fire irons.

He heard the crackle as the coals settled under their new load, and then, a moment later, a hiss as Charlotte thrust the hot poker into a pewter jug of spiced wine kept standing at the side of the hearth. He was aware of her gasp of complaint as she rose slowly and a moment later he looked up to find her standing over him.

'Drink this,' she said, and she offered him his tankard. 'And stay here until I call you. Philip is quite capable of minding the shop. We'll stay open until eleven as usual.'

'But—'

Charlotte tried to mask her irritation with a smile. 'Who knows, some skipper who's sailing on the morning tide might just remember something he's forgotten to buy. He'd not be pleased to find the chandler's closed.'

Even in the state he was in, the pride in her voice brought a faint smile to Samuel's lips. His widowed sister was proud of her only son. And, indeed, she had cause to be. Philip Bertram was only fourteen years old and he did not take after the Walton side of the family. He was hardly a sturdy specimen of virile manhood, but his brain was sharp and his memory phenomenal. He could certainly be trusted to mind the chandlery business for an hour or two.

Samuel roused himself enough to take the cup of wine and smile at Charlotte as he thanked her. Then both of them turned, startled, as a small sigh whispered out from the shadows at the far side of the long room.

'What was that?' Samuel asked, half rising.

'It's only the bairn,' Charlotte told him as she walked towards the settle.

'The bairn?' He frowned, his mind befuddled by worry.

'I mean Josie. Look, she must have fallen asleep.'

'Poor little lass,' Samuel said. 'We forgot all about her.'

Charlotte's voice was sharp as she demanded, 'Well, I've had enough to do, haven't I?'

'No, I'm not blaming you. You've been with Effie and I'm grateful.' He placed his cup of wine on a table beside his chair and stood up. 'I'll mind Josie until Annie can be spared to put her to bed. Now go back to Effie ... please. And tell me when ... I mean ...'

'I know what you mean. Just stay out of the way. And try not to worry. Effie is young and strong, and Jane Brewer is an experienced midwife.'

'But why—' he began.

'Why what?' His sister sighed and looked impatient.

'Why is Effie having such a bad time? There were no problems when Josie was born.'

'Not all births are the same,' Charlotte explained. Samuel could tell she thought it improper of him to ask but she remained patient. 'Perhaps it's a boy, this time. And, like all men, he's starting off by making life difficult for the women-folk!'

Samuel saw that with this attempt at humour his sister meant to comfort him. Charlotte was not usually given to jokes and laughter.

'Perhaps you're right.' He tried to smile. 'Go on, then. You'd better get back to her.' But his sister had only got as far as opening the door when he called, 'Wait.'

She turned to face him. 'What is it?' The unspoken 'now' hung in the air between them.

He stared at her helplessly, her impatient air forbidding him to say anything.

She sighed again and shook her head. 'Sometimes you fuss too much, Samuel,' she said.

Charlotte closed the door briskly. He knew very well that his sister thought he made too much of Effie. Many a time Charlotte had hinted that she believed his young wife to be spoiled. And in his heart he knew his sister was right. But he loved Effie so much that he couldn't help indulging her. Especially as for months now he had been riven with guilt.

Josie sighed and murmured in her sleep; Samuel stirred himself and walked quietly over to where she lay on the settle. He looked down at his daughter and smiled fondly. She was not a pretty child; Charlotte had assured him that the toddler looked just as he had when he'd been that age.

Poor little thing, he thought with humour. She had a mother

who looked like an angel and Josie had inherited the looks and physique of her father's side of the family. But she was not unattractive – at least not to a father's eye. Her face was round and rosy with sleep and her dark lashes, unusually long, lay like silken crescents on her smooth cheeks.

She was clutching her doll. What did she call it? Susan? The poppet went everywhere with her. As he watched, the child stirred and loosened her hold. The doll rolled to the edge of the seat and Samuel leaned over to catch it before it fell to the floor. Not that it would have broken; it was a rag doll with a round, flat face and embroidered features, but Josie loved it and she would be distressed if she awoke and found it missing.

When he straightened up and made to replace the doll next to the child, he saw that his daughter's eyes were open. She stared at him solemnly for a moment as if she was still in the land of dreams and then she smiled.

'Papa,' she said softly, drawing a rueful smile from him.

Such a good little soul his daughter was. So placid and uncomplaining. She never seemed to mind that her mother hardly had time for her. It wasn't that Effie didn't love her little girl, he mused. It was just that she had never truly taken to motherhood. But she was not unkind.

He remembered one day walking into their bedroom to find Effie sitting before her looking-glass as she wound her hair in curling rags. Not that she needed them, but she must have been trying out some new fashion. Josie had been sitting in the middle of the bed behind her mother, watching solemnly. Samuel had remained standing in the doorway, enchanted by the scene.

Mother and daughter had been so intent that they did not notice him and he backed away silently rather than interrupt such a feminine activity. Effie would become more of a mother as the child grew and became more interesting, he was sure of that.

Josie's eyes closed and, after a moment of watchfulness, Samuel returned to his seat by the fire and his cup of spiced wine. And what of this new child? How would Effie take to it? She had not carried it willingly, he knew that.

A gust of wind blew down the chimney and sent a puff of smoke out across the room. Samuel stirred uneasily as he remembered the night of this new child's conception. He had come home from the sea that morning, full of love and anticipation, to find their old house cold and quiet. Effie had not been there to greet him.

Wanting to see her and tell her of his plans, he had made the journey to her parents' home in the village of Moorburn only to find that she was out, walking in the hills, her mother had said. He remembered how flustered Hannah Dixon had seemed when the rain started and still Effie did not return. Hannah sat Josie on his knee and bustled around, warming broth for him and insisting that Effie would not be long.

And eventually his wife had come home. Damp with the rain and flushed from running. How beautiful she had been – and how subdued. He could have wished that she had been more pleased to see him but he put her hesitation down to surprise.

That night when they'd lain in bed he had told her that he would never be leaving her again. That, at last, he had saved enough money to open his own chandlery. They would be leaving their neat but cramped little house in Wallsend and be moving to the quayside, to one of the fine new properties built after the great fire. A property that would provide both the business premises and a fine apartment over the shop.

He had expected Effie to be excited but she had hardly spoken. Perhaps it had been too much for her to take in.

'Aren't you pleased, sweetheart?' he had asked. And, not waiting for her answer, he had gathered her in his arms and begun to kiss her.

'No, Samuel, don't . . .' she'd breathed when she'd realized what was happening. She'd turned away from him.

'Why, Effie? What's the matter?'

'Nothing . . . please wait . . . not tonight . . . not here . . .'

And now he burned with shame when he remembered how he'd ignored her gentle protests. He'd thought he'd understood her meaning. They were sleeping in her old bedroom in the inn, the bedroom she'd had since she'd been a child. Josie was in a crib at the foot of the bed and Effie's parents lay sleeping in the very next room.

The poor girl had been embarrassed but he'd disregarded

her natural modesty. 'It's all right, sweetheart,' he'd whispered. 'You are my own darling wife. And all these long months I have dreamed of our being together again.'

Overcome with longing, he had made love to her. In the heat of passion he had mistaken the sounds she made as soft moans of pleasure. It was only afterwards, when he had held her gently and kissed her face, that he'd realized her cheeks were wet with tears.

His pleasure was spoiled with the realization that he had taken her against her will. She'd turned away from him, holding herself stiffly, and he'd lain awake for most of the night, falling asleep only when he'd vowed to himself that he would make things right between them.

But when he awoke the next morning Effie had already risen and taken the child downstairs to the kitchen. It had not been possible to talk to her, to say what he wanted to say. His wife had not been able to meet his eyes. He'd thought he'd understood why. And, somehow, he had allowed the time to pass without ever telling her how sorry he was.

Once they had left her parents' inn she had never refused him again. Samuel had allowed himself to believe that he was forgiven. But he had never forgiven himself. And now he believed the baby that seemed so reluctant to enter this world must have been conceived that night. It was Effie who was paying the price for his sins.

'Captain Walton?'

Samuel looked up to find that their housemaid had come into the room. 'What is it, Annie?' he asked. 'Has Mrs Walton . . . ?'

'No, sir. Sit down. There's no news yet. I've come to put Josie to bed.' Annie moved towards the sleeping child but Samuel raised a hand. She paused and looked at him questioningly. 'What is it, sir?'

'Do you think . . . do you think it will be long now?'

Annie sighed. 'Poor Mrs Walton is exhausted. Mrs Brewer is letting her rest for a while and then I heard her say she might send for the doctor.'

'Of course she must get the doctor if that's what's needed. Tell them I said so.'

'I will, sir. But if you don't mind my saying, Captain Walton, you look worse than your poor wife.' The maidservant was concerned. 'Why don't you try and get some sleep? I promise I'll wake you as soon as the baby's born.'

Samuel rose from his chair. 'Don't waste time talking like this. Tell my sister not to let Mrs Brewer wait any longer. They must send for Dr Harris straight away.'

Annie's eyes widened with shock at his curt tone. 'Yes, sir.'

He gestured for her to stay a moment and tried to make amends with a rueful smile. 'And it's no use, Annie, I can't sleep. Nor can I settle. I'm going to walk by the river. I won't be far. Send Philip for me when the time comes.'

Samuel watched while Annie gathered up his sleeping daughter and he held the door wide for her to pass through. Then he hurried downstairs, took his overcoat from the stand near the front door and went out into the night.

Effie watched the two women through half-closed eyes. They had propped her up amongst the pillows, covered her loosely with a clean sheet, and withdrawn to the foot of the bed to talk together. Effie pressed her head down a little so that her face was shadowed but she strained to hear what they were saying.

Her husband's sister leaned closer to the midwife as Jane Brewer shook her head. 'The bairn's lying the wrong way,' the woman said quietly.

'Can you turn it?' Charlotte asked.

'I've tried. But I'm not having much success. I think you should send for the doctor, like I said.'

Yes, for pity's sake send for the doctor, Effie thought. I don't think I can bear another moment of that stupid old woman poking and prodding!

She felt tears come to her eyes and scald their way down her cheeks. She turned her face into the pillows, trying to find some coolness, but the linen was hot and damp with her sweat.

She was aware that Annie had come back into the room. Plump, smug little Annie with her fresh pretty face, her neat ways and her air of calm efficiency. Samuel thought her the perfect maidservant and, try as she might, Effie had never been able to fault her. But she had seen the way the girl looked at Samuel from the corner of her eyes; the way she lingered just too long behind his chair at the dining table. Effie knew only too well what it was like to yearn for a man she couldn't have not to recognize Annie's pain.

'Here, Mrs Walton, drink this.' Effie opened her eyes to find the midwife standing over her. 'It will give you some ease until Dr Harris arrives. Annie is going for him now.'

Effie heaved herself up and drank from the cup that Mrs Brewer held. Immediately, it seemed, a wonderful warmth coursed through her tired body. She fell back and gave herself up to a delicious feeling of floating and, when the next pain came, it seemed almost as though it was happening to someone else; to some other poor woman.

'That's right, bonny lass,' the midwife said quietly. 'You sleep if you can. You're going to need the rest.'

Was she sleeping? Effie wasn't sure if she was or not. It certainly didn't feel as though she was properly awake, and yet the bed she was lying in seemed to have detached itself from its proper place and was hovering, not exactly above the floor, but certainly in a different dimension from where the two women had taken their place at either side of the fire.

Effie could hear the low murmur of their voices but they seemed to be so far away . . .

Her lids became heavy and she closed her eyes – and almost sat straight up again because she was so startled. She had closed her eyes, hadn't she? And yet she still seemed able to see her bedroom quite clearly. The bedroom she shared with her husband, Samuel Walton, with its fine oak furniture, oriental rugs and rose-coloured damask curtains.

Suddenly, above the sounds of the fire and the voices, she heard the wind rattling at the windowpanes and she turned her head and noticed that at one of the windows the curtains hadn't been completely closed. She could see the black winter sky and the clouds racing across the face of the moon.

She was caught up in the wild movement. The clouds are trying to drag the moon away, she thought, and she laughed. The two women stopped talking and she heard the rustle of stiff skirt fabric as her sister-in-law rose from her chair; then the creak of floorboards as she tiptoed towards the bed. Effie pressed herself further down into the pillows.

She felt a shadow fall over her and then it moved away.

'Is she all right?' Jane Brewer asked softly.

'Asleep, I think,' Charlotte Bertram answered. 'She must have been dreaming. Do you think she could be delirious?'

'No, it takes them that way, the draught I've given her. It takes away the pain but it brings on dreams. Some say it's wicked to let a woman dream when she's having her birth pangs. They say it's wicked to give her ease; they say the pain is necessary. But I don't hold with that. Let the poor lass dream, I say, and I hope it brings some comfort to her.'

The voices droned on. Effie heard the doctor mentioned and the fact that he shouldn't be long now. Then her attention was caught once more by the rattling windowpane and the view beyond.

The wind is from the sea, she thought. It is blowing in from the German Ocean, in towards the city and then to the hills beyond. It is taking the moon with it. And, if I could reach the window and open it, it would take me too . . .

She smiled as she pictured the amazement on the two women's faces as the wind gathered her up and carried her away. They would rush to the window and shake their heads and then they would call to Samuel to leap up and catch his errant wife by the hem of her nightgown and pull her earthwards.

But he would be too late. She would be gone, flying through the sky as effortlessly as the clouds, with the babe still in her womb, going back to where she had conceived it. For she knew in her heart that Samuel was not the father.

Ralph would be waiting for her in the ruined cottage. The wind would drop her gently on the hillside and she would run, light as thistledown, to the home that her true love would have prepared for them. For the three of them to live as man, wife and child.

She was there. She could feel the cool breeze on her face, lifting her hair and pressing the folds of her nightgown against her swollen body. The frozen grass felt like cool feathers against the bare skin of her feet, and the warmth of the fire in the cottage hearth was drawing her towards the open door.

Ralph was standing in the doorway. As soon as he saw her he ran towards her and took hold of her hands and drew her into the cottage . . . their cottage.

Effie moaned in her sleep. 'Ralph . . .' she whispered. 'Ralph, I knew you would wait for me . . .'

Charlotte had heard her. 'What did she say?'

Jane Brewer glanced at the unsmiling woman uneasily. 'I don't know,' she said. 'I didn't hear properly.'

'I thought she called for someone.' Charlotte placed her hands on the arms of her chair and prepared to push herself up.

'No, I don't think so. But divven't stir yourself, Mrs Bertram,' Jane Brewer told her. 'I'll see to the lass.'

Outside the cottage the wind was blowing across the hill top. Inside Effie could hear occasional crackling from the burning logs in the hearth and Ralph's soft breathing as she lay in his arms.

But where were those voices coming from? Surely they were alone in the cottage? Effie moved away from her lover slightly and turned her head. The walls of the cottage were indistinct. The firelight seemed to cast strange shadows. The shadows moved but took no shape. There was no one there. And yet the voices continued. She strained to listen. Then the voices faded.

The midwife looked down at her patient. She had lied to the captain's sister, for she had heard only too well what the poor lass had said. And now Captain Walton's young wife was moving her head from side to side as if in distress. But Jane had guessed that it wasn't pain that was prompting the fevered movements. It was desire.

It happened sometimes. That's why the doctors – all men, of course – were so against giving certain draughts to ease the pain of childbirth. They were frightened that the poor things would be sexually excited. And most men believed that women had no right to enjoy the pleasures of love. At least not good women.

And what about this poor young woman who was having such a hard time of it? Was she a good woman? It seemed as if she might not be. Who was she dreaming of now in her brief respite from pain? *Ralph*, she had called. That was not her husband's name. Captain Walton, good solid citizen that he was, was called Samuel. Could it be that his beautiful young wife was dreaming of another man?

Jane dipped a clean rag in the bowl of rose-scented water and mopped Effie's brow gently.

'Whisht,' she whispered. She glanced over her shoulder furtively, then leaned closer to her patient. 'Calm yourself, pet. If you can hear what I'm saying then take a warning. Dream on, little lass, but do it quietly. Life's hard and I can't bring myself to condemn you. Old Jane'll keep your secret, never fear.'

'What is it?' Ralph murmured as he drew Effie back into his arms.

'Did you hear something just now?' she asked.

'No . . . we are alone . . . come here . . .'

And he silenced her with kisses.

Jane straightened up and put the cloth back on the bedside table. The young woman seemed to have heard and understood what she had said for, after a moment of stillness, she had smiled as if in agreement.

Seeing that she had settled, the midwife returned to her seat by the fire.

'What were you saying to her?' Charlotte asked.

'Nowt of consequence, Mrs Bertram. Just telling the lass not to worry, the doctor's on his way.'

And I hope he gets here soon, Jane thought. She had been at many a difficult birth and the way this one was going was more worrying than she liked to admit.

'Captain Walton . . . is that you?'

Samuel Walton peered through the mist in the direction of the voice. It was past midnight, and around each gaslamp on the quayside there was a pool of glistening light, but in between them stretched areas of darkness. In one of those areas a light was moving, coming his way.

The light was about three feet from the ground and it swayed to and fro. The beams it sent out, although intense, were blurred and could barely penetrate the fog that had rolled in from the sea.

'Aye, it's me,' he said when a figure emerged and was revealed to be old Ben, the night watchman from a nearby warehouse. 'There's nothing wrong with your eyesight, Ben.'

'Nay, Captain, I guessed it was you. At least I hoped it was. I wouldn't hev liked to take on a fellow your size if you'd proved to be a bad 'un.'

'It's a cold night for you to be out, Ben.'

'For a man of my years, d'you mean?'

Samuel looked down into the old sailor's face and saw the humour there. 'Aye, I suppose I do.'

'I should hev put a bit more by in me youth, shouldn't I? Set meself up in a nice little business like you hev? In a smaller way, of course. I sometimes used to dream of owning a respectable lodging house. Not like one of those in the backstreets up there. I would've had good food and a clean bed always ready for a seafaring man. But I spent all me money on drink and bonny women and me dreams came to nowt.'

The old sailor gazed down at the wet cobblestones for a moment and then, in the ensuing silence, he suddenly raised his lantern and studied Samuel Walton's face.

'Do you regret it, Captain Walton?'

'Regret? What should I regret?'

'Listen,' Ben said, and he swung the lantern towards the river and cocked his head as he stood very still.

'What am I listening for?'

'Whisht and you'll hear it calling.'

The mist swirled around them and at first Samuel heard only the lapping of water against the quay wall. He knew the tide was coming in and he could visualize the swell and the rocking of the many vessels in their moorings. And then he heard voices echoing through the mist. Quiet commands and men calling to each other as they prepared to sail on the turn.

'You know what I mean,' Ben said.

Samuel shook his head.

'Yes, you do. Just think what it would be like to sail on the morning tide with one of these vessels. The wind whistling amongst sails, the spray dashing on the deck. And don't tell me you don't feel the pull of them faraway ports . . . other lands, other climes. That's what's calling you.'

The old sailor held the lantern steady. His gaze was challenging. But Samuel, after a moment of surprised hesitation, began to smile. 'You're quite a poet, Ben,' he said. 'And, aye, I do miss the seafaring life. But there was something, someone, I missed even more.'

Ben nodded. 'Your bonny young wife.'

'That's right.'

'And how is Mrs Walton? She must be near her time?'

'The bairn's on its way.'

'Then what are you doing out here, Captain?'

Samuel grinned. 'I was getting underfoot. They told me it would be a while yet.' The smile vanished and his voice sank almost to a whisper. 'Poor Effie . . .'

The old sailor studied the big man's face for a moment and then he said, 'Divven't worry, Captain, hinny. It's not like it's the first time. Mrs Walton's given you one bonny bairn and this time it'll be easier. Now, I'd best be on my rounds. And if you take my advice, you'll gan back and sit like a good quiet man by the fire. Divven't let the women drive you from your own house! Good night to you, Captain Walton.'

'Good night, Ben.'

Samuel watched the old man walk away. Ben had misunderstood. His sister hadn't told him to leave the house, she had only told him to keep quiet and stop fussing. But he hadn't been able to settle by the fire. How could he when Effie's cries of distress had served to remind him of how cruelly he had treated her the night he'd come home from the sea?

If only Effie had wanted him to stay! He would have ignored Charlotte and taken his young wife in his arms, done anything he could to ease her pain, but he had been banished from her presence.

Suddenly he heard something behind him. Footsteps, running footsteps, muffled by the fog. 'Is that you, Philip?'

Was it his nephew coming to get him? To tell him that his child had been born?

The footsteps stopped. There was silence. No, not quite

silence. Samuel heard the gasp of an indrawn breath. He swung round to peer into the shadows.

'Philip?' he called again.

But he knew it wasn't his nephew. He could almost sense the fear radiating from whoever it was who now appeared through the swirling mist: a small figure, hunched down as if wishing that the ground would open up and swallow him.

'Who is it?' Samuel said softly. 'You have no need to fear me.'

'Captain Walton?' A child's voice quavered through the shadows.

Samuel thought he recognized it as belonging to one of the street urchins who regularly dodged along the quayside seeing what he could beg or steal to keep his pitiful scrap of a body and soul together.

'Is that Tom? Tom Sutton?'

'Whisht! Divven't tell.' It was Tom.

'Tell what?' Samuel asked. The child remained silent. 'Oh, I see. Who's after you?'

'Fox,' came the scared reply. 'Fox Telford.'

And then they both heard the cry, 'Where are you, you little varmint? I'll catch you and I'll thrash the life out of you!'

God help the lad if he's angered Fox, Samuel thought. 'What have you done?'

'Helped meself to a bit supper.' The lad's voice was wavering but, nevertheless, Samuel heard the humour in it. Tom moved uncertainly towards him. 'Will yer help us?' he whispered.

Samuel saw now that he was clutching a whole roast chicken; a bit supper indeed! Tom must have seen the captain's eyes widen for he said defensively, 'I'll be sharing it with me marras.' He meant his pals.

'Here, stuff that chicken down your jacket,' Samuel whispered urgently. 'Do the buttons up tight. Don't drop it.'

Tom looked surprised but he did as he was told and then he uttered a faint yelp as Samuel picked him up and swung him through the air towards the river.

'For God's sake, Captain, divven't drown us!' he gasped. He began to kick out with his matchstick legs. Samuel guessed the poor bairn didn't know what to fear most, being caught by Fox

Telford or being dropped into the freezing river by the man he'd thought was helping him.

'Stop that and hold your tongue!' Samuel urged as he manoeuvred the lad over the side of the quay and began lowering him towards the water. 'The steps,' he said quietly, 'feel for the steps.'

The light of understanding shone in Tom's eyes and he grinned as he stretched his legs downwards. Samuel let go of him the moment the lad's bare feet found purchase on the set of stone landing steps cut at right angles into the quayside.

'Duck down but take care,' Samuel warned. 'Don't slip. I don't fancy coming in after you.'

'God bless you, Captain. I'll not forget this.'

Samuel straightened up and turned to face the moving shadows. Barely a second later Fox Telford burst into the circle of light cast by the nearest lamp. He pulled up sharp and stared at Samuel suspiciously. He took a moment to get his breath back and then he said, 'Captain Walton. Are you alone?'

'You can see I am.'

'I thought I heard voices.'

'No doubt you did.'

Samuel nodded towards a tall-masted schooner dipping and swaying on the rising tide. The murmur of the crew's conversation carried through the mist.

The man scowled but he hesitated as if unwilling to challenge such a respectable citizen. Fox Telford kept a disreputable lodging house, in a narrow backstreet, that catered for light-fingered thieves and housebreakers. There they could both fence their stolen goods and spend the proceeds on food, ale and accommodation. It was rumoured that Fox himself was the mastermind behind many a big robbery and that he had no need to live here, and in such squalor.

The fare was good and Fox asked no questions so long as his customers paid up promptly. But the man had a filthy temper, and it was well known that even the most daring of criminals would not have attempted to cheat him. It was rumoured that one who had had vanished without trace. Murdered, probably, and the body dumped either in the stagnant cesspit, which was never cleared, behind the lodging house, or in the river to be carried away on the tide.

Samuel was aware that the lodging-house keeper had edged closer and was eyeing him suspiciously. The red hair that had earned him his nickname glinted in the lamplight. His sharp features were alert as if sniffing out his prey. Instinctively Samuel drew himself up. He was a bigger man and should have had the advantage, except that the innkeeper was lithe and sinewy and had felled many a hulking brute who had attempted to better him in the past.

'Did you see anyone run this way?' Fox asked.

'Anyone?'

'A lad. A raggy-arsed little brat.'

'What's he done?'

'The light-fingered villain took a roast chicken. The range was hot and I'd left the back door open. I was busy serving suppers. I was in and out of the kitchen.'

'How do you know anything was taken?'

'Because I saw him. I came back in just in time to catch sight of him sneaking out with the chicken under his arm. Fast as lightning he was. Led me a merry dance through the alleys. Lost sight of him for a while but then I glimpsed him heading down to the quayside. But I'm wasting time. Did you see him or not?'

'Yes I did.'

Samuel imagined he heard an indrawn breath from the steps where Tom was hiding just a few short feet away. But perhaps it was only the lapping and sighing of the water.

'So where is he?'

'You're right. You heard me talking to him. I asked him what he was up to and he gave me a mouthful of cheek. Then he took off. That way.'

Samuel pointed downriver towards the older buildings where small businesses and ancient warehouses existed alongside derelict properties.

Fox stared at Samuel as if assessing whether he could believe this information. Then: 'Right,' he said. 'You've wasted my time, Captain Walton. If that's the way he went he could be anywhere in those festering slums along with the other wretched brats that plague our streets. I'll never catch him now, will I? And perhaps that's what you wanted, eh?'

'It's only a roast chicken, Fox. I'll pay for it.'

'Keep your money. That's not the point. No one steals owt from me. Brats like that have got to learn that. I'll not forget this, Captain Walton.'

The lodging-house keeper stared at him balefully for a moment and then turned to go. Samuel was left wondering whether Fox had meant that he wouldn't forget that the lad had dared steal from him or that he, Samuel, had conspired to help the miscreant evade rough justice. Both, probably.

'Thanks, Captain.'

Samuel turned to see Tom's pale face peering over the edge of the quay. He leaned forward to reach out and help him climb the slippery steps. 'You took a risk, there, lad,' he said. He found that he couldn't condemn what the youngster had done. How else was he supposed to survive?

'I know.' Tom was already beginning to edge away. 'I'd better be off. They'll be waiting.'

'Who?'

'You know. I telt yer. Me marras.'

Samuel sighed. Tom could be no more than seven or eight years old and he could well imagine his friends: a ragged bunch of children, orphaned or abandoned and left to fend for themselves. They lived on the streets; huddled in doorways or in long-abandoned buildings, surrounded by filth and squalor. God help them all.

Some good citizens made it their business to try to ease their plight: round them up and send them off to institutions where the poor bairns were cleaned and fed but treated as if it was their own fault that they were poor. Understandably, some of them resisted, preferring to live on the streets, where they ended up either dead or living lives of crime.

And then there were the soup kitchens where good women of the town cooked and distributed wholesome meals. Samuel himself contributed food and money to one of them. But he knew much more would have to be done.

'Go on then,' he said. 'Away with you. And enjoy your supper.'

The lad grinned and then seemed to melt like a wraith into the mist. Samuel shook his head. Poor bairn. He wondered how long Tom had been living like this. Had he ever had a proper home with a mother and father to care for him and worry where he was at night? Or had he been born on the streets to some poor wretch who had either died or left him to fend for himself as soon as he could?

Samuel thought of his daughter, Josie, safely tucked up between clean sheets in a room warmed by a fire. And of the child about to be born. A boy perhaps? A son to join him and carry on the family business. They would prosper together. That would be grand. But whether a son or a daughter was born this night, no child of Samuel's would ever have to live like Tom Sutton.

And then anxiety returned as he remembered why he was out here. Poor Effie. His wife, who was more like a child herself than a grown woman. A wayward child. Well, no matter what Charlotte said, he knew he was willing to go on indulging Effie. He was proud of her beauty and grateful that she had chosen him. And if his desire for her was stronger than hers for him, then that was natural. Women needed to be coaxed. After she was over this birth he would learn how to please her; make her happy.

But now he would go home. Surely the baby would have been born by now.

Effie could hear crying. A baby's cry. The thin wail of a newborn. Was it her baby? Hers and Ralph's?

'Can you hear that, Ralph?' she whispered.

'What did you say, Mrs Walton?'

Effie frowned. The voice that had answered was not Ralph's voice. It was the voice of an older man.

'Mrs Walton, can you hear me?' the man asked.

'Ralph, I don't understand,' Effie said. 'I thought we were alone here. Who is that?'

'This is Dr Harris, Mrs Walton.'

'What are you doing here?'

'I came to deliver your baby. And what a fine child she is. A beautiful daughter.'

41

Effie was silent. She seemed to remember that Samuel's sister and that old woman, Jane Brewer, had told her that they were sending for the doctor, but that was at home – or rather Samuel Walton's home on the quayside in Newcastle. But she was in the cottage now, wasn't she?

She had flown out of the window and been carried by the wind all the way home to the hills that she loved. And Ralph had been waiting for her in the cottage. She shivered. Ralph had built up the fire, hadn't he? So why was she so cold?

'Dr Harris,' she said, 'you came here?'

'I did. And your daughter is safely delivered.'

'Did you hear that, Ralph?' Effie said. 'We have a daughter.'

'What is she saying?' That was Charlotte's voice. Had she come to the cottage, as well?

'Nothing much.' That was Jane Brewer. They must all be here! 'Divven't fret, Mrs Bertram,' the midwife said. 'The lass is delirious. She's talking nonsense. Isn't that right, Dr Harris?'

'Ahem . . . yes.'

'Ralph, what are they talking about? And how did they get here? Ralph . . . where are you? I can't see you . . . I can't see anything. And I'm cold . . . build up the fire . . .'

Effie felt herself begin to shiver violently. It was strange . . . she was cold and yet part of her was warm. She felt a growing sensation of heat – warm heat – flowing through her lower body . . . gushing . . . streaming . . . carrying her away.

'My God!' she heard Jane Brewer cry. 'She's bleeding. Dr Harris, do something. Stop the flow!'

Wearily Effie turned her head to stare into the shadows. It took great effort. The fire had gone out, the hearth was cold and she couldn't see Ralph anywhere. In fact, she couldn't see anyone, or anything. She could still hear voices but they were getting fainter. She sensed that she was drifting away from them.

Perhaps the wind had come to gather her up again and carry her away from the cottage and up into the high hills where she and Ralph used to run free when they were children.

But the wind was cold and growing colder.

'You shouldn't have left me here with these people, Ralph,' she whispered. 'I'll never find you now . . .'

* * *

42

The shop door was closed and all was quiet. After all, it was gone midnight; Samuel had heard the cathedral clock chime. Philip would have locked up an hour ago. He let himself in the house door and hung up his overcoat. Then he began to climb the stairs.

Surely the baby must have been born by now. But, if that was the case, why hadn't his nephew come for him? He'd told them he wouldn't stray far. Well, at least it was quiet. Too quiet. Suddenly the hairs on the back of his neck rose and a sick fear gripped his stomach as he paused on the landing outside the bedroom door.

When the door opened it took him by surprise. Annie stood there, for a moment gazing up at him with something like terror, and then she pushed past him and hurried away down the stairs, carrying a bundle of bloodied sheets.

'Samuel,' his sister called, and hurried towards him.

'Captain Walton, sir. Look, here is your newborn child.'

Jane Brewer also approached, carrying a small bundle wrapped in clean linen. But Samuel stared past them towards the bed where Dr Harris was in the act of drawing a clean sheet up over Effie.

'Stop that!' Samuel bellowed.

But the doctor carried on drawing the sheet up and letting it fall gently over Effie's face.

'No! It can't be!' Samuel cried, and the doctor turned to face him.

'Captain Walton,' he began and then straightened his spine as if to face an ordeal. His face was grey. 'The birth was difficult. I had to use forceps. Everything seemed to go well. But then . . . but then she . . .' The man stopped talking and almost without noticing what he was doing, it seemed, he began to roll down his shirtsleeves and button them. 'Mrs Walton haemorrhaged,' he continued. 'I . . . I couldn't stop the bleeding. I'm sorry.'

No one spoke. Samuel could hear the soft splutter of the fire. He knew the room was warm and yet he felt his body being consumed by cold. It was as if an icy wind was blowing through him and freezing the very blood in his veins. And in his heart.

'May I look at her?' he whispered.

'No, Samuel,' his sister began, but the doctor nodded his head.

Samuel went over to the bed and gently drew back the sheet so that he could see her face. Even in death she was beautiful. He felt the tears well up and was unashamed when they spilled over and began to course down his cheeks. A tear fell on her face and he reached out to brush it away.

'Come now, Captain, hinny,' he heard the midwife say. 'You've lost her but see what she's given you.'

He turned from the bed and Charlotte hurried up to cover Effie's face again. The old nurse was holding something towards him.

'See what your wife has given you,' she said. 'Another daughter. But such a beauty. In all my days I've never seen such a bonny bairn.'

Distracted, Samuel looked down at the face of his child and his eyes widened. The small features were perfect. She was indeed a beauty. She was just like her mother. She had the face of an angel. Good soul that he was, he would never blame the child for the mother's death as some men did. This was a new and innocent being who had not asked to be born in sorrow.

In spite of the worst pain he had ever known, a powerful emotion began to well up inside him. Love for Effie's precious gift to him. His new daughter.

Chapter Three

Summer 1870

'Josie! What have you done?'

'I haven't done anything.'

Josie looked round in dismay as Annie swept into the first-floor room and hurried over to the tall window. The weather was warm and the lower half of the window had been raised. Flora stopped crying and put her thumb into her mouth.

'Don't do that, sweetheart.' Annie kneeled down and put one arm around the younger child. With her other hand she gently drew Flora's small hand away from her mouth. 'You don't want to spoil your pretty face, do you?'

Flora shook her head. Her blue eyes were filled with tears and her cheeks were flushed a delicate rose pink. The nursemaid leaned forward and kissed her forehead.

'Now why were you crying? Tell Annie, there's a sweet angel.' She shot an accusatory look over Flora's shoulder in Josie's direction.

'Annabel,' Flora whispered, and stared down at her toes.

'Your doll? What about your doll?' Annie glanced round swiftly. 'Where is she?'

Flora sobbed and nodded towards the window. Annie's eyes widened. Then, still on her knees, she turned to the window, grasped the sill and, leaning out a little, looked down.

Josie knew what she would see. Just before Annie had hurried into the room, Flora, in a temper with her doll because the ribbons of its bonnet had become knotted and wouldn't untie, had hurled it out of the window. And then realizing what she had done, she'd begun to cry. Flora was only five years old. She often acted hastily and then regretted it almost immediately.

And now the poor doll would no doubt be lying on the cobblestones. Maybe its porcelain head would be broken or cracked. Josie hoped not.

'Here! You! Put that down at once!' Annie startled both sisters by shrieking out of the window. 'No! Wait there. Don't you dare move. Someone will come down and get it.' Then: 'Filthy little urchin,' Annie muttered as she moved back from the window and got to her feet. 'I don't want him going into the shop or the house.'

The nursemaid smoothed down her skirts and adjusted her lace mobcap, which had fallen forward over her face while she'd had her head stuck out of the window. All Annie's hair was tucked up inside the cap, but Josie noticed the end of a curling rag hanging down just before their nursemaid's fingers found it and tucked it up impatiently.

'You go down and get the doll, Josie. There's a lad down there who was just about to make off with it. Lucky I caught him. And so long as the poor thing isn't broken I won't tell your father what you did. Nor will I tell him that you'd taken your little sister to play by the open window.'

Josie stared up at Annie in surprise and the woman's glance slid away uneasily. Josie hadn't thrown the doll out of the window and she hadn't encouraged Flora to play there. Her sister had run over by herself and Josie had tried to stop her. But that injustice paled beside the fact that Annie should not have left them alone in the room in the first place.

As their nursemaid it was her job to look after them. But she had disappeared not long after lunch. Now Josie thought it must have been to put her curling rags in.

Josie hurried down the stairs. The house door was closed and she had the choice of struggling to open it or going through the shop. Her father wouldn't have minded, but Josie sensed that Annie would. Her father mustn't know about the accident with the doll. That had been implicit. She struggled with the door.

The bright sunlight streamed in along with the smells and the sounds of the busy quayside: the shouts from the sailors on board the vessels lying at anchor, and the rattle of the many horse-drawn delivery carts taking goods from the pile of heaped-up merchandise that had just been unloaded from a cargo vessel.

Josie could smell coffee and bacon coming from a nearby stevedores' eating house but, always, there was the underlying smell of horse dung.

'You took your time!'

A ragged boy grinned at her as she stepped out, blinking, into the street. He was holding Annabel by her kid-booted feet, and the doll hung down in a most ungainly – and immodest – fashion, with her skirts falling down to reveal her frilly pantaloons. Josie couldn't help giggling.

The lad followed her gaze and laughed out loud. 'I'm sorry, my lady,' he said. 'I didn't mean to embarrass you.' Josie realized he was talking to the doll.

He righted the poor thing and held it out towards her. Josie didn't take it at first. She gazed at it anxiously. The boy seemed to know what was worrying her. 'It's a bit mucky but it isn't broken,' he said. 'Lucky it didn't land face down. All them golden curls and her fine bonnet saved her pretty head.'

He began to brush little clumps of dried mud and straw from the doll's skirts. Josie bit her lip. His hands were filthy.

'That's better.' He looked up and grinned.

She hadn't had time to change her expression of horror and he scowled as he thrust the doll roughly at her. She grasped it quickly lest it fall again.

'Thank you,' she said.

He looked at her expectantly, as if he were waiting for something more. She was puzzled and she didn't know what to say. After a moment he backed away.

'Ta-ra, then,' he said, and Josie thought he sounded disappointed.

She didn't want him to go. He was three or four years older than she was; she guessed he would be about twelve, but she liked the way he had play-acted just then, speaking as if the doll had feelings. And before she had annoyed him he'd had such a nice smile.

'Wait,' she said.

He turned and grinned. Again she thought he was expecting something. She frowned and he sighed.

'What do you want?' he asked.

'You weren't really going to steal the doll, were you?'

She didn't know why she had blurted that out and she looked to see if he was angry. He wasn't. But he asked, 'Who said I was?'

'Annie, our nursemaid. She said you were just about to run off with it.'

'Well I wasn't. But I might hev done. I could hev sold it on. Got a fair price for it. If it hadn't been your doll.'

Josie was puzzled. 'It's my sister's doll.'

'Well, I thought it was yours. I saw the little 'un throw it out and I thought she was being spiteful. Like she often is.'

'How do you know that?'

'I've watched your nursemaid taking you to school. I've watched how your sister carries on, clever as a box of monkeys.'

'Don't say that. She's only little.'

'All right, then. But I bet you got the blame.'

'Blame?'

'I bet your nursemaid thinks you hoyed the doll out the window. Doesn't she?'

Josie remained silent.

'Well, doesn't she?'

'Yes.'

'And aren't you going to tell her.'

'No. Flora is upset enough. And she's—'

'Only little. I know.' He shook his head. 'So you'll take the blame, then?'

'I suppose so.'

The boy looked hesitant, as if he wanted to say something more but didn't know how to.

'What is it?' Josie asked.

He smiled again. 'I don't suppose your nursemaid gave you something for me, did she?'

'What do you mean?'

'No, I can see she didn't. I'll be off then.'

'No – wait. I don't understand. What did you think Annie would give you?'

'A tip.'

'Tip?'

'A coin or two. A small thank you for catching the doll.'

'But you didn't catch it.'

'I know that. But I didn't run off with it either, did I? I thought she might be grateful.'

Now Josie understood his hopeful look when he had handed the doll over. 'You told me you waited because you thought it was my doll.' She didn't know why but she felt disappointed.

'And that's true. But your nursemaid didn't know that, did she?'

Josie frowned. She thought she knew what he meant but she couldn't understand why he would have wanted money for doing a good deed. Now he was shaking his head again.

'You divven't understand, do you? You with your rich father and your nice house and your clean clothes. You don't understand what it's like to live like me.'

'No I don't.'

'Well, get back inside, then, Josie.'

Her eyes widened. 'How do you know my name?'

'I've telt you. I've watched you now and then when you're out with your nursemaid. Your name is Josie and your little sister is Flora. And your da is Captain Walton, and he's a good man. That's another reason I wouldn't hev run off with the doll. Now I've tarried long enough. I must be off.'

'You haven't told me your name.'

'Tom,' the lad said. 'That's what they call me. I was told once that me name is Tom Sutton. But that was a long time ago and I've forgotten who it was or where we were at the time. Tara, then.'

He was off; dodging along the busy quayside, and Josie was left puzzling over someone who didn't seem to be sure about his own name.

Tom decided it was time to go home and check on Betty. On the way he passed the Milk Market, where, because it was Saturday, just beyond the butchers' stalls there were piles of old shoes and patched second-hand clothes. They were laid out

49

on straw on the cobbles or strung along the railings on the old town wall.

He hung around a pile of working men's boots until the stall keeper was busy negotiating with a customer who was haggling about the price. Then he stooped and snatched up the nearest pair – luckily they were tied together by their laces – and, stuffing them down the front of his jacket, he darted away.

The boots were big, and his jacket was skimpy. There was no way he could hide them completely so he had to rely on melting into the busy throng until he got clear away from the market area.

Soon he began to pass a row of small riverside workshops, all to do with shipping trades. There were painters, block and mast makers, carvers, sail makers, and small chandlers, none of them as grand as that owned by Captain Walton, who Tom knew supplied the agents acting for the more prosperous shipowners.

When he reached the place where the Ouseburn flowed into the Tyne he made a detour to cross the Glasshouse Bridge and went on past the Dead House, where they kept the grappling irons to remove bodies from the river. Then he dived into the backstreets that led to old deserted manufactories and half-ruined tenements long forsaken by all but the desperately poor who could not afford to pay rent. In one of these he had made his home.

As he climbed the stone stairs he had to be careful, for the handrail had long since gone. His rooms were on the top floor, and he'd chosen this dwelling because it was above the stench that rose from the gutters. But the drawback was that it was draughty and cold, even in the summer months. Before he got to the door he could smell a more pleasant odour than those of the streets. Something good was cooking.

Betty and he always kept the door locked but they each had a key. Tom had lifted the lock and keys from a second-hand stall at the market, along with a few carpentry tools, and fitted the lock himself. He fished his key from his pocket and went in, closing and locking the door after him. Then he turned to see his companion leaning over to stir something in a cooking pot on a hob on the fire.

He had never worked out how to approach Betty if her back was turned without startling the wits out of her. But, thank goodness, she seemed to have some sixth sense that told her when she wasn't alone. She straightened up and turned round. She was smiling.

'That smells good!' he said, exaggerating the movements of his lips.

She watched his mouth carefully. Her smile grew even wider and she made a thumbs-up sign. Then she pointed to an old wicker basket by the hearth. It was full of coal. He grinned and gave a thumbs-up in return.

Betty must have gone down to the Ouse bank at low tide to gather coal that had fallen overboard from the keel boats. The coal was heaved into carts, backed axle-deep in the stream. Tom always felt sorry for the poor horses standing in the cold water. But they were patient beasts and seemed simply to ignore the dodging crowd of women and children groping in the water for coal and filling their bags and baskets.

And as for the stew cooking on the range, that would contain bones and scraps from the slaughterhouse, and vegetables that had fallen off the market stalls and were left at the end of the day. Most of the time they lived well without spending a penny earned from odd jobs or thieving.

Betty was prodding his bulging jacket with her fingers. She raised her eyebrows and made a questioning sound. Tom grinned and pulled out the boots he had stolen.

'I'll get a good price for these,' he mouthed.

Betty pursed her lips and wagged her finger, pretending to disapprove, but, in fact, she was a better thief than he was. She looked so pathetic with her shawl and her basketful of bits of ribbons and lace that no one suspected the basket was a hiding place for anything her nimble fingers could lift off the market stalls. She hardly ever sold any of her wares and everything was getting tired and faded-looking. She'd have to get some new stuff soon, Tom thought, or she'd begin to look suspicious.

'Let's hev wor dinner, then,' he said. 'I'm famished.'

Betty had already set the rickety table with a newspaper to serve as a tablecloth, two old spoons and a couple of chipped plates. She pointed to the plates and gestured for Tom to bring them over to the fireplace where she spooned stew into them one at a time.

As they enjoyed their meal together, Tom thought how much his life had improved since the day he'd rescued her from the crowd of taunting children. They were all smaller than she was, but they'd surrounded her, thrown her basket on to the ground and were pulling at her clothes and hair.

Betty had been making noises like a trapped animal and, at first, Tom had taken it for sheer terror. It wasn't until he'd chased the gang of spiteful children away that he'd realized that she couldn't speak properly. And that she was deaf.

She'd been sobbing as he'd helped her to gather up the bits and pieces of bonny ribbons and put them back into her basket and, when he handed it to her, she caught at his arms and moved her mouth, making the strangest noises. It sounded like 'A – oo'.

'A – oo, a – oo,' she'd kept repeating, until at last he'd understood that she was trying to say 'Thank you'.

He was embarrassed and he muttered, 'That's all right,' in the direction of his tattered boots.

She'd caught at his arm again and when he looked up she'd pointed to her ears and shaken her head.

'You're deaf?' Tom had shouted.

And she'd watched his mouth and grinned and nodded.

Since then he'd learned that shouting made no difference at all. Betty was stone deaf and the only way she could understand what he was saying was by watching the movement of his lips.

He said goodbye and left her, but soon realized that she was following him. He turned round and said 'Goodbye' again, as clearly as he could. But she kept on following him. He even tried to scowl and he told her, 'Haddaway!', at the same time making shooing motions with his hands. But it made no difference. It seemed that he'd made a friend for life.

He allowed her to move into his squalid quarters and she'd set about cleaning them and making them more comfortable. Every now and then she'd vanish and return with bits and pieces of household goods as well as personal things such as clothes for herself. Whether she'd brought them from the place she'd been living or whether she'd stolen them, Tom never knew.

'I don't know what to call you,' he'd said one day and she'd frowned in puzzlement. 'What's your name?' he'd said clearly in the way he'd learned to address her.

Immediately she grinned and pulled a scrap of paper from a pocket in her skirt. There was one word written on it. But it meant nothing to Tom.

He'd taken her arm and said quite clearly, 'I've never been to school. I can't read.'

There was no mistaking the pity on her face. There followed an embarrassing few minutes with Betty moving her lips and making sounds again until at last Tom exclaimed, 'Betty!' and her face lit up with joy.

Then she dug a finger into his chest and looked at him questioningly. After she'd repeated the gesture a few times he got it and, pointing to himself, he'd said, 'Tom.'

Since then they'd rubbed along together very well. Betty had taught him some of the signs she used instead of speech, and she certainly made his life easier. He felt sorry for her when he thought how difficult her life must be, not being able to talk properly. And yet he was envious when he saw her spread a pilfered newspaper out on the table and read it. Sometimes what she was reading would make her laugh and sometimes her eyes would widen with horror and she would gasp out loud.

When he saw what pleasure reading gave her he began to steal a book or two from the second-hand bookstalls in the Grainger Market. He had no idea what kind of books he was taking. Some of them had pictures in and some of them had pages and pages of tiny writing. But she always thanked him gratefully and would sit by the fire long into the night, lost in whatever world the book had taken her to.

He wished she could tell him what was so interesting and he wondered how it was that she could read in the first place. She seemed older than he was. He guessed she must be at least fourteen, so he thought that perhaps she had been brought up in the school for the deaf.

As well as reading and writing the children there were taught all sorts of trades so that they could find jobs when the time came to leave the school at twelve. What had gone wrong in Betty's case he would probably never know.

Suddenly, as he mopped up his gravy with a thick slice of bread, he found himself thinking about the solemn little girl who was Captain Walton's elder daughter. She was a strange one. She didn't talk much. In fact, he thought that today might have been the first time he'd heard her string more than two words together. But, young as she was, she had a sort of grown-up air about her, and she didn't look as if she had an ounce of spite in her body. Not like the little 'un.

He wondered if she minded that her little sister was so dazzlingly beautiful while she was just on the right side of plain. Josie Walton was tall for her age, and dark and strong-boned like her father. Her little sister was like the picture of a fairy, a magic being he had seen in one of the books he had brought home for Betty.

He remembered how Betty had pointed to the wings and flapped her arms as if she were taking off like a bird. They'd had a laugh about that. Well, Flora Walton didn't have wings, but she had curls so fair they were almost white and the most beautiful blue eyes. She must take after her mother, he supposed.

He knew that Captain Walton's wife had died. He had watched the funeral procession leaving the tall house on the quayside. Captain Walton was well-liked and respected. He was much more than a simple chandler now. He imported many goods from abroad and was building up a trading empire. That's what folk said. But few envied him because they said nothing could make up for what he had lost.

Many people had gathered to watch the black-clad mutes in their tall hats leading the way, and the black-plumed horses drawing the elaborate hearse up through the litter-strewn streets to the church on the hill.

Listening to the hushed gossip of the bystanders, Tom had learned that the poor lady had died giving birth to a baby daughter. It had not taken him long to realize that she must have died the very night the captain had saved his skin by hiding him from Fox Telford.

Tom still shivered when he remembered how close he'd been to being caught by Fox. He doubted that he would have survived the beating he'd have received, and he thanked his maker – if there was one, and he doubted it sometimes when he thought about the way he and so many other poor people had to live – that the lodging-house keeper had never seen his face.

But he hadn't been caught, thanks to the captain, and he was sorrier than he'd ever been when he saw the grief on the big man's face the day they buried his wife.

He didn't know exactly why, but since then he'd taken to hanging about near Walton's chandlery every now and then. Sometimes Captain Walton saw him and would give him an odd job or two, such as sweeping the street in front of the shop. He'd always pay him with food – bread, cheese, apples – as well as a coin or two. Once he'd given him a whole new tin of biscuits.

Tom still had the tin with its pictures of some grand city on it. He kept it for storing little items of value that he'd stolen until he found a buyer for them. He didn't think Captain Walton would have approved of that but it couldn't be helped. He had to survive as best he could, hadn't he?

Often when he hoped to see the captain he was chased away by that whey-faced shop assistant. Philip, he was called and he didn't half put on airs when his master was out on business. Tom had learned that Philip was the captain's nephew and he lived in the house above the shop along with his mother, the captain's sister.

Often he would dream of what it must be like to have a family and live in a proper house with food and fuel no problem, and new clothes whenever you needed them. And hot water to keep yourself and the clothes clean.

Now he flushed angrily when he remembered how Josie had stared in disgust at his hands. He looked down at them now and then across at Betty. Suddenly he was ashamed. Betty kept herself clean even though every drop of water they used had to be carried back from the pump two streets away; and even if they didn't have coal to heat the water.

Sometimes Betty would take his hands and then push him gently towards the old enamel bowl on the upturned crate that served as a dresser but, mostly, she didn't seem to want to criticize him.

Since Betty had moved in with him he had begun to realize that he didn't want to live this way for ever. But he didn't know a way out of the slums and the sort of life he led. If Betty had to live by thieving, in spite of being able to read and write, what chance was there for him?

When Josie got back with the doll she was surprised to see Aunt Charlotte sitting by the hearth. The screen had been removed and a match had been put to the fire, which had been laid ready. Sometimes the summer evenings were cold, especially here, near the river.

But it was unusual for the fire to be lit this early. Aunt Charlotte looked tired. She complained more and more of her aching joints and she took ages to get up and down the stairs these days. Usually she went to bed to rest in the afternoons; not getting up again until teatime. But here she was sitting with her feet up on the velvet footstall, and a tray beside her on a little table, containing tea and biscuits and two cups of milk.

Annie took the doll from Josie without speaking, dusted it down and gave it to Flora.

'Now be good for your Aunt Charlotte, girls,' she said. 'I'm going out for a while. You can have your drawing books and pencils, and there's some milk and biscuits for you but I'll be back by teatime.

'Are you sure you can manage, Mrs Bertram?' she said to their aunt.

Aunt Charlotte gave Annie a cool glance. 'I suppose I'll have to, since Samuel has asked me to,' she said.

Josie saw Annie bite her lip as if she wanted to say something but she merely nodded and left the room.

Flora usually behaved herself for Aunt Charlotte and she settled at the table with her drawing book. Annabel lay forgotten on the hearth rug so Josie moved her on to the settle in case she should get trodden on.

'Go and join your sister,' Aunt Charlotte said. 'And take the milk and biscuits over. Leave me in peace.' She sounded vexed.

Josie did as she was told and busied herself with her own

drawing book. Flora was scribbling rather than drawing but Josie thought she would try to draw a sailing ship. She frowned in concentration. It was difficult.

She risked a glance at her aunt. Her eyes were closed. She must be asleep. Josie got down from her chair and tiptoed over to the window to look at the vessels moored nearby.

She was so intent on observing them that she did not hear the footsteps behind her.

'Naughty girl,' someone hissed in her ear. 'What have you thrown out of the window this time?'

She turned to see Annie glaring at her.

'Nothing – really I haven't.'

She was pushed aside roughly, then Annie leaned out to survey the scene below before closing the window.

'What's happening?' Aunt Charlotte asked. She had woken up at the noise and looked startled.

'I'm just closing the window, Mrs Bertram. It's safer that way.'

'Oh, of course. I see you're ready.'

'Yes. Will I do?'

There was a strange note in Annie's voice. She's excited about something, Josie thought. As if she's going for a treat of some kind. She was wearing a dress that Josie hadn't seen before. It was dark green and made of some silky material. Her hat was the same colour, with a veil that half covered her face. Her light brown hair was pinned up and back to fall in fat ringlets at the back.

Josie suddenly remembered something from a long time ago. She had been sitting on the bed behind her mother as she put curling rags into her hair. The room had been filled with the scent of her mother's favourite rosewater. Had her father been there too? Perhaps, but he hadn't stayed for very long. When her mother had tied the last rag she had turned laughing as she shook her head, making the rags flop about.

'What do I look like?' she'd asked, not expecting an answer. 'Do you want me to curl your hair too, Josie?'

Had her beautiful mother put curling rags in her hair that day? She couldn't remember. The picture faded and she felt an ache of longing.

'Get back to the table, Josie,' Annie said, and pushed her none too gently.

Then she was gone in a swirl of feathers and silk.

'Hmph!' Aunt Charlotte muttered when the door had slammed after her. 'And I suppose she'll be asking your father to get you a new nursemaid now.'

Josie was so surprised that she blurted out, 'Why should Papa find us a new nursemaid?'

Aunt Charlotte looked displeased. 'Little pigs have big ears!' she said. Then she sat back amongst the cushions with a sigh. 'Never mind, you're going to your Grandma Hannah's tomorrow. Your father has decided it's her job to tell you.'

Josie didn't dare to ask more questions but she couldn't stop thinking about what had been said. Did this mean Annie was leaving? How mysterious. And how strange it would be to have a new nursemaid after all these years.

Next morning Josie woke early. For a while she just lay and enjoyed the sun slanting in through the gap in the curtains and falling across her bed. Flora was still asleep in the other little bed, her hair spread out across the pillow and her cheeks faintly flushed.

Josie loved to lie and listen to the noises from the river, especially when vessels were leaving on the tide. The creaking of the masts and the slapping of the unfurled sails. And also the splashing churning noises the propellers of the steamships made.

And there was always the screaming of the gulls, who treated the tall buildings like cliffs to make nests in. Josie thought their calls sounded like laughter sometimes. Often a gull would perch on the ledge outside her window and look in curiously before soaring away again.

She kneeled on her bed, pushed the curtain aside and looked out of the window. As far as she could see the sky was crisscrossed with a forest of masts and spars and a maze of spidery rigging stretching down to the decks below.

Josie knew the ships had brought in cargoes of grain, timber, tobacco, salt, cotton, fruit, wine, brandy and rum, and so much more. Her father had given her an atlas, a book of maps, so that she could trace their voyages and see where the goods had come from.

He'd told her that he'd voyaged to many of these countries himself and that ships from Newcastle carried not just coal to London, where it kept the fires of the capital city burning, but fine glass and earthenware, paint and lamp black, soda and paper, bacon and hams, beer and porter – oh, so many interesting cargoes to all parts of the world.

And he sounded so sad sometimes, almost as if he'd like to be sailing with one of those vessels. Josie wondered if he ever would again.

Annie came to wake them much earlier than usual. Josie dressed herself while their nursemaid saw to Flora. Then they went down to have breakfast with their father. The table was set for four people. Josie wondered if Aunt Charlotte was coming to join them. Since her bones had stiffened she usually had breakfast in bed, and it took several cups of tea, she said, to get her going.

Or perhaps Philip would join them. He sometimes did. Although he was more likely to have an early breakfast in the kitchen and get down to open the shop first thing, even on a Sunday.

After Annie had set bowls of porridge before Josie and Flora, she returned to the kitchen and came back with two plates of bacon, egg and black pudding. She set one plate before their father and one before the empty chair. Then she sat there herself.

Josie glanced at her father but he had started eating his breakfast. Flora didn't seem to notice anything odd in the arrangement. Only Josie was left wondering why Annie, who had never sat at table with them before, should suddenly be sitting there.

Perhaps it was because she was coming with them to help their father look after them on the journey to their grandparents' home. Or perhaps it was a treat for her because she was leaving. That could be the explanation. But, as no one offered to explain, Josie thought she had best not say anything.

Their father had ordered a four-wheeler to take them to the station. Their luggage had been loaded by the time they all went down. Josie thought there was more than usual. Their father spent some time in the shop talking to Philip and the two young assistants. Then Philip came out with their father, shook his hand and told him not to worry.

Josie knew that Papa was always anxious when he had to go away from the shop. And she knew how cross this would make Aunt Charlotte, who kept insisting that Philip could manage the business very well.

Philip himself never said much. To anyone. He never seemed happier than when he was checking the stock or making long lists in the order books. Sometimes Josie was allowed in the shop when it was quiet and she loved the smells of coffee and tea, wine and vinegar, dried bacon and spices. There was another room full of such things as soap, paint, candles, oil, lamp wick, ropes and sailcloth.

Josie thought one day, when she was grown up, she might like to work in there. If she didn't go to her grandma's and help out at the Bluebell Inn, that was. Josie loved going to the inn at Moorburn. She loved the smell of the fresh country air and the wide skies and the silence when she ventured up the hill behind the inn.

You could hear the birdsong – so different from the screeching of the gulls – and the lambs bleating, and then there was the whistle of the train running along the valley bottom and the huff, puff, huffing sound it made as it rattled over the tracks.

Josie often went to Grandma Hannah's in the school holidays and, as soon as Flora had stopped being a baby, she had come too. That's when Annie had started to come with them, to help Papa look after the smaller child on the journey.

But it was then that they had started going earlier in the day so that Papa and Annie could travel home again. Josie wasn't sure why but she thought that Annie didn't like going to the inn. And Grandma Hannah, although she was pleasant, was always very quiet when Annie was there.

Josie enjoyed the train journey, but the compartment was hot and Annie wouldn't have the window opened in case the steam blew in with bits of soot and grit to soil her fine new clothes. Her hair was curled again and she had on another dress and bonnet that Josie had never seen before. She looked like one of the pretty ladies in Aunt Charlotte's monthly fashion journal. Papa was smartly dressed too but then he always was, even when he was in the shop. If he was in the office he would take his jacket off but he would pull it on if he went through to talk to a customer. Josie knew that her father was considered to be a fine-looking gentleman.

Flora managed to get herself invited to sit on Papa's knee and she played with his watch chain, pulling the beautiful gold watch out of its pocket and putting it back again. Annie soon leaned back and closed her eyes. Josie thought she went to sleep and she must have been having a nice dream because she was smiling.

Grandpa Jack had come to meet the train and he loaded Josie and Flora's cases into the trap. Josie was surprised to see that some of their luggage was left at the station in the porter's office, but her father didn't explain.

The loud clip-clopping of the horse's hoofs and the rattle of the wheels on the country road made talking difficult but Papa didn't seem to mind. Grandma Hannah had a meal ready for them. There was a white cloth on the old kitchen table and Grandma Hannah had brought out her Sunday best dinner plates with the blue and gold rims for the meal of roast lamb.

Papa had brought gifts of coffee, brown sugar and French brandy, but Grandpa hurried away and came back with a bottle of red wine. Grandma had to dust it and Josie watched wide-eyed as Grandpa poured four glasses and raised his own towards Papa before he said, 'I wish you happiness, Samuel and—'

'Whisht,' Grandma said, interrupting him. 'Now let's sit down and eat before everything is spoiled.'

Almost as soon as the meal was over Grandpa said he'd take Papa and Annie back to the station.

Papa hugged Flora and then Josie. He told them to be good girls.

Josie thought that he looked anxious so she said, 'Don't worry, Papa. I'll help Grandma Hannah with Flora.'

She was surprised when her father caught her up in his arms and hugged her more fiercely than usual and said, 'I know you will.'

And then they left.

*   *   *

They had changed trains at Alnwick. Samuel summoned a porter to help them with their baggage. They secured a carriage to themselves but, if she was anticipating any kind of conversation, Annie was disappointed. He would smile at her almost shyly now and then but he seemed distracted as he gazed out of the window. She had to suppress her feelings of irritation . . . and disappointment. This was not how she imagined it would be.

She glanced cursorily at the wild scenery: the hills, the sheep, the rough cliffs giving way to the wide expanse of sea. When they crossed the border into Scotland something stirred in her memory. Romantic couples ran away to Scotland to be married, didn't they? To a place called Gretna Green. Annie had only a vague idea of geography but she knew at least that they were on the east coast and they would not be going near Gretna. And they were not a romantic couple on their way to a secret wedding.

She suppressed a sigh as she pulled the gold chain up out of the neckline of her dress and undid it, slipped off the simple gold band Samuel had bought her and put it on to her wedding finger. She held her hand out as gracefully as she could, angled so that she could see how the ring looked. She expected some sort of gesture from Samuel but, if he had noticed, he didn't seem to think a response was called for. Fretfully she realized that he was still worrying about his daughters.

The motion of the train was beginning to make her weary. She began to look forward to arriving at the hotel in Edinburgh. She had never stayed in a hotel in her life before and, now, in these strange new circumstances, she wondered if she would know what to do; how to behave. She didn't want to embarrass Captain Walton – or rather Samuel, as she should now call him.

She knew that some older couples of Samuel's acquaintance still addressed each other formally. Arthur Williams and Eli Becket, who sometimes came to Samuel's home as dinner guests, referred to and addressed their wives as 'Mrs Williams' and 'Mrs Becket'. And the wives behaved no differently.

Annie's imagination suddenly provided her with a wild and indecent picture of stick-like Eli Becket raising his wife's nightgown ever so politely and saying, 'May I, Mrs Becket?', and his plump wife replying, 'Happy to oblige, Mr Becket. Help yourself.'

She felt herself flush, and she turned her head away so that Samuel could not see her face. She knew it was silly of her but she felt sure that he would be able to see into her mind's eye and be shocked by the shameful pictures he would find there.

She also knew that it would be difficult for her to face the Beckets again. And she would have to. Not just as the captain's maidservant helping to serve at the table, but as his wife. For, even though she was finding it hard to believe, Samuel had married her at last.

She had wanted this for years. Ever since his wife had died and she had made herself indispensable. She had looked after his daughters and tried to guess in advance what his needs would be. As his sister, Charlotte, had become more and more troubled with her arthritis Annie had quietly and unobtrusively taken over much of the running of the household and the ordering of the cook and the two downstairs maids.

At some stage Samuel had acknowledged the extra burdens she had taken on herself and began to appreciate that she was much more than simply nursemaid to his children. Annie wondered if he realized how like a wife and mother she had become rather than a servant. But it took a while.

She had no idea when he had first decided to ask her to marry him – or why. Was it because he was grateful for the many little ways she tried to make his life easier? Partly that, she thought. Or was it because every time he came into the room and she was there with his daughters, she had made sure that it was a happy picture he would see? He adored the girls, especially Flora, although many a man might have resented the child who had been the cause of his beloved wife's death in childbirth.

But not Samuel. It was only himself he blamed. And he had missed her terribly. He wore mourning black for a year and, long after the time most grieving widowers might have gone out and about to enjoy themselves, Captain Walton confined himself to going out to dinner with a sedate circle of older friends and having them back to his home in turn.

In the end Annie was convinced it was sheer loneliness that

had made him look upon her with awakening interest. But she did not fool herself that he loved her. He had given his heart to Effie and there would never be anyone to compare with his beautiful young wife. But as for Annie, she had loved and desired Samuel Walton ever since she had first come to work in his house.

She bit her lip. It had not been the wedding that young girls dream about: slipping out yesterday, just the two of them, to meet his friends Arthur Williams and Eli Becket at the church. No flowers and no attendants. Just the two worthy merchants as witnesses and not even their wives as guests.

Annie had had the uneasiest feeling that Mrs Williams and Mrs Becket might disapprove of Captain Walton's choice of wife – a servant girl. But the two gentlemen had been jolly enough. They had wished her well and pumped Samuel's hand up and down, telling him that he had done the right thing.

A man of his age should have a wife and, while he could have had the pick of any of the merchants' daughters in the town, they quite understood why he wanted to choose someone who had loved and cared for his two little daughters.

And, after all – Eli Becket leaned towards Samuel and lowered his voice but Annie still heard his whisper echo across the empty pews – the lass was a bonny one, wasn't she? Why shouldn't Samuel have his fun like any other man?

So they had married with not even a posy of flowers to mark the occasion. They had hurried home and Annie had spent the first night of her married life in the narrow bed in the little room next to the children's bedroom where she had slept ever since she had come to work in Samuel Walton's house.

Her husband, grown man that he was, had worried over how to tell his daughters that he was to marry again. He had decided that it should be their Grandma Hannah who should tell them. The old woman loved her granddaughters and surely they would see that if she thought it fitting that their father should marry they would be happy for him.

And as for the household staff, he had asked Charlotte to make the announcement after he and Annie had gone. Once more, Samuel had reasoned that if his sister seemed to approve, then no word would be spoken against the match.

In this, he was not being a coward. He was thinking of Annie. For he had realized that the household servants might not altogether approve of one of their number suddenly becoming the mistress of the house. He wanted Charlotte to be seen to give up the reins gracefully.

But Annie had known from the start that Samuel's older sister had not been pleased at all. She would do what she was asked because she was dependent on her brother. Her shop-keeper husband had died and left her very little. So she would comply with Samuel's wishes and hide her true feelings, not only because she would not want to risk losing her comfortable home, but also because of Philip, the son she doted on. Annie had guessed long ago what Charlotte Bertram hoped Philip's future would be.

The train slowed down as it approached Edinburgh, and Annie began to worry and wonder anew about the arrangements for their stay. They were man and wife but he had never kissed her, never held her hand or drawn her into his arms to hold her close. They had spent the first night of their married life in separate beds. Was that the way it was going to be?

Was this marriage simply to give his daughters a mother? She remembered the sly hints and the smiles of his friends in the church the day before. What had Samuel's reactions been? She had not been able to see his face, and his broad-shouldered back had given nothing away.

When the train stopped, Samuel helped her to descend and she stood on the platform, mute amongst the hissing steam and the bustle of travellers, as Samuel called a porter and arranged for a cab.

In no time at all, it seemed, they reached their hotel. Annie became even less inclined to speak. Everything was so grand, so . . . luxurious. Oak-panelled walls, marble floors, rich Turkey carpets, tall, leafy plants in sturdy brass pots as shiny as the stair rods. Jewelled patterns spilled down from a stained-glass window halfway up the wide staircase.

And then they were in their room. The hotel staff had gone. She had heard someone ask if Captain and Mrs Walton – *Captain and Mrs Walton!* – required a chambermaid to help them unpack and Samuel had said that he would ring down a little later.

Annie realized that she had been holding her breath and she let it out in one long sigh as she allowed herself to look around the large room. There were two tall windows heavily draped with creamy lace and framed with dark red velvet curtains, two matching plush armchairs at either side of a marble fireplace, a massive wardrobe and two sets of drawers, as well as ornate tables at each side of the bed. The bed. Annie's eyes took in the large four-poster with its mound of pillows before sliding quickly away.

'That door leads to a bathroom,' Samuel said. 'You'll want to bathe before dinner, I suppose?'

'Yes,' Annie told him, but her voice hardly rose above a whisper.

'I'll send for the chambermaid to help you,' her husband told her, 'but now, let me take your cloak. Perhaps we should rest a while.'

'Yes,' Annie said, and she felt her chest constrict as he took a step towards her.

Samuel removed her cloak and laid it on one of the sofas. Then he began to pull at his cravat with one hand while, taking her hand with the other, he led her towards the bed.

In the little bedroom under the eaves of the Bluebell Inn, Hannah had just settled her granddaughters for the night and she looked down at them as they lay sleeping. Josie lay with a protective arm over her sister, and the little one looked like an angel, just as Effie had looked, with her fine hair like curls of spun gold clustered round her sleep-flushed face. Hannah was anguished to find her grief still raw.

She looks so like her mother, Hannah thought. And she has her nature too. She acts before she thinks. Like the day she made a grab for one of the kittens and when it squealed in terror she burst out crying at what she'd done.

Yes, so like Effie . . . and someone else I know . . .

And then Hannah couldn't stop herself from thinking: oh, Effie, what did you do? And why did you have to die and leave me to carry this dreadful suspicion in my heart? I can't even tell my own husband. Dear old Jack's an upright man and it would grieve him to think that a daughter of his could behave like that.

But perhaps it's just as well – no, I must be wicked to think that! How could I believe that the death of my own daughter at so young an age could be anything but tragic?

It broke Samuel's heart. And yet how much more heart-broken would he have been if you had lived and he had discovered that this is Ralph Lowther's child, as I think she is?

Hannah's sigh was deep as she left the room and closed the door behind her. Now, Samuel had married again. And it was for the best.

He deserves some happiness with Annie, she thought. The poor lass feels awkward when she comes here, I know that. But she has no need to be. She thinks I'll resent her taking Effie's place, but I don't. If I can help in any way, I will. It's the price I have to pay for what my daughter did to him.

Later that night, as Hannah and her husband sat by the fire with cups of spiced ale, he asked her, 'Did you tell them?'

'Aye.'

'And how did they take it?'

'They took it fine. They're only bairns. I'm not sure how much they understand.'

'But they like the lass? They're fond of her?'

'Oh, aye. Annie's always done her best for them.'

Jack took a pull at his pipe. 'Do you not think she sometimes favours the little 'un?'

'What do you mean?'

'Flora. Annie makes a fuss of Flora. I sometimes reckon Josie's left out a little.'

'Do you?' Hannah asked. 'Perhaps you're right. But Flora's just a bairn and Josie loves her little sister. No, Josie wouldn't mind if what you say were true. I'm sure she wouldn't.'

Charlotte Bertram had stayed up late, unwilling to go to bed until Philip had shut the shop and locked up the house for the night. The day had been bright and sunny but now there was a chill wind from the river, and Philip built up the fire before settling by the hearth as they went over the happenings of the day.

Philip had brought his mother a cup of warm milk and she thanked him. He was a good son and she regarded him fondly.

'You told them, then?' he said, as he sipped from his mug of spiced wine.

'Yes. But I think they'd guessed, especially Mrs Dobson.'

'How did they take it?

'Not too well. Maud Dobson and I understand each other. Now she'll have to take orders from someone she regards as her inferior.'

'I never thought of that.'

'Of what?'

'Ever since we came here you have been ordering Uncle Samuel's housekeeping arrangements, although I've noticed Annie's attempts to usurp your position. Now there's no question that she will be in charge.'

'Yes.' Charlotte frowned. Pride prevented her from admitting to Philip how much that grieved her. She changed the subject. 'Have you had enough to eat?'

Philip smiled. 'Mrs Dobson left my supper on the kitchen table, as she usually does before she goes home. A plate of cold meats and cheese. I've had quite sufficient.'

'I wish you wouldn't eat in the kitchen along with Peggy and Joan, Philip. You may work in the chandlery but you're one of the family, not a servant.'

'It suits me. I can sit down at night without having to wash and change. I work long hours, you know.'

'And I hope Samuel appreciates it.'

'I'm sure he does. And you're right about Mrs Dobson and the maidservants having guessed what was up. While I was having my supper Peggy told me that they'd known for a long time that Annie had set her cap at my uncle, and her outing in her new clothes yesterday had set them speculating. Especially as they saw the master leaving at the same time.'

'You shouldn't gossip with the servants, Philip.'

'Oh, I don't know, Mother. I never say very much, you know, but Mrs Dobson thinks I'm a fine young man, and the two girls like to make a fuss of me. And that way I learn things I might not otherwise.'

'What do you mean?'

'Oh, trivialities mostly. But, for instance, did you know that Annie has asked Mrs Dobson if her niece, Patience, would be interested in the position of nursemaid?'

Charlotte Bertram tutted with displeasure. 'I thought as much,' she said. 'Now that she's Mrs Walton Annie won't want to sleep in that little boxroom next to the nursery. Someone else will have to mind the girls at night-time.'

'But that's natural,' Philip said. 'My uncle and Annie are man and wife: they will sleep together.'

Charlotte glanced at her son. He was tall and thin. But she knew him to be strong. His long, bloodless face was not conventionally handsome; but he kept himself clean, dressed well and, in his mother's eyes, his light brown hair, waving naturally, gave him the air of one of those pale romantic heroes in the novels she read secretly in her room at night. The novels that arrived monthly from the private subscription library, parcelled up in plain paper so that no one might guess that Mrs Bertram's taste was more frivolous than her appearance.

'And what do you think of that?'

Philip looked surprised. 'Of what?'

'Your uncle and Annie – I mean they will be man and wife . . .' Charlotte hesitated. She did not know how to convey her fears to her son without being indelicate.

He looked at her gravely and then nodded slowly. 'I see. You are worried that Annie will give my uncle a son?'

'And heir.'

'Maybe she will,' Philip said. 'But why should that concern me?'

'Because . . . because . . .'

Philip shook his head. 'Don't go on, Mother. I know that ever since I started working for my uncle you have hoped that I will inherit the business one day.'

'Why shouldn't you? Samuel has no son.'

'He has daughters.'

'It's not the same.'

'Isn't it?'

'No, and I can't bear to think that all the work you have done, all the years you have helped him, might be in vain if that scheming little madam should have a son.'

'Don't upset yourself. There's nothing we can do about that. But whatever happens, you know I'll look after you. Now, drink up your milk and I'll ask Peggy to help you up to bed. No,' he raised a hand when he saw she was about to protest, 'that's all I'm going to say.'

Philip sat back in his chair and stared thoughtfully into the fire. He seemed totally unworried by their new situation. But Charlotte knew that he was deep. She had no idea what was going on in his mind. His clever mind.

As for herself, she wouldn't be able to sleep that night. Nor perhaps for many nights to come. This marriage of her brother's was going to change all their lives.

Chapter Four

Christmas

Tom had found a job pushing the dobbies on the children's roundabout at the Christmas market and fair on the quayside. The dobbies, or dobbins, were simple enlargements of the penny toy horses. They each had rounded bodies of deal, with a little red-painted saddle and four stick-like legs ending in black-painted hoofs. The heads were cut from flat deal boards slotted into grooves in their bodies, and the tails and manes were made of strips of rabbit skin.

The other lads who were helping him push the dobbies around were all younger than he was, and they were content to work in exchange for a few free rides. Tom had done that himself when he was younger but, this year, Todd Ryan had agreed to let him work each day, shouting up the customers as well as pushing the ride in exchange for a few pence.

It was hard work but at least the effort kept him warm, and Todd and his wife were generous with the leftovers of the hot steak pies and peas that seemed to be their only food. It was while Tom was on his way back from the pie shop, the warmth from the newspaper bundle he carried soothing to his poor cold hands, that he saw Betty threading her way through the crowd with her basket of ribbons and laces.

Tom frowned. The cold air was murky with fog from the river and smoke from the city chimneys, and he wasn't quite sure what he'd seen. But when she slipped away through the crowds as quickly as she could he shook his head in admiration. Betty had just lifted a purse from a man who was part of a group of laughing sailors. The men were young and tough-looking, and Tom was impressed by his friend's daring.

He hurried back to the merry-go-round. The oil lamps hanging from the canopy around the central panels and the bright colours of the dobbies made it look inviting. Todd was waiting for his pie. Maggie Ryan, Todd's wife, had a stall nearby where she sold ribbon rosettes like those that winning jockeys wear, and little toy whips. The children who could afford them bought them before they mounted the wooden horses.

Maggie Ryan was a huge, unkempt woman. She had brewed up a pot of tea on a little stove and, while she and Todd enjoyed their meal sitting behind her stall, Tom was left in charge of the ride. He knew that Todd was keeping a sharp eye on the number of little customers and would know exactly how much money Tom should hand over.

A light fall of snow, more like sleet, did little to thin the crowd. It was Christmas Eve and there was an air of enjoyment and excitement. It wasn't just the townspeople who had come to the market fair. Their number was swelled by sailors from many ports. Laughter and shouts in several languages cut through the cold air. Tom had seen a group of tall fair-haired people – mothers and fathers, grandparents and children – walking about, enjoying the atmosphere quietly but spending very little money.

He knew these people to be Scandinavians. Like many before them they had already made one voyage across the German Ocean in order to get here, and now they were waiting in Newcastle for the next emigrant ship to take them to America – the New World, they called it – where they hoped to make new lives for themselves. Their vessel was ready and waiting. Tom had heard that they were sailing in the morning. On Christmas Day. He wondered what it would be like to go with them.

'Hello, Tom.'

Tom brought his mind back to his work when a child sitting on one of the dobbies startled him by addressing him by name. He glanced at her sharply. It was Josie Walton. He grinned.

'My, you look bonny,' he said. 'Like a princess in a fairy story.'

And she did. She looked like the picture of a little princess in one of the books he had taken home for Betty. Josie was wearing a red velvet coat nipped in at the waist and then flaring out over high-buttoned black boots. The white fur collar matched a hat the same shape as those that some of the Russian sailors wore, and it was tilted forward over her friendly little face, with strands of her dark hair escaping and curling down to her shoulders.

'Do I?' she asked. Her eyes rounded with surprise.

Tom understood then that Josie Walton was not used to receiving compliments, and suddenly he was taken unawares by the strangest of feelings. He realized that in some way he felt sorry for this little girl. And that was crazy. Why should he feel sorry for a child who had grown up in a warm house, who had new clothes probably even before she needed them, had never had to worry about where her next meal was coming from? And whose father was probably the best and kindest man in the world?

'Yes, you do look bonny,' he said gruffly, 'and never let anyone tell you different.'

Josie frowned. But Tom simply made sure she had hold of the scarlet reins. 'Hold on,' he said. 'When me and the other lads get going it can fair spin around. In fact you'd be better to put your arms around Dobbin's neck.'

'Or shall I do that?' Josie asked. She was smiling.

'What do you mean?'

'Look – like the painted lady!'

Josie held the reins with one hand and with the other she pointed towards the gaudy paintings on the panels at the centre of the roundabout. Each picture showed a prancing circus horse, and on the leading horse a lady in a frilly dress stood on the saddle, clutching a long rein with one hand and waving the other in the air above her head.

'Nah, you'd better not try that,' Tom said, and he laughed.

'What's that boy laughing at?' a child's voice asked.

Tom glanced at the horse in front of Josie's and saw her little sister sitting there. Flora too wore a white fur hat, and her coat was of velvet but it was a rich blue that emphasized the blue of her eyes. Yes, she was a beauty, Tom thought, and it was no wonder that folk hardly noticed her older sister. But her glance was sharp, not warm like Josie's, and her delicate features never looked content. At least not on the occasions Tom had seen her. He guessed that she could be a right bundle of trouble if she wanted to be.

'Get a move on!' Todd's booming voice cut into his thoughts. 'You're costing me money while yer stand there idle!'

'Sorry!' Tom grinned as he waved an acknowledgement. Todd was a big, coarse-looking man but he was good-natured and easy-going – unless he suspected anyone of trying to cheat him.

The ragged bunch of lads waiting to help push the round-about looked at Tom expectantly and he grinned again as he pointed to the one he thought had been waiting longest. He was a big lad who had been elbowing the smaller boys aside. Tom thought it best to give him his turn, then his ride, and then get rid of him. 'Hawway, then,' he shouted, 'take yer place opposite me. Ready, steady, go!'

Tom had chosen Josie's horse to push but he kept his eyes forward, not looking at anything in particular. That way he stopped himself from getting dizzy. Soon he realized that the other lad was trying to set the pace. The dobbies began to spin round faster than he liked but he had no choice but to try to keep up. He had a rough idea of how many times they had been round. Soon he would be able to call 'Whoa!'.

The children never wanted the ride to stop. They laughed with excitement as they spun round; waving to their parents and nursemaids each time they passed them. The ride was old and the mechanism began to creak and groan but, even so, all would have been well, if Flora had just kept still.

'Tom!' Josie called, and he looked up. She had turned round to look at him beseechingly.

'What is it?'

'It's Flora – look!'

Tom looked beyond Josie to the dobbie in front. The younger child had swung her leg over and was preparing to jump down. She would have a nasty fall, Tom thought, and, worse, she could easily roll under the ride and be injured.

'Whoa!' he shouted. 'We'll stop now.'

He tried to slow down but the other lad took no notice.

Tom held on to the wooden horse and tried to dig his heels in to stop its momentum but there wasn't enough time. He saw Todd hurrying towards the roundabout and he let go, then dodged forward, reaching Flora just as she launched herself off the dobbie.

He caught her in his arms and flung himself backwards, pulling her with him, away from the ride and into the legs of the crowd. Folk moved back hastily and Tom landed with a thud on the wet cobbles with Flora on top of him. She was crying – yelling blue murder, more like – and Tom screwed up his face in pain from the assault on his ears.

He could hear Todd bellowing at the lad who had caused the trouble and then the lad shouting, 'Divven't hit us, mister – ouch!'

Tom could imagine the clip round the ear he'd received, and managed to grin as the howls receded into the distance. But when a gentle laugh escaped him his chest constricted with pain. He groaned and closed his eyes. Next he was conscious of someone lifting the child off him.

And then a voice he knew said, 'Stand back, everyone. Tom, can you hear me?'

'Aye, I can hear you, Captain Walton, and I'm fine. Just winded.'

He opened his eyes to see the captain bending over him. Flora was in the arms of the woman who had been the nursemaid and who was now the captain's wife. Josie stood next to her father. She looked near to tears. Tom scrambled to his feet, ignoring the pain in his chest.

'Divven't fret, Josie. I'm not hurt.'

'Are you sure?' Captain Walton asked.

'Aye. Just winded.'

'Thank you, Tom,' the captain said. 'You saved Flora from being hurt and I won't forget that.'

'Well, I owed you a favour, didn't I?' Tom grinned as he squinted up between the flakes of snow. The fall was thicker now and, as the day grew colder, Tom guessed the snow might lie.

'A favour? Did you?'

For a moment the captain looked puzzled and then he smiled gravely. 'Oh, yes, I remember. But, nevertheless, I'd like to shake your hand.'

Tom was surprised but he offered his dirty hand and the captain took it in his own warm grasp. Tom felt a slight pressure, something hard against his palm. His eyes widened but the captain shook his head very slightly. Then he withdrew his hand and turned to his wife and children.

'Home, I think,' he said.

Tom watched them go. Captain Walton had taken Flora and she snuggled against his chest, still whimpering. Tom, living on the streets as he did, had witnessed many a family scene and he knew that some parents would have scolded the child for acting foolishly. But not the captain.

Mrs Walton had looked pale, Tom thought. Perhaps she was suffering from the cold; certainly her face was pasty and her nose red. But she was dressed in the smartest of clothes. Tom knew all about fashion, thanks to Betty's collection of pictures torn from ladies' magazines.

Josie turned to wave and Tom was angered by the fact that no one took any notice of her. He forgave the captain, who must still be anxious about the little one, but surely his wife could have taken Josie's hand.

'Right, young Tom. Let's get going again. Time's a-wasting and that means I'm losing money.' Todd lumbered towards him. The big man was grinning. 'You did well, there, me laddo. If the little lass had been hurt I'd hev been in trouble. Here's sixpence for you.'

Tom forgot about the pain that was still nagging at his side and held his hand out for the coin. But not the hand that had shaken Captain Walton's. He hadn't looked yet, but that hand still held the coin that the good man had pressed into it a moment ago. From the size and the shape of it Tom knew it to be a sovereign.

No one must know he had come into such riches; the captain had had the sense to realize that. In the world Tom lived in it was better to keep quiet about such a stroke of fortune.

When Todd turned his back Tom slipped both coins into the small buttoned pocket on his tattered waistcoat. When the roundabout closed for the night there would still be time to buy a treat for tomorrow. He knew Betty had planned some sort of Christmas dinner but perhaps he could buy some sweet mince pies from the late-night baker's. Something to surprise her.

Then, just as he took up his place behind the wooden dobbie, he spied Betty again. Todd shouted, 'Let's go!' but Tom froze in horror. His friend was in the act of lifting something from the coat pocket of a man who was bending over one of the stalls, examining a fine silk scarf.

The goods on the stall were protected by a canvas canopy and the lamps hung on a pole above gleamed through the swirling flakes of snow and illumined the bright red hair of the man standing there. Fox Telford!

Tom went cold with fright. Betty knew fine who Fox Telford was and how vicious he could be. No matter what a tempting target he was as he concentrated on the scarves, surely she had enough sense not to try to pick his pocket.

'Tom, what's the matter with you, lad?' Todd roared. The showman had already chosen another boy as Tom's helper and the children on the dobbies were impatient for the ride to start.

Distracted, Tom glanced at Todd and gave him the thumbs-up sign. 'Right, I'm ready,' he yelled back.

'I should think so. Now – giddy-yup!'

Tom grasped the wooden horse and took a few faltering steps. He glanced back towards the stall and breathed a sigh of relief. Betty had turned and was already darting away as she slipped something into her basket of ribbons and laces. Fox Telford hadn't noticed anything. He was holding one of the scarves towards the stall keeper as if just about to pay.

Thank goodness, Tom thought, and he began to run faster. Some of the children urged the little horses on as they snapped their whips. Not far away a hurdy-gurdy man began to play, and Tom, thinking of the money in his pocket and the money he was still to earn, began to enjoy himself. But wait till I get home, he thought. I'll tell Betty, no matter how good a thief she is, she must never lift anything from Fox Telford again.

Josie trailed along behind her father and Annie as they made their way through the crowds. She would have liked to stay to

77

talk to Tom but Flora was still crying and their stepmama was tired, and Father had decided that they must go home. Josie looked back but all she could see was the brightly painted canopy of the roundabout as it revolved.

She smiled as she imagined her friend pushing the wooden horses and she found herself wondering how long he would stay there. And, when he did go home, she wondered where that would be and if anyone would be waiting there for him.

'Do hurry up, Josie.'

Josie looked up to find that she could no longer see her father and Flora, but that Annie had waited and was calling for her crossly. They weren't far from home, and Annie took her hand and hurried her along until they reached the door of the chandler's shop.

The shop was a blaze of light and, as they hurried in, taking a blast of cold air and snowflakes with them, Josie found that it was crowded. Her cousin, Philip, and one of the assistants were dealing with a queue of patient people, who were all clutching printed lists. None of them looked like sailors.

Josie guessed they were emigrants, people who were going to make homes for themselves in a different land, and the lists they held were of provisions that they would add to the rations given them by the captain of the ship once they set sail. They would buy small portions of sugar, tea, flour and dried fruit – anything they could think of to add to the everyday diet of bread and potatoes.

Sitting quietly in the shop, as her father had allowed her to do sometimes, she had learned that during the voyage they had to cook for themselves and that they had to provide their own pans and kettles and teapots and dishes. Her father kept boxes already packed with everything a family would need.

When he saw how many people were waiting, Josie's father put Flora down and asked Annie to take them upstairs to the living quarters. He told her he would come up as soon as he could but that she could see it was going to be a busy night and he wanted to make sure that these good folk had everything they needed to see them on their way.

Before they went through the door that led to the passage and the stairs, their father gave each of his daughters a kiss and, smiling, told them to get to bed quickly because Father Christmas would not come until all the children were asleep. Josie wondered if Father Christmas would find the children sleeping on the emigrant ship tonight. She would have liked to ask her father about that but he had already shut the door and Annie was urging her and Flora to go upstairs.

Once upstairs Annie handed her stepdaughters over to Patience but told her that before she took them up to bed she must go down to the kitchen and ask her aunt to send up a plain biscuit and a cup of weak tea.

'My aunt was just about to go home,' Patience told her.

'Really?' Annie said. 'I don't remember giving her permission to leave early.'

'No, Mrs Walton. It was the captain. He said that once everything was done she should get home to her family. After all, it's Christmas Eve.'

'I see.' Annie knew that she could not express her displeasure but she was vexed none the less. Samuel had a habit of issuing orders to the servants without consulting her. He didn't do it to spite her – she knew that – it was simply that he didn't think. He didn't remember that she was the mistress here now. She summoned up a smile. 'Of course,' she said. 'Well, could you ask Peggy or Joan to see to it?'

'Yes, Mrs Walton. Just mind the bairns, will you, until I get back?'

She hurried out of the room, leaving Annie more irritated than she had been before. 'Just mind the bairns', indeed! Would no one in this house give her the respect that was owing to the captain's wife?

The trouble was that she had first come here as a servant and nobody could forget that. Patience was new here but she was Mrs Dobson's niece. Annie suspected the cook, her niece and Peggy and Joan gossiped about her in the kitchen.

If only Mrs Dobson wasn't such an excellent cook. If only Annie could think of some way of getting rid of her and taking on someone new. Perhaps she could suggest to Samuel that it would be better to have a cook who lived in? She knew Mrs

Dobson would never agree to that. But, no, they didn't have room for another servant to live in, not with Mrs Bertram and Philip living here.

And that was another problem. Philip took most of his meals in the kitchen and no doubt joined in the gossip. What tales did he carry back to his mother, she wondered.

She sighed wearily and leaned closer to the fire. Her feet were cold from tramping through the slush and she was worried that she had stayed out too long. Not that she could have protested. Samuel had wanted to take his daughters to the Christmas fair and Annie had had to pretend that there was nothing so much that she wanted to do! As if she hadn't done enough over the last few weeks. Although, to be fair, no one had asked her to.

It had been entirely her own idea to make this festive season a happy one for Samuel and his daughters. To celebrate Christmas as it had never been celebrated before in this grand house on the quayside. Weeks ago she had asked Mrs Dobson to start making the pudding and the cake and the sweet mincemeat for the pies.

She had ordered Christmas crackers, tinsel garlands and glass tree ornaments from Bainbridge's, and when the tree was delivered from the stall in the Grainger Market, just a few days ago, she had dressed it herself, climbing the stepladder to fix the glass star on the top.

She glanced over at it, thinking how pretty it looked and how inviting with the brightly wrapped presents arranged artfully round its base. Surely Samuel will notice and appreciate everything I've done, she thought.

'Here's yer tea, Mrs Walton.'

She hadn't heard Peggy enter the room. She turned her head to find her standing with a tray. 'Peggy, you startled me, you should have knocked.'

The girl pursed her lips. She didn't apologize, but at least she went to set the tray carefully on one of the small tables and then lifted both table and tray over and set it beside Annie's chair.

'Will that be all?' she asked.

'Yes.' Annie sighed; she was too weary to reprimand the girl or try to teach her further. Not tonight. And at least the tray had been set up nicely.

When she poured herself a cup of tea she realized that there were two cups on the tray. So that was it. Peggy had thought Samuel was here too. She probably wouldn't have bothered to use the best china if she'd thought it was just for me, Annie thought bitterly.

She sat back in her chair and winced as a sharp stitch-like pain cut through her. She sat still and held her breath but the pain had eased away almost immediately. She sipped her tea and looked across at the tree shimmering in the firelight. It was so beautiful. But perhaps she had been foolish to climb the ladder and stretch up like that to put the star on the top.

And then, later, she had stretched again as she arranged sprigs of holly around the mirrors and along the mantelpiece. She'd had a stitch that night too, a nagging pain that had frightened her, especially after what had happened just after the heat of summer gave way to autumn chill.

To her joy Annie had fallen pregnant straight away after the wedding. It must have happened on their honeymoon. She'd not told Samuel, for she had guessed that Charlotte Bertram was watching her closely and she could imagine why. Samuel's sister would be terrified that Annie would give Samuel a son – and that would put young master Philip's nose out of joint. So, although the signs were unmistakable, she had wanted to be absolutely sure.

And it was just as well that she'd waited, for it had come to nothing. Quietly one morning at the turn of the season, with hardly any pain, she had lost the promise of a child of her own. She knew it happened this way sometimes. Some women might lose several babies before giving birth to a healthy child. That's what had happened to her sister, and now she had three children.

The anxiety grew and coiled within her. Had she been doing too much? For a week or two now she had been sure that what she'd been hoping for was true. She was pregnant for a second time. Samuel and she would have a child of their own. A child who would make her husband realize that this marriage was just as important as his first. And what a miracle it would be if the child was a boy.

81

And, again, she hadn't told him. It was early days. After Christmas Samuel's daughters were going to Moorburn to spend some time with Grandma Hannah. Patience, their new nurse-maid, was taking them. With them gone, she would have Samuel to herself.

Charlotte hardly counted any more. Samuel had moved a table and chairs as well as a small sofa and armchair into his sister's bedroom so that she was spared the stairs, which were becoming more and more difficult for her to climb. And Philip, if he wasn't working late in the shop or sitting at the kitchen table with the servants, would take his meals with his mother when he could.

So Samuel and she would eat alone. That's when she planned to tell him – when they had finished their meal one night and were sitting by the fire. Just thinking about that and imagining what Samuel's reaction might be cheered her up immensely. It was enough to dispel her weariness and her dismal thoughts, and spread a lovely warmth through her whole being.

Setting her cup down carefully Annie leaned over to unlace her boots. When she had eased them off she wiggled her toes to warm them, then reached for the footstool. She owed it to herself to relax for a while. Sighing, she leaned back in her chair.

The pubs along the quayside and the back alleys were full of revellers, most of them drunk. Some of them were singing Christmas carols and Tom paused to listen to one voice that soared above the others.

> 'I saw three ships come sailing in,
> On Christmas Day, on Christmas Day . . .'

He recognized the voice to be that of Daft Bobby, a ragged scarecrow of a man who earned his keep by singing in the streets. Tom couldn't see Bobby so he reckoned he must have ventured into the nearby inn, cap in hand.

> 'I saw three ships come sailing in,
> On Christmas Day in the morning.'

Tom lingered in the shadows for a moment. A light covering of snow lay on the filth of the cobbled alleyway, and the air blowing in from the sea was fresh with the tang of salt water. The revellers in the inn, made tearful by cheap spirits, stopped their tuneless bawling to listen to Bobby.

'And what was in those ships all three?'

As Tom listened his gaze wandered down towards the river. The dark waters glinted in the moonlight, and mast lights glowed from the vessels that were preparing to sail. Tom often wondered about the ships – where they were going, what cargoes they carried, what it would be like to sail with them.

Suddenly he shivered. He had stood here long enough. But it was with reluctance that he turned away from the sound of Daft Bobby's singing. He knew he had heard something wonderful: a poor man singing like the angels surely must sing. And he felt sad that his friend Betty would never be able to share such a moment.

He had often wondered what it would be like to live in a silent world. Never to hear the cries of the street traders, the call of the gulls, soaring high above the mastheads of the ships, and the ordinary conversations with your pals that made life bearable. Still, Betty was his pal now, and they rubbed along as best they could. And they understood each other well enough.

Often they became helpless with laughter when they gestured and mimed to each other the happenings of the day. Neither of them had anybody else, it seemed, so they had become like a family, and life for both of them was more endurable.

Tomorrow he was determined that they would both enjoy themselves. They had got in a good supply of coal and Betty had promised them a feast. He grinned when he remembered how she had pretended to eat, scooping up food with an imaginary spoon, licking her lips and then clasping her hands and holding them out in front of her to signify a big belly full of food.

He imagined her pleasure when he showed her what he had brought home. He'd gone to the baker's as he'd planned as soon as he'd finished working on the merry-go-round and bought sweet mince pies and some little marzipan fancies shaped like stars. He'd tucked the baker's bag safely inside his jacket and the thought of it nestling there warmed him. And he had decided that neither of them would go out thieving on Christmas Day. It didn't seem right somehow. Not on the day that Jesus was born.

Tom wondered, as he often did, if there could really be a being somewhere up on high, beyond the clouds, someone who cared what happened to folk such as Betty and him. Someone whose only son had been born in an outhouse behind an inn to lowly people. He would like to believe the wonderful stories, but it was very hard sometimes.

As soon as he entered the old dwelling house he knew there was something wrong. He didn't know what, or why he felt like that, but he was aware of the hairs lifting on the back of his neck.

Cautiously he made his way up to the top floor, his way lit by the moonlight streaming in through an empty window frame on the top floor and spilling down the stairwell. Even before he had turned the corner to the last flight his suspicions were confirmed. As well as the shadows cast by the moon, dancing shapes flickered on the walls, caused by the fire in their room. Betty had left the door open. And she never did that if she was in alone. Neither of them ever left the door open.

Instinct told him not to call out, and to proceed as quietly as possible. Sure enough, when he reached the top landing, he found the door ajar. He stared in dismay at the splintered wood and the lock he had put there himself now swinging from one nail. Someone had forced the door open; kicked it probably. Who would do that?

He edged himself into a position where he could look into the room. He couldn't see anyone. Had someone broken in and taken Betty? But why? Or perhaps she had found the place like this when she had come home and she had run away. Perhaps she was looking for him on the streets even now.

He had half turned to go when he sensed, although he didn't know how, that someone was listening as keenly as he was. He tensed, growing into himself, becoming smaller as he held his breath. Then he could hear it. Someone was breathing quite close to him. Where?

Behind the open door!

He didn't realize that he'd stretched out his arm until his hand caught the broken lock and sent it swaying to and fro. The slight rattling sound startled him and made him gasp out loud. Then, to his dismay, he realized that the cruel moon had cast his shadow across the floorboards of the room in front of him. Whoever was waiting in there knew very well that he had come home.

He was aware of a scuffling sound and then he heard, 'Ru . . . Ru . . .'

Tom recognized the sounds as Betty trying to tell him to run. But the warning was followed by a slap and a cry.

'Bitch!' a man's voice snarled. 'I told you to keep quiet!'

Tom had no choice. Someone was harming his friend. He shot into the room and, when he was well clear of the door, he turned to see a man gripping Betty by her long hair. The man kicked the door closed. Tom felt his blood run cold. It was Fox Telford.

'Let her go,' Tom yelled.

The red-haired man's eyes widened. He looked amused. 'Make me.'

Tom clenched his fists. To his shame he felt tears gathering in his eyes. But they were tears of rage. 'Why hev you come here?' he asked hoarsely.

'You know.'

That surprised him. 'No, I divven't. Let her go.' Just in time he stopped himself from saying please. It would do no good to beg.

The lodging-house keeper twisted Betty's long hair round his hand like a rope and gripped it more tightly. She squealed with pain and Tom felt sick.

'I saw what she did,' Fox said.

'Saw her?'

'Aye. And I saw you watching.'

'You couldn't hev!'

Fox laughed and Tom realized he had given himself away.

'But I did. There was a looking-glass on the stall. So's you can try on the cravats, or the titfers, hev a look at yerself. Well,

I saw yer pal come up behind me and if it wasn't fer the glass I would never hev known she'd lifted anything. She's good.'

'Why didn't you stop her there and then?'

'Reasons.'

'What reasons?'

Tom felt himself begin to tremble when an explanation suggested itself. Fox had come here to kill Betty. And him too. He said he'd seen him watching from the merry-go-round and Fox was sharp enough to put two and two together. He was going to kill them both.

'What's the matter with you?' Fox barked.

'Nowt.'

'Yes there is. Yer shakin' fit to piss yerself. Now stop that and tell this dummy here to make a cup of tea. We've some talking to do.'

'Don't call her that!' Tom's anger stopped the shakes and he stood up straight.

Fox laughed and he grasped Betty's hair all the tighter, pulled her closer to him and then thrust her forcefully away, letting go of her hair at the same time. She landed on the floor on all fours and crouched there sobbing. Tom hurried over to her. He was conscious that Fox had moved himself so that he stood near the door, barring the way out, although it was nigh on impossible for either of them to escape.

Betty grasped his hands as he helped her to her feet, and looked into his face, desperately trying to make out what was going on. He led her to the fire and gestured for her to make a pot of tea. She looked both frightened and puzzled but Tom made her understand that she had to do it. He didn't want to anger their unwelcome visitor. He had to find out exactly why the man had come here.

A little later they sat at the table. Fox brought a silver flask out of his pocket and poured a generous measure of whatever it contained into his cup. He saw Tom watching him and he grinned and offered the flask.

'Pour a nip into yer tea. Hers as well; I'm feeling generous.'

'No.'

'Manners. But gan on, lad, divven't let pride stop yer. It's good stuff, I can guarantee, and it'll warm yer cockles.'

Tom stared down at the table and shook his head stubbornly but he looked up in surprise as Betty reached over and snatched the flask. She poured more than a mere nip into her cup and Tom's as well, then plonked the flask down on the table in front of Fox and stared at him sullenly.

Fox grinned. 'Not such a dummy after all, then. And if the pair of you do as I say, you'll be able to get used to a few of the good things in life now and then. Fox looks after his own. Now, drink up and we'll talk business.'

At a loss, and wondering what was coming next, Tom sipped his tea cautiously and caught his breath, nearly choking as the strong spirit hit the back of his throat. Through watering eyes he watched in amazement as Betty drank her tea with obvious enjoyment. Then he eyed Fox warily. The man was staring at him and frowning.

'What is it?' Tom couldn't help blurting out.

Fox Telford didn't reply but he shook his head. 'Nowt,' he said. 'I thought mebbes you and I had met before. Hev we?'

Tom's blood ran cold. 'No, never,' he said, and he tried not to look frightened.

Could Fox have recognized him as the lad who had once been foolhardy enough to steal a roast chicken? He looked down into his drink, waiting for the man's wrath to erupt.

But the lodging-house keeper-cum-thief master seemed to shake off his moment of doubt and, because he knew he had them in his power, he grinned as he drew the moment out.

'Right,' he said finally. 'She's good and she's going to work fer me.'

'What?' Tom gasped.

'You heard me. I followed her home and the only reason I was still here when you came back, the only reason I waited, was because I couldn't get a sensible word out of her. No proper words at all, for that matter. I reckoned the lass is some kind of halfwit and I reckoned you've trained her, told her what to do.'

'She's not—' Tom began and stopped himself.

He shook his head and looked down at the table. Betty was far from half-witted. In fact he thought she was probably much cleverer than he was, and he certainly hadn't trained her to pick pockets or be a thief of any kind. Much of the time he didn't know how on earth she did it. But it might not be a good idea to let Fox Telford know the truth of the situation. Tom had better hear him out first and then try to work out what on earth they could do.

'Divven't fret,' the man said. 'I'm not going to spoil yer little life in any way. The pair of yer can stay here and carry on exactly as before, and even make yerselves more comfortable. But everything she lifts – and you an' all – you'll bring straight to me.'

'Why should we?'

'Simple. Because nobody crosses Fox.' The lodging-house keeper hadn't even raised his voice. There was no need to. 'I'll not keep you short,' the man continued, 'because I can get better prices fer anything you pinch than you ever could. And, furthermore, I can put her in the way of better pickings.'

Fox laid a dirty finger at the side of his nose and tapped it. Tom noticed then that Betty was watching the man's lips intently but her face was expressionless. Suddenly Fox reached across the table and took hold of Betty's chin with his fingers. He turned her face towards the light of the fire.

'Pity she's a dummy,' he said. 'She's not bad-looking. I divven't know why she stops with a little bairn like you. I reckon she's ready fer a man to look after her.'

Tom felt sick. He knew what Fox meant and it filled him with disgust. 'Betty needs me to tell her what to do. Like you said.'

'Aye,' Fox sighed, 'I thought as much. So I'll take on the pair of yer. Now I'll hev to go. I've lingered long enough in this hovel. It's Christmas Day the morrer and I'll be busy but, come Boxing Day, I want to see yer both at my place. Yer know where it is, I suppose?'

Tom nodded. There was no harm in admitting it. Everybody knew where Fox's lodging house was, and that it was a right den of thieves.

'First thing Boxing Day morning then, and I'll tell yer where to gan and what to do. Come along the alleys to the back door, mind. I divven't want anyone to know that she's anything to do with me.'

While he was speaking Betty had gone to the fire and poured a little hot water from the simmering kettle into her cup. Instead of going back to her seat she came to stand next to Fox, placed her cup on the table and, with the same hand, pointed first to the cup and then to the silver flask, which still lay on the table.

Fox looked as if he was surprised at her daring but then he gave a shout of laughter. 'So that's the way to her heart!' he said. 'Well, I don't mind obliging the lass but I can see I'll hev to keep her on ration. Divven't want her to take too much and get sloppy. But just this once . . .'

As their visitor unscrewed the top of the flask and concentrated on pouring a drop into Betty's cup he was still smiling. Betty had moved back a little and something about the way she was standing alerted Tom. Her features were drawn, her eyes huge, and her shoulders hunched. Why had she placed both hands behind her back?

And, then, as one of her arms began to move sideways, he had a premonition of what was about to happen. He looked at her face and saw her warning glare. He looked back quickly at his cup and picked it up with both hands, trying to control his trembling.

He couldn't believe Betty was foolish enough to try something, but it would be much worse if anything he did gave her away. All this flashed through his mind in the few seconds it took for her to raise her arm high above Fox's head and bring it down forcefully.

Tom remained rigid, staring into his cup until he heard Fox grunt. From the corner of his eye he saw the man slump forward on to the table, knocking Betty's cup over and spilling its contents. Only then did Tom allow himself to look at his friend. She was holding the flat iron. She must have picked it up from the hearth after she'd poured water into her cup.

Shakily Tom stood up. His chair fell over behind him and he glanced swiftly at Fox but the clatter it made hadn't disturbed him. But how could it? The man was surely dead. Tom stared at Betty wide-eyed. What on earth were they going to do now?

Betty looked at him and must have understood his expression. She pointed at Fox, then at herself and shook her head violently. She repeated the gesture several times until Tom went forward and took the iron from her and placed it on the table before taking hold of both her hands.

'It's all right,' he said, and she watched his lips intently. 'I understand. You were frightened. You didn't want to work for Fox.'

She began to nod eagerly but Tom sensed that both of them knew that Betty had been in danger from Fox in another way as well. Then Betty pulled herself away and, to Tom's alarm, she approached the man lying across the table. What was she going to do?

Tom watched as his friend placed her hand on Fox's neck. He noticed that a dark stain was spreading across the man's red hair. Blood. Tom shuddered. What was Betty doing?

Only moments later she explained. She drew away in terror and mimed with a hand against her own chest that Fox's heart was still beating. Tom understood that she had been feeling for a pulse. And she had found one. Their tormentor was still alive.

Tom realized that thoughts of concealing the body had already been going through his mind. He would have done anything to prevent Betty being hanged for murder. But now the situation was worse for her – and for him too. If Fox survived this night there was no question that he would kill them both.

He looked around the room that had been their home. He thought of the plans they had made for the next day and remembered with a sob that he still had the bag of mince pies and marzipan fancies tucked inside his jacket. Well, there would be no Christmas dinner for them now. Not here. They would have to leave. And there was only one person he could turn to for help.

Samuel Walton had already sent Philip off to bed and he was just about to lock up when the door was pushed open forcefully, nearly knocking him over. He lunged for the cudgel he kept behind the door and swung round, ready to face the intruder. He stared into space for a moment before his gaze dropped and, to his astonishment, instead of a brazen ruffian, he saw a pair of ragged, shivering bairns.

'Tom?' he said wonderingly. 'For God's sake, what brings you here in such a state?'

'Shut the door,' Tom croaked, and he glanced over his shoulder nervously.

His companion, a girl perhaps a few years older, moaned with terror.

Samuel pushed them gently aside and went to the door. He looked out along the quayside. Drunken sailors shouted and stumbled on the frosty cobbles. And there were also silent figures hugging the shadows, men and women intent on relieving fools of their money in one way or another. But there didn't seem to be anyone in obvious pursuit of his late-night visitors.

Nevertheless he stepped back quickly, locked and bolted the door and put out all the lights before shepherding Tom and the girl through to the office. He sat them down by the fire.

'Well,' he said. 'What's up?'

It was a while before their story came tumbling out and, even then, he had to coax them – or Tom, rather, for the girl remained silent.

Samuel was appalled. 'And you left him there?' he asked.

Tom's glance was reproachful. 'What else could we do?'

Samuel shook his head. He knew there was no answer. 'And he's alive?'

'Aye,' Tom said. 'God help us!'

Samuel saw that the girl was watching their lips intently as they spoke. He realized she was a deaf mute. But she was obviously following the conversation and growing more and more restless. When a strangled sob escaped her lips, Tom reached out a skinny hand and covered hers reassuringly before looking at Samuel with a heart-rending mixture of hope and trust.

Samuel thought of his own bairns, Josie and Flora, asleep in their warm beds, dreaming their Christmas dreams, and he decided instantly that he would do whatever was necessary to help these two forgotten waifs. And when he told them so it nearly broke his heart to see the relief that smoothed away the pinched look from their faces.

But it seemed the lad was only asking him to help Betty.

That's what he called her, and he assured Samuel that, although deaf and dumb, she was smart as paint.

After some discussion, Samuel agreed. 'But she'll have to change her ways,' he said, and this brought a wan smile to Tom's face.

'She'll do owt you tell her,' he said. 'All she's ever needed is for someone to treat her right.'

'Very well. I know where to send her.'

'And Fox will never find her?'

'Never. But what about you?'

'Divven't worry about me. I hev a plan of me own.'

'Are you going to tell me what it is?'

'No. But . . .'

'But what?'

'Well, you could give me some provisions, if you like.'

'Provisions?'

'Aye. And one or two things from the store.'

Half an hour later, Tom took his leave of a weeping Betty and slipped out into the night. He was carrying a sack of goods that Samuel had got down from the shelves. As he watched the lad disappear into the shadows he had a pretty good idea of what he was going to do. He'd even dropped a few helpful hints about how to go about it.

Samuel shook his head, surprised at himself but unrepentant. Retired captain though he was, he wished the lad well.

Annie's feet were still cold. She lay as close to Samuel as she could without disturbing him and tried to steal some of his warmth. He had his back to her. They had never lain sleeping in each other's arms in the marriage bed, not even after he had made love to her. There had never been any murmured words of tenderness, not even any smiles. His face would remain composed and solemn and, when he had done, he would feign tiredness and turn from her until the morning.

She had always known when he was pretending. His yawns were false and she knew from instinct that he was not asleep as he lay stiffly staring at the wall. More than once she thought she'd heard a stifled sob.

Effie! she'd thought, and she'd cursed the memory of

Samuel's first wife. Was he never going to forget her? Was he never going to forgive himself for doing what any man would do and taking another wife?

It made it so much worse that this was the very room where Effie had died. The very bed. Annie squeezed her eyes shut and tried to blot out the picture of her predecessor lying here, so beautiful even in death. So pale, so cold . . .

It wasn't fair that Samuel should go on grieving like this. Didn't he appreciate all the things she had done to try to make him happy? She had cared for his daughters, especially Flora, whom he seemed to favour. Well, not exactly favour, but you could hardly blame him for indulging the child who looked so like the woman he had loved so fervently.

And she had tried to make the house more homely. That was something it had never been in Effie's time. The first Mrs Walton had liked fine clothes for herself and fine furniture for the house but she had shown little interest in the day-to-day running of the household. Half the time her mind had seemed to be elsewhere.

It had been just as well that Samuel's sister had been happy to take charge. And lucky for herself that Charlotte Bertram was now too infirm to continue doing so. So, she had been free to try to make Samuel and his daughters happier than they had ever been. And it galled her that he hadn't seemed to notice.

Flora was hard work: light-hearted and joyous one moment and the picture of misery the next. And half the time the cause of her distress would be something she'd done herself in her headlong way of demanding excitement and attention. But it was easy to indulge and forgive her. She could be so loving. She would wind her little arms about your neck and snuggle up and look at you so trustingly that you would have had to have a heart of stone not to respond to her.

And Josie . . . What of the elder child, so quiet and so deep? Yes, deep. Annie suspected that Josie, young though she was, missed nothing. It was hard to know what was going on in her mind. And that irritated Annie. A child of that age had no right to look so wise.

She glanced over at the hearth. The fire had been banked so it would last the night and the glow was reassuring. She could wrap herself in her shawl, she supposed, and sit and toast her toes for a while.

She moved to the edge of the bed cautiously and a wave of sickness hit her. She kept still, willing the nausea to subside but, when it did, the pain that had been nagging at her all day came back and this time it stayed.

Oh, no, she thought, not again. Not now. Perhaps if I lie very still, all will be well. Miserably she lay back amongst the pillows and, even though Samuel was lying next to her, she thought she had never felt so alone.

Josie wasn't sure what had disturbed her but suddenly she was wide awake. She lay quietly and listened for any sign of movement in the house, but there was none. Even the world outside seemed quiet. The voice of a lone reveller rang out for a moment but the usual noises from the quayside seemed to be muffled by the snow.

She pushed back the bedclothes and sat up. She looked across at Flora. Her sister was fast asleep. She was smiling, her misadventure on the merry-go-round no doubt forgotten. Her head would be full of the treats in store for her tomorrow when they would be allowed to open the fascinating parcels that were stacked around the shimmering Christmas tree.

Josie crawled down the bed and examined the stocking that Patience had helped her tie to the bedpost. Flora had one too, and they were both satisfyingly full. Father Christmas must already have paid his visit. Josie sat back and thought for a while.

Did she believe in Father Christmas? Flora did, and Josie would never dream of spoiling things for her little sister by voicing her doubts and her suspicions that it was really their own dear father who filled their stockings with tangerines, sugared almonds and a little net of chocolate coins in gold and silver foil.

Well, whoever filled their stockings, he had been already and she must be careful not to wake Flora, or her little sister would probably want to look in the stocking right now. And it wouldn't do to make a noise and awaken poor Patience. Their new nursemaid had looked tired and miserable. Josie had heard her telling Peggy that it would be her first Christmas away from her own happy home.

But Josie didn't feel tired, and she still didn't know what had awoken her. Instead of snuggling down into her bedclothes again, she kneeled up by the window, pulling back one of the curtains and then letting it fall behind her so that she could imagine she was in a little tent.

It had stopped snowing and the clouds had cleared, and the frosted roofs of the houses on the south bank of the river sparkled in the moonlight. Josie smiled when she saw the moon. It looked as though it had been snared in the rigging of a tall ship lying at anchor and remained captured there while the clouds drifted past.

Then her gaze was caught by a movement down below. She leaned forward against the cold glass and stared very hard. Someone was clinging to a mooring rope, climbing up like a toy monkey on a string, until he reached the ship's deck. Whoever it was climbed over the side and stood there for a moment as if getting his bearings. Josie frowned. The figure was small and he looked as though he had a humped back. And then, in the moonlight, she realized that the hump was a sack tied round his neck. As she watched the figure disappeared.

Josie found she had been holding her breath. She had lived by the river long enough to know that this was a stowaway, and just a boy, by the look of him. She wondered where the ship was going, and whether the boy would be discovered. She hoped not because she knew that punishment could be harsh.

In the olden days stowaways had been thrown overboard. Some said that if the ship had a cruel master, it still happened.

Wherever he was going, Josie wondered if the boy was leaving anyone behind – someone who would be sad to miss him on Christmas Day.

Part Two

For there is no friend like a sister . . .

Christina Rossetti, 'Goblin Market'

Chapter Five

April 1880

Josie looked up from her sketch pad as a small girl came into the art room and walked over to the table. She handed a note to Miss Thomas. Miss Thomas read the note, smiled and said thank you to its bearer, then dismissed her. Only when the door had closed did she rise from her seat and walk quietly past the other girls towards Josie.

Before she spoke she studied Josie's work for a moment. 'Good, as always,' she said eventually, 'if a little anatomical. Forgive me for saying so, but your tulips are more like diagrams in a botanical textbook than a work of art.'

Miss Thomas's smile took any sting from the words.

'Perhaps it's because these tulips don't inspire me,' Josie said, knowing Miss Thomas encouraged the senior pupils to talk to her as if they were equals. After all, she wasn't very much older than they were.

'I know. You prefer to create scenes full of imagined action. Jugs of flowers and bowls of fruit are not your favourite subjects.'

They smiled at each other and then Miss Thomas sighed. 'But, in any case,' she said, 'your work is finished for the day. Miss Garrett wishes to see you in her study and I don't think you will be coming back to your class.

'Don't be alarmed,' she said when she saw Josie's expression. 'You are not in trouble. As if you would be. No, it's some matter concerning your sister . . .'

The word 'again' hung in the bright air between them.

The art room was on the top floor of the big old house, or rather two old houses knocked into one, and the small attic windows had been replaced with larger ones to let in as much light as possible. Today April clouds had cleared and the sky was radiant. The room was warm. One or two of the girls looked as if they were about to nod off over their work.

Miss Thomas went back to her table as Josie tidied her work away. Angela Cavendish leaned over and said quietly, 'Hard luck. I know this is your favourite lesson.'

Josie returned the smile. She and Angela were what was called 'best friends', although she had never really understood why someone so dashing had chosen her as a confidante.

'What do you think?' Angela whispered, and she angled her own work so that Josie could see it.

Josie stared at her friend's drawing of the vase of tulips. Angela's eyes widened as Josie's expression hinted at awe. 'Do you really want to know what I think?' she asked.

'Of course.'

'You have surpassed yourself.'

'Have I?'

'Yes. It's dreadful!'

They both began to giggle and one or two of the girls glanced round and smiled.

Miss Thomas looked up and brushed a stray wisp of hair away from her face as she tut-tutted. 'Really, girls, what behaviour. You wouldn't believe that you are young ladies who are on the brink of leaving school and entering the adult world.' She was trying not to smile herself.

The rest of the class settled down and Josie left the classroom regretfully. Angela had been correct. Art was one of her favourite lessons and she was considering continuing with her studies after leaving school. She had already started assembling a portfolio. She wondered if the tulips would be good enough to be included.

She hurried down the flights of stairs to the ground floor, then along the corridor past hushed classrooms until she came to the headmistress's study. Then she paused to collect her thoughts. What could be the matter this time?

Her younger sister was lively and popular, a natural leader.

But sometimes she acted without thinking and led her poor followers into trouble. Like the time she and a small group had absconded from the nature walk in the park and had been found window-shopping in town. Well, it hadn't just been window-shopping, of course.

Josie frowned as she recalled the incident. A senior assistant at Bainbridge's had telephoned the school to ask if someone would come to collect the miscreants, one of whom had helped herself to a bottle of lavender water. Apparently the bottle of lavender water went missing as they went by. The girls were denying that they had anything to do with it and all knowledge of its whereabouts.

When Miss Curtis and Miss Black arrived they were asked to search their pupils, and the bottle of lavender water was found to be in Muriel Rowe's coat pocket. Muriel had made a big fuss, Flora had told Josie later. She'd protested that one of the other girls must have put it there. But no one believed her and, although the shop was prepared to let the matter drop, Muriel had been expelled from the Girls' High School.

Flora had felt guilty. She'd told Josie that she should never have suggested the lark in the first place. She'd even wondered if Muriel had stolen the lavender water to give to her because she had remarked on what a pretty bottle it was. Josie had tried to reassure her sister at the time. But later she mused ruefully that Flora hadn't seemed to have learned anything from the experience.

Well, it was no use lingering outside the door wondering what had happened this time. Josie breathed in, held herself straight as if preparing for an ordeal and knocked. Miss Garrett's deep tones bade her enter.

The scene that met Josie took her by surprise. Miss Garrett, as straight-backed as ever, sat at her customary place behind her desk, but instead of her usual calm expression she looked troubled. Flora was sitting – *sitting* – on a chair before the desk and Miss Curtis, the history teacher, was standing by Flora's chair, looking vexed and unhappy.

No pupil, and no teacher come to that, ever sat down in Miss Garrett's presence. Josie looked to her sister for an explanation but Flora's face was buried in a clean white handkerchief. Her shoulders were shaking. Was she crying?

'Shut the door, Josie. Don't just stand there,' Miss Garrett commanded, and her usually stentorian voice was edged with anxiety.

Josie did as she was bid but hesitated, not quite sure what she should do or where she should go.

'Flora is . . . ah . . . somewhat upset,' Miss Garrett said.

On cue Flora sniffed audibly and her outgoing breath escaped in a series of stuttering sighs.

As neither Miss Garrett nor Miss Curtis seemed about to say anything further Josie asked, 'But why?'

'Um – ah – Miss Curtis—' the headmistress began.

'I made a mistake,' Miss Curtis said.

'She accused me of cheating!' Flora took her nose out of her handkerchief and turned her head to glare at the unfortunate history teacher, who pursed her lips and shook her head but, nevertheless, seemed reluctant to meet Flora's gaze.

'Flora, calm down,' Miss Garrett said. 'We know now that you didn't copy Sarah's answers. You are vindicated. And I have agreed that your sister should take you home for the rest of the day. That should be sufficient.'

'But it isn't!' Flora exclaimed, and Josie held her breath at her sister's daring. 'I really think Miss Curtis should apologize. She – she jumped to conclusions!'

'You were looking at Sarah's paper,' Miss Curtis interpolated, earning a frown from Miss Garrett.

'I know,' Flora said, 'I saw you watching me. So when you took my paper and found I'd answered everything correctly, which I admit I don't usually, you assumed I'd been cheating. And you said so, in front of the whole class. "My, my," you said, "Flora Walton has answered every question correctly. Could it be because she is sitting next to Sarah Pearce today, I wonder." '

Flora's imitation of the history teacher's nasal tones was masterful and Josie glanced at Miss Garrett to see if it would earn a reprimand. But the headmistress simply pursed her lips and tapped on some sheets of paper on her desk with her forefinger.

'Miss Curtis was too hasty with her judgement,' she said.

'She should have checked Sarah's test paper before saying anything. I think she does owe you an apology.'

'In front of the class?'

Flora had gone too far. 'That won't be necessary,' Miss Garrett said. 'Miss Curtis will apologize to you now and then she will go back to the classroom and say that she made a mistake. She will make it clear that you did not copy Sarah Pearce's answers. Now, Josie will take you home.'

Miss Curtis looked far from happy as she murmured a tight-lipped apology to Flora, who nodded graciously. Josie could tell that this only made the history teacher even angrier. She pitied the rest of Flora's class. Miss Curtis would go back to them in a foul mood and probably make them pay for her humiliation at Flora's hands.

When she had gone Miss Garrett sent Flora to get her coat and motioned for Josie to stay. 'You deserve an explanation of that scene,' she said.

'No, I think I understand. Miss Curtis thought Flora was copying another girl's answers and Flora . . . Flora objected.'

Josie could imagine the scene. No one liked being accused unjustly, and Flora was young for her age. She would take it badly. Nevertheless there was something that didn't quite ring true about all this.

The headmistress sighed. Suddenly she seemed more human. 'This place is like a tinderbox sometimes,' she said. 'All these emotional young women – and I don't just mean the pupils.'

Josie was astonished by the remark and even more so by the conspiratorial smile.

'But the staff, at least, have their positions to consider,' she said wearily. 'Whereas some of these spoiled young madams could persuade their fathers to send them to some other establishment if they chose to and, frankly, my dear, I have my position to consider too. Not to mention my reputation.'

Sun streamed in through the tall windows and fell across the headmistress's desk. It seemed as though Miss Garrett was gazing at nothing more than dancing motes of dust. But suddenly she seemed to be aware of how much she had revealed and she blinked and focused her gaze on Josie.

'I should never have spoken like that. Put it down to weariness. But, then, you are such a sensible and sympathetic young woman. That is why you are head girl. And I believe the principal of any educational establishment is allowed to talk in confidence to the head pupil.' She sighed and seemed to be making an effort to overcome a certain weariness.

'So, to explain,' she continued more briskly. 'Apparently your sister was stung by the accusation of cheating and she burst into tears. Nothing would console her. She ran out of the classroom into the corridor – that's how I heard the commotion. It drew me out of my lair.' Miss Garrett's sense of humour had returned and she smiled at Josie. 'I asked them to come in here and we would try to resolve matters.

'I told Miss Curtis to bring the test papers with her and I discovered at once that your sister was telling the truth. Four of Sarah's answers were incorrect. Miss Curtis acted hastily and I have told her so, although I suppose I can see why she made the assumption she did. Your sister has not proved herself any sort of scholar up till now, has she?'

'No,' Josie said softly. And she realized that that was what had been worrying her.

'However,' Miss Garrett continued, 'Flora assured me that she had determined to do well in this test and that she'd been up half the night learning the stuffy old dates and things – her words. That's why she was so hurt to be falsely accused of cheating.'

'I see.'

Miss Garrett clasped her hands on top of the desk and regarded Josie solemnly for a moment. 'Tell me, my dear, do you know if your sister wants to stay on at school after she is sixteen?'

'No she doesn't. As you know, she wanted to leave as soon as she was fourteen. But . . .'

'But?' The headmistress paused. 'But your father wants her to stay on. Is that it?'

'I'm afraid so.'

'Don't look so worried. I'm sure we'll cope. She's high-spirited and impetuous but there's no real harm in her. And, of course, she's extremely popular with the other girls. She's a

104

natural leader. So we must hope she doesn't lead them astray. That was a joke, Josie. Now off you go.'

On the way to the tram stop on Osborne Road Josie had to hear the story all over again – much embellished, she decided, and the doubts she'd been having about the whole episode returned.

'Flora,' she asked when she was allowed to get a word in, 'why was this history test so important?'

Her sister frowned. 'What are you suggesting?'

'Well, you don't usually work so hard, do you? And, to tell the truth, I don't remember you opening any book at all last night.'

'Oh, it was after you went to sleep. I sneaked into the dressing room because I didn't want to disturb you and I worked by candlelight.'

Josie frowned at this image of her carefree sister poring over her books by candlelight, and her bafflement must have shown.

Flora scowled and then just as quickly smiled. 'Don't you see? I'm so sick of Miss Curtis and her sarcastic comments. She's always going on about girls who don't appreciate the chance of an education, girls who will never have to work, and girls who think beauty is more important than brain power. You know what she's like!'

'Yes, I do, but—'

'Oh, you never had any bother with her. I mean you're not beau— I mean you're brainy, but I could tell that a lot of the time she was getting at me. Sly little digs. And I wanted to show her by coming top in the stupid test. That's why I – that's why I worked so hard.'

'I see. But were you really so upset that you had to make such a fuss?'

'Being called a cheat isn't nice!'

'No, I'm sure it isn't.'

'In front of the whole class!'

At that moment the tram drew up and the girls got on. Josie allowed Flora to go ahead.

'Oh, do let's go up on top,' Flora called, and led the way up the winding stairs without waiting for an answer.

105

By the time Josie had joined her at the front her young sister was smiling out at the passing scene as if she hadn't a care in the world.

'Isn't it marvellous getting out of that prison early?' she asked. 'I know, Josie, let's get off at the Monument and have tea and cream cakes at Tilley's!'

'I thought I was taking you home because you're distressed,' Josie said.

'And don't you think tea and cream cakes would cheer me up enormously? Oh, go on, Josie. Don't be a spoilsport!'

A little later, sitting at the window table in the first-floor restaurant above Tilley's cake shop, Josie watched her sister's enjoyment as she tried to decide which cake to take from the two-tier cake stand, and ended up taking two.

Flora glanced up and, interpreting Josie's questioning expression correctly, she said, 'All right. I admit it. I exaggerated – well, to tell the truth, I put on a grand act.'

'Why?'

'Oh, don't look at me like that. You know why.'

'I don't.'

'Well, you've admitted that Miss Curtis is foul.'

'I've admitted no such thing.'

'Not very pleasant then. And sarcastic.'

'I suppose so.'

'Of course she is. And it really bothers me.'

'So you decided to make things difficult for her? Oh, Flora.'

'Don't be like that. I didn't do it just for me.' Flora's eyes were blazing. 'I did it for all the poor little chumps who don't know how to stand up to her. Who just go home and cry!'

Josie sipped her tea quickly to hide the smile. Flora was acting again. Whether or not it was true at the time that she had been striking a blow for the underdogs, she certainly seemed to believe it now. Josie couldn't bring herself to scold – not that Flora would have taken any notice.

She consoled herself with the thought that Miss Curtis had probably deserved some sort of comeuppance. But, as she took up the cake fork and attacked her vanilla slice with as much enjoyment as her sister was showing, she still couldn't help marvelling that Flora, no matter how hard she'd said she'd worked, had managed to get full marks for her history test.

'Are you warm enough, Mother? Shall I put some more coal on the fire?'

'If you would, Philip. The sun is bright but there's no warmth in it.' Charlotte watched as her son kneeled to busy himself at the hearth. He was a fine young man and he looked after her well. Now that she hardly ever left her room she relied on him more than ever.

'That should do it.' Philip dusted his hands off as he rose to his feet. 'And I've asked Patience to bring us a tray. Tea and a slice or two of raisin cake.'

'Useless girl!' Charlotte muttered as her son took his place in the chair at the other side of the hearth.

'I beg your pardon?' Philip looked surprised.

'Patience. She's useless.'

'Why do you say that?'

'Because she is. I'm afraid her shapely ankles and her flashing eyes have blinded you to her faults, Philip.'

Charlotte glanced quickly at her son. He had leaned back in the winged chair so that his face was in shadow. But then even if she had been able to see his expression she knew that he would never have revealed his feelings. Philip was deep. Still waters, indeed. Sometimes he maddened her, but there was no question that he was a good and caring son. That's why she wanted the best for him. And that didn't mean that little minx Patience.

'And what are Patience's faults, Mother?' She could hear the smile in his voice.

'She's inattentive and lazy. I don't know why my brother kept her on after the girls had no more need of a nursemaid.'

'He kept her on so that she could look after your needs.'

'Exactly.'

'Are you suggesting that she doesn't?'

Charlotte fell silent.

'She brings your meals up, doesn't she?' Philip asked. 'She helps you to bathe and get into bed at night. She takes you out in the Bath chair when you're feeling up to it.'

'And that's all she does.'

'All? Surely that's sufficient?'

Charlotte sighed. She must tread carefully. Her son might not realize it but he had just revealed that his feelings for Patience might be stronger than he would like to admit.

'Yes, Philip. She does everything that she's paid to do, but nothing more. No –' she held her hand up to stop him interrupting – 'I get lonely up here and I suppose I would like it better if the young woman popped in now and then to see if there was anything extra I might need, or just to pass the time of day with me. Can you see what I mean?'

In truth that would be the last thing Charlotte would have wanted – to have Patience dropping in for a chat. But what galled her was the belief that as soon as the young madam shut the door she was pleased to get away and wouldn't have dreamed of climbing the stairs again until she absolutely had to.

'Patience works hard, you know.' It seemed Philip was still determined to defend the girl. 'She helps Mrs Dobson with other domestic duties.'

'I know she does. And I'm sorry I said anything. My bones are aching today. Ah, here she is with our tea.'

Charlotte watched carefully as Philip rose to bring a small table over and then took the tray from Patience. No glance seemed to pass between them but that didn't mean anything. Charlotte was convinced that there was something going on. Otherwise why was the girl content to stay here? She was bonny enough. She surely could have been married long before now.

How old was she? Twenty-four, twenty-five? She must have been fourteen or fifteen when she'd first come here to help with the girls. And Philip – he was twenty-nine. He'd never shown any interest in finding a wife. It was time he did. But not Maud Dobson's niece. He could do better than that – much better.

'Do you want me to stay and pour the tea?'

'Um?' Charlotte looked up to see Patience smiling sweetly at her.

'Shall I pour the tea for you and Mr Bertram?'

'Thank you, dear, that won't be necessary.' Charlotte forced herself to smile. She would get nowhere if she was openly antagonistic. 'Oh, and tell your aunt this cake is delicious.'

'Thank you, I will.' Patience, taken by surprise, shot Philip a startled glance and he raised his eyes.

Charlotte was furious. They talk about me! she thought. No doubt they'll have a little chuckle about the crotchety old woman as soon as they can snatch a moment alone together. Well, that's it. It's time I told him what my plan for him is. I hope I haven't left it too late.

'What are you thinking, Mother?' Patience had gone and Philip was pouring the tea.

'Of nothing in particular. Why do you ask?'

'You were in a brown study just now.'

'Was I? Oh, I was probably wondering why your uncle's wife is so very little at home these days.' It was time to change the subject.

'Good works.'

'I beg your pardon?'

'Mrs Walton is taken up with her work at the mission.'

'Mrs Walton. She's still Annie to me.'

'Yes, well. Not having much to occupy her at home, she has taken to going to work in the new mission that cares for the wives and orphans of men lost at sea. As you well know.'

'Yes.' Charlotte shook her head wonderingly. 'I wonder what on earth she does there?'

'Why don't you ask her?'

'I might.'

'Well, in any case, I'll have to leave you now, Mother, because I have promised to pack up a box or two of groceries to send along there.'

'Annie asked you to do that?'

'No, my uncle did. He approves of their work. And no doubt he is pleased that his wife has something to do with her time. Poor Annie.' Philip rose from his chair and collected the cups and plates. 'I'll take the tray down; I might as well.'

Charlotte stopped herself from making some comment about it being a good excuse for him to visit the kitchen. 'Will you be coming up to have your evening meal with me?' she asked him.

'If you want me to. We can have a gossip about the day's events.'

'You're a good son, Philip, but no. I think you should eat with your uncle this evening. After all, you are one of the family, not a servant to eat in the kitchen or a poor relation to be banished to the attics. Your uncle couldn't do without you.'

'No, I don't think he could.'

She was pleased to see that Philip did not suffer from a sense of false modesty. After all, Samuel trusted him so much that he had begun to leave more and more of the business paperwork to his nephew, even giving him authority to sign contracts with shipping agents.

She smiled at him approvingly. 'So, take your place at his table, then.'

'Very well, Mother, if that's what you want. I'll dine with my uncle this evening.'

When she was alone Charlotte found herself thinking back over the years. Samuel had been good to her, taking her in when her husband had died and promising that he would always take care of her and her son. She wondered if he had ever realized that he had also benefited from the arrangement?

Oh, he had certainly provided a roof over their heads, clothes and good food on the table so that she had not had to touch her meagre savings. But, in the early days, she had run his household for him, and even after his first marriage had continued much as before because Effie had shown no interest at all in housewifely duties.

Charlotte had suspected that the girl had found her other wifely duties distasteful too, and, in that, she had a certain sympathy for her. But a marriage is a contract, for all that, and it had been a blessing that Samuel had not seemed to notice that his beautiful wife was an unwilling partner in the marriage bed. He'd been a seafaring man, after all. He knew the ways of the world and he'd probably put her reluctance down to Effie's innocence and inexperience.

Well, her poor brother had very little time to gentle Effie into acceptance, and he'd never been the same man again after she'd died. And that was why Charlotte could find it in her heart to feel sorry for his second wife.

When Effie had died in childbirth, Annie had done her best to win Samuel's heart. But she'd never succeeded. Oh, Samuel had married her, all right, but that was because he'd been won over by her care for his daughters, especially the little one. And he'd still been comparatively young, with all a man's needs and desires. Charlotte had not begrudged him his comfort.

But, at the time of his second marriage, she would have preferred him to find a nice widow whose childbearing years were over, not a young woman who might have borne him a son. There had been some anxious years for Charlotte.

But although Annie had tried to keep it secret at first, Charlotte had soon realized that, time after time, the poor girl was miscarrying in the early stages of pregnancy. Charlotte had watched her withdraw into her own lonely miserable world as the girls grew older and needed her less. The poor thing seemed to be shrivelling up for want of a bit of attention from her husband.

So when Charlotte had judged that Annie was no longer a threat to her plans for the future, she had offered her a limited sort of friendship. Sometimes when Samuel was working late, or was out dining at his club with business associates, Annie would wander up to Charlotte's quarters like a lost soul. The conversation was mostly domestic.

They would talk about how Maud Dobson, though still an excellent cook, was getting too old to lift the heavier of the pots and pans; how Patience kept her thoughts to herself but hadn't seemed to mind taking on the duties of a general maid when she was no longer needed as a nurserymaid. And how, ever since both Peggy and Joan had left to get married, some years ago now, it had become impossible to keep a servant girl more than a month or so. At the moment they were making do with a little skivvy whose name Charlotte couldn't even recall.

Charlotte approved of Annie's work at the mission. It was the sort of respectable thing the wife of a successful business-man should do, although she hoped she was not being too generous with gifts of food and clothing. Still, Philip would see to it that she didn't take too much – or goods of the best quality.

Her thoughts returned to Philip. Surely now his place as heir to the business was secure, and the fact that Samuel had come to rely on Philip so much must mean that he intended his nephew to take over one day.

Charlotte's speculations always edged uncomfortably away from thoughts of what would happen after Samuel's death. Even though he was showing signs of slowing down, he was her younger brother after all, and would probably outlive Charlotte herself. No, in her musings she preferred to think that Samuel might want to retire one day and live like a gentleman at ease in some tidy house in the country. He could certainly afford to.

And then Philip would be in charge of the business. For who else was there? Samuel could hardly expect his daughters to take over. No matter how clever Josie was, it wouldn't be right. And, as for Flora, she was so beautiful she would make some grand match and Samuel wouldn't have to worry about her.

And here Charlotte's fond imaginings always came up against the same snag. Although no beauty like her sister, Josie would be regarded as a good catch. Some enterprising young spark would court her and marry her in the hopes of taking over Samuel's business one day. And Charlotte couldn't allow that. For a son-in-law might not treat Philip with the respect he deserved. He might even try to oust him from the business altogether.

Samuel could ensure Philip's future by making him a partner, of course. In fact he should have done it before now. Charlotte frowned. Philip was not just hard-working and clever; he was far-seeing and ambitious. Samuel owed much of his present prosperity to his nephew. It was worrying that Philip seemed to be interested in Patience, but if she, his mother, could just choose the right moment, and say the right things, she was sure she would be able to persuade him that there was an even better way to safeguard his position than simply becoming a partner.

Josie was eighteen now, and she would be leaving school at the end of the summer term. Charlotte knew she would have to talk to Philip, and see whether she could persuade him that the best way to further his ambition would be to marry his cousin.

* * *

The remains of the afternoon meal of tea and bread and butter and jam had long been cleared away. The others had gone but one young woman remained, her child on her knee, sitting near the middle of one of the trestle tables that ran the length of the room. Annie paused in the doorway, not knowing whether she should approach her.

Sunlight streamed in through the windows but the dining room of the mission remained shadowy. None of the rooms on the lower floors ever seemed to get enough light. The tall old house was built into the hill that rose above the narrow thoroughfares along the riverside. Above was the castle and the cathedral and the broad new streets of the city.

The house had once been the home of a rich shipowner but that had been a hundred years ago or more. Once the family had moved away, up the hill and on, beyond the city to the prosperous suburb of Jesmond, the house had been divided into flats and one-room dwellings; the tenants becoming poorer and poorer, the fabric of the building more and more neglected, until, eventually, it had been abandoned.

For a while after that there was the danger that thieves and vagrants might move in as they had in many of the older buildings downriver towards the mouth of the Ouseburn and beyond. But just in time, a young man, an American, had been sent by his father, a rich merchant turned philanthropist, to buy the building, restore it and open it as a refuge for the widows and families of men lost at sea.

Often the newly bereaved families were thrown out of their homes because they couldn't pay the rent, and the place became a temporary home for them until new lodgings could be found. Other families visited daily and were given three good meals, and help and advice on how to cope.

Very quickly the house became known as 'the mission', although the women who took refuge there were not expected to go to church, and the prayer meetings that were held there did not seem to follow any particular faith.

The child in the woman's arms began to grizzle softly and his young mother began to rock to and fro silently, holding the child tight in her arms and yet saying nothing, not even making

113

that wordless crooning sound with which mothers comfort their babes.

Suddenly the mother held the child even more tightly and raised her own face to stare unseeingly at the ceiling. It was then that Annie noticed the tears streaming down the girl's face. She hurried forward.

'Let me take the little one,' she said as she sat sideways on the bench next to them. 'You've hardly eaten anything and you must look after yourself.'

The young woman turned on her. 'Why?' she exclaimed, and her expression was savage.

Annie was shocked. 'Because of your child – your little son. Who would look after him if you . . . if anything were to happen to you?'

The woman stared at her for a moment and began to shake her head. The tears flowed more freely and the child, a boy of about two, began to sob convulsively.

'You're frightening him.'

Annie couldn't hide her disapproval and the woman stopped rocking and looked at her in surprise.

Annie took advantage of the moment and continued quite firmly, 'Give him to me.'

Wordlessly the young woman loosened her grip on her son and held him towards Annie, who lifted him on to her knee. His sobs subsided into shudders.

'Now eat something,' Annie said. 'Look, that's good damson jam on that bread. Don't waste it.'

As the child's mother began to pick at the food on her plate Annie leaned over the table and pulled the child's bowl towards her. The boily made of bread and sugar and warm milk had cooled long ago but, almost as soon as the dish was set in front of him, the child grabbed for the spoon and began to feed himself clumsily. He was obviously hungry and, equally obviously, he had been frightened off eating before by his mother's behaviour.

'Here, let me help you,' Annie murmured softly as she took the spoon, ignoring the mess that had already fallen on to her skirt.

'They say he went over the side, you know. Do you think that's true?'

Annie looked up startled to see the child's mother looking at her questioningly.

'I beg your pardon?'

'Nobody saw him go. But when the ship arrived at Boston he wasn't on board. They couldn't even say for sure when they'd last seen him.'

'I know. I'm sorry.'

This young woman's story was like so many others. So many grieving families left behind with nobody to care for them.

'And what do you imagine he thought I was going to do? Me and his bairn?'

'What do you mean?'

'Leaving us to fend for ourselves like this.'

Annie was at a loss. But she had come across this reaction before when grief had turned to anger, the anger directed at the husband or father who had been lost at sea.

'You . . . you mustn't blame him,' she said. 'He didn't do it deliberately, you know. And you're here now. We will look after you. Thanks to Mr Goodwright you will have clothes and food and shelter, you and your son. When he's old enough he will go to school. As soon as you are ready you will be found respectable lodgings and given a living allowance. You will be helped to find employment and if . . .'

'Such a terrible way to die. All alone in the cold sea . . .'

Annie hesitated. What she had wanted to say was that this young woman might marry again. And if she did she would be given a small dowry. But now was not the time to mention it, not when her grief was still so raw. But, in any case, nothing she had said had seemed to make any impression on the poor woman. And why should it when all she could think of was the loss of a beloved husband?

But, in any case, Annie saw that she had eaten what was on her plate and was even reaching for a piece of rice cake. She was young and healthy and, thankfully, her body was telling her what to do.

She reached for her cup, took a sip and grimaced. 'The tea's gone cold.'

Annie suppressed a spasm of irritation at the implied

criticism. 'I dare say Cook will make a fresh pot,' she said, 'if I ask her nicely.'

'No need. I've thought of that.'

They both turned to look at the young man who had just come into the room. It was Jacob Goodwright, son of the founder of the mission, and he was carrying a tray containing a small teapot and a clean cup and saucer.

'This is for you, Mrs Walton,' he said as he placed the cup on the table. 'I should think you're ready for it. Here, let me take the boy.'

He held out his arms and the child went to him readily; he even smiled.

Jacob Goodwright held him with one arm, and with the other he fished a clean white handkerchief out of his pocket and offered it to Annie.

'Your skirt,' he said, indicating the splodges of bread and milk. 'I hope it won't stain.'

'It'll wash,' Annie responded with a smile.

Jacob Goodwright was of average height but in spite of his clean, smooth skin and gentleman's ways, his spare frame suggested a hidden strength and hardiness. His features were fine drawn, his light brown hair had a wave to it, and his hazel eyes sometimes glinted green. No wonder the young women – well, women of whatever age – responded to him with smiles.

But underneath the fine clothes and the drawling American way of speaking, Annie sensed there was integrity and strength that would withstand great hardship, and also that his compassion was tempered by common sense. No matter that Jacob could hardly be much past twenty, his father had chosen well.

She found herself relaxing a little as she sipped her tea. She was tired. Years of pregnancies that had come to nothing had left her body drained and weak. She knew she was doing too much, expending too much of her time and energy on her 'good works', as Samuel's nephew called her activities at the mission. She knew that Philip and his mother discussed her and probably made fun of her but they did not disapprove – even though Philip worried about every little morsel that Samuel gave to charity.

But what of Samuel? What did he think? He had signified his quiet approval of her work at the mission, had told her he would do anything in his power to help, but was it because he considered the cause worthy or was it simply that it kept her out of the house, therefore freeing himself of the sight of her and easing his conscience?

The weak sunlight streaming through the window behind her was strong enough to warm her neck and shoulders. She tried to push from her mind all thoughts of her own life and what it had become, and she closed her eyes and enjoyed the brief moment of rest.

She could hear Jacob Goodwright talking to the young widow. He was coaxing her to respond. She heard him mention the sewing room and the Bo Peep dolls and the toy lambs the women were making to sell, and then she was aware of movement. They're going now, she thought, but she waited a while before opening her eyes. Jacob was still sitting there.

'Oh, I thought you'd gone.'

He smiled. 'I wanted to thank you for everything you've done here, but I was loath to disturb you.'

She knew she was flushing – like a girl, she thought. The maddening thing was he didn't set out to charm. That much was obvious. He just had a way with him.

'I do no more than the others,' she said.

He didn't contradict but he looked at her gravely. 'You're very good with the children,' he said.

'I used to be a nursemaid . . . before I married.'

'And then you had children of your own?'

'No. It never happened.'

She was surprised at her own calmness. She didn't know how long ago she had accepted that she was to be childless but she had never spoken of it until now. No one had ever asked her, of course, until this polite young man who seemed to be genuinely interested in her.

'I'm sorry,' he said.

'But I have stepchildren. My husband—'

'Captain Walton?'

'Yes. He has two daughters. I looked after them when his first wife died. That's why he—'

Annie just stopped herself from saying, 'That's why he married me.' She was horrified at how easy it was to confide in Jacob Goodwright, and beginning to be surprised that he should be asking such questions. But then he seemed to have the gift of easy conversation. She had noticed the way he talked to the poor widows of the drowned sailors: questioning them gently, drawing them out, encouraging them to express their sorrow and helping them to decide what they wanted to do with their lives.

But I'm not a distressed widow, she thought. Why is he talking to me like this? Unless he has sensed my discontent and he's trying to be kind.

'I must be going,' she said. 'The girls . . . they will be home soon.'

'Josie and Flora?'

'Yes.'

Annie couldn't remember when she'd told Jacob her step-daughters' names but she supposed she must have done. Now, by her words, she'd let him think that the girls would expect her to be home to greet them and that wasn't true. Neither of them would even notice if she were there or not.

Sometimes she felt sorry for herself. After all the care and attention she had devoted to Flora the girl hardly spoke to her these days. Not that she was rude or unpleasant. It was simply that she didn't talk to her or confide in her as Annie imagined a girl should to the woman who had taken the place of her mother – the only mother the child had known, in fact.

And as for Josie . . . Annie's mind skittered uneasily away from thinking about Samuel's elder daughter. If she were honest with herself she knew she'd probably neglected her. It was no wonder the girl had grown up reserved and thoughtful. Annie sometimes wondered what went on in that clever mind.

Jacob walked with her to the front door and out into the busy street. 'You will thank Captain Walton for everything he has given us, won't you?'

Mrs Walton nodded and said goodbye. Jacob watched as she walked away. She seemed almost reluctant to leave the mission. He wondered whether he should have walked home with her and thanked Captain Walton in person. He had been to visit the other prosperous businessmen who had been willing to become benefactors and, because they knew him to be Isaac Goodwright's son, the visits had become social. He had been invited to their homes to meet their wives and daughters.

But he had not yet been to see Samuel Walton. He was sure if he dropped a hint poor, sad-faced Mrs Walton would be only too pleased to invite him. Perhaps I will, he thought, but I am not ready yet. He turned to go back into the mission.

Philip did as his mother had suggested and joined the family for the evening meal. His uncle seemed pleased to have him there. As always, Samuel was at his most animated when talking about business affairs. Philip wondered what on earth he and Annie talked about when they were alone.

Josie was quietly pleasant, as usual, and seemed to be genuinely interested in talk of the chandlery and the growing import and export side of the business. She even joined in occasionally with knowledgeable and sensible suggestions.

Flora, however, grew more and more impatient with her father. She tried to steer the conversation towards other things, such as the entertainments at the theatres in town or the latest fashions. Samuel would humour her for a while but it was plain to see he was at a loss how to entertain his younger daughter – although his pride in her appearance and manner of talking was obvious.

And as for Samuel's wife, poor Annie, as Philip's mother now referred to her, she hardly spoke. Every now and then Samuel seemed to remember that his wife was sitting there and he would turn and smile, but he always seemed vaguely distracted – and perhaps a little guilty, as if he knew his wife's air of discontent was really his doing but he could do nothing about it.

It was Philip who introduced the subject of Isaac Goodwright's mission that finally brought some animation into Annie's expression, and Samuel smiled at him gratefully.

'My mother was wondering what you do there,' Philip said.

'Was she?' Annie looked startled and a little defensive. 'Does she disapprove?'

'Not at all. I'm sure she'd find it interesting, as I would.'

Annie flushed with pleasure. 'I just do anything I can. Some of the women are very distressed. So much so that they neglect their children. I help them – wash and dress the little ones, help to feed them. When they leave the mission to go back to their homes or into new lodgings I visit them – so do the other ladies – to see if they are coping.'

'And what do you make of Jacob Goodwright?' Philip asked.

'Make of him?'

'I've heard he's young.'

'Yes.'

'And he's content to do his father's work like this?'

'I'm not sure what you mean?'

'No, neither am I,' Samuel said.

'Well, the story goes that Isaac Goodwright's parents emigrated to America from this part of the world and they prospered,' Philip said. 'Mr Goodwright is a very rich man.'

'Not just rich,' Samuel added. 'Isaac went on to develop a worldwide trading empire and to make a considerable fortune. And because he is conscious that he owes so much to the seafarers who carried his goods across the oceans of the world, sometimes at great risk to themselves, he wishes to repay the debt by helping the families of those who lose their lives at sea.'

'Precisely,' Philip said. 'And I wonder what his son, Jacob, thinks of it. After all, I imagine he is to inherit the fortune one day, and yet here he is, helping his father to spend a great portion of it on charitable works.' He smiled round the table. 'He must be a remarkable young man.'

'He is,' Annie said fervently. 'Most remarkable. I wish you could meet him.'

'Perhaps we should, my dear,' her husband said. 'I've heard he's been invited into the homes of many an acquaintance of mine. Perhaps we should offer him hospitality. Would you like that?'

'Very much. Thank you, Samuel.'

Philip noticed Annie's heightened colour. Well, well, he thought. She's both pleased and embarrassed. Does my uncle's wife have tender feelings for the young man? Or does she perhaps see him as a son?

Then something made him look at his uncle, that good man who had also made a fortune, although it couldn't be compared with that of Isaac Goodwright. Samuel Walton had no one to leave his fortune to except his daughters, and Philip knew very well what thoughts and plans had begun to form in his mother's imagination, although he pretended not to.

She wanted him to marry one of his cousins – Josie, most probably, as she was the elder. He looked across the table at Josie now, calmly drinking her coffee. She had been listening to the conversation with interest, whereas Flora had shown every sign of being restless and bored.

Flora. So beautiful and so wilful. The man who married her would have his hands full. Philip allowed himself to think what it would be like to make love to Flora and had to bend his head over his coffee cup in case anyone should notice the pleasure that suffused his normally impassive expression.

No, neither of them would suit him as a wife. Flora would be impossible unless he could find some way to break her spirit. And Josie? Josie was too clever by far. If only he could confide in his mother, tell her that there might be no need to marry either of them. But his mother would be shocked if he revealed his plans to her. She would try to stop him.

Ah, well, at least he had Patience to bring him the sort of comfort a man has need of.

The dressing table was covered with jars of creams and lotions, bottles of rosewater and lavender water and various instruments of torture for the hair, most of them Flora's.

They had already undressed and Josie had taken a book to bed and was reading by the soft glow of the oil lamp. The sweet smell of rosewater filled the room, and Josie glanced up to watch her sister for a moment. The younger girl's elbows were resting in two halves of a cut lemon as she rubbed and patted her face and neck. Flora had read in a magazine that that was the way to keep the skin of those awkward little joints nice and white.

Josie smiled. But suddenly the image of her sister seemed to fade and merge with a distant memory: that of their beautiful mother, sitting at her dressing table. Josie had loved to watch her brushing her hair or applying the lightest dusting of powder to her face.

Josie's eyes filled with tears at her own sense of loss and also at the fact that Flora had never known her mother, whom she so resembled, not only in her colouring and features but also in the very way she walked and talked. She was so lovely. And Josie had become aware, even if their father hadn't, that his younger daughter was more woman than girl and certainly wouldn't be happy if he insisted on sending her back to school in the autumn term.

Someone else had noticed that Flora had grown up. Josie had caught their cousin Philip looking across the table at Flora only this evening, and there had been no mistaking the admiration – and something else – in his eyes. The memory of that something else – something she couldn't name – made her uncomfortable but she wasn't sure why.

'Oh, that will do!' Flora exclaimed, and stood up suddenly, knocking a little tray of hairpins on to the floor as she did so.

She didn't pick them up but flounced across the room and got into bed. It wasn't long before she was asleep. Flora, highly strung and active throughout the day, never seemed to have trouble sleeping. Like a child, Josie thought. And she wondered what her sister dreamed about.

After a while Josie slipped quietly out of bed. She smiled round at the disorder. First she kneeled to pick up the hairpins and put them back in the dainty silver tray, and then she put the lids back on the various jars and pots.

Then she turned to the clothes discarded and lying just where Flora had left them. She gathered up the underclothes, putting some of them in the laundry basket and draping others over a chair. Finally she picked up Flora's pretty dress, made of grey pin-striped cotton, as the school required, the high neck softened with a lace collar and the long, tight-fitting sleeves deeply frilled at the wrists.

She shook it out before placing it on a hanger, and noticed that something fell from one of the sleeves. A handkerchief probably, she thought, and she kneeled down to pick it up.

It wasn't a handkerchief. It was a piece of paper folded like a bracelet to go round the wrist. Had Flora been passing notes in class? Josie smiled as she glanced at it and then her smile faded. Written on the paper so that the words would circle the wrist was a list of dates and the names of kings and queens. The answers to the history test. Flora had been telling the truth when she'd said she hadn't copied Sarah Pearce's answers. But it seemed she had been cheating after all.

Chapter Six

May

'Well, I'm not sure . . .'

Mrs Forsyth looked undecided. She gazed at Josie through her lorgnette as if this would help her make up her mind. Josie smiled encouragingly.

'Oh, I suppose so,' Mrs Forsyth said eventually. She dropped her lorgnette. It plunged down to dangle over her ample pin-tucked bosom on a length of black velvet ribbon. 'It was only a cold,' she said, 'and it's not surprising the poor girl should have caught a chill, the weather has been so changeable. Angela is much better but a little cross that I did not think it wise for her to travel home this weekend. I think a visit from her friend would put her in a better humour.'

The good woman sighed as if with relief that the decision had been made.

The two of them smiled at each other and then Mrs Forsyth turned and led the way upstairs. She was a large woman but she moved swiftly, her frilled skirts rustling as she walked. It was rumoured that she had once been a dancer who had given up a promising career for love.

Josie wondered what she had seen in Mr Forsyth to change her life's path so dramatically. He was small and precise, too delicate, or too idle perhaps, to work, and grateful that his enterprising wife had had the idea of opening up the house he had inherited from his mother as a boarding house for young ladies. Specifically the young ladies who attended the Girls' High School in Jesmond.

Her young lodgers were all weekly boarders, going home straight from school on Friday and returning to Mrs Forsyth's after school on Monday. They boarded because they lived just too far away to make journeying to school each day practical. Mrs Forsyth looked after them well. The house was clean and comfortable and the food was good. The only quarrel the girls had was that the discipline was strict.

Mrs Forsyth took her responsibilities very seriously, not only because she was genuinely concerned about her young lodgers' welfare but also because she had the headmistress of the high school, Miss Garrett, to answer to as well as the parents. Martinet she might be but, however, her manners were perfect. After all, she could never forget that the girls were the daughters of eminently respectable businessmen, gentlemen farmers and even minor aristocracy. Angela Cavendish's father was a baronet.

When they reached the first landing Mrs Forsyth told Josie, 'I've moved Angela into this little room above the porch. I had to isolate her, you know. I didn't want the other girls to catch her cold.' She knocked on the door. 'May I enter, Miss Cavendish dear?' she asked. 'I have a nice surprise for you.'

Josie was half expecting her friend to be in bed, but Angela was sitting in an armchair by the window, wrapped up like a swaddled baby in a rose-sprigged, white, quilted bedspread. Her slippered feet rested on a velvet footstool. An open book lay on her knee but, from her surprised and sleepy expression, it was plain that she must have fallen asleep while reading it.

'Josie! How wonderful!' Her friend half rose and the book slithered to the floor.

Mrs Forsyth tutted and hurried forward to pick it up but Angela had already stooped to do so herself and the two of them bumped their heads.

'Ouf!' the older woman said.

And, 'Oh, no!' Angela exclaimed as the book skittered away across the floor. Josie stooped to pick it up and was sure she had not mistaken the relieved expression that crossed her friend's face.

Mrs Forsyth straightened up and caught a tortoiseshell comb

that had begun to slither out of her faded auburn hair. Deftly she gathered up the stray locks and fixed the comb back in position before turning to Angela.

'Sit down, my dear . . . here, let me make you comfortable. Now I'll leave you to talk to your friend but I'll send the girl up with some tea and biscuits.'

Josie noticed that the good woman's face was flushed but she left the room with as much dignity as possible. Angela had begun to giggle and Josie turned to find her friend pushing the bedspread aside to reveal that she was robed in the finest nightgown trimmed with deep broderie anglaise frills and flounces. Then she reached somewhere in the folds for a large white linen handkerchief, pushed locks of fine light brown hair back from her face and began mopping her brow. Josie saw that she was flushed.

'Are you all right?' she asked.

'Don't worry. The fever has gone. It was never very high in the first place but dear Mrs Forsyth insists that I wrap up warm – when all I want to do is cast off my clothes and open the windows wide!'

Angela's tone was passionate and Josie was embarrassed at the startling image her words had conjured up. 'Mm,' she said.

'But don't just stand there,' Angela said. 'Bring that chair over – yes, that one – and sit beside me. That's better. And thank you for fielding the book.'

Josie had slipped the small volume into her pocket. She took it out now and looked at it. '*A Shipwrecked Romance or The Captain's Bride*, by Lola Daubery,' she read aloud. She smiled as she handed it over.

Angela laughed. 'It's not that dear Mrs Forsyth would disapprove – I'm sure she reads as many romances as I do – it's just that Miss Garrett has forbidden us to have any but the most sensible reading matter here in the boarding house, and Mrs Forsyth would feel obliged to confiscate it.'

'And read it herself before reporting you!' Josie said.

'Oh, I can't tell you how pleased I am to see you,' Angela said. 'But where's Flora? I was expecting you to bring your sister.'

'I wanted her to come with me. I don't like leaving her on

126

her own but she said she was meeting some of her friends at the art gallery.'

'For goodness' sake, Josie, don't look so anxious. How old is Flora now? Sixteen next birthday, isn't she? She's quite old enough to be left to her own devices now and then.'

'I suppose she is.' Josie could hardly say that Flora had never shown the slightest interest in painting or sculpture until now, and that was what was making her uneasy. After all, it would be like admitting that she didn't trust her younger sister, and of course that was not the case . . . was it? She sighed. 'It's just that we've always been close.'

'You mean you've always felt responsible for her. But I don't know why.'

Josie felt that she was being criticized, however mildly, and she tried to explain. 'I suppose it's because our mother died . . . I mean, Flora never knew her.'

'But you had a nursemaid, didn't you? And then a step-mother?'

'Yes, the nursemaid became our stepmother. But it's not the same, is it?'

'Was she cruel, like in the fairy stories? A wicked woman who didn't love her little stepdaughters!'

'No, of course not. She . . . she . . .'

Josie didn't know how to explain that she had long ago come to the conclusion that the only person Annie loved was their father and that, although she did her duty by his daughters, she was prompted by a need to seek Samuel Walton's approval rather than any genuine feeling for the girls. She was saved from saying anything when there was a knock at the door.

Angela called, 'Come in!'

The only reply was a muffled imprecation. Then silence.

'Would you mind opening the door?' Angela asked Josie. 'It will be the girl with our tea.'

Angela was right. When Josie opened the door she found a young maid standing there. She was barely more than a child; the grey maid's uniform looked too big for her, and this was emphasized by the large, oversized pinafore. Her mobcap was askew over her round face. She was holding a tray the contents of which had slid precariously towards one side.

'Thanks, miss,' she said. 'I was trying to balance it on one arm so's I could open the door without bothering you.'

'That's all right,' Josie said, and stood aside as the girl righted her burden.

The young maid hurried into the room and placed the tray on a table set in the bay window. Her hunched shoulders eased as soon as she straightened up again.

'Do you want me to pour, miss?' she asked Angela.

'No, thank you. We can manage.'

The child hurried away. Josie thought she looked relieved.

'How old do you think she is?' she asked her friend when the door closed.

'Fair, fat and forty I should think,' Angela said with a smile.

'What on earth are you talking about?'

'Who am I talking about, you mean. Mrs Forsyth, of course.'

'Be serious. I meant the little maid.'

'Oh, Sally. I don't know. She must be at least ten or she couldn't have left school. But are you going to pour the tea?'

As Josie obliged she realized that Angela hadn't been joking. Like many of her class she hadn't considered the little servant girl worth wondering about. Angela was neither unkind nor uncaring. Josie was almost sure she would never cause any servant unnecessary pain or suffering, but she had been brought up in a different world from Josie's, a world of luxury and near gentility. If that phrase meant anything at all.

And, as for 'the girl', what sort of world did she come from? Living at the quayside, as she did, Josie was not as isolated as most of her school friends from that other world: the world of hardship and poverty, where some children, even younger than Mrs Forsyth's little housemaid, had neither a job nor a home, and perhaps not even parents.

She knew her father tried to help by supporting charities set up for the welfare of these children and she had sensed that her cousin Philip disapproved of her father's generosity, although he never actually said anything.

Suddenly, unbidden, the vision of a ragged boy, older than she had been but thin and undernourished, appeared in her mind's eye. He had told her his name was Tom Sutton, and she could still see him grabbing Flora from the wooden horse and flinging himself backwards so that her little sister would not be dragged under the merry-go-round.

And then another image arose: that of a small figure climbing up a mooring rope in the moonlight. Josie didn't know why these two pictures should be connected. Perhaps it was because she had never seen Tom again since the day of the Christmas fair. And over the years she had come to believe that she had lost something precious.

'You've gone quiet,' Angela said a few moments later as they sipped their tea and nibbled at the arrowroot biscuits.

'Have I? I'm sorry.'

'You're supposed to cheer me up, remember. Tell me everything I've been missing at school.'

'Nothing very much. There are rumours that Miss Thomas was seen walking along the promenade at Whitley-by-the-Sea with a tall young man in shabby clothes.'

'Shabby?'

'Well, he was dressed like a gentleman but his clothes were old.'

'Miss Thomas is an artist,' Angela said. 'The young man must also be an artist. An impoverished genius, perhaps.'

'You read too many romances.'

'I know. But, seriously, what is wrong with Miss Thomas having a sweetheart?'

'She could lose her job. Women teachers have to resign if they marry.'

'Well, I'm sure Miss Thomas knows the rules.'

'But even if she doesn't intend to marry him, a woman teacher is not supposed to be seen with any man who she isn't related to.'

'Tut-tut, Josie. Surely you mean "to whom she is not related" or some such construction.'

'Oh, do be serious.'

'No, Josie, I won't. What Miss Thomas does in her spare time is no concern of yours. But I must admit she's my favourite teacher so let's hope that the young man in question is her brother.'

Josie saw that it was pointless to carry on with the conversation, even though she knew that the young man probably wasn't

Miss Thomas's brother. At least not according to the two girls who had seen the couple sitting holding hands over the table of a seafront café.

And she supposed Angela was right. Miss Thomas was an intelligent woman who would know perfectly well what the consequences of her actions might be. She supposed it was the idea of the restrictions on a woman's life, the inequality, that bothered her, not this particular case.

Angela sighed and Josie smiled ruefully. 'I'm being a bore, aren't I? Sorry.'

'You're forgiven.'

'Now what shall we talk about?'

'My birthday party,' Angela said.

'But your birthday isn't for ages yet. Not until after the end of the summer term.'

'I know when my own birthday is, but it's going to be quite a grand affair and I've already started to make plans. My father has agreed that I can invite some of my school friends and I want you to help me decide which ones.'

'Oh, I couldn't do that.'

'Why ever not?'

'Well, it's your birthday. You must invite whom you please.'

'But that's just it. I can't have all of them. My mother is so . . . so choosy . . . oh, you know what I mean.'

'Mm.'

Josie knew very well what Angela meant. Lady Cavendish was not at all pleased that her daughter had made friends with girls from what she considered to be the inferior classes. She had never intended her daughter to be educated at the Girls' High School in the first place. She had wanted to engage a governess but Angela's father, perhaps seeing what that kind of education had done for his wife, had insisted that his daughter go to school.

At that point Lady Cavendish had suggested one of the exclusive girls' boarding establishments in the south of England but, again, her husband disagreed. He loved his daughter, he said, and he wanted to see her at least at the weekends, not send her so far away that he would only see her occasionally.

'The trouble with my mother is that she cannot forget her

grandfather was a pitman,' Angela said, and Josie looked at her in surprise. 'Oh, yes, didn't you know? The Robsons were humble mineworkers; they lived in a pit village. And how my great-grandfather came to own one pit and then another, and so on, is something my mother should be proud of. After all, my father would hardly have married into that family if it hadn't been for their enormous wealth. If it wasn't for coal my mother wouldn't be Lady Cavendish.'

Josie wasn't sure how to respond. Perhaps Angela's mother should be proud of her family rather than trying to forget them. And yet, their wealth could not have been won without the toil of other pitmen, and even women and children, who not so long ago had risked their lives for a few shillings a week so that mine owners like the Robsons could live in comfort and even grandeur.

Enterprising men like Angela's great-grandfather had worked hard and, in building their own fortunes, had provided employment for others. But Josie believed they should never be allowed to forget the responsibility that great wealth should bring.

'So will you help me decide which of my school friends I should invite to my party?'

'I told you, I can't.'

'*Now* why not?'

'Well, it seems wrong, somehow, to choose your friends depending on . . . well . . . on social class.'

Angela looked at her solemnly for a moment and then she said, 'And of course that's why I like you so much. Not one of my other friends would say that. And you're right. Here I am, happy to criticize my mother for wanting to forget what kind of family she came from, and yet I'm prepared to go along with her silly rules!

'Pass me that pad of notepaper, would you? That's right, the one on the bedside table – and the pencil. Now, let us decide which girls to invite on the basis of who we like best and who would be the most fun. And the first names I will write will be yours and your sister's. For of course I know you wouldn't want to come without Flora.'

*   *   *

Flora was furious. Not one of her school friends had arrived. She took out her little pocket watch and, opening it up, looked at the time. It confirmed her suspicion that she had been wandering round the art gallery for nearly an hour. While waiting, she had had to pretend to be interested in the boring little watercolours that some ladies' art circle had produced.

The uniformed attendant looked up from his chair near the door and she was sure his glance was suspicious. As if she would steal one of these dreadful daubs! Or perhaps he thought she was going to damage one of them. Well, she certainly felt like doing so!

There were wishy-washy little pictures of flowers and fruit and pet animals, and some perfectly dreadful sea scenes where the sailing boats looked like toys and the sea looked like crumpled tissue paper.

There was one picture, however, that had caught her interest. She couldn't tell whether it was skilful or not – she wasn't artistic like Josie – but it was so much more alive than the other pictures. She went to look at it again and stood still without fidgeting while she took in the view of heather-covered hills with rough stone outcrops under a wide sky. 'A Northumbrian sky', Grandma Hannah would have called it, and as she gazed, she was transported for a moment to her grandparents' inn at Moorburn.

How she loved the holidays she had there. How she enjoyed the simple pleasure of walking in the hills, climbing high above the inn and looking down on the smoking chimneypots of the village. She could never explain the exhilaration she felt when she was all alone with only the sound of the wind soughing through the grasses, the call of the birds and the bleating of the lambs.

Josie would come with her, of course, and she was good company. But Flora would become impatient with her elder sister and run on ahead, laughing as the wind lifted her hair and reddened her cheeks and brought tears to her eyes.

She remembered the first time they had found the ruined cottage, clambering over smoke-blackened stone to the one habitable room. As children they had played houses there with their dolls, taking bottles of water, bread and cheese and apples, and staying there all day until their grandfather would come seeking them and take them home.

Flora loved that cottage. She didn't know why and, even now that she was too old for childish games, she would still go there. Josie would sit and sketch or paint – and Josie's pictures were much, much better than anything here in the gallery – and Flora would sit amongst the sun-warmed stones and daydream.

Dreams of a different life, a life she couldn't quite imagine except that it was wild and free. Sometimes the unformed longings inside her reduced her to tears and she would sob with frustration, all the more intense because she didn't know what she was crying for.

'The moon,' her grandmother had told her once when she had caught her sobbing as she stared out of her bedroom window at the inn long past the time when she should have been sleeping. 'Poor bairn, I think you're crying for the moon and I canna give it to you. And I divven't think there's anybody who can.'

Sometimes she would catch her grandmother looking at her in such a strange way and, once or twice, she was sure she had seen tears in her eyes. But Grandma Hannah would always brush the tears away and hug her and tell her that she loved her, and then get on with her work as if nothing at all was the matter.

'Flora.'

She spun round at the sound of her name. Sarah Pearce was standing there.

'It's about time,' Flora said. 'Where are the others?'

'I don't know.'

Sarah's tone was subdued and she was glancing sideways as if she couldn't bring herself to meet Flora's eyes.

'What do you mean, you don't know? I thought Pamela and Geraldine and you were coming together.'

Sarah, along with the girls Flora had mentioned, lived near each other in Jesmond, and the plan was that they should meet and come into the city on the same tram.

'I . . . they . . . they weren't there. At the tram stop. I waited and then I thought I'd better come.'

'Better late than never, I suppose.'

'Well, you might at least act as if you're pleased to see me! I wasn't going to come but I thought it would be too unkind.'

Flora's eyes widened as she took in Sarah's flushed cheeks and indignant expression. Sarah Pearce was the cleverest girl in the class but she was usually quiet and biddable. She followed happily along behind the other girls and had never, in Flora's memory, answered back or complained.

'What do you mean, too unkind?'

All Sarah's temporary show of spirit seemed to drain away. 'Oh, nothing,' she said.

'No, it can't be nothing. And, look, I am pleased to see you. Of course I am. But I really wish you would explain.'

'Well, don't get angry with me.'

'Of course I won't.'

In reality Flora wanted to slap the stupid girl but she realized that if she did she would never get to the bottom of Sarah's strange behaviour.

'I didn't think that Pamela and Geraldine would come today.'

'Why ever not?'

'Well, we were talking about it over tea last night—'

'Wait a moment. At tea last night?'

'Er . . . yes . . . I mean . . .' Sarah looked as though she wanted to run away. She glanced nervously over her shoulder towards the door and even began to edge backwards.

Flora caught at her sleeve, and smiled through her teeth. 'You had tea together last night? Where?'

'At my house,' Sarah whispered. She was trembling. 'But it wasn't planned. Because, of course, if it had been planned, I would have invited you – like I always do – but we . . . we were just walking home together and you know my house comes first? And we were talking—'

'About me?'

'Yes, well, no, I mean about your idea of meeting here today and when we came to my house it just seemed natural somehow to go in and my mother said they should stay for tea, and—'

'Yes, I understand. That's all right.'

'Do you? Is it?' Sarah began to look more cheerful.

'But do get to the point, Sarah.'

'Oh.' The beginnings of a smile faded. 'Well, Pamela and

Geraldine said that they didn't really feel like going to the art gallery.'

'For goodness' sake, you know I only suggested that we meet at the gallery so that it sounded – well – like a good thing to do. Something our parents wouldn't object to!'

'Yes, I know that, but that's it really. They said they would think about it but that they didn't particularly want to go round the shops either. Not after . . . well, you know . . . not after the trouble at the perfume counter.'

'That was Muriel's fault. We all know that.'

'Mm.'

Sarah's pale face suddenly took on a mulish look, and, in any case, Flora had lost the desire to push the matter further. 'Well,' she sighed, 'I'm glad you came. In fact I think I might treat you to tea and cream cakes. Would you like that?'

'Yes. Oh, I mean, no.'

'I beg your pardon?'

'Look, Flora, I don't really want to go to the shops with you either. I only came because I thought it would be cruel for no one to turn up. I . . . I didn't want your feelings to be hurt. But now I think I'll go home.'

Sarah turned and fled, leaving Flora staring after her open-mouthed. Nothing like this had ever happened to her before. She didn't know what was making her more angry, the fact that Geraldine and Pamela hadn't wanted to spend Saturday after-noon with her, or the idea that silly, ineffectual Sarah Pearce had the temerity to feel sorry for her.

'Well, miss.' She looked up to find that the gallery attendant was walking towards her. 'Your friend has gone and I think it's time that you went too.'

Normally Flora would have replied smartly to anyone she regarded as inferior talking to her like this, but she was so astounded by the way her school friends had behaved that she simply glared at the man and walked out with as much dignity as she could muster.

'It's kind of you to spend time with me like this, Samuel.'

Charlotte was surprised at her brother's reaction to her words. 'Have I been so remiss?' he asked.

'Remiss? I don't know what you mean.'

They were drinking tea together and, although the usual bustle of the quayside could be heard through the open windows, here in the quiet orderliness of Charlotte's room the hurly-burly of the commercial world seemed far away.

Samuel put down his cup and smiled. His sister noticed how handsome he still was when he allowed his features to relax like this. 'Do I neglect you?'

'Of course you don't. Why do you ask such a question?'

'Well, here you are, up in your eyrie, and I have the feeling that sometimes I let whole weeks go by without bothering to climb the stairs to find out how you are.'

Charlotte was silent. Then she realized he was looking at her expectantly and somewhat guiltily. 'Samuel, I know how busy you are, and I don't mind at all.'

'You don't get lonely?'

'No.' That wasn't true but Charlotte had no intention of admitting it. 'Annie comes up to take tea with me, and Josie always asks me if there is anything I need when she goes into town. And, of course, Philip spends as much time as he can with his old mother.'

'Ah, yes, Philip. He's a good son.'

'Indeed he is. And a good nephew too, I hope.'

'He works hard. I have come to rely on him more and more.'

Her younger brother sighed and suddenly Charlotte noticed how tired he looked. She had thought for some time that Samuel might not be well, but he never complained, and she had wondered if it might not simply be that he was unhappy.

She would have asked him why but she knew he wouldn't tell her. He would never admit to her or to anyone else that he had never been truly happy since the night his first wife had died.

Samuel was staring into the mid-distance and she wondered what was going through his mind, what troubled thoughts had taken him so far away. Charlotte found herself thinking back to the night Effie had died. She'd had a hard time of it and there was no question that Samuel had blamed himself. He shouldn't. It wasn't his fault that women died in childbirth.

As the silence lengthened between them Charlotte found herself dwelling on some of the things that had happened the night of Flora's birth. Jane Brewer had given Effie something to ease the pain and, in her drugged state, the lass had become delirious. She tossed about in the bed and moaned and called out . . . what had she called out?

Someone's name. Her voice had been muffled and the words indistinct so that Charlotte had not been able to make out what that name was. But it had not been 'Samuel'. No, Effie had not called out the name of her husband as she lay dying. Charlotte was sure of that.

Samuel stirred himself. 'I believe I have been neglecting my wife, as well as my sister.'

'Mm. Annie.'

'You don't deny it?' Samuel's lips lifted slightly but his smile was strained.

'Well . . . she does seem a little subdued.'

'I know it. And she devotes herself to good works.'

Good works. That was the expression that Philip had used and Charlotte had believed he sounded slightly scornful. 'It is not a bad thing for your wife to be seen to be occupying herself with a worthwhile charity.'

'Is that why she does it, do you think? Prompted by duty?'

'Not entirely. She has told me that she likes to help with the children.'

'Ah, yes.' Samuel looked solemn again. 'Annie has been a good wife, would you agree?'

'Certainly.'

'You know, sometimes I think I was selfish.'

'Selfish?'

'If you had been younger, if your health had not . . . I mean, if you had not become more—'

'If I had not gradually become a cripple.'

Brother and sister looked at each other gravely and he nodded. 'I know you were willing but my girls were growing and I wanted to make life easier – for all of us.'

'So you married poor Annie.'

'*Poor* Annie. That's how all of us think of her, isn't it? And it's my fault.'

'Not at all. She was a servant. You married her. She is the wife of a rich and important man.'

'But we both know she wanted more than that. She wanted something that I could not give. She wanted me to love her.'

'And you never could.'

'No.'

'And you feel guilty. But why now?'

'I have watched her withdraw. She has had no children of her own. The girls are almost grown and hardly need her, and I . . .'

'Don't, Samuel. I don't want to know about your marriage.' Charlotte was uncomfortable. The intimate details of her brother's life were not her business.

Samuel paused. 'I was about to say that I have taken her for granted,' he said. Suddenly he smiled. 'So I have decided to try and make amends. When the girls go to their grandparents' inn in Moorburn in the summer I am going to take Annie away. We shall travel . . . a holiday.'

'Where?'

'Oh, I don't know. Anywhere she wants to go. And I need to know that you will be all right while we are away. I thought I should tell you now in case you want to make arrangements.'

'Arrangements?'

Charlotte felt her throat constrict. Was this a prelude to her brother asking her to move out? Some time ago now, when she had begun to find the stairs more and more difficult, he had asked her if she would like him to find her more suitable accommodation, such as a ground-floor apartment in one of the big houses in Heaton or Jesmond, but she had declined the offer. For if she moved out perhaps Samuel would expect Philip to go with her and that was the last thing she wanted. Philip must stay close to Samuel, always be on hand, always there to prove himself useful.

Samuel did not seem to have noticed her alarm. 'I mean, would you like to engage a companion? A woman who would not only help you from day to day but who would be company for you? Someone other than Patience.'

Charlotte's eyes widened with surprise, and he continued, 'I'm not criticizing the girl – she works hard – but that's it,

138

really. You deserve something better than to be at the mercy of a busy servant. You should have someone who can spend time with you.'

And now Charlotte felt her throat constrict for a different reason. For a moment she could not speak. And then she managed to say, 'You are a good brother, Samuel. And, yes, I would like to choose a companion. I shall be very grateful.'

'Good. I'll start making enquiries straight away, although I've already had thoughts about this. Why don't we consider one of Annie's widows for the position?'

'Annie's widows?'

'From the mission?'

'A sailor's widow.'

'Yes. One of the older women whose children have grown. Some-one who is alone in the world, perhaps? Of course you could choose the person yourself. You would have the final say in the matter. But I'd like to help someone like that. I owe my own prosperity to seafaring men.'

'Of course, Samuel. I agree. One of Annie's widows, then.'

'Good. I'll go to the mission and talk to young Jacob Goodwright; discuss the matter with him. And, of course, in doing so I hope I'll also be pleasing my good wife.'

Samuel rose from his chair decisively and then gasped and clutched his chest. He stood swaying and Charlotte cried out in alarm, 'What is it, Samuel? What's the matter?'

Her brother had closed his eyes, but after a moment he opened them and tried to smile. 'It's nothing. I got up too quickly and I felt the room sway. You must have done that.'

Charlotte laughed faintly. 'Not for a long time,' she said. 'I don't move quickly these days.'

Samuel laughed but Charlotte noticed that his face had drained of colour. He's not well, she thought. His unhappiness drives him to work too hard. He should let Philip do more. I'm glad he's planning this holiday; he deserves it. But when he comes back I might suggest that maybe it's time to make Philip a partner.

The rain started just as she alighted from the tram in Grainger Street. Driven by a cold wind, it threatened to soak Flora and spoil her new hat. A large woman stopped right in front of her to unfurl her umbrella and Flora cannoned into her. The woman turned angrily, nearly pushing Flora over. In fact she would probably have slipped and fallen on the greasy pavement if a tall young man had not caught her arms and held her upright.

'Thank you,' she said when she had recovered.

She was aware that the walking stick he held in one hand was digging into her arm. 'I'm all right,' she said. 'You can let go.'

He smiled and stepped back, at the same time raising the walking stick towards his top hat in a gentlemanly gesture. Flora's attention was caught by the elaborate carving at the top of the cane. Two ivory snakes seemed to coil and writhe upwards around the stick and each other. Their eyes, made from some yellow gem, glistened in the uncertain light.

'Are you sure?' he asked.

Flora frowned. 'Sure?'

'Are you sure that you're all right? You seem somewhat distracted.'

'Oh . . . yes . . . I'm sorry. Of course.' She was embarrassed to have been caught staring. 'I'd better go. You must think me rude – er – thank you.'

'You've already thanked me,' he said, and he smiled. 'But it was my pleasure, I assure you.'

He's teasing me, Flora thought, and she knew that colour was flooding her face. She wanted to glare at him but found that she could only stare in admiration at his lean handsome features framed by reddish brown sideburns, and his smiling eyes. Were they green?

And then he laughed outright and made a mock bow. 'Any time,' he said.

Flora turned and fled before he could see how flustered she was. She dived through an archway, which turned out to be one of the entrances to the covered Grainger Market. Other people had the same idea and hurried into the market to get away from the rain, and for a while Flora was carried along with the crowd, going in no particular direction and not really noticing where she was.

In her mind's eye she could still see her rescuer and she

puzzled over him. He had looked like a gentleman. He'd been dressed in the height of fashion; the gold tiepin nestling in his silk cravat was formed in the shape of a horseshoe studded with what looked like rubies. There were matching buttons on his waistcoat and there'd been a flash of gold and ruby red as he'd raised his hand. So he wore a ring. But no gloves. Surely a man who was dressed so smartly should have worn gloves? Unless he'd taken them off for fear they'd spoil in the rain.

Flora was intrigued. She had never met anyone quite like him. But then that was not surprising. The only grown men she'd met up till now were the sober-suited business friends of her father or the fathers of her school friends. She had an idea that they might think this man was a trifle flashy. She realized they would not approve of him and, for some reason, this disappointed her.

And what had he made of her, she wondered. Flora realized that she had entered the central hall of the market and she made towards the milliner's shop under the overhanging gallery tearooms. While pretending to look at the hats she studied her own reflection.

The bodice of her blue plaid dress was boned in every seam to accentuate her small waist and it ended in a point well below her waistline. The neckline was high, with a standing collar softened with a trim of lace and a bow of velvet ribbon. The full skirt was flounced, but not too much, just sufficient to make it stand out a little from the waist. The plaid wasn't a true tartan, of course. It was just a pleasing mixture of checks and stripes in shades of blue.

She looked down to examine the toes of her pointed boots, which could just be seen peeping from below the bottom frill of her skirt. Thank goodness she was young enough to be allowed to wear slightly shorter skirts. Her sister and her stepmother spent hours cleaning the hemlines of their skirts when they had been out in inclement weather.

Flora considered Annie for a moment. Her clothes were the best that money could buy. Flora's father insisted that she should have anything she wanted, and yet she never looked quite right and Flora knew why. She and Josie had been on shopping trips with their stepmother and they had soon realized that Annie didn't trust her own judgement; she simply accepted anything the shop girls offered.

They weren't exactly cheating her; everything was of the highest quality and latest style. It was as if, faced with a customer who had no opinions, they were determined to sell her the most expensive item, whether it suited her or not.

Flora shuddered when she remembered that it had been the same when Annie used to be responsible for choosing clothes for Josie and herself. There had been more than one dramatic scene in Fenwick's or Bainbridge's when Flora had stamped her foot and refused point-blank to wear something Annie had chosen. And Annie would stand there bewildered, close to tears to be so humiliated in public. She'd usually given in and allowed Flora to have what she wanted.

How grateful Annie had been when Josie, in the nicest possible way, had suggested to Annie that she would take over that responsibility. And Flora had been pleased too, although she had the grace to smile when she remembered that Josie had not been so easy to overcome in matters of taste. But she had agreed that she and Flora were very different and did not insist on dressing them identically, as Annie had done. And at least she had a sense of style, even if it wasn't as glamorous as Flora would have liked.

Glamorous . . . no . . . flamboyant . . .

That was the word to describe the man who had stopped her from falling down, Flora realized. And for some reason he was the reason she felt the need to scrutinize herself so closely now. Well, she hadn't got too wet and the brim of her pale straw bonnet was still quite buoyant. She dropped her head a little and slanted her glance upwards so that she could see the trimmings of pink silk rosebuds, white baby's breath and loops of blue velvet ribbons. The hat appeared undamaged.

As she straightened up she thought she heard a low laugh and she spun round, but could see no one in the crowd who appeared to be looking her way. She heard a rap on the glass behind her and turned back to find that the funny old woman who owned the milliner's shop had come right up to the window and was beckoning her.

When she saw that she had Flora's attention she lifted a hat from one of the stands and held it out. She smiled at Flora and nodded. Flora gazed at the hat. It was a pretty shape with a shallow crown, a wide brim and a mass of fine-tendrilled feathers curling round the brim. But the feathers were dyed in a mixture of violent hues: purple, scarlet, and an impossible emerald green. Unfortunately the effect was vulgar. Flora shook her head. The old woman replaced the hat and looked as though she was going to reach for another one. Flora shot her an apologetic glance and hurried away.

The market was busy and the cries of the stall holders echoed round the high-roofed central hall. The smells of coffee, cheese and spices mingled with the sharp sweet smell of fruit and something more unpleasant: the odours of blood and sawdust coming from the butchers' alley.

Flora hadn't intended to come here. She had planned to walk around town and window-shop with her school friends, and perhaps go into Bainbridge's and Fenwick's to look at the new fashions. And then she had intended to round off the day by treating them to tea in one of the tearooms; perhaps the new one where the dashing young man played romantic piano music while the teacups tinkled.

She was still astounded that they hadn't wanted to come with her. Something like this had never happened before. If the girls were going to be beastly like this it was all the more reason for persuading her father to let her leave school at the end of the summer term.

But what was she to do now? She didn't feel like going home. Josie had gone to visit Angela Cavendish at Mrs Forsyth's school boarding house in Jesmond; Aunt Charlotte was dull company and so was Annie. And, in any case, Annie would probably be out visiting her widows and orphans.

At first Flora wandered up and down the alleyways aimlessly, aware that she was attracting attention, and also that not many young women were as well dressed as she was. In fact the crowd was mostly drab and distinctly shabby. And the recent rainfall hadn't done much for the cut of the cheap coats and jackets.

Then Flora's eye was caught by a display of romance novels on a bookstall. She considered them for a moment, then walked on. For, no matter how exciting the story, she had never managed to read a book right through. She always started well but soon got bored and, although she knew she shouldn't, she usually ended up skipping to the last page to see if all ended happily. And, of course, it always did. At least in that sort of book. She couldn't imagine why a writer would go to all the trouble of writing so many words when the ending was always going to be the same.

Josie, who read just about every sort of book, had tried to explain that the interesting thing was how the happy ending was achieved and that the characters, even in light romances, were just as interesting as the story. But Flora couldn't see it.

She began to grow bored and she had just about decided that she would go home after all when her eye was caught by a glittering display of cheap jewellery on one of the stalls. Sets of necklaces, bracelets and earrings were laid out on velvet cards alongside jumbled trays of second-hand jewellery. Flora stared at these trays in astonishment. She couldn't imagine that any of it was valuable, and therefore wondered who on earth would be tempted to buy it. Although when she looked more closely she decided there were some pretty little brooches amongst the bangles and scarf pins. For example, one brooch was fashioned in the shape of a flower basket with the flowers made from coloured paste. And there was a dainty spray of lilies of the valley with emerald enamel leaves and tiny seed pearls forming the flowers. She knew they couldn't be real pearls but it did look pretty.

Flora picked the brooch up and examined it more closely. The tiny price ticket was smudged and she couldn't read it. She was just about to ask the stall holder the price when another customer, a cheap-looking girl with rouged cheeks, pushed in and took her place. Flora watched in exasperation as the girl and the stall holder began to haggle over the price of a pair of ruby-red drop earrings. First she thought she would interrupt, then, losing patience, she thought she would walk away.

She was just about to drop the brooch back in the tray but, when she saw that no one was looking, she withdrew her hand and coiled her fingers round the brooch so that it couldn't be seen. She breathed in. She could feel her heart racing just as it had on those other occasions. She knew she could do it; she'd never been caught yet.

Well, there had been that incident of the lavender water but she'd managed to get Muriel blamed for that. She wasn't sure why she had started to steal things, especially as nothing she had ever taken was valuable; she only knew that she found it exciting. She enjoyed testing her wits against those of dull shop assistants.

She had an idea that market traders might just have sharper wits than the average shop girl but this one was fully occupied with his awkward customer. Nevertheless, Flora realized that she was holding her breath as she turned to go.

She pushed her way through the crowd, half expecting the stall keeper to cry out. If he did she would drop the brooch, she decided, and kick it away. They wouldn't be able to prove anything if she didn't have it on her person, would they?

No one had noticed. There was no call of 'Stop thief!'. As she turned the corner into another alleyway of the market she let out her breath and began to smile. Believing she had got away with it, she slipped the brooch into her pocket. Then someone tapped her on the shoulder.

She felt the ice forming round her heart as she stood quite still. She couldn't have run because whoever it was who had tapped her shoulder was now holding on to her arms. 'Wait a moment,' a man's voice said. Then her captor let go of one arm and began to turn her round to face him.

She found herself staring at a gold horseshoe tiepin studded with rubies. She was aware of the bustle around them but the noise of the market seemed to recede as she raised her head to meet his green gaze.

'Well, well,' her former rescuer said. 'We meet again.'

Chapter Seven

That night a cold wind swept in from the sea, setting the sail ropes rattling against the masts of the tall ships moored in the river. Bits of torn paper and straw from packing cases were blown along the quayside to wrap themselves round lampposts or fetch up in doorways.

Annie, unwilling to commit herself to the empty bed, huddled over the fire in her bedroom. Samuel was working late again. He and Philip would be sitting in the office on the ground floor, poring over ledgers and bills of sale, and goodness knows what else he could find to keep him occupied until he guessed that his wife would be safely asleep.

Tonight she had decided to wait for him. She'd lit the candles and settled down with the book she'd borrowed from Josie, *Oliver Twist* by Charles Dickens. Josie had said she would enjoy the story of the poor boy born in a workhouse and orphaned so cruelly, but Annie had never been much of a reader and she had soon tired of it.

What was the use of writing about such miseries, she thought, when there was already enough unhappiness in the world? The book lay on the small table next to her, ready to be snatched up when she heard Samuel's footstep on the stairs. She would pretend that she had been so taken up with the story that she had forgotten the time. She would glance up in surprise and smile sleepily, letting the book fall as she rose to greet him. She hoped she could still summon a smile by the time Samuel came to bed.

She stared moodily into the fire and pulled her shawl round

her shoulders. She had not put on her flannel dressing gown. Sensible though it was, it was hardly alluring. Her nightgown of rose China silk was full and flowing, but the material was so fine that it clung to her figure when she stood up. The large collar was trimmed with Normandy lace that framed her face and disguised the growing fullness of a second chin. Rose satin ties kept the garment together at neck and waist; ties that could be undone with one gentle tug to allow the garment to fall open and slip smoothly from her shoulders.

Annie's face flamed with more than the heat from the fire as she imagined her husband's touch. Samuel made love to her so infrequently, and she had to face the fact that whenever he did she was more eager than he was.

But why should I be ashamed of that? she thought. We are married and what we do is not a sin. She had an idea that women were not supposed to enjoy what happened in the marriage bed. In former days, listening to gossip in the kitchen between Mrs Dobson and the maidservants, she had heard mention of wives doing anything to avoid their so-called duties.

Well, she did not find it a duty. She found lovemaking a joy, and it was torture to her that the man she loved so deeply seemed so reluctant. She was sure he had not been like that with his first wife. Even now she could remember the way he used to look at Effie, almost devouring her with his eyes. Following her up to this very room, this very bed, so eagerly.

She remembered with shame how, when she was simply a maidservant in this house, she had sometimes stood outside the door when husband and wife were in bed together and heard his great cries of rapture. He had never cried out like that when he made love to her.

And what of Effie? Annie would bring her her tray in the morning and find her listless, her eyes puffy and her mouth bruised and sulky, her whole attitude suggesting discontent. Samuel's first wife must surely have been one of those women who found lovemaking distasteful. And Annie would never understand how any woman would not have almost died with pleasure to be taken in Samuel Walton's arms.

She looked up with a start when she heard the door open. In spite of her determination not to, she must have fallen asleep.

It was too late to snatch up the book she was supposed to be reading, for Samuel had pushed the door shut with his shoulders and was halfway across the room.

'I'm glad you're awake,' he said, and she looked up in amazement to find that he was smiling. He was carrying a tray.

She watched wordlessly as he hooked a foot around one of the legs of the small table and drew it away from the fire before placing the tray on it.

'What's this?' she asked at last.

Samuel laughed. 'I haven't had my supper and I hoped you would join me.'

'Did you?'

He looked at her solemnly. 'It grieves me to hear how surprised you sound. I shall take that as a reproof – no,' he raised one hand, 'don't say anything. I deserve it. But let's eat.'

He took off his jacket and loosened his cravat before sitting down opposite her at the other side of the hearth. Annie stared at the tray. There was a jug of red wine and two glasses, some soft bread rolls and slices of cold roast beef and a dish of pastries from Olsen's.

Olsen's was the Norwegian coffee house on the quayside, and their cakes and pastries were mouth-watering. Samuel had brought a selection that included Annie's favourites made from sweet dough, shaped as rosettes, then deep fried and sprinkled with brown sugar.

Samuel saw her looking at them and he smiled. 'I went along before they closed,' he said. 'I ordered them earlier. I know you like them.'

Annie's smile wavered and she dropped her head to hide the fact that her eyes had filled with tears. Why do I feel like crying? she thought as she fought to suppress the agony of sorrow that gripped her heart. I should be happy when Samuel pays attention to me like this. When he's like this he's everything I want him to be. And that's it, of course – it happens so infrequently that I can hardly believe he's the same man who walks about his own house as if he were a stranger, or buries his head in business papers so that he doesn't have to talk to me.

Samuel had poured the wine and he held her glass towards her. 'Have a care,' he said when he saw how her hand was shaking. 'It would be a shame to stain such a pretty robe.'

His eyes lingered for a moment on her breasts and Annie felt desire flare. But Samuel set down his wine only to fill two plates with bread rolls and slices of meat. 'I'll make sandwiches of this,' he said. 'That will be easier.'

Annie did not do justice to the food. She left her sandwich half eaten, and even one of her favourite pastries could not tempt her to do more than nibble at it. But she gulped her wine nervously and didn't protest when Samuel filled her glass a second time. She began to feel warm inside and, as the warmth spread throughout her limbs, she began to relax.

She noticed that Samuel drank a little more than usual. He began to talk of something he'd like to do in the summer but she was only half concentrating. It was when he was looking at her expectantly that she realized he must have asked her a question.

'I'm sorry?' she murmured.

'I said, so where should we go?'

'Go?'

'On holiday?'

'Holiday?'

'Annie,' he smiled, 'I said I think we should have a holiday and I want you to choose where we should go.'

'Oh . . . I don't know. Josie would be the one to ask. She's so clever I'm sure she would choose somewhere that we all would like and – what is it?' Annie stopped when she saw that Samuel was shaking his head.

'I'm sure she would, but we are not all going. I mean this to be a holiday just for you and me.'

'Do you?'

She knew she sounded incredulous again, and once more she saw that look cross his face. What was it exactly? Was it guilt? Or at least embarrassment?

'Yes,' he said. 'We spend too little time together. I'm grateful for the way you have taken care of my daughters.'

'They haven't really needed me for some time now.'

'Nevertheless, you took on all the duties of a mother. And you have made my life comfortable in so many ways. I shouldn't like you to think that I have not noticed the smooth running of the household. And . . . and you've been a comfort to me. I thought that when the girls go to their grandmother's you might like it if we went away together.'

'Oh, I would.' Immediately Annie wished she hadn't sounded so eager.

'And would you like to leave the choice of destination to me?'

Annie nodded.

Samuel looked at the dish of pastries and then looked up into her face and smiled. 'Then why don't we go to Norway?'

'Norway?' Annie said wonderingly. 'But that would mean a sea voyage.'

'Yes. Why not? We can sail to Bergen from the Tyne. Almost from our own doorstep. Annie, you'd love it, starting from the moment we set sail. The crossing should be good when we go, and then the country is wild and beautiful. The mountains, the fjords, the fine summer nights . . .'

Samuel's face was shining with enthusiasm and Annie realized, not for the first time, how much her husband still missed his former life as a seafarer. So in spite of her misgivings about a sea voyage she said, 'That sounds wonderful.'

'That's settled then.'

Suddenly the light in Samuel's eyes faded. He had been leaning forward in his chair but now he sat back and raised his glass. He stared into its red depths and then drained it. He reached for the jug.

'Would you like some more?' he asked. His face was flushed.

'No thank you.'

Annie was still clutching her own glass and she became aware that her hand had started to tremble again. This time Samuel did not notice. He filled his own glass and put the empty jug back on the tray.

He seemed irresolute now, almost like a hesitant suitor. And yet she knew that whatever followed there would be no declaration of love. Samuel needed her but only as any man needs a woman to take care of his natural urges. And when it was over he would be grateful. Well, she would be content with gratitude so long as it followed the physical intimacy she craved.

She drained her glass and after she had replaced it on the

tray she noticed that she had spilled some wine on her nightgown after all. She could feel the liquid sinking through the fine silk on to her breast.

Samuel had finished his wine and he pushed the table aside. Then he rose and snuffed out the candles on the mantelpiece before reaching for her hands. He drew her to her feet and when he hesitated she reached for the satin ribbons at her neck and pulled gently until the bow loosened and her nightgown opened, exposing her neck and the rise of her breasts.

Her husband looked at her in the flickering glow from the fire but he could not meet her eyes. Slowly he raised his hands and took hold of the ends of the ribbon at her waist. She felt a tug and then her robe fell away. She gave the slightest of shrugs and felt the silk slip down over her shoulders and arms until it fell to the floor.

She stood there naked, aware of the cracking and spluttering of the coals in the hearth and of the rising wind rattling the windowpanes. But they were the only sounds. Samuel, still without speaking, lifted her into his arms and carried her to the bed. Then he retreated into the shadows to remove his clothes.

When he came to her and took her in his arms and began to make love to her, he was considerate and tender; so much so that she could almost have persuaded herself that this was all she wanted. All she had ever wanted.

And yet, afterwards, when he turned from her, she burned with shame. Shame because she had not been able to stop herself from crying out at the height of her ecstasy, assuring him that she loved him. And he had remained silent. As always.

No matter that he had kissed her brow before turning from her to sleep, what she wanted was for him to say that he loved her too. And she knew he never would.

And now she lay with open eyes, staring at the patterns the flames made as they danced on the ceiling while her husband breathed deeply and contentedly in his sleep. Would it have been different if she had borne him a child? A son? She would never know, for the signs had started that it would not be too long before her childbearing days were over.

So, even though Samuel's lovemaking had given her delight and left her body feeling soothed and at peace, her heart and her mind would not let her be happy. While her husband slept next to her she felt her throat constrict and the tears well up in her eyes. Too weary to wipe them away, she felt them trickle down her cheeks on to the pillow. And outside the tall house on the quayside the wind grew stronger and the rain began.

Samuel breathed deeply and evenly but he was only pretending to be asleep. He knew that Annie was awake and he knew that she was unhappy, but he would never be able to turn to her and take her in his arms, comfort her and say the things she wanted to hear. For he was riven with guilt.

If he had been a better sort of man he would never have married again. But then if he had been a better man his darling wife would not have died so tragically young. Samuel had never been able to free himself of the notion that it was his fault that Effie had died in childbirth.

She had not wanted him to make love to her that night he had come to find her at her parents' home. But he had loved her so much and had yearned for her so much all those weeks that he had been away at sea that he had not been able to stop himself making love to her against her will. Had he forced her that night? Had it been more than that . . . had it been rape? Could you rape your own wife? The law said that you could not, but Samuel was not so sure.

And the resulting pregnancy had not been happy. Even now he could remember how distant and how moody Effie had been. He would have given her everything she wanted, anything in the world that it was within his power to give if only he could have made things right again.

He was a man, and he didn't know how these things worked, but he had convinced himself that Effie would not have died if she had been happy throughout her pregnancy. And he was the cause of her unhappiness. In effect, he had killed her.

And he had not even been true to her memory. In his weakness he had taken another wife. He needed Annie not just because she could be a mother to his girls but also because he was not strong enough to be without a woman for the rest of his life. And better to be respectably married than to visit another sort of woman to assuage his needs and risk bringing disease into the house where his precious daughters lived.

Had he done Annie an injustice by marrying her? He had known at the time that she longed to be his wife. And yet she might have found someone else, someone who would have loved her in the way she wanted and made her truly happy. In his need had he taken advantage of her?

Now, here they were, lying side by side, having just given each other bodily pleasure and yet there was no true comfort for either of them. No comfort of the heart and soul. For Samuel knew that his heart still belonged to Effie and it always would. He would never be able to forget her – not that he wanted to. He had had no portrait painted of his young wife and he had always regretted that. And yet, what need was there of a portrait when her daughter was the living image of her?

Flora . . . In spite of his misery he knew that his mouth was lifting in a smile just to think of his younger daughter. Beautiful and spirited and not half as intelligent or kind as her older sister, Josie. He acknowledged that. He loved them both but just to look at the younger girl filled him with pleasure.

His self-torment began to fade and his eyelids grew heavy and, as he drifted off to sleep, he thanked God that in taking the mother He had at least left him the child to grow to womanhood and bring him delight with every passing day.

When Josie opened her eyes it was dark and she could sense that the space she was lying in was confined. But it was rocking like a cradle. She could feel the splintered wood beneath her and smell the sea-stained tarpaulin that lay only inches above her head.

It was always the same, and it always took her a while to realize that she was not truly awake for she was dreaming. The same dream.

She raised one arm, not her arm surely, for it was skinny and dirty, the arm of a child in tattered clothes, and pushed the tarpaulin aside. She held her breath and listened for a moment before rising and slipping over the side of the lifeboat on to the deck of the ship. There was no one about and she crept to the ship's rail and clung on for dear life as the vessel pitched and rolled.

She gazed out but could see nothing but the swell of the

deep waters. The sea was covered with foam and, as the wind rose, it gathered the spray from the waves and dashed it over the deck, soaking her and making her let go of the rail.

And then the wind gathered her up and tore her away, up into the sky so that she was racing with the clouds and looking down on the gallant little ship, now as small as a toy, seeming to climb up a rolling hill of night-dark water to the crest and then to plunge down into a fearsome trough.

She held her breath until the ship rose again and then the wind carried her away and she watched helplessly as the ship sailed on. She knew it was sailing westwards and that it was carrying something precious. Something . . . someone . . . she had lost and might never see again.

The dream faded, and Josie sighed and turned in her sleep. In the morning she would remember only a sense of melancholy and loss.

Just a few feet away in the other bed, Flora was too agitated to sleep. She didn't know how she had got through the family meal earlier. Philip had chosen to eat with his mother, so their father, unable to talk about business matters, had wanted to talk to his daughters and his wife. Flora had been quite amused to see how pleased their stepmother was to be made the centre of attention as she answered questions about her dreary work with the widows and orphans.

Josie, as usual, tried to make Annie feel important, although Flora had no idea why her sister should feel she should bother like this. After all, Annie had never made much fuss of Josie. But, then, Josie was always kind and considerate. It really irritated Flora sometimes how her sister could never be relied on for a good gossip. She always worried in case they were being unkind when all Flora wanted was to have fun, even if it meant being spiteful.

And then after the meal was over their father had gone back to his office as usual and Josie had fussed about choosing a book for Annie to read. And that was strange. Flora could never remember their stepmother reading a book before – unless it had been a book of recipes or household hints to torture Mrs Dobson with.

While this was going on Flora had murmured something about being tired and wanting an early night and had fled to the room she still shared with Josie. She had undressed as quickly as possible, leaving her clothes where they fell. Then, taking something from her pocket and clutching it tightly in her hand, she went to bed. By the time Josie came up she had her eyes closed.

She felt like tut-tutting out loud when, through half-closed lids, she saw Josie begin to tidy the room, picking up Flora's discarded clothes and folding and hanging them, but she had suppressed her irritation and pretended to be asleep. She couldn't have borne it if her sister had asked her questions about her day. Flora was used to telling half-truths, but today's happening called for concealment if not outright lies.

So, with eyes tight shut she had lain awake for hours. She had listened as the bustle of trade on the quayside below gave way to the different sounds of the night: the shouts and the laughter of revellers visiting the various inns, and the occasional cries and grunts of men fighting.

Then, as the outside world grew quieter, she became aware of the sounds the house made as it settled for the night. The creaks and groans of the floorboards as the heat of the day faded and the timbers grew cold. The constant worrying of the wind at the windows. Footsteps on the stairs and in the corridors.

She hadn't heard Patience come to bed in the little room next to theirs, she thought, but their former nursemaid crept about like a sly cat these days. Flora had no idea why she was being so furtive.

Eventually she realized that her hand was hurting and she sat up and withdrew it from the bedclothes. The curtains were not quite closed, and pale moonlight fell across both beds. Josie's head lay peacefully on her pillow and her face was in shadow. Flora sat very still and listened. Josie's even breathing indicated that she was asleep.

Flora hunched forward and rested her hand on the eider-down. She let her fingers uncurl. She looked at the object that lay on her palm and caught her breath as the white stones that formed the flowers gleamed like real pearls rather than the cheap imitations that they were. So pretty. But hardly valuable.

Why on earth had she taken it? She couldn't imagine an occasion when she would be able to wear it without attracting some comment from Josie.

So, the lily of the valley brooch would have to stay with the other trinkets hidden under a silk scarf in an old hatbox stuffed in the bottom of the wardrobe. She should have put it in there along with her other worthless treasures before her sister had come to bed. If she did so now she might awaken Josie.

She turned and slipped the brooch under her pillow and then lay back, her heart thudding as she allowed the memory of what had happened today play out in her mind like a drama on the stage where she was the leading player.

She'd thought she was going to die of fright when she'd felt someone take hold of her. She'd been so sure that no one had seen what she'd done, that she'd got away safely, and she was still suffused with that feeling of excitement that she always got when she'd helped herself to something from right under a shopkeeper's nose.

She didn't like to think of it as stealing. After all, she didn't need the things she took. And most of them, even the neat little pair of kid gloves she'd taken from Fenwick's, were simply tossed into the old hatbox in the bottom of the wardrobe. No, it was like a game, a duel of wits, which she had to win. And she always had done until . . . until . . .

Unwillingly, for that moment had been so terrifying, Flora allowed herself to relive what had happened after she had felt her arms being seized in the market . . .

Terror flooded through her as she turned to face her captor. She stared at the jewelled tiepin and slowly raised her eyes, knowing who she would see: the man who had saved her from falling not long before.

'Well, well,' he said. 'We meet again.'

Flora almost fainted with relief. This was nothing to do with the brooch. She felt her limbs grow weak, and he must have realized what was happening because he gripped her arms again and his green eyes widened with concern.

'Did I frighten you?' he asked. 'I'm sorry. Perhaps you'd better sit down.'

'Sit down? Where?'

Flora frowned as she glanced around. More people had come into the market out of the rain, it seemed, and the stalls were busy. More than one person had scowled or cursed as they stepped aside and had to walk round the stationary pair.

'In the tearooms. I'll order a pot of tea and pastries too, if you wish?'

'Well . . . I'm not sure . . .'

The idea of tea and pastries was appealing but Flora knew that she really ought not to agree to partake of them with a man she had never been properly introduced to. What on earth would Josie say? Then just as suddenly it popped into her mind that her sister need never know.

'I can see you're going to agree,' the man said, and he let go of her arms but drew one of them through his own in one smooth movement. 'Come along, this way.'

'No, wait a moment. How did you know – I mean, what makes you think that I've decided to accept your offer?'

'Your face.'

'I beg your pardon?'

He smiled. 'It's easy to read. You'll have to learn to dissemble if you are going to continue doing what you do.'

'I beg your pardon?'

He was still smiling but his eyes had grown cold. Flora's feeling of relief vanished. A tremor of fear passed through her, but he neither answered her nor gave her time to question him further. He began to guide her through the market, back to the central hall and along towards one of the exits that led into Nun Street.

'We could go to the café in the gallery,' he said as he glanced up towards the mezzanine floor overhanging that end of the market, 'but it's rather exposed, don't you think?'

'Exposed?' She managed to keep her voice from trembling.

'Well, I know it's fun to gaze down on the passing scene but the drawback is that we would also be seen by anyone who cared to look upwards.'

'You're right. Perhaps I'd better refuse your kind invitation after all.'

'Oh, no! You don't escape that easily, miss.'

'Escape? I don't want to escape. I mean . . .'

He raised his eyebrows and Flora trailed off miserably. The truth was she did want to escape. She was out of her depth and thoroughly flustered, not to say scared. At first she had thought that he had seen her stealing the brooch, but he hadn't even mentioned it. Then he'd said something she didn't really understand about dissembling. He'd been smiling when he said it but there had been a hint of menace.

She'd been excited at the idea of taking tea with him. After all, he was handsome and, by the looks of him, most probably rich. And she was old enough to know the meaning of the way he looked at her. He admired her, he found her attractive, as she did him.

Fleetingly she wished that Josie were here to advise her. But that was nonsense. If her elder sister were here there'd be no question of taking tea with a gentleman whose name she didn't know. She'd be whisked off home without further ado.

'No, not the gallery,' he continued as if her wishes meant nothing at all. 'We'll go in here. It's nice enough.'

He took her arm and guided her firmly towards one of the shops that lined the central hall. A lace curtain covered the bottom half of the large window so that the customers would be able to look out but not be seen clearly.

Flora had never been inside a café in the market and she didn't know what to expect. She was pleasantly surprised to see clean white tablecloths rather than oilcloth, and quite respectable, even dainty, cups and saucers. Her companion guided her towards a table near the back of the room and, without even waiting for the waitress to hand him the menu, had ordered tea and cakes.

While they waited he said nothing, and Flora gazed round at their fellow customers. Most of them were women with shopping bags on the floor beside them or resting on an empty chair. They drank the tea gratefully while they gossiped, and the noise level was such that she was sure the poor waitresses must get headaches after only an hour or two of working here.

When the tea arrived she realized that she was expected to pour. She concentrated on her task but she was aware that he was watching her closely. When she handed him his cup the lift of her chin was almost defiant. He laughed.

'Very pretty,' he said.

'What do you mean?'

'You know very well what I mean. I find the sight of you, even while engaged in something so domestic, or perhaps especially when engaged in something so domestic, very attractive.'

Flora felt the heat rise and she knew that her face had grown pink but she could not help being pleased.

'My name's Vincent, by the way,' he said suddenly. 'And yours?'

'Flora. Flora Walton.'

'How do you do, Miss Walton?'

Vincent bowed his head in a half-mocking gentlemanly gesture. He had removed his hat and placed it on an empty chair. His hair was dark auburn and sleekly dressed. Even through the rising fug of the tearooms Flora could smell the lemony tang of his gentleman's lotion. She felt her level of excitement and anticipation rise, and Vincent didn't disappoint her.

As she sipped her tea and nibbled on a pastry she began to relax and indulge in a game of flirting. At least that's what she thought his banter to be. She had never been in such a situation before. To her surprise she found that she had very soon eaten three of the six pastries on the serving dish. Her companion had not even taken one.

'Oh,' she said, and her embarrassment was genuine. 'You'll think I'm greedy.'

'Not at all. You are young. Your appetite is healthy.'

'But surely you are not much older.'

'Perhaps not. But my taste is not for sweet food. I prefer savoury dishes. But now we've prattled enough. It's time to talk of more serious matters.'

The change in his attitude took her completely by surprise. She looked at him keenly to see if he could be joking but his smile had gone and his eyes were cold again. There was no time to ask him what he meant. In any case, she knew. He leaned towards her and laid his hand on the table, palm up. She

159

stared down at it wonderingly, noting the contrast between the smooth slightly tanned flesh and the white tablecloth.

Flora had had time to notice how lean and strong Vincent's hand was, how graceful the long fingers, before he had said very softly, 'Now, let me see the brooch.'

Wordlessly, she had taken the cheap little ornament from her pocket and laid it in his palm . . .

Ah! Flora gasped with pain. Without realizing she had slipped her hand under her pillow and grasped the brooch. The pin must have been open for it had pierced her skin. She withdrew her hand and stared at it in the shaft of moonlight. A pinpoint of blood appeared in the flesh below her thumb.

She stared as the pinpoint grew into a bead, a dark red jewel like the jewels in Vincent's tiepin. In the other bed Josie sighed and stirred. Quickly Flora turned away from her sister and raised her hand to her mouth. She sucked at the small wound. Her blood tasted bitter. She closed her eyes and tried to blank out all memories of the day. But they wouldn't go away. She knew she would not sleep that night.

Philip sat behind his uncle's desk in the office. He always used Samuel's imposing, leather-inlaid desk rather than his own while dealing with these special customers. His own desk was tucked away in the corner and to have sat there wouldn't have given the impression that he was in charge.

The chandlery was closed for the night, but one customer had been allowed to come through to the office and he stood warming his backside at the fire as he enjoyed a glass of spiced Jamaica rum. The man was tall and well built. His clothes were good quality, but there was a certain roughness about him and he had the weather-beaten complexion of a seafarer.

'By, that's good rum,' he said when he'd drained his glass.

'Only the best for my friends.' Philip spoke without looking up from the papers spread out in front of him. He held a pen in his right hand but with the other he indicated a tantalus on the desk to one side of a leather-bound ledger. 'Help yourself to more, if you like. It's unlocked.'

The man let his coat-tails drop and stepped forward from

the fire. 'That's a fine piece of work,' he said, meaning the tantalus. He lifted one of the decanters from the mahogany stand. 'Bohemian crystal?'

'Yes, it is. We supply the high-class department stores. Now hold your peace until I've totted up. I'm sure you don't want me to make any mistakes.'

But Philip's customer would not be quiet. 'Aye, very fine,' he said. 'You've got good taste, Philip. My wife always says that Philip Bertram knows where to find the finest little luxuries. Didn't I tell you that the last time I was here?'

Philip sighed and put down his pen. When he looked up his smile was dry. 'Of course you did, Captain. And I hadn't forgotten. Look over there, on the other desk. There's a tantalus just the same as this in that box, and it's for you. And because you've brought me regular trade I've already filled the decanters with the best whisky, brandy and rum.'

'No, really? That's grand. Now let me just fill my glass and I won't bother you again.'

The ship's master filled his glass to the brim and retreated to stand by the fire, leaving Philip to tot up the bill.

When he had done he sat back and told his guest what the figures added up to. And then, after a pause, another figure. 'Will that do?' he asked. They looked at each other and smiled before Philip added almost as an afterthought, 'Do you want to run your eyes over this?'

His guest shrugged. 'No, that's all right. You've always played fair with me.'

Philip hid his amusement at the captain's choice of words. It was ironic that he trusted Philip so completely, when they were both engaged in conniving to cheat the ship's owner, and Samuel Walton, of as much money as they could get away with.

Tonight's customer, along with other unscrupulous masters, felt no compunction about cutting the crew's rations to a minimum if they could find a friendly chandler who would then send the owner a bill for the full amount. The chandler and the master would share the profit they made between them. And Philip would have the extra benefit of being able to dispose, at a profit, of goods his uncle thought had already been sold.

Philip was not alone in rewarding such captains with little gifts for the regular trade they brought. And, of course, Samuel Walton had no idea that Philip was engaged in such nefarious activities. Samuel, as a former ship's master himself, had a fine working knowledge of what stock was needed and, because of this, his chandlery business, along with a thriving import and export business, had prospered.

But, almost from the start, he had been grateful to leave the book-keeping to his nephew. He had no idea that there were two sets of books in existence, and that it was not his uncle's welfare that Philip had in mind when he had started encouraging him to leave more and more of the late-night work to him.

When they had completed their business Philip led his visitor out through the shop. They paused in the hushed warmth and Philip fumbled at the lock, the only light being the moonbeams falling through the fanlight above the door. Then, with the door barely open, he turned to see the captain clutching his gift box to his body with one hand and holding out the other.

Philip responded reluctantly. Perhaps a faint stirring of conscience, or regret that he was deceiving his uncle who had been so good to his mother and himself, made him reluctant to shake hands on the night's business. But nevertheless his hand was seized in an iron grip.

'Just between thee and me, remember,' came the hoarse whisper.

And then the burly figure of the captain slipped through the door and vanished into the darkness. Philip was left in no doubt that even to dream of cheating or disappointing such a man would be to embark on troubled waters. And, clever though he might be, it frightened him.

He locked the door, slid the heavy bolts and turned to face into the shop. He stood quite still for a moment and waited until his heart had stopped racing and his breathing had returned to normal before he said softly, 'Are you there?'

'Yes,' someone whispered, and there was a rustle as a slender figure rose from behind one of the counters.

Patience had been lying there quietly on a bed of soft blankets.

'I'm sorry it took so long,' Philip said. 'But he brought a

162

good order. I've done a fine night's business.' He heard her smother a yawn. 'Are you tired?'

'Aye, but not too tired.' She began to laugh.

'Whisht!' he said as, in one smooth movement, he lifted himself on to the smooth counter top and then slipped off the other side.

He took the girl in his arms and silenced her laughter with kisses. He controlled a spasm of irritation. It wasn't because anyone could have heard her laughter – they would all be safely asleep on the top floors of the tall house – but when the girl laughed she sounded what his mother would have called 'common'.

Patience was a good-looking young woman. Of average height, she had a womanly body that was kept trim by hard work. She carried herself well and her features were refined enough to give her the appearance of a lady. Much more so than his uncle's wife, Annie, who, no matter how fine her apparel, still looked like the servant girl she had once been.

No, if Patience had the chance to wear fine clothes she would be a wife to be proud of – until she opened her mouth. Even though she had worked in Samuel Walton's house for years and had been trained in mannerly ways by her aunt, Mrs Dobson, as well as Philip's own mother, she still forgot herself at times and spoke like a hoyden. When she laughed she even sounded like the rough women who haunted the quayside saloons.

But Philip was honest enough to admit that that was part of the attraction she had for him. Patience was warm and earthy. When he pulled her into his arms he could forget the life of toil and duty imposed on him by his mother and his own ambition.

Oh, he knew his mother's hopes for him right enough. He knew very well that she was hoping that he would marry Josie. Well, if he had to, he would, even if he might have preferred Flora. However, it might not come to that. But whatever happened, he had no intention of giving up Patience.

She had stopped laughing and the sounds that escaped her now were soft groans of desire. Still clinging to each other they sank down on to the blankets, and there, behind the shop counter, enclosed in the almost overpowering aroma of tea and coffee and spices from faraway lands, they shed their clothes feverishly and came together with passion.

When it was over they lay for a while in each other's arms before creeping back through the house to their separate beds in the early hours of the morning.

It was long past midnight but the waterside taverns never seemed to close. Jacob made his way along the quayside, moving downriver towards the place where the Ouseburn emptied its black and sullen waters into the Tyne. Every now and then a door would open and a short explosion of noise would burst into the cold, damp air.

Some fellow would stumble out, often falling and lying for a moment staring up at the scudding clouds before rising and stumbling on. Sometimes the wretch would not get up and Jacob would pause and pull him into a more sheltered spot before continuing on his way.

One of the men he tried to help was old. Jacob looked down at his grizzled face and the tattered clothes on the painfully thin frame and realized that if he lay there for even an hour or two he might perish. He kneeled down. He intended to drag the fellow into the shelter of a doorway, but first he slipped something into his pocket. He had hardly withdrawn his hand when the old man came round with a start and began hollering in fright.

'Gerroff! Divven't morder us! I've got nowt!'

Jacob realized that he had been mistaken for a thief, one of the evil blackguards who preyed on drunks, taking what they could and then nudging the bodies of their victims into the river.

'It's all right, friend. Be calm,' he said. 'I'm not going to hurt you.'

He stood up and stepped back. The man scrambled to his feet and was just about to flee as if for his life when he stopped. He hunched down slightly, still ready for flight, but it was as if something about Jacob had caught his attention.

'Who the devil are you? Yer divven't look like a thief.'

'I'm not.'

'What were you about then?'

'I wanted to help you.'

'Whatever for?' The old man sounded incredulous.

'I thought if you lay there you might die.'

'Mordered, yer mean? Nah, they know me. They know I've never got more than a few coppers.'

'Men have been murdered for less. But, forgive me, you're not dressed warmly enough to survive too long a time lying in the gutter. I wanted to move you to a more sheltered spot, a doorway perhaps.'

'Aye, and I would believe you, for you look like a kind gentleman, but how do you explain the fact that your hand was in me pocket?'

Jacob smiled but didn't say anything. The old fellow, perhaps emboldened by Jacob's mild manner, suddenly took a step towards him and thrust out a gnarled hand.

'Give it back,' he said.

'Give what back?'

'Me money.'

'I haven't taken it. Go on, put your hand in your pocket. You'll find it's still there.'

'All of it?'

'Yes, all of it.'

'I stopped you in time, then. Frightened you off.'

The old man slipped his hand in his pocket and brought out the contents. He turned away from Jacob and moved into the circle of light cast by a gaslamp on the gable end of a building. Jacob saw him shake his head in puzzlement.

'Well,' Jacob said, 'all present and correct?'

'Aye.' The fellow slipped his small change back into his pocket and turned round to face Jacob. 'It's all there. And the funny thing is there's a sixpenny piece that wasn't there before.'

'It had probably slipped into a corner.'

'I'm not stupid. But don't expect me to thank you. Frightening a poor old man like that. And let me tell you something else,' he came nearer and looked Jacob up and down with narrowed eyes, 'yer dressed like a gentleman but you don't sound like one. At least not an English gentleman.'

'I'm from America.'

'Aye,' the old man sniffed, 'yer not from these parts. And

that explains why you'd be foolhardy enough to stray round here. Did you never think that you might hev ended up in the river yerself? Robbed of yer watch and yer purse and yer fine walking stick?'

'I can look after myself.'

'Divven't be so sure of yerself, mister. You've hardly got the build of a prizefighter, now, hev you?'

Jacob grinned. 'Brawn isn't everything. I knaa how ter mek the best of what I've got.'

He had slipped into the local way of talking and the old man's eyes widened before he laughed out loud. He shook his head.

'Well, I divven't know what ter mek of you,' he said. 'You're a strange one, and that's the truth. And if you'll tek my advice I would gan back to whichever fine hotel you're staying at. Now I'd best be off. Thanks to you I'll be able to find a bed for the night and mebbes a bowl of soup an' all.'

Jacob watched as the old fellow hobbled away, still chuckling to himself. He had thanked Jacob after all in his own way and he had offered advice. But Jacob wasn't going to take it. He lived at the mission, not in a hotel, but he did not want to return there yet. He wanted to explore a part of the city that he would not like to be seen in by day.

He had come this way before. He crossed the Ouseburn by the Glasshouse Bridge and paused by the Deadhouse. Inside, the bodies of the poor unfortunates who had been fished out of the river were laid out: sailors, drunks and suicides but also victims of violent crime.

In one of the streets behind the waterfront a new building had been erected, a small pottery, but beyond that the earth track led further uphill to a row of ruined and abandoned buildings.

Entering one of the dwellings, he climbed the stairs, his way lit by watery moonlight spilling down the stairwell from a gaping hole in the roof. At the top the door to one of the rooms hung askew on its hinges. The room was bare.

A scatter of splintered wood before the hearth told him that any furniture that had once graced this room had long since been used as fuel by a succession of temporary residents. They had even pulled up some of the floorboards.

Jacob stood in the middle of the room and turned round slowly, trying to imagine the room as it once had been, with a table and chairs, some pots and pans and one or two luxuries such as a funny little painted tin that had once held biscuits . . .

A movement in the corner startled him and his heart thudded as he swung round to face an imagined fate. Then, with a hiss, a black shape shot across the room, out of the door and no doubt down the stairs. A cat.

'I'm sorry, puss,' he said when his breathing had returned to normal. He drew a small packet from his pocket.

The last time he had been here he'd found the creature suckling her kittens in the corner on a bed of old papers. She'd been nervous so he'd retreated quickly. Tonight he'd brought some meat – the scraps from the kitchen at the mission – and a small bottle of milk and a saucer.

He walked over to the corner. The kittens had gone. 'Where have you hidden them?' he asked softly.

He thought he could hear a soft mewling under the floorboards but didn't investigate. Their mother would come back and when she did she would find the meat and a saucer of milk. He stooped to pour the milk into the saucer and arrange the meat on what looked like a torn page from some old book. Others were scattered on the floor. He hoped a rat wouldn't find the feast first.

And then, just before he rose to his feet he noticed something about one of the sheets of paper. He picked it up and walked over to the window. The glass had long since gone and the wind tugged at the paper, almost whisking it out of his hand, but he held on tightly and peered at it.

It looked like a page from a children's story book and it was the illustration that had caught his eye. It was a drawing of a little girl in a long fitted coat, button boots and a fur hat. A little princess. Jacob shook the page gently to rid it of cat hairs then folded it and put it in his inside pocket.

The room had nothing else to tell him. He wouldn't come here again.

Chapter Eight

June

'So Mrs Rodgerson will sleep here, in your room, Charlotte,' Samuel told her. 'I'll put up a screen to give you both some privacy.'

Charlotte gripped the arms of her chair. 'Privacy . . .' she whispered.

Samuel kneeled down beside her and took her hand. The woman he had brought stood back, her hands clasped in front of her, her head bowed respectfully.

'I know it will take some getting used to,' Samuel said, 'but I will be much happier if I know there is someone here with you during the night. If you should need – well, help with anything.'

'I know what you mean.'

Charlotte reflected bitterly on the indignities of needing someone to help her use the chamber pot. As if it wasn't enough that her arthritic limbs were growing more and more useless, now her bladder couldn't be relied upon to last the night. Thank God she wasn't incontinent. At least she could control herself until she reached the chamber pot. But that was the problem – much as she hated to admit it, she needed help to do so.

'I'm sorry, Charlotte.'

'Sorry?' Charlotte looked at her brother and saw understanding in his kind eyes. 'No, *I'm* sorry if I have given you the impression that I'm ungrateful. I don't want to be an awkward old woman.'

'You are a kind and loving sister. I will never forget how you comforted me when . . . when Effie died.'

'Did I comfort you, Samuel?' Charlotte's conscience tugged at her. She knew she had never been the kind of person to express emotion. To be effusive.

'Certainly you did, simply by being here. I was hardly grown when our parents died and you were just a young wife who took me into your home.'

'It was my duty.'

'But it seemed to me you did your duty gladly. That was why I was only too pleased to take you and your son into my home when you were widowed. And then when . . . when . . . Effie died you were here to make my home run smoothly and to care for my daughters. So now it pleases me that I can care for you.'

Charlotte took her brother's hand and motioned with her head towards the woman standing so silently beyond him. 'Whisht, Samuel,' she said softly, 'no need for this talk in front of strangers.'

'You're right. But some things have to be said. Now,' Samuel rose to his feet and seemed to pause and fight for breath a moment before continuing, 'we must discuss some practical arrangements, for Annie and I will be sailing for Norway within the week.'

A little later, when Samuel had gone, Charlotte asked her new companion to bring tea for both of them so that they could be more informal as they talked. Janet Rodgerson was in her early forties but she looked older than her years. She was tall and thin – there didn't seem to be an ounce of spare flesh on her – and yet she looked strong. Otherwise Samuel wouldn't have chosen her for this position, Charlotte supposed.

He had gone with Annie to the mission to meet the woman that Jacob Goodwright had recommended. Jacob had not been there. He had left word that he had had to visit a recently bereaved family who were taking it hard. But Samuel was welcome to interview Mrs Rodgerson in his absence.

They had learned that Janet Rodgerson had been recently widowed. Her husband, Douglas, had been lost at sea during a voyage to Valparaíso. Janet had a grown son but he was married and his wife did not wish to provide a home for her mother-in-law.

'Don't you mind?' Charlotte asked her now as they sipped their tea.

'Why should I mind?' Janet replied. 'There's hardly room in their little house. Not with the three bairns and her crippled sister.'

'But you're his mother.'

Janet Rodgerson shook her head. 'She's a good wife to him. She doesn't want to share him with his ma.'

'That's a strange thing to say,' Charlotte said.

'Is it? You've got a son, haven't you, Mrs Bertram?'

'Yes, Philip.'

'I seen him in the shop afore we came upstairs. He's a fine-looking lad. Well, he'll tek a wife one day, and you know what the saying is: "A daughter's a daughter for all your life, but a son's a son till he takes a wife." Well, it's true.'

Charlotte sat back in her chair and considered Philip. He had been a good son, always considerate to his mother. Surely that wouldn't change when he married. But suddenly she realized that would depend on who he married.

She knew without doubt that Patience had set her cap at Philip, but she mustn't be allowed to snare him. Not just because of Charlotte's hopes and plans for her son, but because a wife such as Patience would have no time for her husband's mother. Charlotte was sure of that.

'Let me take your cup, Mrs Bertram, before you spill yer tea. Here, I'll fill it up for you.'

Charlotte watched as Janet poured the tea. With her gaunt frame and her craggy features she looked what they called 'hard-bitten', and yet Charlotte sensed there was an underlying sense of humour and compassion in the woman.

'Now, I'll pull this little table up and put yer cup there. And before we say owt else I want to tell you how grateful I am to you and the captain fer giving me this job. Living in a house like this, with folk like you, is more than I could ever have hoped for.

'I married young and the only work I ever did outside the house was a bit charring. I never expected to be anyone's

170

companion, but I'm clean and I'm honest and I'll do everything I can to make your life easier, Mrs Bertram. There, I've said me piece.'

Janet Rodgerson sat back in her chair and drank her tea. Charlotte stared at her bemusedly. She had never supposed that Samuel would bring anyone unsuitable into the house so she had been a little surprised at the rough appearance of the woman. But now she saw that she was indeed clean, and Charlotte was ready to believe that she was as honest as she claimed to be. She decided that, although she had never met anyone quite like her, she was inclined to think that Samuel had found a gem. A rough diamond, as they said. Charlotte found herself smiling.

'Well, Janet,' she said eventually, 'I only hope you won't find the work too onerous.'

'Difficult, you mean?'

Charlotte nodded.

'I'm used to hard work.'

'I need quite a lot of help . . . personal help, I mean.'

'Divven't fret, Mrs Bertram, hinny.'

Charlotte winced at the rough endearment but decided not to say anything.

'Nay, you've nowt to worry about. I nursed me mother until she . . . I mean, I nursed me mother and she was a giant of a woman, not a nice slim lady like you. I'll manage fine.'

A nice slim lady . . . Well, Charlotte thought, that was a polite way of putting it. In reality she thought she was more like a skinny old bag of bones these days. But she did have fine clothes, she supposed. Samuel had been generous, and she must certainly look like a lady to this funny, plain-spoken woman whose own clothes showed signs of much washing and mending and making do.

It would be a pleasure to be generous, Charlotte thought. I'm sure Samuel will agree to my buying my companion some new clothes, some apparel more suitable for her place in this household. But how to do it? She'll need guidance and I certainly can't go shopping with her.

But, of course, I'll buy her clothes the same way I buy mine. I'll order them from the Army and Navy Stores' catalogue.

We'll have an amusing time choosing them together. Charlotte looked at her new companion, who was tidying their cups on to the tray prior to taking it down to the kitchen.

She had never met anyone quite like Janet Rodgerson, she thought. The woman had had a hard life and probably nothing more than an elementary education, and yet she was obviously intelligent and, although polite, not at all in awe of people who would be thought by the world to be her betters. Charlotte realized suddenly that, servant or not, this woman would lighten her days in more ways than one, and the thought lifted her spirits considerably.

Companion . . . Charlotte thought. Surely a companion is only a short step away from being a friend? I don't think I've ever had a friend, at least not since my school days. As a young wife and mother I had no time for the girls I used to know. Perhaps that was a mistake. And when I was widowed my brother took me in.

Now Janet had gone. She'd said quietly that it was time she introduced herself to Mrs Dobson, the cook. She had lifted Charlotte's feet gently on to the footstool and said, 'Put yer feet up, Mrs Bertram, pet, and hev a little shuteye. When I come back I'll sit quietly and start on that mending if yer like.'

Charlotte had nodded and smiled. But in spite of the fact that she had sensed that her own life was about to change for the better she felt a sense of melancholy stealing up on her. Samuel, her kindly thoughtful brother, did not look well. He'd probably been working too hard and it was just as well that he'd decided to take a holiday.

She hoped the voyage would bring the roses back to Annie's cheeks too. It was strange, she thought as her eyes grew heavy, and unjust somehow that so good a man as her brother had not been able to make either of his wives happy.

Charlotte had long suspected that Effie's affections had been given elsewhere. She had never been able to understand why the girl had married a man so much older and more settled in his ways than she was herself. And, as for Annie, she must have realized from the start that her husband would never love her. How could he when he had never stopped loving the beautiful, wild girl who, in dying so young, had broken his steadfast heart?

When Janet came back into the room Mrs Bertram's eyes were closed and she was snoring gently. Janet took some of the clothes waiting to be mended, and the workbasket, and moved a chair and a small table over to one of the windows. Her eyesight wasn't as good as it used to be and she needed every scrap of available light.

There were stockings to be darned, new drawstrings to be slotted in a couple of pairs of drawers and buttons to be replaced on bodices. Everything she needed was in the sewing box, including tapes, and spare buttons.

What an interesting household she had found herself in, Janet reflected. And for all kinds of reasons she could not believe that she had been so fortunate. When the ship had come home without Douglas on board she had sunk into the deepest pit of despair, made all the worse by the suspicion that her husband had not been washed overboard as his mate, Albert, had claimed, but had lain doggo in a lifeboat after the storm and then jumped ship in Valparaíso.

Douglas Rodgerson had been the best-looking lad in their class at school and Janet had started walking out with him when they were only twelve. Everyone had remarked what a bonny pair of bairns they'd been. Douglas had gone to sea as a cabin boy and he'd asked her to wait for him. They'd married young and, as they grew to adulthood, Douglas had grown even better-looking, with his sea-weathered skin, sun-bleached hair and far-seeing blue eyes, whereas Janet had never fulfilled her early promise.

She'd known she was plain. She'd heard the spiteful whispers of so-called friends, but Douglas had always assured her that he still loved the girl he'd married and that she'd always be beautiful to him. Huh! He certainly had a way of talking. And from the way he behaved when they were in bed together she'd always believed him.

Until the day she'd found the photograph. Douglas had been packing his sea chest. It was a fine day and he'd stood the chest on an upturned crate in the backyard while he put in everything he would need for the next voyage. Janet stood at the sink in the scullery, washing a few pots as he went in and out.

She watched as he put a blanket on the bottom and then his clothes, his hairbrush and comb, his shaving things, mending materials, a shoemaker's last and some tacks, his tools, a sharp knife and all the usual things he would need for a long voyage, including a bottle or two of Richardson's stomach pills. None of his shipmates would have dreamed of sailing without them. The standard of the meals produced in the galley was always unpredictable, especially if the voyage went on longer than expected.

Suddenly he looked up and saw her watching through the window and he smiled. He came into the house and told her that he was nearly finished but needed to pop along to the corner shop for some pipe tobacco. He wouldn't be able to survive the voyage without ample supplies of his favourite Rubicon Twist.

When he'd gone Janet wandered through to the only other room downstairs in the house, the kitchen-cum-living room. She hated it when Douglas was preparing to sail again. Long before he had finished packing his chest she sensed that he had already taken his leave of her and that in his mind he was already on the high seas. She knew he loved the life and so she would never reproach him for making her feel that he was glad to go.

She went over to the hearth, deciding to sit for a while and quiet her thoughts, but before she could sit down she noticed that Douglas's Bible was still on the mantelpiece. He never sailed without it. She took it down and went out to the yard. He had left the chest lid half on and she moved it aside so that she could put the Bible in. She saw that his writing paper and pens were on top of everything else. And on top of the sheets of lined paper there was a plain piece of creamy-coloured paper, which had been folded over to form a sort of packet.

Janet had no idea what it could be and neither did she have any conscience about picking it up and unfolding it. When she had opened it she saw that there was a piece of oval pasteboard, a photograph, glued to the middle, and the paper itself was decorated with a pretty printed border of flowers. But it was the photograph that made her chest constrict and her blood turn to ice.

When her mind had rejected every possible explanation except the one she dreaded, she folded the paper carefully and put it back in the chest. She had not mentioned finding the photograph to her husband. In those dreadful moments in the backyard she had known without question that she was willing to pretend that all was well so long as he always came home to her.

But he hadn't come home, and when Albert had come with the story of Douglas having been washed overboard in the storm she hadn't believed him. But she'd put on her mourning black and acted like a widow. And when hardship had struck and her son had made it clear that he couldn't help she had been forced to seek aid from the new mission.

It hadn't been long before the young American Jacob Goodwright had told her that he had found a live-in position for her. She'd not had to think long. Of course she'd take it. She knew damn fine that Douglas was never coming back but not because he'd been lost at sea.

If Douglas was dead she'd know it, she was sure of that. No, he was alive and well and no doubt shipping out of Valparaíso under a different name. And wherever his voyaging took him he'd make damn sure he never sailed into the Tyne again.

While Mrs Bertram dozed in her chair Janet sat quietly getting on with the mending. She had never been good at darning. Douglas had been much better than she was, and he had laughed at her clumsy efforts and told her how he'd had to learn from the start not only to darn his socks but also to sew on buttons and patch his breeches while he was away at sea.

But Janet was pleased that she had to concentrate. She didn't want anything to be too easy. For that might give her time to think and time to call up that picture to her mind's eye. The photograph of the bonny young woman with big dark eyes and a white flower in her long black hair. Janet would never forget the smile on the young woman's beautiful face as she gazed at the child sitting on her knee. A little lad with dark hair and dark skin like his mother but who, nevertheless, was the image of Douglas Rodgerson.

'It's very kind of you to help me choose the clothes for my holiday, Josie.'

'But I'm enjoying myself,' Josie said. And she meant it. However, she hoped her stepmother had not noticed her lack of total concentration.

'Well, then,' Annie said, 'which is it to be, the dark grey or the light grey?'

Josie brought her mind back from the worrying moment in the haberdashery department and gazed at the two linen costumes without much enthusiasm. They were well cut, comprising a skirt and a fitted jacket, which would undoubtedly flatter Annie's rather stocky frame, but they were unquestionably sensible, if not severe. 'Neither,' she said eventually.

'Oh, do you think I have enough clothes already? Perhaps you don't think I need any more?'

'No, it's not that,' Josie smiled as she contemplated the list of garments in the young saleswoman's hand – underwear and outerwear that had been deemed suitable for the journey and sent off to be packed carefully before being delivered to the house on the quayside. 'You will be away from home for some weeks,' she told her stepmother, 'and will not always be able to have things laundered. But I wouldn't advise either of these ensembles because I think they're too old for you.'

Annie's eyes widened in surprise and, with a rare flash of humour, she smiled and said, 'I'm no spring chicken, you know.'

'Neither are you an old woman – nor even properly middle-aged. And I think you should have the same style of costume – the cut is flattering – but in some lighter material.'

'I know just the thing,' the senior saleswoman said. 'If you care to follow me . . .'

They formed a small procession as they walked through the ladies' gowns department – the senior assistant, Annie, Josie and the very young junior assistant, who, in her severe but elegant shop uniform dress, looked like a little girl dressed up in her mother's clothes.

The floor was richly carpeted, tall marble columns soared up towards the ornate ceiling and, here and there, there were luxuriant waxy-leaved plants in large brass pots. A temple to the god of commerce, Josie thought. But she was not so hypocritical as to deny that she loved shopping as much as any other woman of her class.

'What do you think of these?' The senior assistant stopped before an alcove near a tall window where there was a display of glazed cotton two-piece costumes. 'Lovely and fresh-looking for the summer, don't you think?'

Interestingly she had addressed her questions to Josie rather than Annie.

'They're lovely,' Josie said. 'What do you think?' She turned to her stepmother. Annie looked impressed but doubtful, so Josie continued encouragingly, 'The pale blue striped cotton would suit you, especially as the darker trim matches the colour of your eyes.'

Annie flushed. 'You don't think it's too young . . . too girlish?'

'Not at all.' Josie and both sales assistants spoke in unison.

'And what about the lavender?' The senior assistant spoke to Josie again. 'I'm sure Mrs Walton would look charming in that.'

Josie turned to see that Annie was smiling with delight at the lavender skirt and jacket. 'Oh, it's lovely,' she said. 'Just look at the embroidery on the collar and the cuffs – the little flowers. Yes, I think the lavender. What do you think, Josie?'

'Definitely.'

Annie's smile vanished as quickly as it had arrived. She frowned. 'But, before you said the blue . . .'

'Brings out the colour of your eyes. And so it does. We'll take both ensembles,' she said to the assistant. 'You have them in Mrs Walton's size?'

'I do.'

'Then please add everything we have bought today to Captain Walton's account and have them delivered as soon as possible.'

'Will tomorrow do?'

'Thank you.'

Annie seemed only just to realize what was happening. 'But, Josie—' she began.

'No "buts", for now I deserve some refreshment, don't you think?'

'Yes, but – oh, I'm sorry. Of course you do. Trailing round like this and giving up your afternoon when you might have wanted to visit your school friends as Flora has done.'

'Not at all. I'd rather be here with you.'

'Really?'

'Yes, really.'

Annie flushed with pleasure, and Josie found herself moved by the unexpected moment of closeness. So she smiled and tried to conceal her unease, for her stepmother's words brought back the unpleasant thoughts that had been darting in and out of Josie's mind. Had it been Flora she had seen as they had walked through the haberdashery department? Her view had been obscured by the crowds of shoppers but Josie had glimpsed a young woman who looked like her sister.

At least in profile she looked like Flora, and the hat she was wearing looked like one of Flora's hats. But she was also wearing a hip-length cape over her coat that Josie had never seen before. The young woman had taken a silk scarf from a display at the far side of the hall and was holding it up as if to examine it for drawn threads.

What had happened next? Josie still couldn't be sure. A tall, well-dressed man had walked past, behind the person who looked like Flora. He had been looking straight ahead and it had taken no more than an instant for him to disappear amongst the other shoppers and yet, by the time he had gone, the young woman was walking in the opposite direction and there was no sign of the scarf.

The obvious explanation was that she had replaced the scarf on the counter, having decided not to buy it, and Josie would have thought no more about it if she had not seen the sales-woman behind the counter appearing to be puzzled as she looked at the other scarves still on display. All this had taken no more than a few seconds but the unease had lingered.

Over tea and pastries in the Palm Court rotunda Josie tried to forget the strange incident when she realized that her stepmother was still worrying about the amount of money they had spent. She told Annie her father would want his wife to look as attractive and as fashionable as possible during their forthcoming voyage and visit to Norway.

Which was nothing but the truth. Her father was a generous man who delighted in indulging his wife and his daughters. But Josie had her own reasons for wanting Annie to look attractive. Samuel Walton had no idea how handsome he still was and Josie wanted to make sure that his wife would not attract curious stares or whispers about her fashion sense.

It's strange, she thought, I am the child, not the parent, but I want to wave them off and be proud of them. And, of course, I want them to be happy. Suddenly she realized that Annie was looking solemn again.

'What is it?' she asked. 'Are you still apprehensive about the voyage?'

'No, it's not that. I have been thinking how kind you are to help me like this.'

Josie laughed gently. 'And that is a reason to make you look sad?'

'I don't deserve it.'

'Why do you say that?'

'I think perhaps I have neglected you over the years.'

'You haven't. You have been a good stepmother.'

'It's kind of you to say so but I know very well that I favoured Flora.'

'Well . . . maybe.' Josie was too honest to deny it. 'But she needed you more than I did.'

'Mm, that's true. But then, Josie, you were such a good little child. You never seemed to need anyone.'

'Oh, but I did. In a different way, perhaps. I think, small though I was, I enjoyed having a little sister to look after. But now please start thinking about all the marvellous sights you are going to see: the mountains and the fjords and the waterfalls tumbling over sheer cliffs, and the glaciers – the frozen rivers of ice. Aren't you excited at the prospect of your holiday?'

'Yes, I am. And I want to thank you for your help today. We've had fun, haven't we?'

They looked at each other and smiled.

'Yes, we have,' Josie said. And she realised that they had both been surprised to discover how much they had enjoyed each other's company.

'Go on, drink it, it's not poison.'

Flora picked up the glass and stared at the dull red liquid for a second longer before sipping it cautiously.

'Well?' Vincent asked. 'Do you like it?'

She didn't answer straight away but took another sip and savoured the full sweet taste before saying a little uncertainly, 'I think so.'

He laughed. 'You're such a child sometimes.'

Flora flushed. She nearly said that she *was* a child but stopped herself in time. I am fifteen, she thought, nearly of marriageable age. The thought made her blush, and Vincent raised his eyebrows but remained silent.

He drank from his own glass and then surprised her by apologizing. 'I'm sorry, I shouldn't tease. But, seriously, have you never had a drink of wine before?'

Flora was pleased to see that he was looking at her in what she considered to be a respectful manner. 'Yes,' she said. 'Sometimes my father will bring a bottle of Madeira or some such to the table but he has always added a little water to my glass. He says he will do that until I am sixteen.'

'Ah.'

Again Vincent fell silent and Flora sipped her wine but enjoyed it less. She reflected uncomfortably that not only was she here in a private sitting room of a hotel with a man her father had never met but she had accepted a drink of wine from him, and as for what had gone before . . .

She began to feel warm and, putting her glass down on the low table between them, she raised her hand to unfasten the ribbons of her cape.

At that moment the waiter arrived with the refreshment Vincent had ordered. Flora lowered her head. She pretended to concentrate on adjusting one of the buttons of her coat. She did not want the man to see her face.

'That's fine,' she heard Vincent say as a silver tray appeared in her line of vision and was lowered on to the table top. On the

180

tray there were plates containing sandwiches, wedges of game pie and slices of rich dark fruit cake.

Flora could not tell whether the waiter was still there or not so she kept her head down. She heard a sort of flapping sound and then saw a white napkin edging its way on to her knee.

'There you are, madam,' a strange voice said. 'And if you fiddle with that button any longer you will twist it right off.' The voice changed its timbre and now she recognized it as Vincent's. She looked up to find him hovering over her.

'Where? What?' she spluttered.

'It's all right, we are alone,' he said, his voice returning to normal. 'But in any case you needn't have worried. The waiters at this establishment are most discreet.'

His words made her feel more uncomfortable not less, with the idea that she had put herself in a situation that called for discretion.

'That . . . that's a lot of food,' she said.

'Yes, isn't it?' Vincent returned to his seat. 'But hard work always makes me hungry. Come along, you have done well today, exceptionally well. You would have thought you were born to it.' His smile was touched with mild astonishment. 'That's why I brought you here,' he continued. 'You deserve more than the usual tea and buns in the market café.'

Flora looked at the food spread out before her and found that she was hungry. But before starting to eat Vincent shed his topcoat, laying it carefully across a chaise longue near the wall and then placing his hat on top.

'Give me the cape,' he said, and laid it just as carefully near his coat.

She was glad to be rid of the burden, and at the prospect of the delightful food she relaxed sufficiently to undo the buttons of her coat to make herself more comfortable.

Flora hardly noticed when Vincent poured her a second glass of wine, but it was when he removed the carafe from the table and took it over to a cabinet that Flora looked around the room properly. She had been overawed by the novelty of the situation when they had first arrived. Now, replete with good food and wine, she was relaxed enough to analyse her surroundings. She noticed there was another door on the wall near the cabinet and wondered where it led. She thought she might have guessed.

'Do you live here in the hotel, Vincent?'

'Sometimes.'

'Sometimes? What does that mean?'

'I keep these rooms because it's convenient to have a place in town but I'm not always here, in Newcastle.'

'Then . . . where . . . ?'

Flora hesitated. She was aware that, in the few weeks she had known him, Vincent had revealed little about himself. There had not been much time for conversation – he had been too busy instructing her – but only now did she realize that whenever they had chatted over 'tea and buns', as he'd put it, he had drawn her out to offer information about herself.

She had told him about her sister, her stepmother and the cousin and aunt who lived with them, and even about her father's chandlery business. But he had confided very little in return – except that he had been sent away to boarding school.

What else did she know about him? She had guessed from his appearance when they first met that he was prosperous. Well, he was, but the cause of his prosperity was shocking. And, in any case, she had only been able to guess at it; he had not actually told her in so many words that he was a thief. He spoke well – that would be the result of the boarding school – and he seemed to have time on his hands.

Now he was frowning. Had she angered him by asking where he lived? A moment later, however, the frown cleared and he smiled.

'I don't suppose there's any harm in your knowing. We have a house in Yorkshire.'

'A country house?'

He laughed. 'I suppose you could call it that.'

'I mean a grand house?'

'No. Just somewhere quiet. Up on the moors.'

'And do your parents live there?'

Vincent's smile grew thin and Flora realized that he was losing patience with her questions. Nevertheless, he answered her. 'My mother and my grandmother live there.'

'And your father?'

'When his business allows.'

And with that she knew that he would say no more. But now she had so much more to wonder about. What could Vincent's father's business be? Was he a thief, like his son? Is that why they needed somewhere isolated? A bolt hole? Her imagination skittered about uneasily. She knew she was out of her depth but did not know how to extricate herself from this situation.

Her mind flew back to the day they had met, as it often did in her unquiet moments. The day that had changed her life, she thought dramatically. Vincent had seen her stealing the cheap little brooch and he had followed her and frightened the life out of her when he had seized her arm from behind.

But then he had given her a sense of false security when he had taken her for tea at the café in the Grainger Market. Only when she had relaxed and started to enjoy the strange experience of sitting taking tea with a man to whom she had not been properly introduced had he sprung his deadly surprise . . .

'Let me see the brooch,' he'd said, and wordlessly she had taken the cheap little ornament from her pocket and laid it on his palm.

She had thought she was going to faint, right there in the café, collapse on to the teacups and the milk jug and the sugar basin, and perhaps send them flying on to the floor.

She held her breath as he stared at the brooch and a slow smile spread across his handsome face. He shook his head. 'Pretty,' he said. 'But of course, you know it's worthless?' He'd looked up at her and his eyes had crinkled with amusement. 'I suggest you let out your breath slowly and then breathe in and out equally slowly until you regain your composure. And don't worry, I am not going to call for a policeman. Far from it.'

And he hadn't. Flora still could hardly believe the conversation that had followed. Vincent had suggested that they take a walk as he had a proposal to make to her and it was confidential. While Vincent had called for the waitress and paid the bill, leaving a generous tip, Flora had speculated wildly about what his 'proposal' might be.

Was he going to blackmail her into marrying him like some villain in a gothic novel? Common sense told her that sort of thing didn't happen in real life, but, in the event, it might have been better than what followed.

He had trained her to be an accomplished thief – was still training her – and she had agreed because blackmail was indeed involved. Although he had presented his plan to her as some kind of adventure – a bit of fun that would provide excitement in her dull life – he had left her in no doubt that, if she didn't agree, he would have called the police there and then and left her to face the consequences.

And if she did not agree to meet him next week at the same time in the café they had just left he would come to her home and tell her father the whole story. She had made one feeble protest that he did not know where she lived but he had laughed and told her that would prove no problem.

The worst of it was that she had found it fun. And each time she met Vincent she knew she was getting in deeper. She tried not to conjecture where it was all leading . . .

'What are you thinking about, Flora?' She looked up to see Vincent, in his shirtsleeves, standing over her, staring at her speculatively. She must have been deep in thought because she had not noticed he had taken off his jacket. 'Oh, nothing in particular.'

She tried not to look into his eyes but, instead, focused on the gold watch chain looped across his waistcoat.

'I can send you home in a cab right now,' he said, 'but I thought you might like to see what we have . . . acquired today.'

He didn't wait for an answer but picked up the tray, making sure that all the plates and the napkins were upon it, and carried it to the door that led to the hotel corridor. Vincent opened the door and placed the tray on the floor outside, then he closed the door and locked it. The sound of the key turning made Flora catch her breath but Vincent did not seem to have noticed.

Next he went to the chaise longue and picked up the cape that Flora had been wearing for their excursion around the department stores. It was dark blue, a fetching contrast to her light blue grosgrain coat, but it had not been chosen as a fashion accessory.

Deep pockets were skilfully set into the lining and it was into these pockets that Flora slipped the items that she stole.

Usually she would shed the cape in the tearooms and, when they left, Vincent would pick it up and casually depart with it over his arm. She had never before been present when he had emptied the pockets.

Sometimes, if the pockets were full, or if the object was too bulky, she would pass it to Vincent, who would be casually walking by, and then the stolen item would end up in an inner pocket of his topcoat.

These pockets he emptied now and laid everything on the table, along with the things he'd taken from the cape pockets. Flora stared at them in fascination.

A wristwatch with a jewelled bracelet, cufflinks and a matching tiepin in a fancy box, a set of gold and silver waistcoat buttons on a card, a pair of pearl drop earrings, a necklace set with semi-precious stones – all these lay on the table next to a silk scarf and a pair of dainty kid gloves.

'Very good,' Vincent said softly. 'They should fetch a good price.'

Flora's sense of wonder and excitement vanished at his words. Even though she had realized almost at the start that Vincent was a thief, to her it had been a game. She did not need any of the items she had stolen and she did not care what price they fetched. She had never cared to dwell on what happened next – or who Vincent sold them to.

'I think I should go now,' she said.

'Of course.' Vincent reached into a pocket in his waistcoat and took out a small drawstring purse of soft leather. 'Here you are.'

'What's that?'

Vincent held the purse towards her and jiggled it up and down. The coins inside it clinked.

'Let's call it your commission.'

'But I don't want anything.'

'Why not? You've earned it.'

'I . . . don't need it. I have an allowance.'

'Oh, I'm sure your father – the good Captain Walton – is most generous, but wouldn't you like to have something you have earned yourself?'

Flora gazed at the purse dangling in the air just in front of her eyes. She frowned, looked indecisive, and then she said, 'No. I don't want it, and I must go.'

'Very well.' Vincent seemed to give way graciously. He stood up and offered his hand to help her rise. This was simply a mannerly gesture; she was young and lithe, she needed no help. 'I'll escort you down,' he said. 'There's a cab waiting in the stable yard to take you home and I insist you will at least allow me to pay for that.'

A pity, Vincent thought as he watched her do up her coat buttons. She turned and walked over to a mirror on the wall. She lifted her arms gracefully towards the back of her head, pulled out her hat pin, adjusted her hat and then put the pin in more securely. That done she pulled the half veil down over her eyes. Such lovely blue eyes and such shining golden hair. Yes, a great pity that she was so young – and, as yet, so innocent.

He contemplated what it would be like if he persuaded her to stay; plied her with more wine, then led her through that other door into the bedroom. Would she be as willing a pupil in the arts of love as she had proved in the craft of larceny? He felt a stirring in his loins. Vincent sensed that she would indeed be an eager pupil but he acknowledged regretfully that, if anyone were to become her tutor, it should not be him.

She was too young, not yet sixteen. And, although that would not have been a problem in the sort of woman he had consorted with in the past, in a girl of Flora's upbringing it would be like making love to a child. He was surprised to find that he had these scruples but there was no denying them.

And, in any case, if Flora became his lover she might become too demanding. He sensed that as yet she had not realized how potent her attraction was. Once she did, the balance of power between them would shift. No, it was to his advantage to keep her sexually innocent, the better to corrupt her in other ways.

It was not as if he wasn't enjoying the game. There was no doubt that she was a skilful thief and that he was profiting from their partnership. But he didn't really need her. There were plenty of others – although none who looked quite so unlike a thief as Flora did. Her appearance was a great advantage.

No, he would go on with this game for as long as he could and he would try to bind her a little more securely. He had tried to implicate her more deeply by paying her and she had refused to take the purse. Well, when she got home she would discover the purse in her coat pocket. It had been so easy to slip it in without her noticing when he helped her to rise from her chair.

Would she return it to him next time they met or would she keep it? He really couldn't say. And that was part of the fun.

'What are you smiling at, Vincent?' Flora had turned from the mirror and was looking at him suspiciously.

'At you. I was thinking how pretty you are.'

'Oh.'

He could see that she was disconcerted, but before she had time to work out a proper response to his words he turned from her and crossed to the door. 'Come along,' he said. 'It's time you went home.'

When the cab turned into Dene Street Josie prepared herself for the steep descent to the quayside. She knew from experience that it would be a rough ride over the cobbles. Her stepmother looked apprehensive and clutched the edge of the seat. Goodness knows what she'll be like on board ship if there's a heavy swell, Josie thought.

Most of their purchases were to be delivered the next day but the one or two small parcels Annie had wanted to bring with her were stowed under the seat and they had already started to rattle to and fro.

Josie glanced up at the tall handsome buildings – expensive shops, business premises and shipping offices – but Annie stared straight ahead, not even able to make any attempt at conversation. Just past Dog Leap Stairs the cab veered round to pass under the soaring railway viaduct that carried the main lines north and south to Edinburgh and London.

People living in these buildings, Josie thought, must find it strange to have the trains thundering by over their heads or, in some cases, if they lived on the upper floors, to be able to look out of their windows straight into the carriages of the passing trains.

By the time they reached The Side they could glimpse the ever-present view of tall masts, and hear the puff and snort of the steam cranes and the rattle of carts and horses as the quay was cleared of the heaped-up mass of merchandise.

Josie's school friend Angela Cavendish had asked her more than once why her father continued to live on the quayside when most of the prosperous businessmen had moved their families up the steep bank sides, away from the river and out to the pleasant suburbs such as Jesmond and Gosforth. But Josie understood why her father didn't want to move. It wasn't that he desired to 'live above the shop'; it was simply that he couldn't keep away from the river and the sight of the ships that had once been part of his way of life. She often wondered if he had ever regretted coming ashore but she knew he would never tell her.

Josie sensed Annie's relief when they reached the bottom and began to make their way along the riverfront. As they approached her father's chandlery, Josie saw that another cab had just stopped there and a girl was alighting. It was Flora and she was wearing the same hat as the young woman Josie had seen earlier in the department store, the person she had thought for a moment might be her sister. But that person had been wearing a fashionable dark blue cape. Flora had no such garment and certainly wasn't wearing one now.

She supposed Flora must have a double and, as for the hat, the style certainly wasn't exclusive, so it was just a coincidence. The cab in front pulled away and, just as Josie was about to descend and help her stepmother with her parcels, a young man appeared from out of the crowd and stopped and, it seemed to Josie, stared at her.

He was slim and perhaps not much taller than she was, his hair was light brown and his eyes were hazel, almost green. She knew that because he made no attempt to drop his gaze when he saw that she was looking at him. She was disconcerted by the intimacy of the moment and she had only the vaguest impression of his clothes: sober but good cloth and well cut, she would have said if asked later.

She was aware that a stranger should not stare at her like this and yet for some reason she was not offended. At first he had looked as though he were startled. His eyes had widened and Josie was almost certain that he had gone pale. But he recovered quickly and began to smile. Josie found herself responding and, as she did so, something flickered in the corners of her mind, telling her that she had smiled at him like this before.

All this had taken only seconds since the cab had come to a stop, and she had almost remembered something that she knew to be important when her stepmother leaned across her and said, 'Jacob, how nice to see you.'

Jacob, Josie thought. That's the young American from the mission, isn't it? Her surmise was confirmed when he spoke. It seemed to Josie that he tore his eyes away from her reluctantly and, a moment later, he was smiling at her stepmother.

'Good day, Mrs Walton.' His voice was low and pleasant.

'Have you come to see us, Jacob?'

'I came to see Captain Walton. I wanted to ask him if Mrs Bertram is pleased with Mrs Rodgerson.'

'Oh, she is,' Annie assured him. 'We all are. Did my husband assure you of that?'

'Unfortunately, no. Captain Walton is at the warehouse.'

'Well, I'm sorry you missed him but I can assure you he would have told you that he is more than pleased. And I can tell you that Mrs Bertram has quite taken to her companion.'

Jacob Goodwright smiled, then the cabbie gave an impatient cough, prompting the American to say, 'But let me help you down, Miss Walton.' He offered his hand to Josie and she took it.

She felt the warmth and strength of his hand through the fine fabric of her lace gloves and the strangest surge of sensations took her by surprise. She stumbled as she stepped down from the cab and would have fallen if he had not been standing so close.

He put both his hands to her waist to save her from falling. She stood close to him, breathing quickly and knowing that her face had flamed. Their faces were level and she could feel his breath on her cheek.

'Thank you,' she whispered. She was incapable of speaking any louder for she sensed that her voice would betray her heightened sense of emotion.

'Not at all.'

Josie didn't know why it pleased her to hear the break in his voice. She moved away quickly and then watched as he helped

189

her stepmother collect her parcels from the floor of the cab. He assisted her to alight with them. Annie grew flustered when Jacob Goodwright insisted on paying the cabbie but he did so with such confidence and ease that it reminded Josie that he was said to be the son of an extremely wealthy man. And that was puzzling.

A ragged boy was standing looking up at the patient cab horse. The horse was steaming gently and the boy's face was filled with wonder. As the cab pulled away, the wheels racketing over the cobbles, the lad began to follow and was soon racing after the horse and cab, presumably just for the fun of it.

Suddenly Josie remembered another boy and another horse, a wooden one, and she felt an ache in her throat and tears pricking at the back of her eyes. She heard her name called and she blinked the tears away. Annie was waiting for her at the door.

'Are you coming in, Josie?'

'Oh . . . yes. Where's Mr Goodwright?'

'He's gone. He said goodbye to you. Didn't you hear him?'

'No.'

And the fact that she'd missed the moment he'd taken his leave made her inexplicably and profoundly sad.

Chapter Nine

July

'Do I have to come with you to Angela's party?' Flora asked.

The sisters were supposed to be packing their clothes but, so far, Flora had made no attempt to help.

Josie stared at the younger girl in surprise. 'I thought you'd be delighted.'

'Did you?' Flora snapped. 'I really don't know why.'

Josie was perplexed. Her school friend's party was going to be a grand event in the Cavendishes' country house. Those girls who hadn't received an invitation were disappointed. Favoured guests, including Josie, were staying for three or four days. Angela had included Flora in this list to please Josie, and Josie had been convinced that Flora would be thrilled. But here she was scowling out of the window as if going to the party was a tiresome duty rather than a treat.

'I don't understand you, Flora. This is a party in a lovely home. There will be dancing and picnics in the grounds and organized games and the chance to meet new people.'

Her sister didn't respond. Instead she went over to the window and glowered crossly out at the falling rain. It was merely a summer shower and the sun was still shining through the watery clouds. Josie went over to stand behind her sister and caught her breath when she saw the rainbow soaring over the tall masts of the sailing ships moored in the river.

'Look, Flora.' She took hold of her sister's shoulders from behind and squeezed them gently. She didn't understand why her sister was being so gloomy and she wanted to lighten her mood. 'Isn't that beautiful?'

'What?'

'For goodness' sake look out of the window – now look up.' Josie had to work hard to control a growing sense of irritation.

Her sister obliged and then sighed before she said, 'Oh, yes, the rainbow. Very pretty. I suppose you'd like to paint it.'

'Well, yes, I would, as a matter of fact, but I won't have time, will I? Not if I'm going to have to do the packing for both of us.'

Flora turned to look at her and her eyes widened with surprise. 'Are you cross with me, Josie?'

'To tell the truth, I am.' Josie let go of her sister's shoulders and went back to the task of packing.

'I'm sorry,' Flora said. She sounded contrite. 'I'm being a pig, I know. And I am grateful to Angela for inviting me to her party, it's just that – oh, I don't know!'

There was such a note of anguish in Flora's voice that Josie stopped what she was doing and turned to look at her. 'What on earth is the matter with you?'

'Matter?'

'You sound so miserable.'

'Do I?' Flora shrugged, and then went on quickly, 'No, I'm not miserable and there's nothing the matter – *really*.' She emphasized the last word as if in response to Josie's sceptical air. 'It's just – well, all the girls there will be your friends, not mine. They'll probably ignore me.'

'They wouldn't be so unkind. You will be made welcome, you know you will.'

Flora sighed. 'I know. And that makes it even worse.'

'What on earth do you mean?'

Suddenly Flora couldn't meet Josie's gaze. Her glance skittered sideways. She looked as though she knew she'd spoken hastily and had immediately regretted her words. But then she laughed self-consciously and said, 'I mean those girls will be making me welcome only because I'm your sister, not for myself.'

Flora bit her lip and looked away. Josie stared at her. Flora's words made sense in a way. Josie loved her younger sister but that did not mean she was blind to her faults – and one of those faults was a sense of her own importance. And yet Josie couldn't help feeling that Flora's statement didn't ring true. That she wasn't upset because she had been invited simply because she was Josie's sister, there was another reason but, for the life of her, Josie couldn't fathom what it was.

'You must be sick of sorting and packing clothes,' Flora suddenly said, and there was a forced brightness in her tone.

'Why so?'

'Well, I mean, you helped our stepmother and it seemed to take days. You would have thought they were going to the ends of the earth, not just Norway.'

Josie laughed. 'You're right. But I enjoyed it, really I did.'

'Rather you than me. To tell the truth I find our dear stepmother more than a little tiresome. I'm very pleased Father has taken her away for the summer.'

'That's cruel. Annie has always been kind and caring towards you.'

'Oh, I know.' Flora sighed. 'And I'm sorry. I just don't have such a sweet nature as you do. You are like our father: you think well of everyone and you always want to help people.'

'For goodness' sake don't talk like that. You make me sound so boring.'

'No, you're not boring. A little intimidating, perhaps.'

'Surely not!'

'Oh, yes. The younger girls at school are all in awe of you. They think you're clever, artistic, sweet-natured. A veritable saint! It's quite an ordeal being the head girl's younger sister, you know.'

'Then I'm sorry to have made your life so difficult.'

The sisters looked at each other and laughed, and Josie sensed that whatever was troubling Flora had been banished for the moment. But although her anxious look had vanished it was suddenly replaced by a more thoughtful expression.

'Josie . . .' she began, and then hesitated.

'What is it?'

'Do you . . . do you remember our mother at all? No, I don't suppose you do. I mean how old were you when she died? Two?'

'Mm. But I do remember . . . certain things.' Josie paused. 'She was . . . I don't know how to describe it . . .'

'Try.'

'She was restless. Always moving, never settling for long. I seem to remember Grandma Hannah scolding her as if she were a child.'

'But you were the child.'

'I know. And I'm sure our mother loved me. She was never unkind. Just . . . perhaps she wasn't ready to be a mother.'

'Can you remember what she looked like?'

'Oh, yes. She was beautiful. Very beautiful; with long fair hair and blue eyes. But come here.'

'Why?'

'Just do as I say. That's right.' Josie took her sister's arms and guided her towards the looking-glass set in the door of the wardrobe. 'Look at yourself.'

'All right. Well?'

'That's what our mother looked like. You are the image of her.'

But Josie wasn't seeing Flora. Her mind's eye had taken her back to a day when, as a small child, she had been sitting in the middle of her parents' bed, watching as her mother had combed her hair. The intense feeling of love this image brought with it somehow spilled out and enveloped the younger girl standing next to her. The girl who so heartbreakingly kept Effie Walton's memory alive in their father's heart.

'Have my nieces finished packing?' Charlotte asked.

Janet Rodgerson put down the newspaper she had been reading aloud to her employer. 'I don't know. Do you want me to go and find out?' she asked.

'I told Patience to help them but—'

'No doubt the lass is busy,' Janet interjected quickly.

She wanted to save Mrs Bertram embarrassment. Since Captain and Mrs Walton had left for their holiday the maid-servant had been taking liberties. She knew very well that Mrs Bertram was a prisoner in her room these days so she took very little notice of her. And Janet suspected there was another reason why Patience felt confident enough to do this. And that reason concerned young Mr Philip Bertram. She guessed his mother would not be at all pleased if she knew how close the pair of them seemed to be.

'Would you like me to go and lend a hand?'

'Yes, Janet, I would. I know what Flora is like and I suspect Josie has been left to see to everything.'

'Very well. Do you want this newspaper?'

'Yes, please, and I'd better have the magnifying glass.'

'Here you are then. And don't worry about your nieces. I'll see they get packed up for their little trip and I've already ordered a four-wheeler to take them to the Central Station in the morning, like you said.'

'Would you like to go with them to the station, Janet?'

'What me? Ride in a carriage?'

'You would be doing me a favour. You could help the girls with their luggage, call a porter and see them on to the train. They will be met at the other end, of course.'

'Well, if you think it's necessary . . . I mean, Miss Josie seems very capable to me, you know.'

'Capable or not, I'd like you to do it. I would have gone myself but . . . well, it's impossible, isn't it?'

'Divven't fret. I'll gan with them. It'll be quite a treat. Oh . . .'

'What is it?'

'Am I to pay off the carriage at the station?'

'Certainly not. You shall ride back.'

Janet flushed with pleasure and she left the room promising to take care of everything. When she knocked and entered the girls' bedroom she wasn't surprised to find Miss Flora sitting on her bed doing nothing at all while Miss Josie tried to bring order to the mass of clothes lying across the chairs and hanging from the door of the wardrobe.

'All this for less than one week!' she couldn't help saying.

'We're not taking all these to Angela's,' Josie said. 'The rest are to go with us to Moorburn.'

'Oh, yes, you're going to yer grandma's for the rest of the summer, ain't you?'

'Yes. So when we get back from Angela's I shall have to unpack one lot of clothes and then fill up the trunk again.'

'Heven't you got another trunk? If you hev I could hev this lot packed and ready for you.'

'I think my stepmother commandeered all our luggage for my father and herself.'

'Oh, yes.' Janet smiled. 'You'd hev thought they was setting off on a royal progress, the amount of stuff she had. And she was that excited. I divven't think she slept a wink the night afore they sailed. That morning her eyes were like pis— like dirty holes in the snow.'

'What were you going to say just then?' Flora asked.

Janet grinned. 'Something I shouldn't. Not in front of you young ladies. But now, this little problem with your clothes. Your pa sells cabin trunks in that shop of his, doesn't he?'

'Yes,' Josie said. 'All sizes.'

'Well, I'm sure he wouldn't begrudge his daughters a nice new trunk, would he?'

'No, I don't think so.'

'Right. I'll gan up and hev a word with your aunt. After all, she's in charge here while your da's away, isn't she?'

'Yes. That's kind of you, Janet.'

'Kind? Well, I suppose so. But to tell the truth I'm glad to find things to do – keep meself interested, like.'

And that was nothing but the truth, Janet thought as she hurried back to Mrs Bertram's room. Looking after Captain Walton's elderly sister was easy for a woman used to hard work like Janet was, and there were hours when the poor old thing was sleeping in which her companion had nothing to do but see to the mending.

She had started looking for other little jobs she could do: helping Mrs Walton now and then; cleaning silver, tidying shelves and cupboards, or sorting out clothes the family had finished with to send to the mission. In her quiet way she had begun to make herself indispensable and, while she was about it, she had learned quite a lot about the family she was working for.

Josie was a grand lass, good-natured and patient, but her own woman for all that. She just got on with anything that needed doing but there was an air about her that would stop anyone trying to take advantage. And she was the only one who could handle Flora, flighty miss that she was. Oh, the younger lass was beautiful – the apple of her father's eye – but there was something about her that made Janet uneasy.

Sometimes, when Miss Flora Walton came home, there was a closed look on her face as if she'd been up to something while she was out; something that she didn't want to talk about. Could she be meeting a lad? The sort of lad her father wouldn't approve of? That was usually the case with wilful young madams. Captain Walton and his wife were good people. Janet hoped Flora wasn't going to do anything that brought shame on them.

Luckily Mrs Bertram hadn't fallen asleep over the newspaper as she sometimes did, and she agreed readily that Philip should give her nieces a suitable trunk. The only person who objected was that sly puss Patience, who sighed and shrugged when Philip asked her to help Janet carry the trunk up to his cousins' bedroom.

Janet didn't say anything because it was not her place, but she wondered what the housemaid had been doing in Master Philip's office in the first place when her duties lay within the house.

Oh, she'd been sitting at one of the desks right enough, holding a pen and pretending that she was checking a stock list, but Janet didn't believe that's what she'd been doing. Not for one moment; not if you went by the lass's pink cheeks and the fact that the buttons on her blouse were done up all skewwhiff.

The lads in the shop had told Janet that Mr Bertram was in the office and then they'd looked at each other and grinned.

'Mind you knock!' Eric Hopkins had called as she went through the back shop. And the other one hadn't been able to control a burst of laughter.

Well, of course she'd knocked. She would have done so even if she hadn't been told but, as it was, she hadn't been a jot surprised when Philip had taken his time to answer and then told her to wait a moment because he was busy. Busy indeed! She could guess very well what had been keeping him occupied, and his ma wouldn't like it at all.

But at least he had agreed straight away that his cousins

should have the best trunk he could find. Anything to help, he'd said. He'd smiled and been that obliging, and Janet had formed the impression that in fact he was mighty pleased that Miss Josie and Miss Flora were going to be away from home for weeks on end. Just like their da and stepma. It would give him the run of the place, she supposed. And somehow that made her uneasy.

'Janet, you're a marvel,' Josie told her later when one trunk was packed and lists had been made for the contents of the other. 'I don't know how I'd have managed without you.'

'Get away with you. You'd hev managed fine,' Janet said gruffly. But she smiled and coloured a little.

'And if I label the trunk properly you can have it sent in advance to my grandmother's. I'll give you a letter so that you can charge the delivery to my father's account. Is that all right?'

'Of course it is. Now, as you and your sister will be off early in the morning why don't you come up and say goodbye to your aunt now?'

'Better still,' Josie said, 'Flora and I will take our evening meal in Aunt Charlotte's room with her and you, if that wouldn't be too much trouble for you to arrange.'

'No bother at all, pet. Mrs Bertram would like that. I'll see to it straight away.'

That was thoughtful of Miss Josie, Janet thought as she hurried down to the kitchen to consult with Mrs Dobson. She must know how lonely and frustrated the old woman was becoming. But, as for Miss Flora – Janet had heard the sigh and seen the way the lass had cast her eyes ceilingwards. Little madam. Well, at least she hadn't put her objections into words.

Then Janet frowned as she wondered why the younger sister had looked so out of sorts. All this packing and preparation was because the girls were going to a party, wasn't it? And a grand party in a country house with moneyed folk, at that. You would have thought the lass would be happy and excited. Janet shook her head in wonderment. A more miserable face she'd never seen on any lass. And that was a mystery.

'What's this?' Philip asked, and Patience suppressed a twinge of exasperation.

'It's the table set for your evening meal,' she replied.

'I can see that. But why is it set for two?'

'Because Josie and Flora are taking their meal with your mother.'

'Are they?' Philip looked surprised. 'And why is that?'

Patience sighed. 'That interfering busybody Janet Rodgerson said it was because Miss Josie thought it would be a nice thing to do before they go away.'

'Did she? Well, that was kind of her. No doubt my mother will miss the girls while they are away.' Patience pursed her lips and Philip smiled. 'You don't like Mrs Rodgerson, do you?'

'No I don't. She interferes.'

'She looks after my mother. That's why my uncle has employed her.'

'Of course.' Patience realized that she would have to tread carefully. She knew Philip was close to his mother and, so long as he thought Mrs Rodgerson was making life easier for her, he would not have her criticized. 'But, well, I'm not sure how to put this . . . I mean, she's devoted to your mother and that – well – that might be the problem.'

'How could that be a problem?'

'She might carry tales.'

'Ah.'

Patience saw that Philip had guessed what she meant and she lowered her voice, became more confidential. 'I mean, you have to admit she has cau— I mean, seen us together now and then.'

'Yes.'

'And you . . . I mean, you've told me that you don't want to tell your mother about us until you judge it to be the right time.'

'Did I say that?'

'You know you did!'

'But what is there to tell?'

Patience stared at him in exasperation. 'What is there . . . ?' she began and then she saw the look in his eyes. 'Stop teasing. You want us to be together, don't you?'

Philip nodded.

'And we'll be married one day, won't we?' When he didn't

answer immediately she hurried on, 'And you've told me more than once that we have to be careful. Well, that's why I'm wary of Mrs Rodgerson. Wherever I turn she seems to be watching me and I don't want her spoiling things for us by saying something out of turn, that's all.'

'You're right,' Philip said decisively, and Patience sighed with relief. But his next words set her nerves on edge again. 'We've been careless. We'll have to be more careful.'

Patience sighed. Philip could be determined, and she could see she would get no further with him in his present contrary mood.

'Shall I serve the meal now?' she asked.

'Yes, do. But you still haven't fully answered my question.'

'Question?' Patience frowned. What was he talking about now?

'Why is the table set for two?'

She smiled. 'Oh, it's for you and me. I thought that with your cousins taking their dinner with your mother we could have our meal together.'

'Here in the dining room?'

'Why not?'

'You don't take your meals in the dining room. What will Mrs Dobson say?'

'I told her she could go home early and that I would see to the meal.' Patience felt herself flushing. Philip had reminded her of the difference in their stations in life. He was a master and she a servant. She stared at him rebelliously and was infuriated to see his smile.

'And the girl? The little skivvy?' he asked.

'It's not her place to say anything.'

'But you've just told me at length that my mother's companion might be spying on us. What if Mrs Rodgerson came down and found us eating together? Or my cousins – what would they think?'

Patience knew there was no answer. Philip was right. She took the tray from the sideboard and began clearing the table.

'What are you doing?' he asked.

She tutted in exasperation. 'Clearing the table, can't you see?'

'Leave my place set.'

'But why? You can eat in the kitchen with me. You often eat your meals in the kitchen so that you can get back to work more quickly. No one will think it strange.'

'Well, tonight I will eat here. Alone. I will sit at the head of the table in my Uncle Samuel's place.'

'Very well,' Patience said.

'Don't sulk. We will observe the conventions. We will give no one any cause for gossip. Don't you agree that's for the best?'

Patience moved one set of cutlery to the head of the table and replaced the other set in the drawer, and pursing her lips in the effort to restrain an angry retort she flounced out of the room. But when she heard Philip's soft chuckle she couldn't stop herself from slamming the door behind her.

Very well, she felt like saying to Philip. Eat your meal alone, treat me like a servant instead of . . . and here her thoughts floundered. Instead of what? He had never acknowledged that they were sweethearts, not openly. Oh, he was full of soft promises and hints but Patience was beginning to grow weary of waiting. And frightened. Could she trust him? She knew very well what his mother's hopes for him were and a way would have to be found to thwart them.

When Patience stormed into the kitchen she scared the little skivvy half to death. The girl had had the temerity to sit herself in Mrs Dobson's ample chair by the fire and she'd fallen asleep.

'You!' Patience snapped. 'What's yer name, wake up!'

The girl scrambled to her feet and the kitten that had been curled up on her knee mewed in fright and fled across the kitchen to hide under the table. 'Violet, miss,' she said when she'd collected her wits.

'What?' Patience glared at her.

'Me name's Violet, miss.'

She rubbed at her eyes with the backs of her dirty hands, whether to brush the sleep away or to hide her tears, Patience didn't care. 'Wash your hands and comb your hair,' she ordered. 'I want you to take Master Philip's dinner up to him.'

'Me?' The girl's eyes widened and her jaw dropped in astonishment.

'Yes, you.'

'But I've never done that. I've never waited on table. I mean I might drop the dishes on the stairs.'

'God help you if you do. Now, go on, tidy yourself like I told you to.'

Violet did as she was bid while Patience donned a large pinafore and filled the various serving dishes with the meat and vegetables that Mrs Dobson had left in the warming oven. She became aware that the little skivvy was staring at the tray doubtfully.

'What is it?' she asked impatiently.

'Ee, I'm sorry, miss, but I don't think I'll be able to manage all that.'

'No, I don't suppose you will.' Patience sighed. 'Get that other tray from under the bench and we'll share the load between us. Hurry up or the dinner will get cold.'

'Are you coming up as well, then?' Violet asked.

'Only as far as the top of the stairs. You will carry your tray in and then come back for this one. Then we'll come down again and you can take the pudding up yourself. It's only a trifle and a jug of cream.'

Outside the dining room Patience watched impatiently as Violet knocked at the door with one of her bony elbows. The tray slanted sideways and the serving dishes skidded disastrously but the frightened child managed to right them just as Philip called for her to enter.

Patience heard the humour in his voice. She knew he would be expecting her to enter the room and she didn't usually knock if it was only Philip present. And then she heard the astonishment as he said, 'Oh, er . . .' He paused and seemed to be puzzling over something, then he gave up. 'Er, what are you doing here?'

'Violet, sir. Me name's Violet and here's yer dinner.'

'Here, let me take the tray,' she heard Philip say. And then, 'Is this all?'

Patience couldn't make out the girl's mumbled reply but a moment later Violet appeared on the landing and took the second tray from her and disappeared into the room again.

Now Patience leaned over slightly and peered through the

crack in the door. She leaped back when she saw that Philip was staring in her direction. He knows I'm here, she thought. That's why he's grinning like that.

'I'll be back in a jiff with yer pudding, Master Philip,' Violet said, but by the time she had left the room, Patience was halfway back to the kitchen, her emotions churning.

She shared out what food was left between her and Violet and sat down at the kitchen table. No matter how appetising the roast beef and how rich the gravy, she found she couldn't eat any of it. She looked up and saw Violet casting glances her way as she mopped up the last scrap from her own plate with a crust of bread.

'Here you are.' She pushed her plate across the table towards the child.

'What?'

'Don't say what. Say, I beg your pardon.'

'Sorry, Miss Patience. I beg your pardon? But what do you mean?'

'I mean I'm not hungry and you can have my dinner.'

'Really?'

'Yes, really. Now remember you'll have the dishes from Mrs Bertram's room to wash as well before you go to bed.'

'Yes, miss. Thank you, miss.' Violet started on the second plate of dinner.

Patience climbed the stairs to the tiny room – more like a cupboard, in truth – next to Josie and Flora's bedroom. She found herself treading carefully. She did not want Philip to hear her. Let him guess what she was doing. But she had decided she would not be seeing him again tonight.

Usually she would lie in her narrow bed and wait until she judged everyone to be sleeping before slipping down to the shop where Philip would be waiting. Often they would have a bite of supper together. A few little luxuries. She liked a glass of port-wine and Philip would drink brandy. He would open a box of her favourite rose and lemon Turkish delight. *Rahat lokum*, Philip told her it was called and that it had been invented in a city called Constantinople many centuries ago.

Patience loved the delicately scented, coloured squares of

confectionery covered in powdered sugar. Ignoring the little wooden fork lying under the first layer of greaseproof paper, she would pick each square up with her fingers to place it in her mouth. Then she would lick the sugar off her fingers before chewing the soft jelly. She loved the way it slid down her throat.

Philip had once told her that the name *rahat lokum* meant 'rest for the throat', and then he had taken her in his arms and stroked her neck with his fingers, pretending to be following the course of the jellied sweet as she swallowed it. When they had kissed their lips had been sticky with sugar, and ever since then Patience could not eat her favourite confection without thinking of Philip's lovemaking.

She had made her decision not to go to him but she couldn't help wondering if he would wait for her in his office after he had locked up the shop. If he did and if he said anything in the morning, if he asked her why she had stayed away, she would pretend that she had simply fallen asleep and not woken up until it was almost time to help Josie and Flora dress and set off for the country. She would not give him the satisfaction of knowing that her feelings had been hurt.

Nevertheless she could not help entertaining the forlorn hope that he would come for her. That sick of waiting and impatient for her embraces, he would tiptoe upstairs in the dead of night and, entering her room, put his finger to his lips before drawing her out of her bed and bidding her follow him down to their cosy place by the hearth in his office.

He had never done that and she knew in her heart that he never would. It was hours before she finally sank into a troubled sleep.

Flora sank into a troubled half-sleep. She had accepted she would have to go to Angela's birthday celebrations. Unless she feigned illness there didn't seem to be any way of getting out of it.

Could she pretend to be ill? She was good at acting. It would be easy enough to cough and splutter. But Josie or Aunt Charlotte would only insist on calling the doctor and she wasn't sure that she would be able to fool him. And, even if she could, and she was allowed to stay at home, Vincent would discover what she had done and he might call here.

She shuddered at the thought. Vincent would never believe that she was ill. He would know immediately that she was dissembling and he would be angry. Flora turned her head into her pillow to stifle a groan.

If only she hadn't told him about Angela's party!

At first she had been surprised and pleased that he had been so interested. He had smiled and asked her questions about the other guests. Drawn her out . . . laughed and joked about the wonderful time she would have. And then he had spoiled everything by telling her what she must do when she got there . . .

Chapter Ten

'Do you mean one of your ancestors had a whole village demolished just because it spoiled the view?'

Josie could hardly conceal her disapproval, and Angela laughed. The two friends were walking in the grounds of Cavendish Hall. The day was warm and the air smelled of meadow grass. As they strolled slowly through the parkland Angela had been telling Josie some of the history of the place.

'Well, the answer to your question is yes and no.'

'Yes and no?'

'Josie, please remove that head girl look from your face. We've left school now, you know. And please let's sit down for a moment. I can't keep up with you.'

'Where shall we sit?'

'There – in the little summerhouse by the lake.'

The 'little summerhouse' that her friend indicated had been built to look like an old temple from classical Greece or Rome, with graceful pillars and a cool marble floor. Inside, a stone bench was set along the back wall and Josie marvelled to see that there was a jug of lemonade and glasses set out on a small wrought-iron table. Angela removed the clean cloth that protected the contents from flies and midges, and poured them a glass each.

'Here you are.'

'Thank you.' They sat down. 'Now tell me about the village.'

'Ah, yes, it was like this. You've gathered that the Hall started out as something rather humble, no more than a bastle – that is, a fortified farmhouse – perhaps, but as the family prospered throughout the ages, they kept adding bits on.'

'I can see that.'

'And quite often a rich bride was needed in order to carry out the latest grand plan.'

'I see.'

'Well, one of these rich brides, sometime in the middle ages, I think, actually had royal blood and she'd been used to an exalted way of life. She simply couldn't stand looking out of her bedroom window at the huddle of ramshackle dwellings that formed the village.'

'So she had the whole lot knocked down!'

'There's no need to condemn her. She had a new village built – over the hill and out of sight, of course – but the dwellings were much more comfortable than the old ones, which had been allowed to decay.'

'Mm.' Josie found it hard to contemplate that one family could have so much power over fellow human beings.

Angela sipped her lemonade and added slyly, 'And, of course, the estate provides work for several villages, not just that one. Why, the house and grounds alone must give employment to at least a hundred souls.'

'That's positively feudal!'

'Not quite. They are all free men and women, aren't they?'

'I suppose so.'

'My mother was another rich bride, of course.'

Josie sensed a change in her friend. Her voice had lost its light-hearted tone. She glanced round to find Angela looking pensively across the lake. Some of her other guests were strolling by the shore. Josie could hear soft talk and laughter. The girls were dressed in pastel colours and one or two of them carried parasols. The young men were jacketless and some had rolled up their shirtsleeves. The scene before them was like a painting by Renoir, Josie thought; especially as there was a skiff drifting on the placid waters.

It was there, on the skiff, that Angela's gaze seemed to focus, but instead of seeing the two young men it contained it was as if she were looking at something that existed only in her mind's eye. And what she saw there troubled her. Was it something to do with her mother?

'And has she not been happy?' Josie hazarded.

'Who?' Angela asked distractedly.

'Your mother?'

Angela's frown cleared and she looked at Josie in surprise. 'What on earth are you talking about?'

'Well . . .' Josie felt awkward, 'you've just told me that your mother was another rich bride and—'

'That's right. Her father was happy to have his daughter marry a title, even such a modest one, and my father's father was more than happy to have a substantial portion of the Robson coal fortune flow into his ancient coffers.'

'But . . . ?'

'What do you mean by "but"?'

Josie sighed but decided to plough on. 'Immediately after telling me that your mother was another rich bride, you turned pensive on me, gazing out across the lake as though something was troubling you. So, forgive me if I'm wrong, I assumed—'

Angela smiled and interrupted her. 'Assumed? You mean you jumped to the conclusion that my poor mother was a bartered bride?'

'Oh, no!'

'Or at least unhappy with the arrangement?'

'Well, that's more like it. I suppose that is exactly what I assumed.'

'No, you're quite wrong. Both my parents were well pleased with the arrangement. My mother was enchanted with the idea of being Lady Cavendish, even though we are a very minor branch of a noble family, and would have married my father even if he hadn't been good-natured and handsome into the bargain. And my father found himself with a beautiful, spirited bride. I think it's safe to say that they fell in love with each other almost immediately and have remained in that blissful state ever since.'

The fact that her parents were happy did not seem to have eased Angela's air of melancholy. 'But there is a problem, for all that,' Josie said.

'I'm afraid so, my perceptive friend. The problem is that I am an only child.'

'Ah, I see. No son to inherit the title.'

'Mm. The title will go to a distant cousin who already has more titles than he needs and as many houses. I don't think my father minds that so much as the fact that his own descendants may no longer be able to live in this house – on this land.'

Angela's eyes flickered towards the lake again. The two young men had moored the skiff and were in the act of stepping on to a wooden landing jetty.

'Why? Does the house go to your cousin too?'

'No, the house will be mine, but I may not be able to afford to keep it. The family is in need of another rich bride. Or in this case, a rich husband.'

'Ah, I begin to see the problem.'

'Do you?' Angela turned to look at her friend. The two young men were walking up the gentle slope towards the summerhouse.

'Well, yes,' Josie said. 'You are worried that your father may find a husband for you whom you cannot love.'

To her surprise Angela laughed. 'Oh, Josie, if you could hear yourself. That was like a line from one of Mrs Braddon's romantic novels. It's nothing to do with love.'

'Isn't it? I should have thought that marriage was everything to do with love.'

'How innocent you are. How can I say this without sounding as if I'm trying to be superior . . . but people of my class often marry for practical reasons to do with property or lineage. The best they can hope for is respect.'

'But your parents—'

'Were lucky.'

'And you are worried that you might not be?'

'Yes, I suppose so, but I am also worried that the man my father has chosen might not know the rules.'

'Rules?'

'He may not even have guessed why he has been made welcome here. After all, he's an American. Perhaps they conduct things differently over there.'

Josie could not tell why she suddenly felt uneasy. 'So your father has already chosen a husband for you?'

The two figures approaching them up the gentle slope towards the summerhouse became lost for a moment as they left the bright sunlight and walked into the shadows cast by the massive branches of some ancient trees.

'A prospective husband, yes,' Angela said. 'My father is modern-minded: he would never force me into marriage with someone I objected to.'

'You mean, "with someone to whom I objected", or some such thing,' Josie said, slipping into their old schoolgirl game of correcting each other's grammar.

Angela's answer was a brief smile.

'And he is American?' Josie asked.

'I've told you, yes. And he is immensely wealthy. At least his father is.'

'And *do* you object to him?'

Angela looked away and paused before saying softly, 'That would be telling.'

'Oh!'

'What is it?' Angela must have been alerted by the shock in Josie's voice for she looked at her friend with real concern.

'Nothing,' Josie said. 'That is, I think these two young men are coming here to see you.'

Josie stared at the two men who had emerged from the dimness. One hand had risen involuntarily and she shaded her eyes as she looked at them. One was tall and well made; he had a large head and a mane of reddish brown curls. His rolled up shirtsleeves revealed brawny arms. His companion was smaller, slighter, but the way he walked gave an impression of controlled strength. Josie was glad that her face was obscured by her hand for she could see that he was looking directly at her and his gaze was intense.

The sounds and the sights of the summer day faded. Josie's whole being focused on the man walking towards her. And, as he drew nearer, she was taken completely unawares by a surge of excitement such as she had never experienced before. She realized that the hand shielding her eyes was trembling. And all this happened in the course of one heartbeat.

Angela turned and looked at the two men and gave a dry laugh. 'There's no need to be alarmed. It's only my cousin Forbes Robson and Jacob.'

'Jacob?' Josie whispered. Her mouth felt dry.

'Yes.' The men were now within earshot so Angela leaned towards Josie and murmured, 'Jacob Goodwright. My American.'

Vincent sat on the rim of an ornamental fountain and watched the activity with some amusement. He had walked from the railway station, still without any real idea of how he was going to get in. But once he reached the massive gateway of Cavendish Hall, he found there was no problem. The carriages bringing late guests were still arriving, as were numerous delivery carts. The gatekeeper was directing the carriages one way and the carts another round the semicircular drive as they entered the grounds.

It was easy to slip past the scene of activity and vanish into the shelter of a grove of trees. Then he walked away through the shade until he saw the glimmer of the lake. He took care not to go too near any of the guests who were walking in the grounds and laughed softly to himself when he came across a couple locked in an embrace in a small clearing. He moved away quietly, as unwilling to spoil their fun as to have them look too closely at him.

He saw two young women sitting in a summerhouse by the lake. Two young men had stopped to talk to them. He watched the scene for a moment and saw that one of the girls was Flora's sister, Josie. He had observed the sisters together on several occasions when they had gone shopping or to church, although Flora did not know this. The other girl was not Flora. Perhaps she was already waiting for him in the rose garden.

He wandered on until he reached the lawns and gardens in front of the house. Smartly dressed as he was, he could have been any of the guests who had been invited to Angela Cavendish's birthday celebrations. So far so good. But where was the famous rose garden?

He found it easily enough and there was the summerhouse, built to resemble a Chinese pavilion. You could hardly miss it, with the columns painted lacquer red and the dragons of sheet metal guarding the upper and lower columns of the roof. There had been an article about it in the *Newcastle Daily Journal* and Vincent thought the reporter had described it well.

Never having been to Cavendish Hall before, Vincent had had to choose somewhere that they would both be able to find without too much difficulty. Now he saw that it had been a good choice. In spite of its faux Chinese appearance the pavilion was a solid structure, and when he walked round to explore what lay behind he discovered an area where the gardeners kept their tools. It would be safe enough to meet there if they were careful and didn't take too long.

But Flora was nowhere to be seen. He glanced at his watch. He had told her what time to slip away from the house and she had disobeyed him. Or perhaps she was caught up with one of the groups strolling about the gardens and had not yet been able to make an excuse.

He waited for a while and, when it became apparent that she had disobeyed him, he made his way to the wide expanse of lawn behind the house. He stopped by the fountain with its carved sea nymphs and dolphins, and watched the activity and bustle taking place on the long terrace that ran along the back of the building. A procession of musicians carrying instruments and music stands was rounding the corner and heading along the terrace towards some huge glass doors, which had been opened wide.

Judging by the number of men and the amount of equipment, it looked as though a whole orchestra had been hired for the ball, which was to take place that evening. Vincent enjoyed the passing show for a while and then he took off his jacket, folded it neatly and laid it tidily and out of sight under one of the curved stone benches that were arranged in a circle at a short distance from the fountain.

He strolled towards the house and mounted the steps that led up to the terrace. It wasn't long before a short tubby man, sweating profusely as he carried some sort of musical instru- ment in a large case, a music stand and a bulging satchel no doubt full of sheet music, staggered slightly and looked as though he might fall over.

Vincent moved forward swiftly and steadied the man. 'Let me help,' he said, and took the music stand.

'Thank you,' the man said gratefully. 'Lazy man's journey – my own fault.'

'You look as though you could do with some refreshment,' Vincent said. He had already spotted the trestle table laid out just inside the doorway and the jugs of lemonade. As they went inside Vincent saw a couple of young maids offering drinks to the grateful musicians. 'Let's put these down safely – over there, I think – and then do collect a drink and sit down for a moment.'

'Thank you, I will.'

No doubt the man took Vincent for one of the house staff, or even one of the family, but he certainly did not suspect that he had no right to be there. And neither did any of the servants or genuine members of the household. If they had noticed him at all, they had seen him enter with one of the orchestra carrying a piece of equipment. It had been as easy as that.

Vincent waited a moment before going over to the table. He had no wish to get into conversation with the man who had innocently assisted his trespass. A round-faced maidservant poured him a glass of lemonade and, when she handed it to him, she appeared startled. Vincent experienced a moment of unease but, when he saw colour flooding her face and her shy smile, he realized that it had not been suspicion that had prompted the widening of her eyes.

No doubt she thinks me a handsome fellow, he thought. He knew he was good-looking and he knew the effect he had on women; at least those innocent enough not to be made wary by the way he dressed and his worldly-wise manner.

As he drank the cool refreshing drink he studied his surroundings. This room was obviously the ballroom. With a certain amount of chaos the orchestra was setting itself up on a raised stage at one end while servants arranged gilded chairs and small sofas around the walls. Two men wearing green aprons were arranging huge tubs of flowers at various intervals and another two used ladders to drape floral garlands from pillar to pillar.

The flowers were white and most of the foliage a dark glossy green. Very tasteful, Vincent thought, and suffered a pang of envy. He would like to live like this but, no matter how successful a thief he was, he knew it was unlikely that he would achieve such grandeur.

'Have you finished with your glass, sir?'

The round-faced maid hovered in front of him. She carried a tray and had been collecting empty glasses. Vincent saw that other servants were folding up the linen cloth and dismantling the trestle table. Others had started to give a final polish to the floor.

'Here you are,' he said, and he smiled at her.

He set his glass on the tray but she lingered. 'Are . . . are you part of the orchestra?' she asked.

He was surprised at her boldness and chagrined to realize that she obviously did not think of him as a gentleman guest, otherwise she would not have spoken to him.

'Certainly not,' he said coldly, and he saw colour suffuse her cheeks.

'I'm sorry, sir.' She bobbed a curtsy and the glasses on her tray rattled and threatened to slither off.

'Have a care,' he said, but not unkindly.

She righted the tray and was about to hurry away when he said, 'Wait a moment.'

She turned to face him but there was a truculent look on her face. 'Yes, sir?'

'I shouldn't be here, you know,' Vincent said, and he saw her eyes widen.

'Shouldn't you?'

'No, but I couldn't help myself.'

She frowned and gave every sign of being about to back away uneasily.

Vincent sighed and tried to look melancholy. 'I wonder if you would help me,' he said.

'Help you?'

'You see I haven't been invited but my—' he caught his breath and paused as if he had just stopped himself in time from saying something. 'A young lady friend of mine was. I mean, she is one of the guests, whereas I . . .' He allowed his voice to trail off miserably.

'Oh, I see, sir. But I don't know what I can do about it.' She looked uneasy. 'And I really think you ought to go now,' she added.

She looked over her shoulder in the direction of an officious older manservant who was directing the floor polishers. Vincent caught her arm and she almost dropped her tray again.

'You're right,' he said. 'I'll go immediately. But I wonder if you would do something for me? If I write a note to my – to my friend – would you deliver it?'

'No, I couldn't do that, sir. I don't know who she is.'

Vincent couldn't decide whether she was being stupid or deliberately provocative but he suppressed his irritation. 'Of course you don't. It's Miss Walton, Miss Flora Walton. An extremely beautiful young lady with blue eyes and hair like an angel's.'

Vincent pretended to be overcome suddenly with the memory of Flora's beauty but when he glanced at the maid-servant he saw she was completely unimpressed. But then she murmured, 'I think I know the lass you mean, but it still wouldn't be right. And in any case how am I supposed to find her if you can't?'

'Perhaps she's in her room?'

'Mebbes she is, mebbes she isn't, but I don't know which rooms they're in.'

'But there must be a list? You could find out, couldn't you?'

'Mebbes I could. But who's to say she'll be there? She could be anywhere.'

'You're right. But presumably all the young ladies will have to change in time for the ball tonight? She'll go to her room eventually.'

'Well, that's a bother, I must say.'

'I really would appreciate it.'

She looked as if she was just about to object again when she caught sight of the coin Vincent was holding up. In the silence that ensued Vincent deliberately took another coin out of his pocket and dropped both of them on the tray. They clinked against the glasses.

'Be quick,' she said, 'or someone will notice that I've been standing talking to you for too long.'

Vincent took a small notebook from his pocket, wrote a few words on one of the pages and tore it out. He folded it and dropped it on the tray near the coins. It wouldn't matter if curiosity overcame the girl: she would make nothing of what he'd written.

She hurried away and, as Vincent watched her go, he frowned. He'd read her wrong. He'd thought at first that her round young face and fresh complexion might denote a certain sentimentality, that she would be pleased to help a forlorn lover. He should have realized that her wholesome appearance was the result of her country upbringing. And country folk were no innocents. They were supremely practical. He would have saved time if he'd offered to pay her straight away. And now he resigned himself to waiting.

Flora was alone in the sweet little bedroom they'd given her. This was such a big house that most of the guests had rooms of their own. If Angela had ever had a sister she would never have had to share a bedroom with her like Flora and Josie did in their house on the quayside.

She had pretended that she was tired and needed to have a rest after the picnic luncheon and she had yawned so convincingly – behind her hand, of course – that she was sure Josie had believed her. Her sister had come up with her so she'd had to keep up the pretence and take off her outer clothes. Now Josie had gone and, wearing a light-weight silk robe over her petticoats, Flora was lying on top of the bedspread as far from sleep as it was possible to be.

Now and then she would get up and go over to the window and look at the other guests strolling in the gardens or sitting in happy chattering groups. She would have loved to be out there with them. Some of Angela's smart family had come from London and were full of delicious gossip about fashions and people who appeared in the society pages of the newspapers.

Flora knew she was prettier than any of the other girls and she knew she had caught the eye of more than one young man. Especially that of Forbes Robson, one of Angela's cousins on her mother's side, whose father was a coal baron. Forbes himself, although still in his twenties, owned a fleet of colliers, the ships that carried coal from the Tyne to the Thames, and, as well as being the heir to the family fortune, he was wealthy in his own right.

After catching sight of his distinctive figure heading towards the lake with a smaller, slighter man, Flora flounced back to bed and almost screamed in anguish. If only she hadn't helped herself (she had never thought of it as stealing) to the cheap little brooch in the market that day! If only Vincent hadn't seen her doing so! And, worst of all, if only she hadn't been weak enough to allow herself to be drawn into his daring games!

That's how he had presented his plans to her at first, as a daredevil enterprise to stretch her skill. But she wasn't stupid and she had soon come to realize that what she was doing was no game. It was stealing. And some of the objects she stole were very valuable. Vincent was a criminal and he had taught her to be a thief. He had even tried to share the rewards for their activities with her.

The first time she had found the little purse of coins he must have slipped into her pocket she had dropped it as if it would burn her flesh. She had agonized about what to do with it. She knew that Vincent wouldn't take it back. So each time he 'paid' her she had accepted the purse with ill grace but she had never spent the money. Neither had she kept it. There were plenty of beggars on the streets of Newcastle and many of them had benefited from her criminal activities. She had the grace to blush when some of the old and the ill called her their own 'angel'.

But why hadn't she put an end to it all by now? That very first day, in the Grainger Market, when she had tried half-heartedly to refuse to co-operate Vincent had said he would expose her as a thief. And he'd repeated that threat whenever he'd thought she was wavering. And when she'd found the courage to tell him that that would mean exposing his own activities as well, he had simply laughed at her.

There were ways to incriminate her without endangering himself, he'd said. And, in any case, he'd told her, he had friends who would help him disappear. He would simply vanish and stay away from Newcastle for as long as need be. It was *her* reputation that would be ruined and all her father's wealth might not be able to keep her out of prison. She had believed him.

So now, instead of being able to enjoy this treat, all she could think of was how to avoid doing what Vincent had told her to do tonight. She'd been supposed to meet him in the rose garden this afternoon. He'd said she wouldn't mistake the place because it was famous all over the county – if not the country. There was not another rose garden like it.

'What if there are other people there?' she'd asked.

'Bound to be,' he'd replied. 'Then you'll sit for a moment and discourage anyone from talking to you. I'll find a way to speak to you. Trust me.'

Trust him! What a strange choice of words, she'd thought. Could you ever trust a man like Vincent?

Restlessly Flora left the bed again and went to look out of the window. Then she gasped and took a step back as she saw the figure beside the fountain. He was bending down to take something from underneath one of the stone benches and Flora had caught a glimpse of red hair. But it wasn't the golden red of Forbes Robson's hair. It was the dark, fox-like colour of Vincent's. So he was here as he had promised. Well, of course he would be. And no doubt he'd been looking for her.

Would he believe her if she told him she was ill? Too ill even to attend the ball tonight? Oh, but how annoying if she had to miss the fun! She walked back to the bed, still anxiously worrying over what she was going to do, and then there was a knock at the door. She gasped with fright, but realized immediately that it could not possibly be Vincent so she called, 'Enter.'

A maidservant appeared with a tray bearing a jug of lemonade and a glass. 'Miss Walton, is it? Miss Flora Walton?'

'Yes.' Flora was bemused at first but quickly realized that Josie must have sent this girl with the lemonade for her. That was kind. 'Please just put the tray on the little table – that's right – by the bed.'

'Yes, miss.'

Flora sat down on the bed and stared moodily at nothing in particular.

'Shall I pour it for you?'

She looked up in surprise to see the girl still standing by the table.

'No thank you. To tell the truth it was kind of my sister but I don't feel like a drink right now.'

'Your sister?' The girl looked puzzled.

'Mm. Josie sent the lemonade, didn't she?'

'No, miss, she didn't. It was my idea. And I wish you would just come and look at this tray for a moment, then I can go.'

Flora was so surprised by the maidservant's words and her attitude that she did as she was bid. She stared down at the tray and saw that as well as the jug of lemonade and a glass there was a folded slip of paper. 'Why, what's that?' she asked.

'What?'

'That note.'

'I don't see no note and if there is one I have no idea how it got there. Right?'

'Oh . . .'

Flora was at a loss. But now the strange girl was smiling. In fact Flora could have sworn she winked before she turned swiftly and left the room.

Suddenly she snatched up the piece of paper and held it tightly against her breast. Forbes had sent her a note! A billet-doux! That's what they were called in the sensational novels, weren't they? He had sent a romantic request for her to dance only with him, or at least to meet him on the terrace or some such thing. He had bribed the maidservant to bring the note to her and the impertinent creature had probably read it – that's why she had acted so strangely.

With her head full of music and moonlight Flora opened the note and read it. Her hopes vanished immediately and all the torment returned. There were very few words:

I'm waiting.
V

Flora crumpled up the note and howled with rage as she flung it across the room.

'So you are a school friend of Angela's?'

Forbes Robson had invited Josie to walk by the lake shore. He was large and good-natured, and his clumsy attempt to leave Angela and Jacob alone had caused his cousin to blush.

'No, don't go,' Angela had protested politely, but Josie had almost leaped up and taken the arm Forbes had proffered, grateful to him for giving her a means of escape.

'Yes,' she replied to Forbes's question as they strolled by the gently lapping water's edge. A froth of fallen blossom drifted on the undulating water. How different this was from the flotsam riding the tides of the river that flowed past her home on the quayside. Josie lifted her face towards the sun and, breathing in the sweet country air, she tried to get over the shock of finding that Jacob Goodwright was a guest here – and perhaps more than a guest. 'But school days are over now,' she forced herself to add in as normal a voice as possible.

But perhaps Forbes had caught the catch in her voice for he asked, 'Does that make you sad?'

'A little.' She risked a smile although she knew her lips might tremble.

Forbes, obviously mistaking the cause of her discomposure, smiled sympathetically. 'And have you any plans?' he asked.

'Plans?'

'Angela told me that you were the head girl and that you are amazingly intelligent. I don't suppose you want to sit at home and wait about until you marry, do you?'

'Like Angela, you mean?'

To her consternation Josie realized how waspish that had sounded and she glanced at Forbes apprehensively. He looked surprised.

'Well, it's true that Angela has no intention, nor any need, of a career, but that's not unusual in her circumstances, is it?'

'I suppose not.'

'You know, Miss Walton, I was trying to pay you a compliment and, somehow, you have taken it the wrong way. I'm not sure why, but shall we start again?'

She glanced up to find him looking so concerned that she was filled with guilt. 'I'm sorry,' she said. 'Perhaps it was because I had no idea until today that Angela had . . . I mean . . . I don't know how to put this . . . a suitor.'

'Ah, I think I see. You are a little jealous, perhaps?'

'Good heavens, no! Why should I be jealous?'

'Oh dear. I've been clumsy again. It's just that I know how close you and Angela have been and I thought you might be worried that the nature of your friendship will change when she marries. That you will not see so much of each other.'

'Oh.'

Josie couldn't have explained to herself why she had reacted so sharply, but she sensed it was nothing to do with being jealous because someone else was important to Angela. Somehow it was tied up with the shock she had felt when she realized the rich American Angela might be going to marry was Jacob Goodwright.

'My cousin tells me that you are a gifted artist.'

Forbes was valiantly trying to change the subject and Josie made an effort to smile. 'That's kind of her,' she said. 'I like to draw and paint but I don't know about "gifted".'

'So I wondered if you might be going to drawing classes or something like that. That's all I meant when I asked if you had any plans.'

'I'm sorry.'

'No, don't apologize. No doubt I was clumsy.'

'Not at all. And, as a matter of fact I would like to study further,' Josie said. 'I thought perhaps I might apply to the School of Science and Art.'

'The Art I understand, but why the Science?' Forbes asked.

'Because I'm interested in the practical side of life too. I like to know how things work – even objects of great beauty.' Josie smiled to see Forbes's surprised expression.

'And your father would agree?'

Josie imagined that, in Forbes's world, young ladies would be encouraged to study drawing, painting and music but nothing more practical. They certainly wouldn't consider entering a technical college.

'My father approves of women being educated. Don't you?'

Josie had not been able to resist the question and she was amused to see the difficulty it caused Angela's good-hearted cousin.

'Well, of course I do. I mean, a man wouldn't want a wife

221

who was totally ignorant, would he? Got to be able to read and write and do her sums – and carry on a decent conversation, of course.'

'But no more than that?'

'I don't follow you.'

'For example, what about women who become teachers?'

'Oh, of course. But they don't marry, do they? Not allowed to, as far as I understand.'

'Doctors? Women are allowed to register as doctors now, you know.'

'Miss Walton, are you trying to pick a quarrel with me? If so I should tell you that I really wouldn't mind if either of my sisters was to become a doctor or a teacher or, God help her, a lawyer, if that's what she really wanted, but when a man marries it's natural for him to want his wife to stay at home and bring up the children, isn't it?'

Josie relented. 'I know. Of course, you're right. It's just I wonder sometimes if that really is the way it has to be.'

Forbes was silent, and after a while Josie stole a glance at him. He looked thoughtful and then he asked almost hesitantly, 'And does your sister feel this way? About further education, I mean?'

Josie smiled. 'Oh, no. In fact, my father is fighting a losing battle in trying to persuade her to go back to school, at least until she is sixteen.'

'And when will that be?'

'In January.'

'Ah.'

Forbes stopped walking and looked out across the lake. Josie studied his face in profile. He was good-looking, she supposed, almost handsome, and he had the sort of powerful frame that often looked clumsy in formal clothes. But this was not the case with Forbes. He carried his fashionable attire well and his manner was that of a gentleman. But why shouldn't it be? There had now been several generations since the Robsons had been humble pitmen.

Of course, Josie had seen how taken he was with Flora. He had joined their group for the picnic lunch earlier and he had seemed to hang on the younger girl's every word. Josie was used to Flora being the centre of attention wherever they went. She was so beautiful and, today, dressed in the palest blue muslin, she had looked almost like a fairy child. But Forbes had not seen Flora as a child. Josie realized that now.

And what of Flora? Josie was sure that she had noticed Forbes's admiring glances and she had responded to his efforts to amuse her with his gossip of London society. So Josie had been all the more puzzled when her sister had decided to go to her room and rest. She had seemed genuinely tired but could she have been flirting? Perhaps hoping to make Forbes all the keener by withdrawing for a while? Was her little sister capable of playing such grown-up games?

Next year Flora would be of marriageable age. Josie wondered what Angela's cousin was thinking now as he gazed so steadily across the lake. Suddenly he seemed to gather himself together and he turned his head and smiled at her before he bent down to pick up a smooth flat stone. He examined it carefully, then sent it skimming across the water.

Josie watched it bounce several times on the surface, gradually slowing down and then sinking near the centre of the lake.

'How did you do that?' she gasped.

'Have you never seen that trick before?'

'No. Show me how you did it.'

Forbes took his time gazing at the assorted stones on the shore; when he straightened up he had two in his hand. 'Here, this one's for you,' he said. 'Now watch.'

Josie watched as, in a half crouching position, Forbes swung his arm back and then forward. He seemed to flick his wrist as he released the stone.

'Count them,' he shouted, and grinned like a schoolboy.

'One, two, three, four, five, six, seven, eight!' they called in unison before the stone finally sank.

'Now it's your turn,' Forbes said.

Josie had observed him keenly and now she tried to imitate his actions, half stooping before swinging her arm back. This was made a little difficult by the restriction of her corset. How she wished she had left it off on this warm day as Flora had done.

'Keep it flat to the water,' Forbes said just before she released it, and then he watched in disbelief as the stone bounced five times. 'Very good!' he said, his eyes widening. 'For a woman, that is.'

Josie saw the teasing look on his face and laughed. 'How about a challenge?' she asked.

'No, I think it's probably time we returned to the house,' he said. 'I believe light refreshments will be served before we retire to our quarters to get ready for the ball.'

Other guests were making their way back to the house through the grounds and gardens. Josie had a sneaking feeling that Forbes, for all his good nature, had not wanted to continue the game in case he was bettered by a mere woman, but she liked him, for all that. He seemed cheerful as he started to hum one of the fashionable waltz tunes of the moment and Josie wondered if he was looking forward to dancing with Flora.

Immediately that thought came into her head she saw a picture of waltzing couples in the ballroom. Forbes with Flora, Angela with Jacob, but who would she, Josie, be dancing with?

Angela and Jacob . . . Josie let the image of them linger in her mind's eye and she discovered that it pained her. 'My American', her friend had said. Suddenly Josie was engulfed by a powerful emotion. She had been fighting against it all the time she had been by the lakeside with Forbes but she had not known what it was. Now she knew. She *was* jealous, as Forbes had surmised. But the cause of her jealousy was not quite what he supposed. Incredible as it might seem, she was in love with Jacob Goodwright.

'What do you want?'

Flora's face was flushed and her eyes slightly wild. Vincent tried to take her hand but she snatched it away.

'To talk to you.'

'What about?'

Vincent paused before answering. She knew very well what they had to talk about. But Flora was obviously in a strange mood and he would have to humour her. 'Walk with me and I'll tell you,' he said pleasantly, hoping she would not catch the edge of irritation.

'Walk?'

'Yes. If we stand here in the centre of the rose garden we will attract attention. Especially if you are going to shout at me like that.'

'I wasn't shouting.'

Vincent suppressed his growing anger. She would be no good to him in this unsettled mood and he didn't want to make her worse. 'Very well,' he said, 'but you must admit that anyone looking out of the upper windows of the Hall could see us here.'

That seemed to frighten her and she glanced over her shoulder towards the house. The afternoon sun glinted on the windows, making it impossible to see if there was anyone standing looking out. Taking advantage of her obvious nervousness he leaned towards her and said softly, 'If you go back to the house I shall follow you. Do you want to have to explain to your sister who I am and, more importantly, how we met?'

Flora's eyes widened and he heard her indrawn breath. 'Where shall we walk?' was all she said.

'That way,' he said. 'Towards the Chinese pavilion.'

He'd watched as the gardens had gradually emptied and guessed that some sort of meal was being served in the house so perhaps by delaying things Flora had been wise without intending to be, for he could not help thinking that she would not have come at all if he had not sent the note.

Sure enough, as soon as they had left the formal beauty of the rose garden for the workaday tidiness of the working area, she turned towards him and said, 'Do I really have to do this?'

'You know you must.'

'*Must?*'

A bonfire smouldered on a patch of stony ground, giving off the smell of wood smoke and early leaves. The fire was almost out but Vincent could see the remains of small branches forming ash skeletons that would collapse any minute into the embers. Smoke drifted across towards them. Was that what was causing Flora's eyes to fill with water? She saw his glance and brushed her face with the back of a hand.

'Yes, Flora,' he said patiently, 'you must.'

'Oh, please—' she began, but Vincent did not allow her to

go on. Tonight was too important and he could not have her in such a state that she would not be able to concentrate.

'Listen to me,' he said. 'What if I say this is the last time?'

'What?' Flora's eyes widened and one hand flew to the base of her throat. Her fingers were trembling.

'Do this for me tonight and I won't ever ask you to – to do anything like this again.'

'To steal things, you mean!'

Vincent shrugged.

Flora looked at him for a long while before she asked, 'Do you mean it?'

'Yes.'

'I will be free of you?'

'If you want to put it that way.'

'What other way is there to put it? I tried to tell you many times that I didn't want to go on. It wasn't – it wasn't fun any more!'

'Poor Flora. Did you think it was a game?'

'You encouraged me to think so. But I soon realized that it was – it was criminal. I had become a thief. And when I wanted to stop you resorted to blackmail.'

'That's putting it a bit strong.'

'But it's true!'

'Well, now I'm telling you that you are free – after tonight, that is.'

'Why should I believe you? Why should I trust you?'

'Because the jewels you will st— will take tonight will be so valuable that I shall be able to go away. In fact I will have to.'

'Where will you go?'

'There's no need for you to know that. But I can at least tell you that I will be leaving England.'

'Really?' Flora's eyes filled with hope.

'Really. Help me tonight and it will be as if you'd never met me, I promise you.'

Vincent watched the emotions that played across her face. 'No one will be hurt by this, you know. The insurance company will pay up. No one loses.'

'Are you sure?'

Vincent lowered his gaze. This was not the moment to fluster her. But he heard a soft sigh and he sensed the moment that she was tipped, unhappily, into making her decision.

'Very well.'

'You know what to do? You'll follow our plan?'

'As well as I can. But afterwards? Have you decided where I am to meet you? And how shall I get out of the house?'

'As for getting out of the house I've made sure that one of the doors that leads from the ballroom on to the terrace will not lock properly. The door at the end near the orchestra platform. And as to where, right here.'

'You'll wait here all night? What if it rains?'

Vincent laughed. 'It will be easy enough to break into that tool shed under the trees. In fact, I don't even believe it's locked.' He strode over to the shed and, sure enough, the door opened easily. 'Perfect,' he said. 'Now off you go, it's time for Cinderella to get ready for the ball. Perhaps you'll meet your Prince Charming. Who can say?'

'Don't tease!' Flora exclaimed, and the way she flushed told Vincent that perhaps she had already met Prince Charming.

Well, well, he thought. I wonder who he is. And I wonder if there's any profit in it for me? I'd better find out.

He thought Flora had seen the speculation in his expression for she suddenly looked alarmed. 'Of course I haven't met anyone,' she said. Then she turned and hurried away.

Vincent waited until he judged she would have reached the house before leaving. He had no intention of waiting in the tool shed. He knew that there were so many visiting servants here tonight that no one would notice him if he mingled with them.

He wouldn't enter the house, of course. That sharp-tongued little maid would recognize him. Instead he made his way to the stable yard. As he had hoped, one of the tack rooms and the room above it were full of the valets and servants of visiting gentlemen who had sought escape from the female chatter in the servants' hall by visiting the grooms and stable boys.

The Cavendish family had been generous and good food and ale had been provided for all the servants. If the latter was a little weak, the former was rich: game pies, sliced meats, strong cheese and savoury pickles. All served on the remaining pieces of once-grand dinner services. No one noticed when Vincent helped himself; they were all busy filling their own plates. And the mood was jolly.

Not only did Vincent find this congenial company but there was much valuable information to be gleaned about other rich families if you listened carefully and did not appear to be too curious. It was the sort of information that his father would be pleased to have. Yes, he thought, the hours spent waiting for Flora would not be wasted.

Chapter Eleven

The minstrels' gallery was not an original feature of the house. The ballroom at Cavendish Hall was part of the Palladian wing that had been added after some eighteenth-century Cavendish had taken his bride to Italy for their honeymoon journey and had been greatly influenced by the classical buildings there.

He had returned to Northumberland full of enthusiasm to extend the family home yet again. Fortunately he had followed the family tradition and married a rich wife, so he had been able to indulge his extravagant plans. But, unable to free himself entirely of the old ideas, he had asked the architect to add several 'traditional' features.

Hence the minstrels' gallery, which was too small to accommodate more than a handful of musicians and which looked entirely out of place in the grand new reception hall. Sadly the gallery had hardly ever been used except to store a few old pieces of furniture.

However, it provided a marvellous view of the ballroom, and over the years the children of the house had hidden there to watch the grand entertainments below.

This evening the housemaids were taking it in turn to slip away from their duties and watch the dancing, two at a time. Alice Fairbairn and her younger sister, Eva, had just changed places with the previous two girls and now they crouched down in the shadow of an old chaise longue and peered through the gilded rails.

'Aren't they beautiful?' the younger girl whispered. 'All the lasses in them bonny frilly frocks. They look like flowers in a garden.'

'Whisht,' Alice hissed. 'Not so loud. And you and me would look just as grand if we could afford clothes and jewels like that.'

Eva lowered her voice as she'd been told to. 'Do you think so?' she asked. Her eyes were round.

'Well, of course I do. I've seen some of them getting ready, remember. Had to help out if they hadn't brought a maid of their own. Some of them's not so handsome close up, I can tell you. And they have to put curling rags in their hair or use the tongs; not like you and me.'

'Really?'

Eva looked pleased and the fingers of one hand strayed to play with a wayward curl that had escaped from her mobcap. Suddenly Alice was filled with rage because girls like her sister, who was as pretty as a china doll, should spend their days scrubbing and cleaning and fetching and carrying while some of those spoiled young madams dancing down below were waited on hand and foot every day of their lives.

Angela Cavendish, whose birthday ball this was, was the same age as Eva, and she had only just left her private school in Newcastle, whereas Eva had left the village school at twelve years old, just as Alice herself had done, and she had been working for her living ever since.

Young Miss Cavendish's bedroom was the same size as the only room in their mother's cottage and by the time she woke up each day the fire had been made up and her clothes laid out ready for her. She only had to pull the bell rope and her breakfast arrived on a tray and, often, she didn't even remember to say 'thank you'. Although she always smiled, Alice conceded.

Oh, the lass was pleasant enough, as were her mother and father, but most of the time the family behaved as though the servants didn't exist – at least not as living, breathing human beings just like themselves.

They gave orders but, apart from that, they never spoke to any of the below-stairs staff or even looked at them if they passed them on the stairs. Indeed, if any of the family came into sight, the housemaids had been told to turn their faces away and stand still without fidgeting until they'd gone.

Perhaps the Cavendish family and people like them thought the people who cleaned their houses and cooked their meals and even helped them put their clothes on were like mechanical fairground dolls in that they didn't have feelings or hopes and dreams of their own – or worries and concerns, for that matter.

Alice's angry musings made her scowl. The heady perfume of the flower garlands seemed to rise and engulf her, and it no longer smelled so sweet. The lilting music jarred and the swirling couples below faded into a muddle of inharmonious shapes and colours as she contemplated the injustices of the world.

She didn't realize her sister had been talking to her until the younger girl nudged her none too gently. 'What's the matter, Alice?' Eva hissed.

'Matter? What do you mean? There's nowt the matter.'

'Well, you wouldn't think so. Not the way you're glowering. Are you tired? Do you want to gan now?'

'No, it's all right. We'll stay a few minutes longer.'

Alice knew how much Eva had been looking forward to coming up to the gallery to watch the dancing, and she didn't want to spoil things for her. Besides, if they went back to the servants' hall now, they would only be put to work, and she could do with a break.

'Doesn't Miss Angela look ravishing?' Eva whispered.

That made Alice smile and she looked at her sister with some amusement. '*Ravishing*? My, that's a big word when it's out. Where did you hear that?'

Eva flushed. 'Don't tease. They all say it when they're talking about each other. The young ladies, I mean.'

'Do they indeed? Well, take my word for it, they don't mean it half the time. Oh, they might sound sweet but they're little cats, some of them.'

'Just like you, then.'

Alice's eyes widened at her sister's sharp words. 'I beg your pardon?' she said.

Eva smiled placatingly. 'Honestly, our Alice, you should see yourself. You've got a face that would curdle milk. And you've done nowt but find fault since we came up here.'

'I'm sorry, pet. I divven't want to spoil your treat. And, yes, I do think Miss Angela looks bonny: all in white and sparkling with diamonds. They say the diamonds used to belong to her Grandmother Cavendish; she left them to Miss Angela when she died.'

'I know that!' Eva's eyes sparkled. 'And I know why. They say Angela's ma was hoping to get them but the old lady didn't think they should adorn the descendant of a common pitman! That's how the story goes.'

'Aye, and it's probably true.' Her sister seemed to have forgiven her for being so sour and she was pleased that the younger girl was enjoying herself. 'And do you know what, our Eva?' she added.

'What?'

'That just proves how stupid the high-and-mighty gentry are, doesn't it?'

'Does it? Why?'

'Well, Miss Angela is her mother's daughter, isn't she?'

'Of course.'

'Don't you see? That makes her a descendant of a common pitman too, doesn't it?'

As Eva nodded her head wonderingly, Alice grinned. 'So don't you ever go thinking these folk are better than you, because they're not. Promise me?'

'All right.'

Eva looked doubtful and Alice put her arm round her and hugged her. 'But we shouldn't waste our time up here. I know, let's see if we can decide who is the belle of the ball.'

'And what's the belle of the ball when it's at home?'

'The prettiest lass here tonight.'

'Well, that would be Miss Angela, wouldn't it?'

'Do you really think so?'

'Well . . . she's . . . I mean, she's "our" young lady, isn't she?'

'Oh, Eva, you are a loyal little thing, aren't you? Yes, I know you admire her but do you really think she's the prettiest here tonight?'

'Yes. Don't you?'

Alice shook her head and then asked, 'What about Miss Walton? Don't you think she's pretty?'

232

'You mean Miss Angela's school friend?' Eva looked surprised. 'Oh, no. I mean, there's nothing wrong with her – she's got nice eyes and a kind face and lovely thick brown hair – but she's not what you would call a beauty, is she?'

'No, she isn't. But I didn't mean the elder Miss Walton. I meant her sister, Flora. Look at her now.' The elder girl leaned forward and, keeping low, she pointed down the length of the ballroom. 'She's over there near the doors to the terrace talking to Miss Angela's cousin Forbes. Don't you think she looks lovely in that baby-blue frock with all them little blue flowers in her hair?'

Eva studied Flora Walton for a moment and then she said, 'Yes, I can't deny the lass is beautiful. But . . .'

'But what?'

'Beauty is only skin deep,' Eva said. 'That's what our mam says, isn't it?'

'Aye, she does. But remember what wor dad says: "It's only the skin you see." '

The sisters looked at each other and grinned, and suddenly, homesick for their parents' cottage and the companionship of their parents and their brothers and sisters, Alice put her arm round the younger girl and hugged her.

'All right,' she said after a moment. 'If we're going to choose the nicest lass to be the belle of the ball I would give the crown to the elder Miss Walton. There's no side to her at all and she always remembers to say please and thank you.'

'Oh, but—' Eva began, and Alice held up one hand.

'But we'll agree to differ, shall we?' she said. 'Now we mustn't stay here much longer or we'll be in trouble, so feast your eyes on the fine ladies and gentlemen so's that you can tell our mam every little detail of what they were wearing next time it's your turn to go home for the day.'

Eva spread her forearms along the rail in front of her and rested her chin on her clasped hands as she gazed at the twirling pairs of dancers. Soon she began to hum the tune quietly to herself and Alice smiled to see her sister's head begin to sway very slightly from side to side in time to the music.

Well, it was all very splendid, of course, and Alice only wished she could enter into the spirit of the occasion like the other servants here. Even though this birthday celebration had meant so much extra work nobody had complained, and the gossip amongst the maidservants had been all about the fashionable clothes the young women guests had brought with them – approving and disapproving, agreeing with that little detail, or offering their own opinions of what might have made a certain ensemble better still – as if it mattered.

Alice was of the opinion that, as neither she nor any one of her fellow servants would ever be able to afford clothes like that, there was little point in even taking notice of them.

But the music was catchy, she had to agree. She allowed herself to relax for a moment and she leaned forward and peered over the rail and looked straight down on to the heads of the musicians. She smiled to see how energetically they were playing. How uncomfortably warm they must be in those formal clothes, she thought, and how they must be looking forward to the intermission, when they would be allowed to file into the room behind the stage and partake of cool drinks.

This made her remember the incident earlier with the good-looking stranger. At first Alice had taken him for one of the musicians. He had certainly come into the ballroom carrying some sort of musical instrument in a strange-shaped case. But he had reacted so haughtily to that suggestion that she had been forced to consider that he was one of Miss Angela's guests.

But not for long. He had admitted almost immediately that he had no right to be there and Alice had not been surprised, for although he spoke like a gentleman, the cut of his clothes was not quite right. Alice had not been able to pinpoint the reason for this assumption but it was something to do with the fact that he was a little too showy, like an actor. Yes, that was it, he reminded her of one of those players in the troupe that came round the countryside putting on shows in village halls and barns.

Then he'd persuaded her (her mind skittered away from the word 'bribed') to take the note to the younger Miss Walton. Uneasily she considered what she'd done. There had been no harm in it, had there? She frowned as she called up the words he had written – for of course she had read the note.

'I'm waiting.' That was all.

Waiting where? Alice wondered now. Had Miss Walton got dressed and hurried out to meet him at some prearranged place? Or was he still waiting out in the gardens or down by the lake while the young madam danced the night away with Miss Angela's cousin?

For whatever the truth of the matter, from the way Flora Walton was looking up into Forbes Robson's eyes, she couldn't be very enamoured with the man who signed himself 'V'.

The waltz came to an end and the couples made their way off the floor. Below the gallery the musicians wiped their brows and tuned their instruments.

'Eva,' Alice said softly, 'we'd better go and give someone else a turn.'

'All right,' Eva said reluctantly.

They were just about to leave by the little door at the side of the gallery when the music started up again. Alice and her sister glanced down towards the dancers one final time.

'Look,' Eva whispered, 'Miss Angela looks so happy, doesn't she?'

'Of course she does. It's her birthday ball, isn't it?'

Eva smiled. 'Aye, but that's not the reason she looks as if she's floating on air. I reckon she's got the man she fancies. She's just about to dance with the rich American.'

Josie watched Angela sail by in Jacob's arms. Without a partner for this dance, she stood back and studied her dance card. It was a double card with a list of dances on one side and on the other blank spaces to be filled with a list of partners. So far she had danced every dance with young men she hardly knew and, tired of the inconsequential chatter they felt obliged to provide, she was pleased that she was not promised for the waltz that had just struck up.

The ball had begun traditionally with Angela and her father leading the couples four times round the ballroom in the stately grand march. Then there had been a selection of quadrilles, waltzes and polkas and there were to be more of the same. In fact, there were at least ten more dances to come before the intermission. The composers listed were Schultze, Musard and Lumbye; but at least a third of all the dances were by Strauss, the King of the Waltz, as he was known. And his melodies certainly made the ball a lively affair.

No music or descriptions of the dances were entered on the cards after the intermission, although another twelve spaces were provided to write in the names of prospective partners. Josie had asked Angela why this was so, but her friend had merely smiled and said, 'Wait and see!'

All the female guests had been given little silver cases containing their dance cards. Inside each case was a tiny pencil attached to a cord. The idea was that the gentleman should request a specific dance and then his name would be written next to the dance in question. The card case with its list of dances and dancing partners would then be a memento of the event for ever more.

Flora's card was full. Every dance listed had a gentleman's name beside it, even those mysterious empty spaces after the intermission, and one name appeared more often than any other: that of Forbes Robson. Oh, Forbes had done his duty. No doubt prompted by his aunt, Angela's mother, he had done the rounds and politely signed the cards of those young ladies who were in danger of being wallflowers.

He had requested that Josie dance with him twice and she had wondered for a moment if he considered her a wallflower, but as he had spent each entire dance questioning her tactfully about her sister, she had soon realized that he had another motive.

But as was usual at the beginning of these events, there had been a degree of muddle that had left some dances free on some of the guests' cards, and so there was a scramble in between dances to right the matter. Josie had no partner listed for the present dance and she was pleased to be able to get her breath back. Forbes, in spite of his non-stop chatter, had just danced her almost off her feet in the preceding polka. Now he had waltzed away with Flora.

Josie glanced up and looked for them as the couples went spinning by. The frills and flounces of the ball gowns swayed in time to the music and the vibrant colours were like splashes of paint on an artist's palette. The various light scents that the girls were wearing gave off powdery fragrances that mingled sweetly with their partners' hair lotions and the more exotic perfume of the garlands twisted round the columns and draped in loops below the cornice.

Now Josie closed her card case and dropped it to let it hang on the silver ribbon pinned to her dress. It settled into the chiffon flounces of her pale green gown. She felt a welcome breeze somewhere behind her and turned to see that the doors opening on to the terrace had been left open. The soft night beckoned but, just before she could leave the ballroom, someone called her name. She turned to see another of Angela's cousins approaching her, Forbes's younger brother, Ambrose.

'I say, Miss Walton. This is a piece of luck.'

Ambrose Robson was smaller than his brother and perhaps a little overweight. Instead of red-gold, his hair was dark brown. His long-fingered hands were white and soft and his smile almost girlish. At the moment he looked like an appealing young puppy dog anxious for approval.

'Why is that?' Josie asked.

'Erm . . .' he smiled with his head on one side, 'what exactly do you mean?'

'You said that this was a piece of luck,' Josie explained patiently.

'Ah . . . er . . . yes, of course.' Ambrose's smile widened until it lit up his face. 'Finding you, I mean.'

'Oh.'

Josie wasn't sure how to react. Ambrose was two years older than she was and yet he seemed so much younger. He was completely guileless. It was almost as though he hadn't grown that protective skin that everyone should have before they are let loose in the world. Every honest emotion showed in his face, his voice and his gestures. Ever since she had been introduced to him only the day before he had done nothing to disguise the fact that he had taken a liking to her.

Thankfully, Angela's mother had kept him busy overseeing the floral decorations, for Ambrose was a gifted artist, otherwise he would have been by Josie's side all the time. And, even more thankfully, Angela's father had played on his good nature and persuaded him to sign the dance cards of spinster aunts and elderly widows, otherwise he might have demanded to dance every dance with Josie.

'The next dance is mine, you know,' he said now.

'I hadn't forgotten.'

'Hadn't you!' Ambrose coloured and Josie saw that the ridiculous boy had taken this as a compliment.

'No, of course I hadn't. But now I was just about to go out on the terrace to seek some cool air.'

'Oh, of course. Good idea. Have you seen the Chinese lanterns? They're genuine, all the way from Shanghai courtesy of a local importer.'

'I know. My father.'

'Oh, of course. Captain Walton. How interesting that must be.'

'Interesting?'

'To live where you do by the river. To see the ships setting off and returning from all the corners of the world. I intend to travel, you know.'

'Do you?'

'Next summer. But only as far as Italy.'

'A holiday?'

'Not quite. I'm going to paint.'

'How wonderful.' Josie was genuinely interested.

'My cousin says you are an artist too.'

'Well . . .'

'But let me escort you on to the terrace. It's quieter out there and we can talk properly.'

Josie took the arm he offered and they walked out into the moonlight.

No one saw them leave except Jacob. He was making a bad job of keeping polite conversation going with Angela as they swirled around the floor. Luckily the tempo had increased and his partner began to appear a little breathless. Although attractive, she was a little on the plump side, and Jacob suspected she had laced herself in uncomfortably tightly in order to be accommodated in her fashionable gown.

She was a good dancer. No doubt she had had lessons as part of her expensive education, and she rested in his arms trustingly, even closing her eyes now and then so she was

238

unaware that he had been glancing round the room looking for Josie Walton. Unaccountably he had not been able to find her to request a dance. Had she been avoiding him?

When he finally saw her deep in conversation with Ambrose Robson, he wondered if she had. Perhaps she had been making sure of keeping enough dances free for Forbes's young brother. Jacob suppressed a niggle of irritation that came close to fully fledged jealousy. Ambrose was nice enough but surely Josie couldn't be attracted to him as her sister, Flora, was unmistakably attracted to his older brother. That would be a neat arrangement, he supposed, if Captain Walton's daughters could be matched with the sons of one of the region's greatest coal magnates.

Forbes and Flora would make a good couple. Forbes was a handsome man and intelligent enough to make his business prosper. But he would demand no more of a wife than that she be beautiful – and aware of the social graces. Flora was still young, but that was good too. Jacob knew there was wildness in the younger Walton girl and that she would need guidance from an older and a stronger man. The marriage – if that was what was in Forbes's mind – could be successful.

But Ambrose and Josie! He could see why Ambrose would be attracted to Josie – any intelligent and sensitive man would be – but what on earth did she see in him? Oh, he was artistic. According to Angela he was talented, and Jacob had learned that Josie liked to paint. And Ambrose would be rich enough and liberal thinking enough to encourage Josie's talent. But he was nowhere near man enough for her.

And now they had walked out on to the terrace, which was romantically lit by oriental lanterns, not to mention an obliging moon.

What were they doing?

Jacob fought hard to suppress the image that sprang to mind.

The dance had come to an end and the couples were leaving the floor. 'Just one more dance before the intermission,' Angela told him as he led her back to the row of gilded chairs down one side of the room. He noticed that she was breathing heavily and she looked at the chairs longingly, but her next partner was already making his way towards them.

She was too unsophisticated to hide her regret as he handed her to the brawny red-cheeked young man who looked like a prosperous gentleman farmer. Jacob gave a half-bow and melted away between the couples on the floor, who were already taking up their positions for a gallop.

Jacob was not engaged for this dance and he hoped Josie might be free too. No matter that she had gone out on to the terrace with Ambrose. He would go out there boldly and ask her to dance. The young fellow had been brought up properly and he might be taken aback by the rude manners of the American visitor but he would be too courteous to object.

He heard the conductor tap his music stand with his baton and the music began. He had to push his way through the couples and earned several surprised frowns. Then just as he reached the doors the couple he was seeking came back into the ballroom. They were laughing.

'Josie – Miss Walton—' he began, but they swept past him.

Josie turned her head briefly and looked at him. Her laughter died. Then she and Ambrose joined in with the couples who were following the lead of Angela and her partner in the gallop. The headlong charge would wend two or three times round the ballroom before heading for the supper room and the refreshments provided for the intermission.

Jacob kept his eyes on Josie, and he saw her glance back in his direction once more. But he turned away, unable to meet her gaze. He was trying to rid his mind of the image of her and Ambrose smiling and laughing as they had come back into the ballroom. They had been holding hands.

The gallop ended in the supper room with everyone flushed and laughing and ready to enjoy the refreshments. Angela escaped from her dancing partner as soon as she could without seeming impolite and wove her way through the crowd, making her way back to the ballroom.

Jacob, unlike the others who had not been dancing, had not followed them. The last Angela had seen of him he had been lurking behind a pillar, looking very much as if he was sulking.

Was that possible? Could he be annoyed because she hadn't saved enough dances for him? She would have done so willingly had he asked her to. But perhaps they did things differently in America. She had heard that the young ladies were more forward there. Perhaps there was some new etiquette that allowed them openly to encourage a partner rather than drop the ladylike hints that was the practice here in England. Or at least this part of England. She had heard that matters were much more advanced in London.

The ballroom was empty. Even the musicians had gone to their own room behind the stage to enjoy a rest and the meal that had been provided for them. Where could he be? Angela noticed that the flower garlands were swaying slightly and remembered that the doors to the terrace were open. Should she go and look for Jacob there? Would he think her forward? Surely not. She was, after all, the hostess, and it was her duty to look after a guest; especially a guest from overseas who might not be sure what was expected.

The Chinese lanterns looked like giant oranges strung along the terrace and on wooden poles set up on the lawn – but oranges that were glowing with a mysterious inner light and that had long silky tassels that shimmered in the breeze.

The breeze, coming up from the lake, was chill, and Angela shivered and clasped her bare arms. Now that she was beginning to cool down she suspected she might come up in goose pimples. That wouldn't do. She was just about to turn back when she saw Jacob leaning on the stone balustrade, gazing out across the grounds.

He must have sensed her approach for he turned towards her before she had taken more than a couple of steps.

'Miss Cavendish,' he said. His face was in shadow and she couldn't tell from the tone of his voice whether he was pleased to see her.

She wished it wasn't so important to her what this man thought of her, and her anger at her own vulnerability robbed her of her usual social poise.

'Aren't you coming . . . ?' she began and faltered.

'Coming?'

'Yes . . . for supper.'

'Is it expected?'

'But of course.' She forced herself to sound both

encouraging and yet amused. 'My mother would be desolate if you did not partake of the amazing feast she has provided. She hopes to impress you, you know.'

'Impress me?'

'Well, you are a visitor from America and she imagines that everything there will be a little . . .'

'Primitive?' Jacob moved towards her and she saw with relief that he was smiling.

Nevertheless she was embarrassed. Furthermore she knew how artificial the whole exchange had sounded. Jacob Goodwright was no fool. He must be aware that her concern for him was more than that of a hostess and that her interest in him was personal.

'Oh dear,' she said, 'have I offended you?'

'Of course not. And I assure you I am ready to be impressed.'

'Very well, then.' She tried to inject a certain matter-of-factness into her tone. 'You'd better come with me to the supper room. We're having a "perpendicular", you know.'

'What on earth is that?' He sounded both puzzled and amused.

She allowed herself to glance at him and saw that he was smiling. She began to relax. 'Well, it's a sort of buffet with sandwiches and cakes and exquisite little tempting mouthfuls laid out on a long table.'

'Oh, I see. And the guests remain standing? Hence the "perpendicular"?'

'Mm, well, at any rate the gentlemen do. There are chairs scattered about for the ladies, who must rely on the gentlemen to fill plates for them.'

'Ah. Then I hope you'll allow me to do that for you.'

'Oh, well, I suppose so. Although that's not why I came looking for you.'

'Of course not.'

Angela was aware that her cheeks were burning. This was not what she had expected to happen when her mother had told her she was inviting the rich American to the birthday ball: the young gentleman of great wealth whom everyone was talking about. In fact Angela had actually been angry because her mother's intentions had been all too clear. She had muttered something about it being a cattle market and her mother had simply laughed and told her that marriage market was the more appropriate phrase and that it was nothing to be ashamed of.

How infuriating, therefore, that when she had actually met this unimposing and seemingly unassuming American she had immediately been stricken like any of the foolish heroines in the romances she so loved reading. And to her utter chagrin she knew that she had done a very poor job of concealing her attraction. Perhaps that was why she was suddenly prompted to say rather imperiously, 'Do you have anything like that at home in America?' Her tone implied that she would be very surprised if they did.

Jacob was not at all put out. 'Oh, yes,' he said. 'Mrs Goodwright is an avid follower of fashion. She has all the latest books on ballroom and dinner party etiquette. There's probably no one in New York or Boston who knows as much as she does about "the well-dressed table"!'

'*Mrs* Goodwright? Your – er?'

'My mother. I'm not married.'

Again she realized she'd been clumsy and perhaps Jacob sensed her discomfort for he hurried on in a light-hearted manner, 'Most of the time Mrs Goodwright is taken up with good works. She's utterly devoted to any of Mr Goodwright's projects, so he's more than happy to indulge her wish to be part of society.'

'Oh.' Angela could think of nothing more to say. She was surprised and puzzled by the fact that Jacob referred to his parents as Mr and Mrs Goodwright. She supposed it must be the American way but she had not imagined that they would be so formal.

Well, she hoped that he would be impressed with her mother's table and perhaps even write to his mother about the fine linen, the elegant china, the crystal and the deceivingly simple yet most eye-catching flower arrangements that Cousin Ambrose had overseen.

Once in the supper room Jacob did his duty. He brought her food and drink and kept up a flow of easy chatter, but Angela could not rid herself of the feeling that he would rather have stayed on the terrace. What on earth had he been doing out there? Even from behind, the way he was standing had suggested that he was brooding about something. That he was unhappy.

It wasn't until they heard the musicians tuning their instruments prior to beginning the dancing again that she had one of those moments of intuition that told her why. Jacob had been silent for a moment and she glanced up to find him gazing across the room to where her cousin Ambrose was talking to Josie Walton.

Ambrose was flushed and happy and animated about something. He was waving his arms about in that ungentlemanly and yet endearing way of his as he made his point, but Josie was not paying attention. She had risen from her chair and was holding her plate awkwardly, trying to keep it out of the way of Ambrose's enthusiastic gestures, but she had half turned her head and was staring in Angela's direction.

But Josie was not looking at her old school friend. She was looking at Jacob. And he was looking at her. Angela's glance went from one to the other; at first she was unwilling to acknowledge what she saw. Then her heart grew cold when she realized there was no mistaking that look of suppressed longing on their faces.

Angela stood up so quickly that her chair fell over. By the time Jacob had turned to pick it up she had stormed off to the ballroom.

'Oh, how marvellous!' Flora exclaimed as she gazed at the musicians. They had rearranged themselves on the platform and some of them had taken up different instruments such as a melodeon, a tin whistle, a piccolo and a harmonica. But the most significant change was that centre stage had been taken by a Northumbrian piper.

'Look, they're taking off their jackets,' Flora continued. 'We're going to have country dancing!'

Her eyes were sparkling. Forbes felt himself falling even more deeply in love. She's still a child, he thought, and I must wait, but I shall make it my business to see her father as soon as possible and make my intentions clear. Surely he can have no objections to such a match – apart from her youth. And if he asks me to wait a year or two longer then I shall wait. But I must have her.

'Wasn't it clever to keep this a surprise?' Flora asked.

'Actually, it was my idea.'

'Was it?'

Forbes was ridiculously pleased to see the admiration in her eyes. 'Yes. As Angela has no brothers, her mother dragooned Ambrose and me into helping organize the celebration.'

'Did you mind?'

'Not at all. And especially not now when I see I've pleased you so much.'

'Oh.' Her cheeks flushed with colour and she lost her poise for a moment. Then she raised her chin and said, 'You're flirting.'

'Do you mind?'

To his consternation she suddenly looked as though she was going to burst into tears. He wondered what on earth had brought about the change in her. He'd been so positive that she liked him. It's vanity, he thought, but why not? He knew he was passably handsome and he prided himself on his appearance.

But, truth to tell, Flora had been blowing hot and cold all night. She'd delighted in the dancing, responded to his friendly conversation one moment, and then for no apparent reason she would distance herself from everything as she seemed to be contemplating something deeply troubling.

By God, he hoped she wasn't already promised to somebody. Some callow lad. Could that be it?

'Flora,' he said, 'what's the matter?'

'Matter? What do you mean?'

There was no mistaking the look of panic on her face but he was prevented from questioning her further when the musicians took up their instruments and crashed into the opening bars of a reel. Flora flung up a smile as she grabbed his hand. 'Come along,' she said, and she pulled him on to the floor to join the other couples in the Morpeth Rant.

After that Forbes claimed Flora for every dance, simply waving away any unfortunate youth whose name appeared on her card. Such was his seniority in North Country society that no one wanted to oppose him. And, in any case, as the strathspeys, the jigs and the reels got wilder, the system of etiquette failed altogether and young men and women simply stayed with one partner or settled for the nearest person with a smile and a polite nod of the head.

Ambrose, not nearly so ineffectual as his appearance suggested, just like his brother, managed to see off any young man who came to claim Josie. He was also a very good dancer. Surprisingly graceful and light on his feet, he became more and more animated as the tempo increased, and was prepared to go on dancing long after some of the guests had collapsed on to the chairs and sofas set at the sides of the ballroom.

Well, at least the young women were seated on the chairs as they fanned themselves madly. Many of the young men were on the floor, either sitting at the feet of their partners or, in some cases, lying flat out as their friends laughed at them and stumbled over their prostrate bodies.

When the music began for the heel-and-toe polka, Josie would have liked to have sat down, but Ambrose put his arm around her waist and off they went. She heard a gasp and she looked across the room to see her sister and Forbes nearly come to grief as they collided with another couple.

There was a moment when it looked as though both couples would fall down but the other pair whirled away, hardly missing a step, whereas Forbes stopped and pulled Flora close to his body as if to save her. She held on to him tightly until they had regained their balance, then they seemed to pull away reluctantly and there was a pause before they began dancing again.

Josie had not missed the way they had clung to each other, nor the way Flora had looked up at her partner dreamily in that long moment before they had started to dance.

'Forbes is so clumsy!' Ambrose said laughingly. 'He's like a bull in a china shop when he dances. Not like me.'

'You shouldn't boast.'

'I know. It's a failing of mine. But if I don't sing my own praises nobody else will.'

Ambrose smiled so engagingly that once more Josie found herself warming to him. The process had begun before the intermission when they had walked out on to the terrace. The steps of the polka, learned at dancing school, were easy and repetitive, so as she danced she allowed her mind to wander back to her conversation with Ambrose just a short while before.

Whether he had sensed her pensive mood or not, his spontaneous chatter had seemed designed to lift her spirits. He had admitted to her that he had no interest whatever in commercial concerns and he'd had the grace to acknowledge that he knew how lucky he was to have a secure income. He had an allowance and an eventual inheritance so generous that he would never have to work for a living.

'Don't you feel guilty?' Josie had asked him.

'No, for I shall not be idle. I intend to travel and paint, and I have enough faith in my own talent to believe that my work might even bring pleasure to many people. My paintings might hang in provincial galleries and cheer their dreary lives. That would be worthwhile, wouldn't it?'

There had been something in his tone that made her look up into his face. They had been standing at the end of the terrace, well away from the light spilling out of the tall windows, but they were caught up in the warm glow of a Chinese lantern. She saw from the way he was looking at her that he genuinely wanted her approval.

'Yes, I think it would be worthwhile,' she said. 'But why do you ask me?'

'Because I value your opinion.'

'But you've only just met me. We don't really know each other.'

'You are an artist. We are alike. Furthermore I shall take you to Italy with me and we shall rent an old house in Naples and sit on the roof and paint views of Vesuvius.'

She knew he was teasing but she entered the game and she laughed as she exclaimed, 'But that would be scandalous!'

'To paint views of the volcano? Oh, I think not. But if you really object to that then we shall paint views of the orange and lemon groves.'

'But—'

'No? Not the groves. Well, how about the Bay of Naples?'

'Ambrose – my reputation . . .'

'Ah, I understand. Yes, it's true. All the lesser artists produce paintings of the bay. You wouldn't want to be associated with such daubs. Well, I know what we shall do. We shall sit on our sun-warmed rooftop and we shall paint views of all the other rooftops, with the pots of geraniums, the sleeping cats, the lines of washing, the green shutters and the raspberry-pink and yellow-ochre peeling from the old walls. That would be original, wouldn't it? Say you'll come with me. Please.'

'Ambrose! Stop talking this nonsense. You know very well what I mean. You know why I couldn't possibly come with you.'

'Of course I do. But it would be wonderful, wouldn't it? If it were possible?'

'To go to Italy . . . ?'

'You and I together . . .'

'To paint.' She knew she sounded wistful.

'There is a way, you know.' Ambrose moved nearer to her. His expression was serious.

'And what's that?'

'I could persuade my mother to take a villa and make up a house party. If she did, would you come?'

'I don't know.'

'Why is the decision difficult?'

'Well . . . my sister . . . we've never been apart for more than a day.'

'That's no problem. Flora would also be invited. And then my brother would want to come too. Oh dear.' Ambrose sighed. 'That spoils it.'

'Why?'

'All those people. My mother would feel obliged to make up parties for excursions to Pompeii and Herculaneum and Capri and the grottoes.'

'Grottoes?'

'Oh, there are sure to be grottoes. And it just wouldn't do.'

'Why not?'

'Because we wouldn't be left alone for one moment. We'd never get the chance to paint the tabby cats sleeping on the rooftops.'

He had turned away from her while he was speaking and

leaned on the stone balustrade to gaze out across the grounds. Josie hardly knew whether any of this had been serious or whether it was all a fantasy made up to amuse her but he suddenly turned and smiled.

'I know,' he said. 'I know what we can do. We'll elope!'

'We'll what!'

'We'll run off to Gretna Green and get married and then no one could object to our going to Italy together. Will you marry me, Josie? I'll go down on bended knee, if you like.'

Before she could stop him he did just that and, taking up the pose of an actor in a melodrama with one hand on his heart and the other stretched towards her in supplication, he declared, 'Oh, wondrous girl, oh, love of my life, marry me or I die!'

He looked so droll that Josie began to laugh. 'Please get up,' she said. 'You look ridiculous.'

'What, dear heart? Do you spurn me? Then life is over.' Ambrose pretended to draw something from inside his coat and held the imaginary object up in the air. 'Come, trusty dagger!' he declared. 'Find your target!' He brought his arm down in a stabbing motion and then stopped, raised it again and looked up and asked in his normal voice, 'You're sure you won't change your mind?'

By now Josie was helpless with laughter. She shook her head, indicating that she couldn't speak.

Ambrose scrambled to his feet. 'Very well,' he said. 'I'm heartbroken but I'm also hungry. If you won't marry me then at least gallop along with me to supper.'

'Gallop?' Josie managed to say.

'Yes, gallop. Can't you hear the music?' Ambrose put his hand to his ear and adopted a stagy pose again.

As Josie began to laugh anew Ambrose took her hand and hurried with her into the ballroom. As she danced with him she remembered how her feelings of gaiety had evaporated the moment she'd seen Jacob looking at her.

It was well past midnight when the musicians finally packed away their instruments. They would be given supper and then taken back to the station in the coaches and wagons that had collected them. There they would catch the early morning train back to Newcastle, the milk train.

Most of Angela's guests had either departed in their own carriages or, in the case of those who were house guests, had gone wearily to bed. A few lingered in the supper room where a supper of bouillon and sandwiches and tea and plain cake was being served by housemaids who could barely keep their eyes open.

Angela sat at one of the small tables that had been set out and stared round the room disconsolately. Etiquette demanded that she stay until everyone had gone to bed but now that she and Forbes were the only members of the family left, she had a mind to ask her cousin to see if he could hurry everyone along.

'Here you are.' Forbes approached her now with a plate of sandwiches and, hooking a foot round an empty chair, he pulled it closer to the table and sat down. 'I thought we could share these. I've asked the girl to bring over some cake and tea in a little while.'

'Thank you, Forbes.' Angela sighed but, nevertheless, she helped herself to a sandwich. She usually found it comforting to eat and, sadly, she realized she was in need of comfort.

'You look a little glum,' he said.

'Well, so do you – positively chapfallen, in fact!'

They smiled at each other briefly and then Forbes said, 'Is it because the young American fellow has been neglecting you?'

'Neglecting me? I don't know what you mean.'

Forbes looked concerned. 'You don't have to pretend with me,' he said. 'You like him, don't you?'

'I suppose I do.'

'And Jacob?'

She shook her head. 'Don't ask.'

'I'm sorry. I know what your parents were hoping for.'

'Well, they hoped in vain. But what about you? You and Flora seemed to be getting on famously and then she suddenly vanished.'

'You noticed? She was like Cinderella on the stroke of midnight. One moment we were dancing and then she fled.'

'Do you know why?'

'I have no idea.'

'You didn't frighten her, did you?'

'Frighten her? How?'

'Well, she's very young, you know, and you . . . you are a grown man.'

The cousins stared at each other. Angela was too modest to be more explicit but she didn't have to be. Forbes knew very well what she meant. He smiled.

'Nothing I said was unsuitable for a young girl's ears. And, in any case, the younger Miss Walton may be an innocent – indeed, I'm sure she is – but she is old enough to appreciate the fact that I would be a very good catch. And, furthermore, I got the distinct impression she was agreeable to the idea.' He stared moodily at a sandwich before taking a bite. Then he shrugged and smiled. 'So, like Prince Charming I shall have to find the glass slipper.'

Angela laughed. 'She was probably just very tired.'

'That's what she said.'

'Well, there you are then.' Forbes frowned and Angela continued, 'Why don't you believe her?'

'She didn't look tired. She looked . . . oh, I don't know. It was as if she suddenly remembered something. Something that agitated her. I wondered . . . I wondered if there might be a complication.'

'Complication?'

'You know. Some young fellow she's promised herself to.'

'Oh, no, Forbes, I don't think so.'

'What makes you say that?'

'Her sister, Josie, is my friend, remember. She would have told me.'

'She might not know. Flora could have been conducting some secret romance. She might have kept it secret from her sister.'

Angela thought for a moment and then said, 'It's possible but not probable. I'm sure you'll find that she was simply overcome with excitement and sheer fatigue. When you see her in the morning she will be all smiles again.'

'I hope so.' Forbes grinned. 'I shouldn't like my younger brother to be more successful in affairs of the heart than I am.'

'Ambrose? What on earth are you talking about?'

251

'Ambrose and the elder Miss Walton. Don't say you haven't noticed.'

'Josie and Ambrose?'

'Didn't you see them dancing together? Didn't you see how happy he looked?

'No, I can't say I noticed. But Josie, did she look happy too?'

Forbes drew his brows together in concentration, then shook his head. 'Do you know, I can't say I looked at her. I was too busy looking at my brother and wondering if he and I were going to make it a family affair and both go courting the good captain's daughters.'

'Hm.' Nothing Forbes had said had reassured her.

At that moment one of the maids, Alice, appeared at the table with a tray containing the tea and cake her cousin had ordered. Forbes thanked her and told her what a good girl she was and Angela noticed how the girl responded with a scowl. She wondered if she ought to reprimand her but decided not to.

She's tired and out of sorts, she thought. Just as I am. She looked round the room and saw to her relief that she and Forbes were now the only people left in the ballroom.

'Alice.' She called for the girl to return.

'Yes, miss.'

'Fetch me another piece of cake,' she said.

She saw Forbes glance askance at her but she didn't care. This had been her birthday ball and instead of feeling elated she was tired and miserable. Well, at least she could take comfort from an extra piece of cake.

Chapter Twelve

The Chinese lanterns had been extinguished and the grounds of the house were lit only by starlight. Clouds raced before the moon and it seemed to Flora that the shadows came alive, advancing and retreating across the lawns and gardens like ghosts or trespassers.

She imagined that the occasional rustlings must be caused by wild creatures but she had only a hazy idea of what these creatures might be. Field mice, hedgehogs, badgers, perhaps. Just as she entered the rose garden she heard an unearthly shriek echoing from the direction of the trees near the lake. Flora nearly died of fright. She stopped and clutched her white lace shawl about her shoulders. It was several moments before she was composed enough to go on.

It must have been an owl, she thought, half remembering something she had been taught at school about mother owls shrieking in the moonlight. She looked back at the dark bulk of the house, its haphazard pattern of towers and chimneys thrown up in sharp relief against the night sky.

She turned again and descended the stone steps into the rose garden. She stepped on a loose stone or piece of gravel. It felt almost as though it had penetrated the flimsy sole of her dancing shoe and she had to stop herself from calling out in pain. The sound of her intake of breath almost drowned out the sharper sound of a twig snapping. Once more Flora looked all round and saw nothing. Another creature, she thought, before taking the path that led towards the Chinese pavilion and her meeting with Vincent.

She expected him to be waiting behind the pavilion in the gardeners' hut so she was totally unprepared for what happened next.

'For God's sake come here!' Vincent reached for Flora and pulled her roughly into the shadowed colonnade.

'Ah!' she shrieked.

'Be quiet!'

She recognized the controlled fury in his tone and she shrank back. 'What is it? Why are you angry with me?'

'First of all I expected you at least an hour ago and secondly, just look at you! Didn't you have enough sense to put on a cloak?'

'It's warm. I didn't need one. This shawl is all I needed.'

'*I didn't need one!*' He mimicked her voice and she felt herself flushing. 'It's not your welfare I'm worried about, you stupid child. Have you any idea how visible you are walking about the gardens in the bright moonlight in that pale-coloured dress? It's almost as though you want to be discovered. As if you want to be caught red-handed and branded as a thief!'

'Don't say that!'

'What? Don't call you a thief? That's what you are, isn't it, Flora?'

'Only because you made me do it.'

'Oh, no. You can't blame me. You were already an accomplished little criminal long before I caught you out that day in the Grainger Market.'

'No . . . no . . .' Flora began to sob and Vincent took hold of her arms and hurried her round to the back of the pavilion and towards the gardeners' hut. When she saw where they were going she stopped suddenly, refusing to go any further.

'What's the matter?' he asked.

'I'm not going in there with you!'

He stared at her for a moment and she forced herself to hold his gaze. He laughed softly. 'Why ever not?'

Flora glanced at the open door of the shed, saw the darkness inside and imagined the musky smells, the garden implements. Some of them would have sharp blades. She pressed her lips together and shook her head. She could feel her heart beating against her ribs – in fact, she could hear it echoing in her head.

It hadn't crossed her mind until the very moment that she dug her heels in that Vincent might hurt her. It would be so easy for him to murder her there, she thought. After all, he had promised that this would be the last time she would have to steal anything. What if, her usefulness over, he had decided that it was too dangerous to let her live?

'Ah,' he said. 'I see. But surely you don't imagine that I would hurt you?'

'Just take the – just take them and go,' she said.

'Very well. Show me what you've got.'

Flora raised one arm slowly towards him. A beaded Dorothy bag hung from her wrist on its twisted silk cords. Vincent drew the loop over her hand and took the bag. He weighed it in one hand and smiled at its weight. Then she watched as he pulled at the drawstrings and looked inside. Holding the bag with one hand he reached in and took out a glittering rope of diamonds.

'That's Angela Cavendish's necklace,' Flora said. 'The earrings and the brooch are in there too. And that's why I was late. Angela was the last to come up to bed.'

Vincent was peering into the bag and smiling. 'But it all went to plan?'

'They dismissed the maids as soon as they'd undone their corsets and then just flung everything down. Clothes on the floor or over chairs, and jewellery on the dressing tables, sometimes not even put back inside the cases.'

'I told you it was like this after these events. All a thief needs is an accomplice in the house. Sometimes a maid and sometimes a guest. It's better if it's a guest; the police are too ready to suspect the housemaids of being in league with the criminals.'

'Don't.'

'Ah, sorry. I forgot.' He paused. 'You don't like being reminded of what you are. But you were able to slip into the rooms without being noticed?'

'They fell asleep as soon as they got into bed.' Suddenly Flora giggled.

'What is it?'

'Some of them were snoring! Not very ladylike, I'm sure!'

'So nobody saw you?'

'Well . . .'

'Someone did see you? Who?'

'Oh, don't worry, it was only a maid.'

'Only a maid?'

Alarmed by the sudden hint of menace Flora hurried on, 'I don't think she saw me. Really I don't.'

'You'd better explain.'

'I'd been waiting for Angela to go to bed. I needn't have bothered,' she said, suddenly defiant, 'my bag was already full, but you'd been most particular about wanting Angela Cavendish's necklace.'

'All right, hurry up, tell me about the maid.'

Irritated to be spoken to like this Flora drew the explanation out, knowing she'd annoy him. After all, she'd been expecting praise for her efforts, not this constant fault-finding.

'You just can't imagine how difficult it was for me. I'd gone up to bed early – like you said I must. I told Josie, my sister, not to come and say good night because I was very, very tired. But it was just as well that I got into bed and pretended to be asleep – and very uncomfortable it was in all my clothes – because she looked in on me when she came up.'

'There's no need to tell me all this.'

'No, I want you to know. I had to keep peeping out of my room until the house was quiet—'

'Flora!'

'All right. It was easy, just like you said it would be. Except when I went to Angela's room.'

'What happened?'

'I listened at the door before I opened it. There wasn't a sound. I was sure she was asleep so I went in.'

'She was awake?'

'No. Fast asleep, but there was a maidservant in there folding up the clothes – at least that was what she was supposed to be doing.'

'What do you mean?'

'Well, she stood in front of the mirror and held up Angela's ball gown – you know, close to her body as if she was trying to imagine herself wearing it.'

256

'Did she see you?'

'She was too busy admiring herself. Well, I backed out and hid behind one of those ridiculous suits of armour they have along the landing. I waited until the girl went away. So that's why I was late – and I didn't expect you to be cross with me.'

Suddenly she looked forlorn, just like the child she really was, Vincent thought. 'You did well,' he told her. 'And I am pleased with you.'

To his dismay she looked as though she was about to burst into tears. He had lingered long enough. He knew he must go as soon as possible but he couldn't leave her in this state. She had to get back to the house and into her bedroom without being discovered.

'You must go back now,' he told her. 'Back the same way you came. Can you do that?'

'Yes, but promise I won't have to do this ever again.'

'I told you. This is the last time.'

'But promise!'

'Very well. I promise. You'll never see me again. And will you take some advice from me?'

'What advice?'

'You were only a good thief when you didn't have a conscience. Something has happened to make you worry about what you're doing. Whether it's genuine remorse I don't know. Perhaps it's no longer exciting. Perhaps some other prospect has opened up for you and you have no desire to do anything that puts that prospect in jeopardy. But whatever it is, it will make you a clumsy thief. You had better stay on the straight and narrow from now on.'

'Oh, I will!'

'Goodbye then, Flora.'

'And I'll never see you again.'

'That's what I said.'

Vincent took a black velvet bag from his pocket and carefully shook the jewellery into it. 'Here you are,' he said, giving Flora back her Dorothy bag. 'Now, hand them over.'

'Hand what over?'

'Your necklace and your earrings.'

Flora's hand flew to her throat. 'But why? They're not

valuable. Only pearl and amethyst. They were a gift from my father.'

'Nevertheless, it will look strange if your jewellery is not stolen.'

'Oh, of course. Very well.'

'Turn around then.'

Vincent reached towards her as if he were about to unclasp the necklace but she flinched away from him.

'No ... I'll manage. There you are.' She dropped the necklace and then the earrings into the bag he was holding. 'What will you do now?' she asked. 'How will you get back to the station?'

Vincent slipped the velvet bag into an inside pocket of his jacket. 'The same way I came here,' he said. 'I'll walk. But no more questions. Go back to the house. I'll watch you.'

Flora looked as if she were going to say something more but he held up his hand to stop her and then pointed in the direction of the house. She took one last look at him and then turned to go. He watched her. She looked back once and then she began to hurry. When she reached the steps that led up on to the wide expanse of the lawns there was a loud scream that sounded almost human, although Vincent recognized it as the call of a vixen in the woods by the lake.

It caused Flora to stumble on the steps. She put both her hands down to save herself. Then she righted herself and began to run across the grass. Her pale clothes made her highly visible and Vincent held his breath, only relaxing when he saw her mount the steps to the terrace and then disappear into the house. The moonlight glinting on the glass panes showed the door opening and closing behind her. Good. He could go. Vincent began the long walk to the station.

Only then did the person who had been watching and listening emerge from the shadows. He had not been able to sleep and had been walking in the gardens when Flora, looking like a ghost, had emerged from the house. Thinking she might be on her way to an assignation he had wondered whether he should follow her or not.

But something about the way she was walking, nervously starting and stopping, suggested dread rather than eager anticipation so he found himself drawn to follow her. The skills of evasion he had learned many years ago came back to him. She did not know he was there.

Once Vincent had taken her round to the back of the pavilion, it had been easier. He had kept close to the building and managed to remain within hearing distance. The only wonder was that Vincent, obviously a practised criminal, had not sensed he was there.

What he had seen and heard had been deeply disturbing but he had already decided what he must do. Once Flora was safely in the house, he let Vincent have a head start – after all, he knew where he was going – and he set off after him. Somehow he had to save the situation for the sake of the woman he loved.

Soon both men had gone, leaving the nocturnal animals to explore the grounds of the old house in peace. But neither Vincent nor the man who was now pursuing him had noticed the pale blue satin evening bag lying on the steps that led down into the rose garden.

Vincent kept up a steady pace along the country roads. He tried to contain a growing feeling of exhilaration. The night's work would bring in a good profit and his father would be pleased with him. But he wasn't home yet.

He didn't hurry as he did not want to arrive at the station too long before the train. His footsteps striking on the gravelled surface sounded unnaturally loud and this made him slightly nervous, especially when he passed a lone farmhouse and set the dogs barking. Wherever he could, he walked along the grass verge, but sometimes the proximity of the hedge or the existence of a ditch made this impossible.

There was a faint mist floating over the fields and the grey early morning light was strengthening by the minute, although the road was still shadowed by the overhanging branches of the trees. Vincent had no idea that someone was following him. Someone so skilled at stealth that the farm dogs never even opened one sleepy eye as he passed.

When the road began to dip down towards the valley bottom the sooty smoke from the village chimneys rose to mingle with the clean air blowing down from the hills. There were lights showing in cottage windows and he could hear the clip-clop of horses' hoofs and the rattle of carts over cobbled streets. Some of them, like those containing the musical instruments, would be making for the railway station.

The station was busy. Along with the shop workers and office workers heading for a long day's toil in the city, there were the musicians who had played at the ball. Some of the latter were sitting on the benches around the village green, and those who were not dozing with heads resting on their instrument cases were annoying the good people in the adjacent houses with their jocular chatter.

Vincent kept his head down. The tiny waiting room was full. But, in any case, Vincent would not have gone in there. Oil lamps, almost redundant now as the sun grew stronger, cast pools of light along the platform. It was easy enough to mingle with the good-natured crowd without actually being part of any one group. Most of them were sprawled tiredly across benches or station trolleys or were even sitting on the ground.

But when they heard the train whistle as it approached the station the easy-going atmosphere changed. Everybody leaped up, seized whatever luggage they were personally responsible for, and began to push and jostle to get a good position at the front.

This suited Vincent. He kept himself in the middle of the crowd and as the train drew in and stopped with a hiss of steam he let others jostle at the carriage doors, allowing himself to be carried along in the surge.

Then suddenly someone's temper snapped. 'Out of the way,' a voice called, and Vincent felt himself being shoved sideways. He righted himself, only to be pushed again and his foot slipped. He had a terrifying vision of going down and being trampled underfoot – or even worse, slipping between the platform and the train to be horribly mangled when the train started up again – when two strong arms reached out from behind and hauled him upright.

'Thank you,' he gasped, and turned to see who his rescuer was, but the man kept his eyes down and turned away quickly, then slipped through the crowd in the direction of the exit.

Vincent frowned but before he could marshal his thoughts

another voice asked, 'Are you all right?' He looked round to see the musician he had helped to carry his music stand into the ballroom.

'Perfectly, thank you,' he muttered and, turning his face, he pushed his way through the crowd a little. The last thing he wanted was to strike up a conversation with someone who might put two and two together if last night's events got into the newspapers.

He found that his carefree mood had evaporated. He didn't want to draw any more attention to himself so he waited patiently until one of the compartments was almost full and then slipped in, taking the one remaining seat.

He leaned against the cold window and slanted a look down the platform. He could see the musical instruments being loaded into the goods van, along with the milk churns and the mail sacks. He heard the guard's whistle and steam eddied along the platform as the train pulled away.

Good, he was on his way. So why did he feel uneasy? As the train picked up speed and the rattle of the wheels along the track began to echo in his tired brain, the sound they made seemed to take on the rhythm of some words he had just heard: *Out of the way . . . out of the way . . . out of the way . . . out of the way . . .* What was it about that voice that was bothering him? It was different, that was it, different from the voices you usually heard in this part of the world.

Then suddenly Vincent put the voice together with the face he had half glimpsed as the man who had saved him from falling had turned away. Saved him from falling or pushed him down in the first place? Which had it been?

But why would he do that?

Vincent was even more puzzled now that he realized where he'd seen that face before. The face belonged to one of the guests at the ball, the American; the same man who had set up the new mission on the quayside. Jacob Goodwright.

The lake was as smooth as glass and it reflected the images of the surrounding trees almost as perfectly as a mirror. Josie wondered if the swan knew how beautiful and strange it looked as it moved through the water on top of its own reflection. Mist

261

had risen from the surface and seemed to hang in the branches of the trees but it was already dispersing as the sun rose higher.

Josie shivered slightly. It was cooler here by the water, and she was glad she had brought her shawl. She pulled it more securely round her body and hid her hands and arms in its folds.

She had not been able to sleep. It was strange, being in a room on her own, and she missed her sister's company. Even a sleeping Flora would have been better than no Flora at all. As soon as she'd heard sounds of domestic activity Josie had got up and, unwilling to pull the bell rope to summon one of the maids, she'd poured water left in the jug from the night before into the washing bowl.

She dressed quickly and made her way downstairs. Only when she was standing in the baronial hallway confronted by the massive locked and bolted door did she realize that she would have to summon help if she was to get out of the house that way.

Remembering the doors that led on to the terrace, she wandered into the ballroom to find several maidservants already sweeping and tidying. One of the manservants was standing at the door. He was moving the handle up and down as if puzzled about something but, on seeing Josie and guessing her intention, he opened the door for her and smiled respectfully.

He didn't speak and Josie realized he would not have expected her to say anything to him. She wondered, not for the first time since coming to Angela's, what it must be like to have other human beings living in your house whose name you probably didn't even know.

In the pearly light the dew-sodden grass looked like silver and, when she left the stone path and set out across the lawns for the lake, her skirt left trails of a darker green. How beautiful this is, she thought, and yet how different this tamed and ordered landscape is from the wild countryside where our grandparents live.

And so, lost in her own thoughts, she had taken a solitary walk by the lake. Perhaps it was the almost unnatural stillness of the water or the brooding reflections of the trees, but Josie realized she was being overtaken with melancholy. She turned away from the water.

However, still unwilling to return to the Hall, she sat for a while in the summerhouse. It was here that Angela had told her the day before that her parents were hoping she would make a match with a rich American. And then, almost immediately, Josie had discovered who that American was: Jacob Goodwright, who, in truth, she hardly knew, and yet she felt that she had known for years.

She wondered how this could be. Perhaps some people were so in tune with one another that they could be friends immediately, even if they had never met before. But Josie realized, sadly, that with Jacob she wanted much more than friendship. And that could never be. Angela was hoping to marry him, and if she did, she might lose Angela's friendship too, for she didn't know if she would be able to bear seeing him married to someone else.

I'd better go back, she thought. If Flora is up she'll be wondering where I am. Josie smiled as she remembered her sister's high spirits of the night before. And how beautiful she had looked as she danced in Forbes's arms. Forbes's intentions were clear. He obviously intended to marry Flora. As yet she was too young but Forbes would be patient. He would act correctly. And if that is what Flora wants I'm sure Father won't object, Josie thought.

On the way back to the Hall she remembered her conversation with Angela the day before, and she wondered how many men were employed to keep the grounds in such an immaculate condition. They were almost too perfect. If these were my gardens, she thought, I would keep one part completely wild. I would banish order, forbid weeding and let nature take its course.

While thinking this she paused at the entrance to the rose garden and acknowledged that a certain amount of order was pleasing to the eye. A young man was already working in the rose garden; he was sweeping the paths, no doubt making everything neat and tidy before any of the house guests emerge, Josie thought.

At that moment he saw Josie and stopped his work. He walked towards her. 'Good morning, miss,' he said.

Josie was surprised. She had already got used to the idea

that the servants in the Cavendish household were, like children, to be seen but not heard.

'Good morning,' she replied.

'I found this on the step,' he said as he dusted off his hands on his waistcoat and then reached into an inner pocket. 'Perhaps you would take it to the house for me.' He held something towards Josie and as she realized what it was her eyes widened.

'Of course, I will. Thank you.'

'You'll be able to find out who it belongs to.'

'Yes.'

The young man raised one hand to his bare head as if he were touching a cap and smiled. 'Thank you, miss. I'd best be off.'

He returned to his work, leaving Josie staring down at the blue satin evening bag she held in her hands. She wouldn't have to enquire who it belonged to. She already knew. Apart from the colour it was identical to hers. They had ordered them together, along with their evening gowns. One bag was ice blue and one pale green. Both bags were decorated with an identical pattern of seed pearls.

Josie tucked the bag into the folds of her shawl as she made her way back to the house. She wondered why the discovery of her sister's evening bag in the garden had made her so uneasy.

She had expected everyone to be tired this morning so the noise level, as she approached the dining room, surprised her. The minute she entered she saw that everyone was in a state of great excitement, as they filled their plates and settled down in gossipy groups. She imagined they would be discussing the dancing and the socializing of the night before.

The breakfast dishes were set out on the sideboard. Josie had already discovered that breakfast in a house such as this was quite different from the more homely meal served at home. Family and guests alike were left to choose from a bewildering display. Cold roast meats, poultry and even game pies all seemed to be deemed suitable, along with hot dishes of broiled herring, mutton chops, kidneys, bacon, sausage and scrambled eggs.

Josie didn't feel that she could face anything so substantial this morning so she helped herself to a slice of toast and a serving of honey. Once she was seated at the table a maidservant appeared as if by magic and offered her tea or coffee. She settled for tea. All the while she was looking round for her sister but she was nowhere to be seen. It was possible, of course, that Flora had been down early and had already left the dining room but Josie didn't think so.

As she nibbled her toast Josie glanced around at her fellow guests. She realized that none of the family was there. Perhaps it might be too early for the aged aunts, but neither of Angela's parents had appeared, nor her cousins, nor, in fact, Angela herself. She frowned. Surely this was unusual? Surely at least one of them ought to be here to greet their guests? And someone else was missing from the breakfast table: Jacob Goodwright.

But just at that moment she heard a familiar voice. 'Miss Walton, may I sit with you?' She looked up to see Ambrose Robson standing behind the chair next to hers.

'Please do.'

Ambrose put his plate down. It was a full-sized dinner plate. Josie stared at its contents. Bacon, kidneys, sausages, devilled chicken, herrings in mustard sauce, and scrambled eggs. Ambrose saw her expression and grinned good-naturedly.

'I hate going back and forth,' he said. 'It looks so greedy. And before you say anything, I know, so does this full plate. But only the people sitting next to me can see it.' He didn't sit. 'Wait a mo,' he said. 'I'm just going to get some muffins. If you can catch that girl's eye get me some coffee, will you?'

But the maidservant in question was already bustling forwards, and by the time Ambrose returned his cup was full. 'Here, I've brought these for you,' he said as he put one of the plates he was carrying down before Josie.

'But I don't—'

'Of course you do. These muffins are delicious. Go on, try one.'

Ambrose had hardly eaten a few mouthfuls when he turned and said, 'I hope you haven't lost anything valuable?'

'I beg your pardon?'

'Sorry, shouldn't talk with my mouth full. Nanny would be horrified.' He smiled and Josie thought he looked concerned when he said, 'Your jewellery, you know. Dreadful business. Fancy the dastard sneaking round the house at night when everyone was asleep and just helping himself.'

Josie shook her head in bewilderment. 'I'm sorry, but I don't know what you're talking about.'

Ambrose stopped with his fork halfway to his mouth and stared at her in astonishment. Then he lowered his fork to his plate and, taking up his napkin, he dabbed at his lips before continuing.

'My dear girl,' he said, 'you mean you really don't know what has happened here?'

'No, I don't.'

'There has been a robbery. My cousin's diamonds were stolen.'

'Oh, poor Angela!'

'Not just poor Angela. Poor everyone. Well, the young house guests, that is. Lady Cavendish and the older ladies seem to have been spared the indignity.'

'Indignity?'

'Of having some villain come into their bedrooms at night when, no doubt, most of them would be lying there with their hair in curling rags. But what am I saying? The thief must have visited your room too. Don't tell me you haven't noticed if anything is missing.'

'No, I haven't.'

'Did you put your trinkets away last night?'

'I always do.'

'And you haven't checked your jewel case this morning?'

'No.'

'Then your pearl drops . . . ?'

Josie's hand went to her ear. 'These earrings have a little box of their own. The necklace and earrings I was wearing last night are kept separately.'

'Are they valuable?'

'Compared to Angela's diamonds my necklace and earrings of pearls and amethyst are valuable only because they were a gift from my father.'

'So you would mind if they had been stolen?'

'Yes I would. But how was the theft discovered? Did

everyone wake up and immediately see that their jewellery was gone?'

'No. Those who are still sleeping don't even know yet. Lady Cavendish will have to tell them and then immediately reassure them that the jewels have been recovered.'

'What are you saying?' Josie was utterly confused.

Ambrose had resumed eating his breakfast and was obviously enjoying both the food and the drama of his tale. 'I know I should have told you at once before I set you worrying about your father's gift but that would have spoiled the story. I wanted to draw it out. Especially as there is a happy ending.'

'The thief has been caught?'

'Not exactly.'

'And yet you say the jewellery has been returned?' Josie could see that Ambrose would not be hurried. He was like an overgrown schoolboy and no doubt he had been delighted to find that Josie knew nothing about the robbery so that he could win her undivided attention.

'Yes. It seems as though the American is quite a hero.'

'Jacob? How is he involved? And where is he now?' Josie rose slightly in her seat and scanned the room anxiously. 'Has he been harmed?' She tried to conceal her agitation.

'No, not he. At this very moment he is closeted with my uncle, and the local constable, who arrived from the village just a short while ago. But earlier this morning Jacob Goodwright had my uncle roused from his bed to tell him that he'd chased and apprehended a thief.'

Ambrose reached absent-mindedly for one of the muffins he had brought for Josie and he frowned as he smothered it in butter. 'Mm, this is good,' he said when he'd taken a bite.

'You were telling me that Jacob got the jewellery back from the thief,' Josie prompted. She stared at the muffins on her plate, not wanting to let Ambrose see how concerned she was.

'That's right. My uncle asked Forbes to join them and Goodwright told them the whole story. And my brother obligingly told me.'

'But I still don't understand what happened.'

'Actually, I'm not sure if I do.' Ambrose signalled for the maid to fill up his coffee cup and, when she had gone, he continued. 'I mean, it must have been very late – the early hours of the morning, in fact – but Goodwright said he couldn't sleep and decided to take a turn about the grounds. That's when he saw a shadowy figure slinking away. He thought the man was behaving suspiciously.'

'So he challenged him?' Even though she knew Jacob was safe she found her heart beating faster.

'Not immediately. He says the blackguard sensed he was being watched and took off pretty smartly. So then our hero gave chase. When he caught up with him there was some sort of tussle and he managed to wrest the jewels back from him before the wretch escaped.'

Ambrose was still frowning as he gazed into the middle distance.

'What is it?' Josie asked.

'Well, I suppose he did the right thing, didn't he?'

'What do you mean?'

'To bring back the jewels.'

'Of course he did. What's wrong with that?'

'Well, Forbes told me that he would have tried to catch the fellow and given him a good trouncing, then secured him until the police arrived. Quite right. I would have done that too!'

'Would you?' In spite of her agitation Josie couldn't help smiling at the image that came into her mind of the slightly portly Ambrose tackling a hardened thief.

'Why are you smiling? Don't you believe me?'

'Oh, yes, I'm sure that's what you would want to do.'

He tilted his head on one side and stared at her for a moment and burst out laughing. 'You're right, of course. I would only make myself look ridiculous if I attempted such a thing. In fact, only someone big and strong like my brother would stand a chance of overcoming such a fellow. And, in any case, we have a happy ending. My aunt will preside in her sitting room after breakfast and all the young ladies will be able to go and reclaim their jewels.' He smiled. 'Now, can I get you something else?'

Without waiting for her reply, Ambrose, who had quite forgotten that he himself had by now eaten the muffins from Josie's plate as well as his own, rose and hurried to the sideboard to fill both his plate and hers. When he returned Josie was standing by her chair.

'Oh, are you going? What about these muffins?'

'Thank you but I really couldn't manage any more. And, you know, I think I'd better go and check my jewellery case, don't you?'

'Oh, of course.'

Ambrose nodded and sat down once more. Just as she was about to leave another of Angela's guests approached. The newcomer smiled hesitantly at Ambrose and said, 'Ambrose, can you tell me what on earth the uproar is about?'

'Good morning, Matilda, dear. Don't you know? Do sit beside me and I'll tell you all about it. But aren't you eating anything?'

While Matilda murmured that she wanted only a cup of coffee Josie slipped away. Before she reached the door Ambrose called her back. She turned to find he had hurried after her.

'What is it?' she asked.

'Did you drop this?' He held the evening bag out towards her. 'When Matilda sat down she saw it next to the chair.'

'Thank you.' She took the bag from him and tried to leave once more.

'I thought you must have dropped it,' he said. 'But it belongs to your sister, doesn't it?'

'Yes, that's right.'

'She was wearing blue and you were wearing green. But I noticed your bags were identical apart from the colour. My artist's eye, you know.'

'Thank you, Ambrose, but I must go. I'm anxious to check my jewellery. I told you.'

'Oh, of course.'

She noticed he was frowning slightly as he turned to go. He's probably wondering what I'm doing with Flora's evening bag at this time of the morning, she thought. But somehow I didn't feel like telling him that it had been found in the rose garden.

Josie was almost certain that no intruder had come into her room during the night. She had slept badly – in fact, hardly at all – and at one stage she had risen and gone to the window to gaze out over the moonlit gardens.

269

And now, when she opened the slim jewellery case, she discovered her necklace and earrings were safely inside, just as she thought they would be. So the thief had not come to her room. And surely he could not even have opened the door and peeped inside, for she was sure she would have awoken at the slightest disturbance.

She closed the case and decided it was time to seek out Flora.

The other girls were waiting on the landing outside Lady Cavendish's morning room. Flora was amongst them. Josie could not help thinking that her sister looked surprised to see her.

'Josie? Why have you come? Your necklace hasn't been stolen, has it?'

'No, it hasn't. Yours has, I take it?'

'Mm.'

'But what made you think that mine had not?'

'Oh, I don't know. I mean, I didn't know whether it had or not. It's just that you went down to breakfast quite calmly and you haven't bothered to come along here until now.'

'I went to breakfast because I knew nothing about the theft. I hadn't looked at my necklace and earrings since I put them away last night.'

'You put them away? Oh, clever you.' Matilda had joined them. 'Ambrose Robson told me that some of the girls hadn't even returned their jewels to their cases and even those who had had left them on the dressing table.'

'But I—'

Josie was about to say that she too had left the jewellery case on top of the dressing table when Flora interrupted her. 'So you could say they were to blame – just leaving things around for a thief to find?'

'No,' Josie said. 'Careless, perhaps, but no one would expect that a thief would be so audacious as to enter a house like this and wander at will from room to room while everyone was sleeping.'

'And it's almost as if he knew which rooms to go to, isn't it?' Matilda said.

'Why do you say that?' Flora asked.

'It's obvious, isn't it? It was a pretty daring thing to do and he would have to be quick. He couldn't waste too much time searching around.' Matilda looked thoughtful. 'I think he must have had an accomplice!'

'Whatever are you talking about?' Flora looked startled.

'Someone inside the house. I read all the latest sensational novels, you know, and that's what would have happened in a detective story.'

'Detective story!' Flora said dismissively. 'No wonder you talk such nonsense if that's the sort of book you read!'

Josie looked at her sister with surprise. Flora's tone suggested that she wasn't just teasing. There was some other emotion underlying the caustic tone and Josie had no idea what it was. 'No, Matilda is right,' she interjected. 'Many of those stories are based on real cases. I believe one of the most successful authors is a reformed jewel thief himself.'

'The more shame him!' Flora declared.

'Why do you say that?' Poor Matilda looked bewildered.

'To be making money out of crime.'

Fortunately Matilda took this as a joke and began to laugh but Josie knew her sister well enough to discern that something was upsetting her and was grateful that she had the sense to attempt to join in the laughter. She shot her a warning glance and turned to smile at Matilda.

'Your theory may be right,' she said. 'Has Mr Goodwright suggested that there was an accomplice?'

'Oh, I don't know about that,' Matilda said. 'Ambrose told me only that Angela's beau saw the sneak thief in the grounds of the house. He didn't mention anyone else.'

From the corner of her vision Josie saw Flora move back and take a seat on one of the chairs that had been put on the landing. She seemed to have lost interest. But Josie had one more question to ask.

'Angela's beau? Has Mr Goodwright proposed marriage, then?'

'Oh, I couldn't say.' Matilda smiled and her eyes gleamed as she moved closer and inclined her head towards Josie. 'I mean, I know I shouldn't gossip but Ambrose told me that Angela is very keen, and her parents are hoping that he will come up to scratch. And, of course, Sir Roger thinks him quite the hero for rescuing the Cavendish diamonds.'

'Of course.' Josie felt the need to change the subject. 'You didn't tell me, Matilda, did you lose anything in the robbery?'

'Oh, goodness, yes. I went straight up to my room after I'd drunk my coffee and discovered that they'd gone: necklace, earrings and matching brooch. Not as valuable as Angela's diamonds, of course. Only tourmalines and seed pearls. But the awful thing is they're not mine.' Here she paused and confided in a hushed tone, 'They belong to my older sister and she doesn't know I've borrowed them. Thank goodness for Mr Goodwright! But what about you? What did you lose?'

Josie was saved from answering when the door into Lady Cavendish's sitting room opened and the Curtis sisters came out. Immediately they were surrounded by the other girls, who questioned them about what had happened. Apparently there was a police officer in the room who was making a careful list of the jewellery set out on a table and questioning each guest as she went in.

'Oh, how exciting!' Josie heard someone exclaim.

'I do hope he is respectful,' another girl said.

'Absolutely. But I suppose he has to write some sort of report,' the elder Curtis girl said. 'He's taking names, making notes, that sort of thing. Oh,' she said suddenly, 'we were supposed to send someone else in.'

'I'll go,' said Matilda. And then, 'Oh, I'm sorry, Flora. You were here before I was.'

'Oh ... thank you,' Flora said. Josie thought she looked tense.

'Would you like me to come with you?' she asked her sister. After all, Flora was very young. No wonder she felt a little apprehensive in such a strange situation.

'No, I'm perfectly all right. You needn't wait for me.'

Flora raised her head and walked into the room.

Josie felt as though she had been dismissed. She went downstairs again, wondering what to do. The programme of entertainment seemed to have been abandoned. Indeed, some of the guests had decided to go home. Servants were carrying luggage down to the main hall and the sound of wheels on gravel could be heard as carriages were brought to the main entrance.

Angela had not made an appearance, and it was Forbes who was acting as host to see that the guests departed safely with feelings smoothed. He smiled when he saw Josie and paused from his duties long enough to say, 'Ah, Miss Walton, there you are. I have a message for you. Someone is waiting to see you in the rose garden.' Then he left her to escort a young woman to her carriage.

Josie had not really believed that the message had come from Jacob but, nevertheless, she was disappointed to see Ambrose rise from the bench and smile widely as she approached.

'I'm glad you came. I had to get out of that madhouse. Fortunately my elder brother said he didn't need me. Indeed, he was adamant that I get out of the way!'

Josie couldn't help smiling at his cheerfully self-deprecating manner.

'Have you recovered your jewels?' he asked. 'All done and dusted?'

Josie nodded. She couldn't have explained to herself why she didn't want to admit that she seemed to have been the only young guest who had not had her jewellery stolen.

'What do you think?' he asked as he held a sketch pad towards her. Only then did she notice his artist's paraphernalia set out on the bench. She looked at his drawing and saw that it represented the Chinese pavilion.

'It's very good.'

'Of course it is.' He laughed. 'But look closely.'

Josie did as she was bid and then she smiled. Ambrose had made a faithful drawing of the pavilion but, instead of setting it in the rose garden of Cavendish Hall, there was a snow-capped mountain – it looked like a volcano – behind it and the trees and plants surrounding it were distinctly foreign. The figures he had placed before the building were wearing formal and yet graceful wide-sleeved robes.

'Chinese ladies,' Josie said.

'From my imagination. I've only seen them in picture books. Perhaps I should go to China.'

'Before or after you go to Italy?'

'You decide. Where shall we go first?'

Josie sighed and shook her head.

'Ah, I see you're not in the mood for teasing this morning and I don't blame you. But it's not really teasing, you know.' His smile was wistful. 'If I thought you would accept me I would come to see your father along with my brother.'

'Forbes?'

'Yes. He woke up this morning more determined than ever to lay siege to your sister's heart. Look – there they are now.'

Josie turned to look in the direction in which Ambrose was pointing. Forbes must have finished helping with the departure of guests for now he was escorting Flora across the lawns in the direction of the lake. Even at this distance Josie could see that both of them were in high spirits. This morning Flora was wearing a light blue skirt and a fitted darker blue jacket. Her hair was pulled back and up, and tied with a wide blue ribbon; a plain unfussy style and yet on Flora the effect was ravishing.

'When are you leaving, by the way?' Ambrose asked.

'Tomorrow. Flora and I are going to our grandparents' inn at Moorburn. At least that was the plan, but I'm not sure whether we ought to go today. Perhaps we're no longer welcome.'

'Why do you say that?'

'Well . . . with the robbery . . .'

'Of course you're still welcome. Those guests who have gone have left because they wanted to. My aunt and uncle certainly didn't ask them to.'

'But Angela . . .' Josie didn't quite know how to say that her friend appeared to have been avoiding her.

Ambrose seemed to know what she meant. 'My cousin has had her birthday celebrations ruined. I don't imagine she's feeling very sociable at the moment.'

'No.'

'Would you like to sketch the pavilion?'

Josie was startled by the change of subject.

'I should like to see your work,' Ambrose added.

'Oh, very well.'

Josie agreed because she needed distraction. She allowed

Ambrose to direct her to the best position and settle her with his own sketch pad and pencils. She tried to banish the unanswered questions from her mind. She still had Flora's evening bag; she had slipped it into her pocket. When exactly had her sister dropped the bag? Had she been walking in the rose garden with Forbes either during or after the dance? But if that was the answer why was the bag empty? Where was her handkerchief, her comb, her scent bottle?

But drawing came naturally to Josie and, although her movements were driven by habit when she began, she was soon taken up with her work. So much so that she was unaware of the way Ambrose was looking at her with a mixture of envy and admiration.

As soon as Jacob could get away from Sir Roger and the police officer he set out to find Josie. He tried to work out what he was going to say. He was sure that he had managed to spin a believable tale to the others. He had been able to say with truth that the intruder was not one of the guests. And because he was a stranger here they had believed him when he had said that he had not recognized the man.

And now he acknowledged that the last part was not quite true. Because although he had never seen the thief before he had been shocked to discover that his features were familiar. An old memory had stirred. A face that had haunted him over the years had come floating up from his troubled past.

This could not be the man – he was too young – and yet there was a likeness. And that had disturbed Jacob enough to make him careless. He knew he had not turned and slipped away quickly enough at the station. Maybe the thief had seen him. That was not what he had planned.

For he had known he must do everything possible to protect Flora. Not because she deserved it, but because of Josie. By the time he came across her in the rose garden he still had not decided how exactly he was going to break it to her that not only was Flora a thief but she may be in danger. He was sure that that was now the case.

After trying all the public rooms of the house he decided to try the grounds, and so he found her in the rose garden. With

Ambrose. Jacob stopped and observed them. She was seated on one of the benches, her dark hair hanging forward over her face as she bent to draw something. Her concentration was intense, her movements quick and graceful. This would have been a moment to treasure if it had not been for the presence of the other man. Ambrose was standing beside her, but out of her light, as he watched her at work. They were so intent that it was almost as if they had entered a different world. Jacob knew that he could not talk to her now. He would have to wait until she was alone. He turned and walked away.

'Lamebrain!'

Vincent saw the blow coming and ducked, but his father was quicker and his clenched fist caught him flush on the jaw. Vincent staggered back across the kitchen and fell across the table and the remains of a roast joint of beef. He could feel the hot blood trickling from the corner of his mouth but, in spite of the pain, he was more concerned about the state of his clothes.

He righted himself groggily and twisted round to survey the damage. He groaned as much at the dark stain of grease on his coat as at the pain that was pounding through his head. But at least his dismay brought a twisted smile to his father's face.

'How could you let that happen?' his father snarled.

Vincent took a handkerchief from his pocket and dabbed at his lip. He winced. He could feel it swelling. The noise of raucous voices from the room beyond made it hard to think clearly. 'I wasn't expecting it,' he said.

It was the wrong thing to say. His father clenched his fists again and took a step towards him. The general stench of the place, combined with fear, made Vincent gag. He felt the bile rise in his throat and his head began to pound. He stumbled backwards until he found himself cowering against the wall.

'Divven't hit us, Da,' he snivelled, his terror making him regress to the voice and manner of the little lad he had once been.

His father shook his head. 'What hev I raised?' he said. 'Just look at you. I've sent you to school, I've educated you like a gentleman, I've lined yer pockets with silver and taught yer how to make even more. And the first time you get a chance to rise above petty thieving it all comes to nowt because you didn't stay on yer guard.'

'But how was I to know someone was following me? No—' He raised his arm to ward off the blow he thought might come when he saw his father's face suffuse with rage. 'Just listen, Da.'

'Go on.'

'I got away from the house – nobody challenged me. By the time I got to the station I was bound to think I was well clear, wasn't I? I mean, why follow me all the way there? Why not stop me before I left the grounds of the house?'

His father nodded. 'Aye, you've got a point.'

Vincent took heart from the thoughtful expression on the older man's face.

'And, most of all, why take the jewels the way he did? Lifting them from my pocket, I mean? That was the action of a practised thief.'

His father's expression grew stern again. 'We should hev thought of that. Perhaps I should hev warned you. But I never thought anyone would hev the nerve to take owt from a son of mine.' He shook his head. 'I divven't think it's anyone local.'

'No, Da, I know who it is and that's the puzzle. He isn't local but he isn't a thief either.'

'You saw him?'

'Just a glimpse.'

'How do you know it was the man who pushed you?'

'I can't say for sure – but why else had he come to the station? And why didn't he get on the train?'

'So who was it?'

'The American. The fellow that runs the mission. Jacob Goodwright.'

His father's eyes widened in surprise. 'They say he's rich as Croesus – at least his father is.' He paused and frowned. 'Do you think that's how they made their pile? Thieving? I've heard there's rich pickings in New York.' Then he shook his head. 'No, I divven't think so. Isaac Goodwright's a genuine merchant. He's known worldwide.'

'So do you think Jacob Goodwright took the jewels for himself or to give back to their rightful owners?' Vincent asked.

'You're assuming it was him, but I'm inclined to agree with you. And, you're right, there's a mystery here. But divven't fret, I'll get to the bottom of it. Here, sup this.' His father reached for a bottle of brandy and poured a generous measure into a pewter jug. 'Are you hungry?'

'Yes.'

'Sit down. I'll make you a sandwich.'

Vincent sat at the table and watched as his father sliced the bread and carved the meat. The older man's hands were filthy and Vincent had long since got used to a better way of life. A way of life made possible by his father. He was grateful for that, and grateful at this moment because the puzzle of why Jacob Goodwright had taken back the stolen jewels the way he had was keeping his father's mind occupied and away from Vincent's failings.

'Here, eat this,' his father said as he placed the sandwich on the table before Vincent. 'And then you can haddaway. Best be off to your mother in Yorkshire for a while. For if you only got a glimpse of him it's plain as hell he got a good look at you. Lie low until I send word it's safe to come back.'

They both fell silent for a while as Vincent ate his sandwich, then his father asked, 'Can you trust the girl?'

'Flora Walton? She won't say anything.'

'How can you be sure?'

'She's got too much to lose. Especially now.'

'Why's that?'

Vincent smiled. 'She's in love.'

'Be serious.'

'I am. I think she hopes to hitch up with Forbes Robson.'

'Well, well. Forbes Robson. No, I can see she wouldn't want to put that match in jeopardy. I wonder . . .'

Vincent could see what tack his father's thoughts were taking and knew it didn't bode well for Flora – or her father. He knew there was some reason why his father hated Captain Walton. He'd hinted that the man had once got the better of him and Vincent's father was good at bearing grudges.

And, whatever his father decided to do, there would be nothing that Vincent would be able to do about it. There would be no hope of opposing him. He had promised Flora that she would never see him again after tonight. But she must know by now that after what had happened that promise no longer meant anything. Not that it ever had, he acknowledged. Promises were easy to make, especially when you made them to a silly young girl. And just as easily broken.

'Are you finished?' his father asked.

'Yes.'

'Off you go then. And take the usual route. I divven't want anyone to see you leaving here. After all my efforts to make you a gentleman it wouldn't do for anyone to find out that you're Fox Telford's son.'

Chapter Thirteen

August

'Where are you going?'

Flora stopped with her hand on the latch. She glanced back over her shoulder and said impatiently, 'Out.'

'Flora, hinny, wait a moment.' Hannah put both hands on the table and began to push herself up.

Her granddaughter ignored her. She opened the door and hurried out. The door banged shut behind her and opened again. It began to creak backwards and forwards in the slight breeze.

Hannah continued to rise stiffly and painfully but the young woman who was peeling potatoes at the sink turned and raised a hand, gesturing for Hannah to sit down again. Then she wiped her hands on her apron and walked over to the door. She closed it and secured the sneck.

The older woman smiled a thank you, then sighed wearily as she sank back on to her chair. She rested her clasped hands on the scrubbed wooden table in front of her and shook her head. Ever since Flora and Josie had arrived at the inn, her younger granddaughter had been restless and moody. And the older girl had not been much better. Even the letters that had arrived regularly from Samuel, describing his and Annie's excursions, had not seemed to cheer her.

Josie had been subdued and thoughtful. Hannah had noticed that she would try to engage Flora in conversation now and then, and this usually resulted in Flora making some impatient reply and then flouncing out of the inn and staying out for hours on end.

Hannah knew that Flora had friends in the village; girls she had played with when she'd come to Moorburn as a small child, and that she was still welcome in their homes. But Hannah also knew that her younger granddaughter liked to be free from restrictions. Just like her mother.

At least Josie was usefully occupied most days with her drawing and painting. She would set off with her easel and all the paraphernalia that her father had bought for her. Hannah was amazed at Josie's talent and she had had some of her pictures framed to hang in the parlour.

Today Josie had gone out first. She had come down early, looking pale and drawn as if she hadn't slept and, after trying but failing to eat the bowl of porridge Hannah had placed before her, she had taken her sketching materials and slipped out quietly.

Hannah looked up and smiled ruefully at the comely young woman, her housemaid and companion, who had just come silently to the table with a tray bearing the teapot and two cups. 'Aye, sit down, pet,' Hannah said, and watched as the tea was poured. 'But I wish I knew what was the matter with those two lasses.'

After placing Hannah's cup on the table before her the young woman got her attention by touching her on the shoulder. Hannah looked up to see her companion smile as she placed one hand flat on her chest to cover the area of her heart and then put the other hand on top of it, making beating motions. At the same time she looked up towards the ceiling with big eyes in what Hannah could only describe as a soppy manner.

'What . . .?' Hannah said. And then she laughed. 'You think one of them might be in love?'

The young woman smiled and nodded.

'Do you mean Flora? That would explain the moods. But she's only a bairn.' However, even as she said the words she remembered that Flora's mother had imagined herself in love with Ralph Lowther at about the same age.

But the question had brought a new expression to the young woman's face. She looked as though she was considering the matter. Then she pursed her lips and her brow puckered as if to say 'perhaps'.

'Josie, then?' Hannah asked.

Her companion grinned and nodded.

'Well, I never, my sensible little Josie,' Hannah said. 'And that would explain the pale face and the sighs, I suppose. You know, Betty, I think you may be right. Now fetch two of those currant scones from the cooling tray. You and I deserve a little treat.'

The two women sat with their tea and scones in companionable silence. Hannah could hear the ticking of the old clock, the crackling of the fire and the purring of the mother cat. She reflected, as she often did, what a shame it was that Betty could hear none of these comforting sounds.

She thought back to the day Samuel Walton had brought the strange little lass to the inn. It was Christmas Day and, because Samuel wanted to get back to his family, it had been very early in the morning. Hannah and Jack had barely finished their breakfast. Jack, easy-going as always, had left Hannah to deal with his son-in-law and he'd gone to the cellar to check the barrels.

The kitchen had been warm and full of the comforting smells of roasting meat. The lass had sniffed appreciatively and looked around with a sort of half-starved look that had gone straight to Hannah's heart.

At first she'd thought the girl was overawed by her circumstances. She sat at the table without uttering a word. But Hannah noticed how the lass watched carefully, following the movements of their lips, when someone spoke.

Samuel explained that Betty was deaf – and therefore she had never learned to speak properly. But that, nevertheless, she had all her wits about her and might prove a grand help to Hannah if only she would take her. He offered to pay for her keep.

Hannah refused this offer. She told Samuel that the girl could earn her keep by working and, furthermore, she wouldn't be expected to work for nowt. But there was one condition. She had to know why he'd brought her to Moorburn and if the lass was honest.

And then Samuel looked grave and said he couldn't guarantee that Betty might not have resorted to thieving in order to survive, and the reason he had brought her here was to get her away from such a life – and from someone who might harm her.

So it had been with misgivings that Hannah agreed to take Betty. Samuel promised to find somewhere else for her if she didn't behave herself. Neither of them had noticed that while they were talking the girl had begun to cry until the sobs and sniffs became too loud to ignore.

'What is it?' Samuel asked.

The lass wiped the tears from her face with the corner of her shawl and made a writing motion with her hand. Hannah understood what she wanted and got a notepad and a pencil from the dresser drawer.

A moment later Samuel read the words the girl had written and looking straight at her he mouthed his words slowly and clearly. 'Tom will be all right,' he said. 'He wants you to be safe. You must try to be happy, for his sake.'

And that was all Hannah had ever learned about the girl's past life. That there was someone called Tom, who obviously cared for her. And she for him. Hannah had never thought it right to ask – that would have been prying – and the girl had never offered any information. But she had settled in uncomplainingly and worked hard.

Samuel had found other ways to help: gifts of fine cloth for Betty to make herself new clothes, and parcels of books. For although the lass couldn't speak she could read and write.

And she had certainly made a difference to Hannah's life. She'd watched and copied and learned until she could have managed the house and the kitchen by herself. She even helped Jack in the inn sometimes. There'd been one or two incidents: a fool or two who'd thought it grand sport to mock her. But Jack gave them short shrift and, no matter how good a customer the fellow might be, he was banned from the Bluebell Inn, the best hostelry for miles around, until he'd learned better ways. Hannah was proud of her husband for that.

But straight away, it seemed, Jack had realized that although Betty might be dumb, she was no dummy. He'd even taught her how to tot up the accounts and was pleased to relinquish some of the burden. Just as I have been myself, thought Hannah.

'Aye,' she murmured softly as Betty rose to gather up their empty cups and plates, 'she's a grand lass. I divven't know what I'd do without her. She could never take Effie's place in my heart, of course, and yet she's like a daughter to me. Mebbes she's the daughter I should hev had . . .'

Betty had seen Hannah's lips moving and she touched her on the shoulder again and looked at her questioningly. Hannah shook her head. 'It's all right, pet,' she said, mouthing the words plainly. 'Just an old woman muttering to herself.'

To Hannah's dismay she felt the tears well up in her eyes. Betty immediately put both her hands, one on top of the other, over her heart and then gestured with them towards Hannah. The meaning was clear. The lass was telling her that she loved her.

Josie saw her sister coming up the hillside towards her. She stopped sketching and watched, waiting for the moment when the younger girl would notice her and then, no doubt, veer off, leaving the path to climb up and beyond the outcrop of stone that Josie had chosen as a vantage point.

She had brought her sketch pad and was attempting to capture a view of the village below. A sort of bird's-eye view, she thought, and she wondered what it would be like if she could really fly over the winding streets, the smoking chimney-pots, the lines of washing flapping in the breeze.

But it seemed that today Flora was not going to avoid her. She had stopped to wave and now she began to run faster and faster, even though the way grew steeper. By the time she arrived where Josie was sitting on a large, smooth-surfaced stone, she was out of breath and rosy-cheeked. She collapsed, laughing, at Josie's feet.

Josie surveyed her warily. Ever since they had come to stay with their grandparents at Moorburn, Flora had been uncharacteristically quiet. And, when they were forced to be together in their shared bedroom or at the table, she had been unresponsive and sometimes downright crabby.

Flora didn't speak at first. She rolled over so that she was lying on her back. She put her hands behind her head and closed her eyes as she lifted her face to the sun. Josie saw her breathe deeply and smile as if she were enjoying the sweet country air. How beautiful she is, Josie thought. And how different we are. She is so slight and fair, just like our mother, and I am more robust and dark like our father.

Josie wondered if Flora's present mood meant that they would be able to talk more openly about what had happened at Angela's birthday celebration. Most of all she would have liked a satisfactory explanation as to why her sister's evening bag had been found in the garden. She'd returned it to Flora before they'd left Cavendish Hall. Her sister had been packing and she'd thanked her and mumbled something about not realizing it was missing.

Unwilling to quiz her, Josie had been about to go when Flora had blurted out that perhaps it had been stolen along with her necklace and then the thief had dropped it. She hadn't looked up when she said this and Josie knew she was lying. But she still hadn't been able to bring herself to question Flora further.

Perhaps I'm frightened of what I'll hear, she thought now as she gazed down at the peaceful scene in the valley below.

'What are you thinking?'

She turned her head to find Flora staring up at her.

'Why do you ask?'

'You looked so serious just now. Is something the matter?'

In spite of Flora's apparently sympathetic smile Josie was aware of an undercurrent of tension. She sensed a challenge. Her sister was giving her the opportunity to ask questions and, at the same time, willing her to deny that anything was troubling her.

'No, nothing's the matter,' she said. 'I'm just a little tired.' And that was true. She wasn't sleeping well and, in fact, she realized she was most unwilling to sail into dangerous waters and risk the tempest of her sister's reaction.

'Not too tired to come with me to the Hall?' Flora asked.

'The Hall?' Josie frowned. She was confused.

Flora laughed and sat up. 'I mean Four Winds Hall. It's only a couple of miles away – three miles at the most.'

'But why would you want to go there?'

'To have a proper look, of course.'

'We've looked at it before.'

'From the outside.'

'Of course from the outside. It's been shut up for years.'

'But we often wondered about it, didn't we?' Flora got to her knees so that her face was almost level with Josie's as she sat on the rock. 'When we were children and Betty took us for walks across the moor top we would peer in at the windows, and imagine there were all kinds of treasures in there.'

'Pictures, books . . .' Josie smiled as she remembered.

'Beautiful clothes belonging to the family,' Flora added. 'Don't you remember how we would wonder about the family?'

'We knew that they'd gone to live in London,' Josie said. 'And they hardly ever came home to Northumberland. And we would wonder why.'

'You told me once that they must have forgotten about the house,' Flora said.

'Did I?'

'Yes – and then you said what if they'd forgotten the kittens and we both began to cry. Do you remember?'

'Mm. I don't know what made me think there were kittens in there.'

'But you said you'd heard them! Do you mean to say there weren't any, after all?'

Josie frowned. 'I don't think so. I think I just assumed that every house had kittens.'

Flora shook her head. 'But that's dreadful. You had me breaking my heart over something you just imagined!'

'But I really believed it at the time,' Josie said wonderingly. 'And, do you remember, we tried to persuade Betty to break a window so that we could go in and rescue the poor creatures and she almost had to drag us home? Poor Betty. What a trial we must have been to her.'

Flora looked thoughtful. 'I wonder how much of that nonsense she understood. I mean, you were looking at her and saying, "Puss, puss, puss." And I was meowing pitifully!'

'I'm sure Betty understood everything. And, what's more, if there really had been starving kittens in there she would have broken the window without our urging.'

They looked at each other and smiled, and Josie was

286

suddenly overcome by a surge of love for her younger sister. The unresolved questions that lay between them faded into the background as she contemplated these scenes from their shared childhood.

'Move over,' Flora said, and she got up and joined Josie on the sun-warmed stone. 'Do you ever wonder where Betty came from?' she asked when she had settled. 'I mean she was suddenly there, wasn't she? And yet I remember a time when she didn't live at the inn.'

'Me too. But we were just small children. I suppose we didn't question things.'

'My friends in the village told me that our father brought Betty to Moorburn,' Flora said.

'Really? When? I mean, when did they tell you?'

'Oh, just the other day. I'd never thought to ask before. But they say one Christmas, many years ago, he was seen getting off the early morning train with this ragged girl – and the girl was crying – and he took her to our grandmother. They think she must have been some sort of charity child he'd taken pity on. It sounds like the sort of thing he'd do, doesn't it?'

'I suppose so. Perhaps Grandma Hannah had told him she needed help and he thought he'd do two good turns.'

'But as Betty can't speak I suppose we'll never know the full story.' Flora leaned closer and rested her head on Josie's shoulder. 'He's a good man, isn't he?'

'Our father?'

'Mm.'

'Yes. He's kind and he's just.'

'And he loves us.'

Josie didn't know whether that was a statement or a question, but she answered, 'Of course he does.'

She could have added that she had always felt that he loved Flora even more than he loved her but she sensed that whatever was troubling her sister was near the surface again and she was unwilling to risk losing this moment of friendly intimacy. Besides, when she thought about it, she accepted that she had never minded that her younger sister had a special place in their father's heart. For she knew why.

Flora was the living image of their mother, the only woman

that Samuel had really loved. And for Josie too, this was enough to forgive the younger girl almost anything.

'So he would want me to be happy,' Flora murmured softly and Josie thought she knew what had prompted Flora's questions.

'Does this mean that you want to marry Forbes?'

'Yes.'

'Well, you have no need to worry. After all, apart from being a good and clever man, Forbes is amazingly wealthy. What sensible father could object to such a match?'

'Really? You think so?'

'Of course. Oh, but I think he may ask you to wait a year or two. After all, you are very young.'

'No! I don't want to wait. My father married my mother as soon as she was old enough; surely he won't object if I marry at sixteen!' Flora stood up and moved forward a little to stare down into the valley.

Josie was taken aback. Her sister had always been spirited and a little wild, wanting her own way, but Josie sensed there was something more to this.

'Do you . . . do you love Forbes so much? Are you anxious that he'll forget you if you have to spend time apart?'

'Of course not. He won't forget me. And of course I love him. But it's not just that.'

Josie was amazed at Flora's confidence in Forbes's intention, amused that her voice had faltered only a little when she had assured Josie of her own love for Forbes, and worried by the anxious look that had invaded her sister's eyes when she had finished speaking.

'What is it then?'

'Forbes has promised me that we can live in his house in London and I . . . I want to go there as soon as possible.'

'Oh . . . I see.'

But Josie didn't see. And she didn't think that Flora was being completely honest. Oh, it was easy enough to imagine that her sister would be attracted to a more fashionable life in London, but that in itself was hardly a reason to rush into marriage. It was almost as if there was something she wanted to run away from.

'And it won't be long now before Father returns from his holiday, will it?'

'I'm not sure. Did he and Annie ever set a date for their return? I thought they were simply going to travel for as long as the fancy took them.'

'Well, whenever Father comes home, Forbes has asked me to write and inform him. Then he'll come to see him and, oh, Josie, I just can't wait!'

Again Josie got the feeling that there was more at stake than simply wanting to be married as soon as possible. But before she could even work out how to question Flora, her sister's mood changed once more.

She turned to face her with a brilliant smile. 'Anyway,' Flora said, 'I came to ask you to come to the old house with me. To Four Winds Hall. Please say you will.'

'But my drawing materials . . .'

'Leave them under this overhang. Look, it's quite sheltered. And, in any case, it's not going to rain.'

'Isn't it?' Josie smiled at her sister's confident attitude.

'Oh, come on. It'll be just like when we were children.'

'All right.'

Josie closed her sketch pad and put it back in the beautiful burgundy wood artist's box that her father had given her, along with her pencils and charcoals, and she tucked the box away under the overhang of rock as Flora had bid her do.

She wanted to recapture the closeness of a few moments ago, and if going to peer in the windows of the old house was enough to please her mercurial sister then she would do it. By the time she straightened up Flora was running up the track ahead of her.

It was easy to see how the house had got its name. Standing on a rise overlooking the purple sweep of the moors it was indeed exposed to the elements. Many years ago there had been an attempt to plant a stand of trees on the north side of the house. They hadn't flourished and the prevailing winds had forced them to lean at an angle towards the buildings as if they were looking for shelter. The branches tapped and scratched at the windows and, whenever Josie saw them, she was always reminded of a scene in Emily Brontë's novel, *Wuthering Heights*.

Even now, on a bright sunny day, the place looked forbidding, and Josie didn't really blame the Lowther family for preferring their London home. She'd heard that the Lowthers were distant relatives of her grandmother. She wasn't quite sure how she'd come by this information – probably through village gossip – but, once, when she'd been quite small, she'd asked Grandma Hannah why they didn't go visiting.

The answer had been that the connection was way back and that two brothers had fallen out during the days of the Roundheads and the Cavaliers. Anyway, the families didn't keep in touch, especially now that the heir to the Hall had married the daughter of a rich London merchant.

Flora ran ahead across the rough grass and heather. Now and then she swerved sideways to avoid a craggy outcrop. And it seemed to Josie that the clouds high in the wide blue sky were also racing, their shadows speeding across the dramatic landscape.

And then Flora stopped and turned to face her. 'See?' she cried.

'What? What is it?' Josie asked when she caught up. She was out of breath.

'Look!' Flora flung one of her arms out in a wide arc towards Four Winds Hall. 'I told you!'

'Told me what?'

'We're going to have a proper look. Oh, don't you see?'

Josie sensed the excitement in her sister's voice and she looked at her face. Flora's eyes were sparkling as she nodded excitedly. So Josie looked again at the house. The sun was bright and she had to bring a hand up to shade her eyes. At first nothing looked different. The dull red sandstone of the house stood out clearly against the blue sky. The sun shone on the many windows. The windows . . . there was something different about the windows. Some of them were open.

And even as Josie took in the significance of this, a figure appeared in one of the windows on an upper floor and leaned out to shake a large white piece of cloth, a bed sheet. There were people in the house. Had the family returned?

Then Flora took her hand and tried to pull her forward. 'No,' Josie said as she grasped her sister's intention. 'We haven't been invited.'

Flora laughed. 'There's no need for that. There's nobody there yet.'

'But . . .'

'I found out yesterday. The master of the Hall is returning. His land agent has engaged some of the village women to prepare the house.'

'But we can't . . .'

'Yes we can. They're my friends. They'll let us in.'

Flora lost patience and let go of Josie's hand before taking off again. Josie hesitated for only a moment longer and then she too began to run, and as she did she began to laugh. 'Wait for me!' she called.

They arrived at the imposing entrance gates almost at the same time and, after pausing for only a moment, they walked up the short gravelled driveway hand in hand.

The old oak door was ajar and when they pushed it creaked like a door in a ghost story. They hesitated on the threshold, looked at each other with big eyes and then walked in.

They found themselves in a stone-paved entrance hall. It was lofty but not as grand as Josie had been expecting. Maybe that was because it was so gloomy. To one side there was a huge old fireplace, which once must have made visitors welcome with its crackling heat, but now the hearth was filled with the sad ashes of old fires. As her eyes became accustomed to the dim light Josie realized that the shadowy movement in front of the hearth was a young woman, little more than a girl, who was on her knees trying to clean out the grate.

The girl turned when she heard their footsteps echo on the stone floor. She pushed back a lock of hair with the back of her hand and managed to leave a sooty trail on her cheek. Pale sunlight filtered down from a many-paned window halfway up a massive oaken staircase and the girl peered at them through the dancing motes of dust.

'Oh, it's you, Flora,' she said. 'And is that Josie? Hev you come to lend a hand?' Her grin showed that she knew how improbable this would be.

Flora didn't even answer the question. 'Hello, Margery. Your mother said we could look around,' she said.

'Only because you pestered her. But gan on. There's no one

here but the women who've come up to clean. Mam and me sister, Hetty, are upstairs. They've started airing the linens – they smell that mouldy we might hev to take them home and wash them. And the whole place'll hev to be scrubbed through. This job is going to take us a month of Sundays!'

'Well . . .' Flora began to back away, 'Josie and I will leave you to get on with your work.'

'Oh, aye.' The girl laughed good-naturedly. 'Divven't offer to do owt!' She turned back to her task.

'Where shall we start?' Flora asked. And then, when she saw Josie's expression, she added, 'What's the matter? Why do you look so solemn?'

'Do I? It's just this is so sad, isn't it?'

'Sad?'

'Yes. Look around you. Those rugs . . . they're threadbare.'

'Yes, well, Margery's mother told me that the best things had been sent to the house in London years ago,' Flora said.

'And those old tapestries,' Josie continued. 'They must have been beautiful, once. Can't you imagine the rich colours? And now they're faded and dirty. And that chest . . . and the carved chair. They haven't been polished for years and once they must have shone and smelled of beeswax. Now the whole house just smells dusty and sad.'

Flora shook her head. 'I don't know how a house can smell sad. It just smells fusty to me. Now, come along do. Margery's mother told me yesterday that they can work only as long as the light lasts. If the sky clouds over they'll have to go. They're not trusted to light candles.'

As they wandered through the house they found some of the rooms completely empty while in others there were pieces of furniture that were probably too big or too unfashionable to warrant their removal.

'I wonder why the master is coming back now,' Josie said.

'They think he's going to sell the place,' her sister answered. 'His parents are dead and his wife won't hear of living here. And I don't blame her – not if they have a big house in London!'

Flora swept ahead again, occasionally stopping to smile at the village women as they swept and scrubbed and began to polish. These women like Flora, Josie realized, for all that she acts like a spoiled child. They've always liked her ever since Grandma Hannah allowed us to totter down to the village on our own for an hour or two. My sister has a gift for attracting people. Maybe it's because she's so beautiful.

So Josie trailed behind Flora as they went from room to room and, eventually, the younger girl declared herself disappointed.

'I suppose it's because I've been wondering about this place for so many years,' she said.

She plonked herself down on an old velvet chaise longue that had been placed in an alcove on the first-floor landing. It was an unwise thing to have done. As she sat down forcefully, clouds of dust rose and set them both coughing. Flora leaped to her feet again and began to shake the skirts of her pretty summer dress.

'Disgusting!' she exclaimed when she had caught her breath. Her eyes were streaming. 'How could anyone let a house get into such a state? It's a scandal!'

Josie suddenly had a vision of a house-proud Flora some years in the future. When she was married to Forbes and no doubt mistress of several mansions, each dwelling would be both fashionable and immaculate. And Forbes would be happy to indulge his young wife.

And what of me? Josie thought. Will I be the spinster sister who is allowed to visit the fashionable couple and bask in reflected wealth and glory like a young woman in one of Miss Austen's novels? Or will I lead an altogether more exotic existence, travelling and painting and bringing gifts from strange lands for my growing brood of nieces and nephews?

Josie allowed herself to contemplate what life would be like for her if she married Forbes's younger brother, Ambrose. But, even though she knew he would make a kind and considerate husband and, furthermore, he would be far from conventional, which would suit her independent disposition, she knew that she could never marry him. Liking someone would never be enough for her. She would resign herself to remaining single if she could not marry a man she loved.

And without warning Jacob's image appeared before her. She closed her eyes but this only made the image more intense.

How can it be? she wondered. How can I love a man I've only just met? A man I've barely spoken to. I hardly know him and yet I cannot rid myself of the notion that he has long been part of my life.

'Josie! Come here!' Flora's excited tone roused her from her reverie, and Jacob's image faded.

'What is it?'

'Look what I've found.' Flora had wandered away and opened a door at the end of the landing. Even as she spoke she vanished into the room beyond.

Josie followed her and found herself in a long gallery that led to another wing. There were pictures on the walls but she couldn't see them clearly, for the curtains were drawn at every window. Flora hurried from window to window, opening the curtains.

'When we were children you always said there would be beautiful pictures in the house,' she said excitedly. 'Well, here they are! Oh . . . they're all of people.'

'They're portraits,' Josie said. 'I think they're family portraits.'

'Look at the clothes some of them are wearing,' Flora said. 'They look like fancy dress costumes.'

'No, it's not fancy dress. Some of these portraits are very old. Those would be the proper clothes of the day. I think we're looking at generations of the Lowther family,' Josie said.

The sisters began to walk along, looking at each painting in turn. They were of different sizes, some very small, of round-faced children, and one or two very large with whole family groups and the dogs and sometimes horses as well. Josie soon decided that none of this was great art. The Lowther family had probably employed several generations of the sort of jobbing portrait painters who travelled the length and breadth of the land recording the existence of people who would otherwise live and die unheard of and important to no one but themselves.

'Look!' Flora shrieked suddenly. 'That old woman looks a little like Grandma Hannah. But what a funny tall-crowned hat she's wearing. It's like a witch's hat, except it's flat on top.'

Josie looked at the painting of a serene apple-cheeked old woman in a full-skirted, plain, dark-coloured gown with a wide white collar. 'That's the sort of clothes Puritan women wore,' she said. 'This branch of the Lowther family must have been Roundheads.'

'Well, whatever they were, you can see that Grandma Hannah is related to them. And have you noticed how many of them have such bright fair hair? Oh!'

'What is it?'

Flora didn't answer. She was staring at the portrait of a young girl in a flowing high-waisted gown of green velvet. The low square neckline was trimmed with fur, as were the sleeves. One of her hands was resting on the head of a long-legged hound. But the striking aspect of the portrait was the girl's abundant fair hair, which cascaded down over her shoulders, free from all restraint except for a circlet of tiny white flowers and dark green leaves.

'She looks like someone from a fairy tale,' Flora breathed. 'No . . . not a fairy tale . . . a princess from an old legend like "The Knights of the Round Table".'

She does indeed, Josie thought. But the true cause for wonder was that it could have been a portrait of Flora herself. She wondered if her sister realized this as she gazed so rapturously at the girl and the hound. 'She's beautiful, isn't she?' And Josie smiled at her next words. 'Of course I realize that she looks like me – that there's a family resemblance – but don't you think she's a little like our grandmother too?'

'Perhaps.'

'But of course she is. Don't you see? Grandma Hannah's hair is faded now, but it must once have been nearly as bright as that. And her eyes are still as blue, aren't they? And although she's old and wrinkled, her face is still heart-shaped, just like this girl's. She must have been, well, not exactly beautiful, but quite pretty once.' Suddenly Flora looked sad. 'It's dreadful, isn't it, that we have to grow old? Do you think Grandpa Jack remembers how pretty his wife once was?'

'Of course he does. I'm sure that in his eyes, she's still beautiful.'

'Really?'

Josie nodded. For in truth she was fighting tears just as Flora was.

'Well, I know one thing for sure!' Flora exclaimed.

'What's that?'

'I'm never going to have my portrait painted.'

'Why ever not?'

'Because when I got older, I wouldn't be able to bring myself to look at it for fear of being reminded of what I looked like when I was young. It would break my heart.'

Suddenly Flora hurried to the windows and began to close the curtains again. Josie stayed where she was, grateful that the resulting shadows obscured the tears that were now streaming down her cheeks. She wasn't crying at the idea of growing old and beauty fading. It was the family likeness through the ages that had unsettled her.

First of all the picture of the old woman in Puritan garb who looked like their grandmother as she was today, and then the girl, probably from medieval times, who, as Flora said, could have been their grandmother when she was young; or Flora as she was today. But most of all, the picture had reminded her of their mother, the mother who had died on the night Flora was born, but who would never truly die as long as Flora lived. Josie wondered why it didn't break her father's heart every time he looked at his younger daughter.

'Let's go,' Flora said at last. 'I don't want to see any more.'

'There's not much more to see,' Josie said, 'except the attics. Don't you want to go up there and see if there's any hidden treasure?'

'Don't be childish, Josie.' But Flora paused and Josie saw the speculative look in her eyes. 'Oh, all right, then,' she said. And she whirled out of the room and along the landing until she found a set of stairs that led to the top floor.

There was no hidden treasure, of course. Josie hadn't expected there to be. Some of the attic rooms contained iron bedsteads and simple chests of drawers that told her that they had been used for servants in more recent times. Others held broken furniture: chairs that must have been placed there waiting to be mended but had been forgotten about, a table with one leg missing and a little dressing table marred by a scorch mark. Josie could imagine the careless moment when a pair of curling tongs had been placed there.

Flora was beginning to look dispirited again. The escapade had appealed to her and probably managed to take her mind off whatever had been troubling her, Josie thought. But now the younger girl had wandered over to the window and was gazing out across the countryside.

'Why do you think the Lowther family have neglected this house so badly?' she asked without turning her head.

'I can't imagine. Perhaps they simply don't like living here.'

'It looks so grand from the outside that I've always believed it would be quite splendid inside. Well, we both did, didn't we? And yet it looks as if it hasn't been cared for for years and years.' Flora leaned her head against the window and then suddenly she straightened up and appeared to stare out intently. 'Oh,' she said softly.

'What is it?'

'Come here . . . look . . . way over there beyond that ridge.' She placed a finger on the windowpane and took it away again quickly when she realized how dusty the glass was.

'What can you see?' Josie asked.

'The old ruined cottage. Remember Grandma Hannah forbade us to play there when we were children? She terrified us with tales of wild beasts having a den there!'

Josie smiled. 'I'm sure that was only because she didn't want us to fall or have stones tumble down on us.'

'Shall we go and look at it now? On the way home?'

'Well . . .'

'We won't go inside if you think it's dangerous.'

Flora didn't wait for an answer and Josie followed her out of the room and down two flights of stairs. Her sister called goodbye to her friends from the village and then sped out into the sunshine.

Ralph Lowther, now Sir Ralph since the death of his childless uncle, oversaw the unloading of his luggage from the guard's van of the train and sought out the stationmaster to find him a trap. But once his cases and boxes were loaded, he paid the driver and told him to set off along the country road. He wouldn't be coming with him because he'd decided to take the short way up the hill out of the village and across the moor. It was only about four miles as the crow flew and he needed the exercise after the long journey from London, which had started not long after dawn.

He knew he couldn't hope to pass through the village unnoticed and he walked as quickly as he could, giving no more than a curt nod to anyone who recognized him. And, although he hadn't been back to Moorburn for many a long year, there were plenty who did.

No doubt every family in the surrounding countryside will know before morning, he thought. They'll know that I'm back and they'll all be wondering why and speculating that I'm probably going to sell the estate at last.

For it wasn't just Four Winds Hall that Ralph Lowther owned. There were acres of land, all rented out to farmers, and providing him with enough income to make him feel not totally dependent on his rich wife to maintain his property, and to stop it from being a drain on his London business.

It was good to be out in the country air. Here in Moorburn the smoke rising from the chimneys was soon blown away over the hills, not like the cloud of soot that sometimes shrouded the city. And the farmyard smells were nothing compared to the stench of the part of London near the docks where Ralph worked in his father-in-law's head office. But at least the new home Caroline and he had just bought in Kew benefited from sweeter air.

The garden was so large that you could almost imagine you were in the country, Caroline said. Just perfect for the children when they came along. Poor Caroline. She still believed she was going to be a mother but, as the years went by, her hopes were fading. And Ralph's too. At least his parents were no longer alive to grieve over his childless state. There was only Ralph to care that his line of the Lowthers was going to die out and, therefore, as there probably wasn't going to be anyone to inherit Four Winds Hall, he'd decided he might as well sell it.

He'd asked Caroline if she would like to come with him but she'd said there was no point. She trusted him to make all decisions regarding any furniture or paintings he might wish to salvage. She was far too polite to express a hope that he would not bring anything from the Hall to their beautiful new home but he could see it in her anxious expression.

And she didn't exactly tell him that she'd never liked the place but Ralph could remember even now her shock when her parents had brought her for a visit as a young girl before they were married.

'How old-fashioned everything is,' she'd said wonderingly. 'And how inconvenient.'

They'd never been here together after they'd been married, and Ralph's necessary visits to see that everything was kept in order became fewer and fewer. There was nothing to draw him to Moorburn. Not since . . . but he always repressed the thoughts of what might have been. If only he'd realized in time that his childhood friendship with Effie had grown into something deeper.

So this would be his last visit to Moorburn. Soon he would hand over the keys to the agent from Hexham and leave everything in his hands. The house would be cold, he thought. He'd not warned them he would be arriving today so no fires would have been lit. Even as he realized this he found that he was passing the opening of the short track that led to the Bluebell Inn. He paused for a moment. Should he seek a comfortable bed there with Hannah and Jack?

Hannah had been kind to him when he was a child, left to run wild by his neglectful parents. But, no, how could he stay with them? It would be too painful to sleep in the home of his lost childhood companion. He hadn't seen Hannah since he'd heard that Effie had died in childbirth. There would be nothing they could say to each other now. Surely there would be kindling and logs in one of the outhouses. He would make his own fire.

Perhaps it was the thought of this fire that made him remember other times he had kneeled at a hearth; a much more humble hearth than any of those in Four Winds Hall. So, without even realizing that he had made a decision, he found himself veering off the rough track and heading uphill at an angle. He was going in the direction of the ruined cottage. He would visit it one more time.

* * *

'So those are the wild beasts Grandma Hannah meant. But they're adorable!'

Flora was just about to hurry forward when Josie put a hand on her arm to restrain her. 'Don't go near them,' she said. 'They could be vicious.'

'Vicious? Those sweet little kittens?'

'They're not like ordinary cats. They're feral, completely wild. And, besides, I'm sure their mother will be nearby and she won't be pleased with anyone who goes near her babies.'

'Oh.' Flora looked disappointed. 'I would so like to have stroked them, or sat with them on my knee.'

'Well, don't,' Josie said. 'But there's nothing to stop us looking at them. Oh, how I wish I had my sketch pad with me.'

'Would you like me to run and get your drawing things for you? They're not far away.'

'No, it's all right. I don't think we should stay too long. Neither of us has been home since breakfast time and I don't like to worry Grandma Hannah. Besides, surely you must be hungry?'

'As a matter of fact I am.'

Flora's smile was wide and genuine, and Josie guessed that her sister had managed to push whatever was troubling her to the back of her mind for the moment. She was still so much a child. And in spite of her headstrong ways she was vulnerable. Josie had always felt protective towards her younger sister; perhaps that was why her senses were so attuned to Flora's moods. Suddenly Josie wished their father would come home.

'My friends in the village say the last person to live here was a witch and she burned the place down when she was making one of her spells in a cauldron over the fire,' Flora said as she looked around the ruined cottage. 'Perhaps those kittens are descended from her familiar and they don't want to leave the place that was once home.'

'Maybe that's so,' Josie said, and she pretended to examine the kittens closely. 'No, perhaps not. They're not black.'

Flora stared at her with wide eyes and then she smiled. 'You're teasing me.'

'Of course I am. Those cats are wild cats who've taken advantage of the ruin for a bit of shelter. And I don't believe in witches. The poor old woman was probably just a lonely old soul who'd annoyed the villagers. You know how stories can be exaggerated as they're handed down through the years.'

'I suppose so.' Flora sighed. 'But it's strange that no one ever wanted to live here again. I mean, it would have been easy enough to put it in order.'

'Perhaps the local people felt guilty.'

'Why should they feel guilty?'

'For allowing whatever it was to happen. For standing by when the poor old woman burned the house down.'

Flora shivered. 'Do you believe in ghosts?' she asked suddenly.

'No I don't,' Josie retorted sharply. 'So please don't tell me any of your friends' stories about the old woman haunting the cottage.'

'I wouldn't do any such thing.' Flora looked indignant. 'Because I haven't heard any such stories. No, I suddenly had one of those moments. A sort of shiver. I suppose it was what people mean when they say they felt someone walking over their grave. But it wasn't quite like that.'

Josie wanted to tell her sister not to be silly. Not to give way to foolish imaginings just because they were standing in a ruined cottage that had a sad history. But she saw that Flora was standing quite still, her attitude almost trancelike as she appeared to be listening to something.

'What is it?' Josie asked. 'What can you hear?'

Flora didn't answer at first and then she said, 'I'm not sure . . . voices . . .'

'Outside? Do you think someone is approaching the cottage?'

Josie half glanced behind her but her sister shook her head.

'No . . . not outside . . . I thought I heard someone – a woman . . . perhaps just a girl . . . it sounded as if she was calling for someone . . . then she started to cry. It sounded over there.' She nodded towards the doorway that led into a tiny room at the back of the cottage.

Sending a half-frightened smile in Josie's direction, Flora walked towards the open doorway. If there had ever been a door it had long vanished. Flora rested her hand on the old stone of the door jamb and, leaning forward, she peered into the dimness beyond. 'No, there's no one here,' she said after a moment and she turned and smiled at her sister. Josie thought her smile was rather sad. 'But I'm almost sure I heard something . . . Didn't you?'

Josie was perplexed. Flora had never been fanciful and her earlier talk of witches had been inspired by her friends in the village rather than belief. So now what was she imagining? That she could hear ghosts?

'No, I didn't hear anything,' Josie said. 'Just the wind.'

'Perhaps that was it,' Flora said. 'But do come and look. What a sweet little room.'

Josie joined her sister in the doorway and then, as their eyes became accustomed to the shadowy light, they entered the room.

'I hardly think it's sweet,' Josie said. She stared around at the earthen floor, liberally covered with rabbit droppings, the window, long since bereft of glass, where a piece of ancient canvas flapped, and the cold hearth where an old dented cooking pot was the only sign that someone had once lived here.

'Look, a witch's cauldron!' Flora exclaimed.

'No, some wandering tinker probably left it here,' Josie told her.

'Oh, I know that. But it's nice to make believe sometimes, isn't it? Like we did when we were children, remember?'

Josie almost said that that wasn't so very long ago, but Flora might not have appreciated being reminded of how young she still was. Not now that she considered herself almost old enough to be married.

Before Josie could think of a suitable reply Flora exclaimed, 'I know! Let's bring a picnic here tomorrow!'

'Here?'

'Oh, do say yes. You can bring your sketch book and draw the kittens. It will be fun.'

Josie didn't think it would be fun. The cottage was dark and dank and depressing. She couldn't understand why Flora was so taken with the place. But it was obvious that Flora meant to have her way. And if she agreed to the plan perhaps they would grow close again and Flora might be more likely to answer some questions.

'Well, perhaps,' she said. 'If the weather holds. But now we must go back to the inn.'

The wind had risen and, in spite of the bright sunshine, Ralph knew that he would have to make a fire of some sort if he was going to be comfortable in his childhood home tonight. He wondered if the village women would still be there when he arrived. If they were he could always persuade one of them to light some fires and prepare some kind of meal for him. His goods and chattels would have arrived by now and there was a box of provisions. He wouldn't go hungry.

The old cottage was in sight, and he remembered the picnic meals that he and Effie had eaten there – all provided by Hannah. Except for the bottle of brandy-wine that time . . . neither Hannah nor Jack knew that Effie had helped herself to that.

And then, as he drew nearer, he heard Effie call his name. He stopped in his tracks and his heart lifted. She was waiting for him there. But how had she known he was coming home today? He began to run towards the cottage. The old stones seemed to be glowing in the summer light. For a moment the sun shone even more brightly and his eyes were dazzled. He couldn't see where he was going.

Then a cloud passed across the sun and the light faded and his reason returned to him. Effie could not possibly have called to him, could she? Not from this world. But as Ralph stood and looked at the ruined building he became aware that the air was still. Even the winds that always worried away across the moor top had grown quiet as if they were waiting for something to happen.

As he looked at the cottage a slender figure stepped out from the deep shadow of the doorway and the air brightened again. Ralph gazed at the bright-haired girl and his chest constricted. He couldn't breathe. Had he died? Was that it? Had Effie truly called him and here on the hillside had he answered the call? Were they to be together at last?

Chapter Fourteen

Josie followed Flora out into the sunlight and almost collided with her. Her sister was standing quite still and, until Josie's eyes adjusted to the light, she couldn't see why.

'Who are you?'

She heard the man's voice and, squinting a little, she put up a hand to shade her eyes. She looked beyond her sister to see a stranger standing there. He was tall, with very fair hair, and he was dressed like a gentleman, although there was something about him, a sinewy strength, that suggested he would be just as at home in the hills as in the city. Josie had assessed all this with her artist's eye in the instant before she realized that the lines of his handsome face were etched with shock.

'Flora,' she heard her sister answer his question. 'But who are you?'

Before he could answer he caught sight of Josie and his gaze shifted. He seemed to relax a little. Or, if not relax, at least to have conquered some of the tension that had kept him riveted a moment before.

'And you?' His question was directed at Josie.

'I'm Flora's sister, Josie.'

'You're sisters?'

He looked from one to the other. He thinks we don't look very much alike, Josie thought. 'Yes. Flora and Josie Walton.'

'Captain Walton's daughters?'

'You know my father?'

'We've never met.'

'Then how . . . ?'

'I know your grandparents,' he said quickly. 'In fact, Hannah Dixon is a distant relative of mine.'

Flora said suddenly, 'You must be Sir Ralph Lowther!'

'And how do you know that?' the stranger asked. Josie noticed that whenever he looked at Flora his blue eyes seemed to brim with wonder and pain.

'We've just been to Four Winds Hall – to look around. Oh . . .'

At last Ralph Lowther smiled. It was almost as if he was coming alive again after being in a trancelike state, Josie thought. And then wondered at herself for being so fanciful. It must have been Flora's talk of witches and ghosts, she thought. And then Sir Ralph arriving on the scene so unexpectedly.

'You've been to the Hall?' he asked.

Josie stepped forward. 'Flora is friendly with some of the women who are working there today,' she said. 'We've always been curious about the Hall, ever since we were children.' It was her way to be honest and, instinctively, she knew that this was the best way to deal with Ralph Lowther.

'So you decided to have a look?'

'I hope you don't mind.'

He smiled. 'What did you think of the place?'

Flora had left Josie to deal with the awkward situation but now she burst out, 'Why have you left it to moulder away like that?'

'Flora!' Josie said. And then, 'I'm sorry.'

But Ralph Lowther shook his head. 'It's all right. The criticism is justified. Even as a boy I knew my home was not like the homes of my school friends.'

'But why? Were you poor?' Flora asked.

Josie clutched her sister's arm but Ralph Lowther saw the movement and sensed her embarrassment. He gave her a reassuring smile. He didn't seem to mind Flora questioning him like this – as if they knew each other, as if they had known each other for some time, in fact. And, furthermore, as if they were equals rather than a grown man and a girl who was not quite a woman.

'No, we weren't poor. But neither were we as rich as my

mother would have liked. And any money we did have she spent on travel, when she could, rather than the upkeep of the Hall.'

'But you own the Hall now,' Flora said.

'I have done since my parents died some years ago.' He raised a hand when it looked as though Flora was about to question him further. 'But long before they died I did exactly what my father had done before me. I married a girl who did not want to live here. In fact she never has lived here.'

'Why is that?' It was Josie who asked the question, encouraged by the easy intimacy that seemed to have developed between the three of them.

'Because, after my fine education, it was decided that I should work for her father, a city tea broker, rather than languish in the country collecting rents from my farms.'

'City?' Flora asked.

'London. We live in London.'

'Do you?' Flora smiled radiantly. 'I'm going to live in London – when I'm married, that is.'

'Married?' Ralph Lowther looked surprised. 'You are going to be married?'

'Well, not immediately,' Flora said. 'But Forbes – Forbes Robson, that is – is going to ask my father if he can court me as soon as I'm old enough.'

'I see.'

Ralph Lowther's easy manner suddenly changed but Josie couldn't fathom what had made him suddenly become so distant. Well, not distant, perhaps, but certainly distracted. And Flora – she had lost her smile also. She had obviously expected some sort of reaction when she had announced that her intended suitor was Forbes Robson. She would know very well that a man of such immense wealth would be known in London, especially by a fellow merchant.

But, getting no reaction, she turned to Josie and said, 'Perhaps we ought to go, now. Grandma Hannah will be wondering where we are.'

Josie raised her eyebrows. Since when had Flora worried about their grandmother? But she smiled and agreed.

'Wait a moment,' Ralph Lowther said. 'How is Hannah? I hope she's well.'

'Yes, she's well,' Josie replied.

'We are cousins, you know,' he added.

'Very distant cousins, I think,' Josie said.

'That's true. But she was kind to me when I was a boy.'

'Was she?' It was obvious that Flora was intrigued.

'Yes. My poor mother was forgetful. If my father was away she would forget to feed herself – and me too.'

'But surely you had servants? I mean a cook . . . ?'

His smile was rueful. 'I think they took advantage of the fact that my mother didn't seem to care.'

His expression became bleak, and Flora suddenly took both him and Josie by surprise by moving forward and taking his hand. 'Oh, poor Sir Ralph,' she said. 'I'm glad that Grandma Hannah was kind to you.'

Josie thought the man was going to faint. His face lost all colour and he gripped Flora's hand so tightly that eventually she frowned and snatched it away. 'We must go,' Flora said. 'And thank you for not minding that we visited the Hall.'

He seemed to make a great effort to pull himself together. 'You must come there again. You and your sister.'

'Perhaps,' Flora said. 'Come along, Josie.'

When Josie came down the next morning there were two letters on the kitchen table. Both were for her. She examined them and put them aside without opening them because Betty had placed a bowl of porridge on the table and now she gestured to her that she should sit and eat.

'Aye, eat your breakfast, Josie,' her grandmother said from her rocking chair by the fire. Grandma Hannah was drinking tea and Josie thought she looked tired. It was as well she had Betty to help her, she thought.

As she spooned a dollop of black treacle into her porridge she noticed that Betty was preparing sandwiches. Before they'd gone to bed Flora had mentioned that she wanted to go out sketching with Josie the next day. She hadn't mentioned where they would be going, and Josie had been torn. She couldn't understand why Flora wanted to return to that dismal place –

no matter how sweet the kittens were – but she wanted to keep on good terms with her sister so she hadn't objected. Neither had she told her grandmother where they were going. After all, whatever Hannah's objections might once have been, she didn't think there was any danger in the old building now.

Almost before she had finished her porridge Betty had placed toast and marmalade before her and a large mug of tea. When the young woman took Josie's empty bowl to the sink she leaned over to look out of the window and then she turned and frowned and shook her head. Josie knew what she meant. The sky was dark and unpromising, but although a slight breeze was causing the windowpanes to rattle, it hadn't started to rain.

'It's not the day for a picnic,' Hannah said, 'but it won't be any use trying to dissuade Flora. Once she's made up her mind there's no shifting her. I don't know how you put up with her.' Her grandmother was smiling, for all the implied criticism in her words. 'And by the time she's finished titivating and gets down for breakfast the best of the day will be over.'

Betty had finished the sandwiches. She wrapped them in a clean teacloth and put them in a wicker basket along with two generous slices of raisin cake, some apples and a flask of home-made lemonade. Then she looked towards Hannah, who nodded, before the young woman poured herself a cup of tea and sat down at the table.

Flora had still not come down and, as Josie had finished her toast, she reached for the letters. One had a foreign stamp; she recognized her father's writing. The other had a local postmark and, again, Josie recognized the handwriting. The letter was from her old school friend Angela.

She had not heard from Angela since the birthday celebrations and, still fretting that she hadn't even seen her to take a proper leave of her, she was glad to have the letter and she decided to open it and read it while she waited for Flora.

'Dear Josie,' the letter began, and Josie frowned. Angela usually began her letters to her with, 'My dearest friend'.

Already feeling anxious, she started to read it again.

Dear Josie,
    I am sorry that I did not see you before you left

Cavendish Hall. But, as you can imagine, I was upset that my birthday celebration had ended the way it did and there was much to sort out with my father and the local constabulary.

And now it will be some time before you and I meet again because I have decided to go travelling. My cousin Ambrose has persuaded his mother to get a party together, and as soon as the weather is cooler we are going to Egypt. Egypt! Can you imagine it? Of course you can. In fact, you will be much better at imagining it than I could be for you were top of the class in geography, whilst I remained a little hazy about continents and hemispheres and all such things.

Well, anyway, Ambrose wants us to discover the splendours of the Nile. We shall begin our visit in Cairo where we shall see the pyramids and then we shall embark on our voyage back through time – those are Ambrose's words – as we sail down – do I mean up? – the Nile to Upper Egypt, to Luxor and the Valley of the Kings where all those long-dead pharaohs are entombed in the desert.

Ambrose will be painting, of course. He will bring home sufficient paintings to fill a gallery, he says. And here, my dear Josie, I am supposed to plead with you to come with us. Ambrose says it will be a wonderful opportunity for you to develop your talent. (He's so pompous sometimes!) But don't worry, Josie, I know you will not want to come, so I shall tell him I've asked and you can write a polite reply saying you couldn't possibly leave Flora.

At this point Josie laid down the letter and sipped her tea. It was cold. Betty must have seen her frown, for she appeared at her side with the teapot, topped up her drink and went to sit down again. As Josie drank her tea she considered the fact that, for all the light-hearted tone of the letter, her former school friend had made it plain that she did not want her to join her aunt's party on the trip to Egypt. Oh, she was pretending that she believed Josie would not come without Flora, but if she had any real regard for her old friend surely she would have tried to persuade her – urged her, in fact – to come with them?

What could have happened to make Angela grow cool towards her? Uneasily Josie returned to the letter and found that her friend had changed the subject entirely.

> Do you know, Josie, I find myself embarrassed that I confided in you during our chat in the summerhouse that day. Looking back on it I believe I may have given you the impression that I am fond of Jacob Goodwright. That I was hoping to marry him, in fact. Let me assure you, nothing could be further from the truth. Well, to be honest, my father may have considered him a suitable match and I would like to have been able to please my parents but, once I got to know him, I decided he simply wouldn't fit into the life I am used to.

Again Josie paused. She entirely agreed about Jacob not being comfortable in the stratum of society occupied by the Cavendish family. That much had been obvious all the time they were at the Hall. But, then, it was hard to imagine where the American would feel at home. He was so different from anyone Josie had met before – and yet there was that nagging and inexplicable feeling that she knew him well . . . that they would always be at ease together like old friends . . . and more . . .

But she knew instinctively that Angela was not telling the truth about not wanting to marry him. She had seen the way her friend looked at Jacob as he walked towards them when they'd been sitting in the summerhouse by the lake. For the briefest of moments Angela had been exposed and vulnerable.

So what had happened to change things? Perhaps Jacob had not responded as he should have done. Perhaps he simply hadn't realized that he was being regarded as a prospective suitor or, if he had, perhaps he had made it plain that he did not want the role? Josie was aware that the hand that was holding the letter was trembling.

> But, of course, [the letter continued] we shall always have to be grateful to Jacob Goodwright, for foiling the jewel thief and saving the Cavendish diamonds! How

dreadful if my birthday celebrations should have gone down in history for entirely the wrong reason. If it had not been for Jacob my poor father would have had to recompense all our guests and, even though he told me we are covered by insurance, some of the pieces were ancient family heirlooms and could never have been replaced.

Well, I am sure you will agree with me that it was a stroke of fortune that Jacob could not sleep and was walking in the grounds. But I wonder what it was that was keeping Jacob awake, don't you?

And, something odd, when my father and I sorted out the necklaces, the earrings, the bracelets and the brooches in order to return them to their rightful owners, I discovered that nothing of yours had been stolen. Well, you didn't report anything and there was nothing left on the table after everything had been returned safely. So I can only assume that you escaped the thief's attention. Lucky you, not to have been upset like my other guests were – including your sister.

And there's another strange thing. After the police decided there was no more to be done we tried to settle into our normal routine, but servants always gossip amongst themselves, you know, and a strange story began to circulate concerning one of my guests. Eventually it came to the housekeeper, Mrs Barton's, ears and she brought the story to my mother.

The story concerns one of the junior housemaids, Eva Fairbairn, not that her name makes any difference as my mother tends to call every one of them Mabel. Forgive me, I digress. Well, Eva had apparently been dawdling as she was tidying up in my bedroom. I was fast asleep and, apparently, she held my ball gown up in front of herself while looking in the mirror.

And that's when she saw someone standing in the doorway behind her. She saw the reflection, rather, and that person was your sister. The girl said she was quite sure it was the younger Miss Walton because, earlier that evening, she had taken good notice of how beautiful the young lady was and how her hair was angel fair. There's no one who has hair quite like your sister's, is there, Josie?

To go on with the tale, Eva got a fright – I think she imagined that she might be scolded for what she was doing – but, strangely, Miss Flora simply backed out of the doorway, she said, and young Eva no doubt breathed a sigh of relief. In fact, she was so relieved that it didn't occur to her to wonder what on earth Flora was up to. And that wasn't the last time she saw her that night. Later, when she was making her way to bed, she saw Flora again, coming out of another of the guest's bed-rooms.

What with all the excitement of the next few days and Mr Goodwright's tale of derring-do, Eva forgot all about it. But as the gossip in the servants' hall became more speculative, Eva must have started to exercise her brain cells and, eventually, she told people what she had seen and, as I said, Mrs Barton told my mother.

Have you any idea what your sister was doing wandering around after everybody else was tucked up in bed? Well, everybody except Mr Goodwright, that is.

My mother and I have decided not to mention this to my cousins Forbes and Ambrose. Because, and this is rather delicate, it did cross our minds that Forbes may have made some assignation with Flora and that was why she was wandering about – lost, so to speak. Turn that over in your mind. No, it's not very likely, is it? However, knowing how smitten with your sister Forbes is, we do not want to put any obstacles in the way of his courtship when there may be a perfectly reasonable explanation for Flora's behaviour. Perhaps you could ask Flora about it?

In any case, if you ever get to the bottom of this little mystery, you will have to write and tell me what the answer is and, sooner or later, the letter may catch up with me on my travels. I'm going to keep Ambrose company and, after the Egyptian trip, he intends to wander where his fancy takes him for a year or two. My aunt will return if there is to be a wedding, of course.

And I suppose Ambrose will want to be there for Forbes.

But now I must get back to studying the catalogues that have arrived from the Army and Navy Stores. Isn't it amazing that I shall be able to order all the clothes I need for my travels, and the luggage too, without leaving my home?

So, goodbye for the while.

Your former school friend,

    Angela

Josie's gaze was unfocused as she folded the sheets of paper and returned them to their envelope. She was aware that her sister had come down at last and was being persuaded by Grandma Hannah to eat a bowl of porridge but she did not dare glance in Flora's direction for she knew that she would not be able to disguise the alarm and unease that had taken over her mind.

In spite of the fact that the letter had ended with the words 'goodbye for the while', what Angela was really saying was 'goodbye'. Surely there was some significance that she signed herself a 'former' friend, and there was even the implication that she would not return for her cousin's wedding.

Josie's friendship with Angela was over. The letter left her in no doubt of that. If Angela still cared for her she would have done her best to persuade her to go to Egypt with them, no matter that she would probably have declined. Angela was right about that although not for the right reason. Josie might have brought herself to leave Flora but, if she had gone, it would have given Ambrose false hope and that would not have been fair to him.

But was Angela's reason for wanting to end the friendship something to do with Flora's eccentric behaviour or was it something else? Once more Josie recalled the moment Jacob had walked towards them through the dappled sunlight. It had been plain to see from Angela's face that she was attracted to him. But what of me? Josie wondered. Did my expression reveal something too? And maybe Angela saw and understood that.

Josie immediately tried to repress the troublesome thoughts that came into her mind. There was something else to worry about: Flora's behaviour on the night of the ball. Why had she been wandering about the house? Why had Josie's jewellery not been taken? And why had Flora's evening bag been found in the rose garden?

What a muddle. But it was plain that Angela was suggesting that Flora had something to do with the robbery. Perhaps she believes that I am involved, too, Josie thought, and that along with Jacob, Flora and I have staged an elaborate charade. But what would have been the purpose of that?

And yet there was something else troubling Josie about Flora. The idea that although she may genuinely have fallen in love with Forbes and wanted to marry him as soon as possible, she was also giving the impression that she wanted to escape something.

Josie was unaware how tightly she was gripping the envelope that contained Angela's letter with both hands and that she was twisting it backwards and forwards as if she were about to tear it in two.

'Are you going to sit there all day?' Josie looked up to see Flora smiling down at her. 'But what's the matter? You look as though you've seen a ghost?'

Josie frowned. A ghost? No, only my sister of flesh and blood when a moment ago I was visualizing her wandering like a wraith in the moonlight on the night of the ball.

'Or has something in that letter upset you?' Flora continued. 'Who's it from?'

Josie dragged up a smile. 'It's bad manners to ask but I don't mind telling you. It's from Angela.'

'Oh, Angela. Now I know why you're upset.'

'Do you?' Josie was startled.

'Of course. You're very fond of Angela, aren't you? And I imagine she's been telling you how miserable she is that the American doesn't seem to want to pay court to her.'

'How do you know that?'

'Forbes told me.' Flora adopted a superior air. 'He's like a big brother to Angela and, I suppose, he feels responsible for her. He said he could see very well what was going on the night of the ball and he felt sorry for the poor girl.'

'And what exactly was going on?'

'Well,' Flora relaxed into an easy gossipy manner, 'Angela was casting soulful glances at Jacob but she could see that he was casting equally soulful glances at someone else.'

'And who was that?'

'Don't you know?'

'I wouldn't ask otherwise.'

'You really don't know, do you? I told Forbes that I didn't think you'd realized but he said you were probably dissembling and that like many young women you were probably leading the poor fellow on.'

'You mean . . . ?'

'That's right. Jacob Goodwright didn't seem to be able to take his eyes off you. Poor man.'

'Why do you say "poor man"?'

'Because I can tell you're not interested.' Flora sighed. 'Isn't it sad?'

'What's sad?'

'This whole business of misplaced affections.'

Josie looked at her sister and had to suppress an urge to laugh – or cry. She felt as if she could give way to both emotions quite easily. Flora felt so grown up and important because Forbes Robson had chosen to court her that she was already attempting to speak and behave like a sophisticated young woman instead of the delightful child she really was.

But what was she to make of Forbes's belief that Jacob Goodwright was interested in her? Forbes was not the sort of man to imagine such things. Could it possibly be true? Her thoughts were reeling but she didn't have time to explore her reaction to this news because Hannah bustled over to them.

'If you two lasses divven't get yourselves away and out before much longer the best of the day will be over,' their grandmother said. 'Now, here's your painting box, Josie. Flora can carry the picnic basket.'

They all turned as Betty suddenly clapped her hands for attention.

'What is it, Betty, hinny?' Grandma Hannah asked.

Betty smiled and held up two umbrellas.

'Aye, you're right, pet. The girls had better take a brolly each.' Grandma Hannah not only insisted on their taking umbrellas but she made them each take a light paisley shawl. 'The weather's uncertain,' she said. 'I divven't want you catching a chill, not when your father trusts me to look after you.'

They got to the door before she said, 'And where are you off to, by the way?'

'Nowhere in particular,' Flora said breezily. 'When I came across Josie yesterday she was drawing a view of the village from above. It was very good.' And so, without lying, she had avoided telling their grandmother that they were going to the cottage. Grandma Hannah clearly didn't like the ruined cottage, else why had she tried to scare them away from the place when they'd been children? Perhaps, like some of the villagers, she thought it haunted.

Flora had already stepped outside and a slight breeze was blowing chaff across the threshold when Betty caught up with Josie and touched her arm.

'What is it, Betty?' Josie mouthed.

Betty held up the other letter that Josie had left lying on the table. The letter from her father.

'Oh, thank you.'

Josie took the letter; she would read it later. Her father wrote wonderful letters and she wanted to read it when she was alone and had time to savour the vivid descriptions of the places he and Annie had visited.

The two of them set off and took the usual path that led away from the village and up towards the moor top. Flora seemed to be in a good mood and Josie wondered whether she should wait until they were enjoying their picnic, perhaps, and then try to ask some of the questions that would solve the mystery of what had happened on the night of the ball.

It wasn't the fact that Flora might resent being questioned and go into a sulk that was making her nervous, it was the fear that by asking those questions she might discover something that would jeopardize Flora's chance of happiness with Forbes. What distressed Josie most was that she didn't have enough faith in her younger sister to be able to dismiss all these ridiculous ideas from her head. And so she decided the questions would have to wait.

'Tell the girl to go.'

'The "girl" has a name. She's called Betty. And she stays.'

'I want to talk to you.'

Hannah stared at Ralph Lowther wearily. She supposed she ought to have expected this as soon as she had heard he was coming home to Moorburn. 'You say whatever you want, Ralph. The poor lass is deaf and dumb.'

Ralph's eyes narrowed as he looked at Betty. She looked back at him curiously. 'She looks normal to me.'

Hannah was vexed. 'She is normal. As normal as you or me. She just can't hear you. Although . . .' Hannah bit her lip.

'Although what?'

Hannah, cross with herself for doing it, nevertheless turned her head a little to the side before she said, 'She can work out what you say by looking at your lips.'

'I see.'

'Well, don't loom there like that. Come in and shut the door, then. You'd best sit down or I'll get a crick in me neck.'

Ralph Lowther had been standing in the doorway that led to the inn yard. Now he closed the door and neither he nor Hannah noticed that the sneck hadn't quite dropped home.

Hannah smiled reassuringly at Betty and gestured for her to get on with the meal they had been preparing. Then, while the younger woman carried on chopping meat and vegetables for a stew, Hannah wiped her hands of flour and motioned to Ralph to sit at one side of the fireplace while she lowered her old bones into her rocking chair at the other. She watched Ralph uneasily, waiting for him to speak.

The kettle steamed on the hob and the old cat, stretched on the hearthrug between them, twitched in its sleep, a soft growl coming from its throat. Betty had taken over Hannah's task and she moved rhythmically as she rolled the pastry at the table. This should have been a peaceful time – Jack in the inn parlour and her granddaughters out for their picnic. But instead Ralph had come – as she'd feared he might. And now he was sitting as if he'd been carved from stone as he stared down at the floor.

'It's been a long time, Ralph,' she said at last. 'A long time since you've been to see me.'

317

He raised his face and she recoiled from the misery she saw there. 'I couldn't come,' he said. 'Not after Effie died.'

'Aye, I know,' Hannah said as she began to rock gently, seeking comfort, although what she knew she couldn't have put into words.

'Why didn't you tell me?' he asked at last. His hands were gripping the wooden arms of his chair and his knuckles were white.

'Tell you? What should I tell you?'

'About Flora. About Effie's younger daughter.'

'I divven't ken what you mean. You knew fine well she had another bairn. You knew I had two granddaughters.'

'Yes, I knew there'd been another child. And that Effie . . . that Effie did not survive the birth.'

They looked at each other and, for the moment, were united in grief.

'But I'd never seen them, either of them, until yesterday,' Ralph said when he was able to speak once more.

'You saw them? Where?'

'I felt like walking to the Hall from the station. I passed by the witch's cottage. They were there. I . . . spoke to them.'

'Ah.' For a moment Hannah couldn't speak. Of all the places Ralph should come across Flora it would have to be there. It was almost as if Effie had called to him . . . no . . . she shook her head and tried to rid it of such fanciful thoughts.

Ralph's next words took her by surprise. 'She says she's going to be married.'

'What?'

'Flora is going to be married. Didn't you know?'

'Of course I did.'

'To Forbes Robson?'

'If her father agrees.'

'And he hasn't agreed as yet?'

'He doesn't know. Samuel and Annie are away, travelling.'

'He married again.'

It was neither a question nor an accusation but, nevertheless, Hannah felt the need to defend her son-in-law. 'That didn't bother Jack and me. He needed a mother for the bairns. And a man needs a wife.'

'Of course.' Ralph paused. 'And you think he will agree to this marriage?'

'I can't speak for Samuel, but why shouldn't he? I've never heard anything against Forbes Robson and it would be a grand match for the lass.'

'She's very young.'

'No doubt Samuel will tell them to bide a while.'

'How old is Flora, Hannah? Exactly?'

'Why do you want to know?'

'Just tell me.'

'She's fifteen.'

Ralph grew very still. 'What month was she born?'

'For heaven's sake, why does that matter?'

'You know why it matters.'

'No I don't. And I don't see why I should tell you. And, anyway, what brought this on?'

Ralph gripped the arms of his chair even more tightly and leaned forward. 'You know why I'm asking. Of course you do. I believe you know what happened in the cottage that day – the last time I saw Effie.'

'No . . . stop this!'

'I won't stop and you'll hear me out because it's the truth I'm after.'

'We'll never know the truth.'

'It's staring you in the face!'

'What do you mean?'

'When you look at Josie and Flora together, what do you see?'

'My granddaughters.'

Ralph clenched his fists and banged them on the arms of his chair. 'And do you think they look like sisters?'

'They are sisters. And divven't you shout at me!'

He closed his eyes for a moment as if controlling his emotions and when he opened them his voice became low and reasonable, persuasive. 'But how unlike each other they are, Hannah. Josie, I imagine, looks like her father but Flora—'

'Looks like her mother,' Hannah said quickly. 'That's not unusual – for bairns to favour different parents.'

Ralph's eyes were glinting, whether with fervour or with

319

unshed tears Hannah couldn't tell. 'Oh, yes. Flora is the image of her mother,' he said. 'When I first saw her yesterday I thought I had died and gone to heaven – or that my longing for her had made Effie come to life again in the very place where we—'

'Don't!'

Ralph gave a great sigh and sat back in his chair. He shook his head. 'It's more than simply taking after her mother, isn't it? Flora is a Lowther through and through.'

Hannah's throat felt dry, her tongue too big for her mouth. Her voice wavered when she forced herself to speak. 'There's a family likeness, aye. But I'm a Lowther, remember?'

Hannah sensed a movement at the table. She heard the rolling pin drop with a clatter. But she couldn't turn to see what Betty was doing because Ralph Lowther was compelling her to give him all her attention.

He laughed. 'Oh, no, Hannah, don't fool yourself. It's much more than some distant family connection. The likeness is too strong. Look at me. Look at my hair. Look at the colour of my eyes. Don't pretend any longer that you don't know what happened in the cottage between Effie and me on the very day that her husband came home.'

Ralph Lowther got to his feet and Hannah shrank back as he glared down at her. 'Flora is my daughter,' he said. 'Don't try to deny it!'

And then several things seemed to happen at once. Hannah felt her heart thudding but, as she tried to form a denial, she found Betty at her side. What had brought her? The girl had been working at the table with her back to them; she couldn't have fathomed any of what had been said.

But the lass was pulling at Hannah's sleeve urgently and when Hannah looked up, she pointed towards the door. What Hannah saw filled her with dismay. The door was open – no one had knocked – she hadn't heard the sneck lift – those thoughts chased through her mind even as she saw what was happening.

Samuel Walton was standing there, his face the colour of parchment. Annie was behind him, her eyes expressing deepest shock.

Hannah got to her feet. 'Samuel,' she breathed, 'how long . . .'

Samuel turned his head towards her and he frowned. His lips moved sluggishly but all that came forth was a jumble of words that made no sense. Then he moved his head slowly until he was staring at Ralph Lowther. There was no mistaking the glare of hatred in his eyes. Then, without warning, Samuel pitched forward and crashed to the floor.

'. . . have you been standing there?' Hannah found herself finishing her sentence.

'Long enough,' she heard Annie sob. And then the woman sank to her knees, moaning with pity and terror as she tried to lift her husband's head from the cold flagstones and cradle it in her arms.

Chapter Fifteen

October

'Josie, wait for me!'

Josie turned to see Flora running down the track from the inn. She hadn't put her hair up and it was blowing wildly in the wind. Loose gravel and dead leaves scurried along in front of her. When she reached the spot where Josie was standing, she stopped and pulled strands of hair away from her face impatiently.

'Flora . . .' Josie began.

'Why didn't you wait for me?' Flora exclaimed.

'Flora, you'll catch cold. You should have put a coat on.'

'I would have if you'd given me time. I told you I was going to come with you this morning but you just sneaked off without telling me!'

Flora began to shiver. She was dressed simply in a grey flannel skirt and a high-necked white blouse. The wind pushed her clothes from behind so that they flattened against her back and the folds of her skirt billowed out in front of her. She looks like an untidy schoolgirl, fresh from hockey practice, Josie thought.

'I didn't tell you because I thought I'd made it clear last night. Annie hasn't changed her mind.'

'But you did ask her?'

'Yes. I wouldn't lie to you.'

To Josie's dismay Flora began to cry – huge racking sobs that shook her slender frame. 'Don't,' Josie said. 'Please don't.'

She unwound her own scarf, a large tartan affair almost like a shawl, and put it round her sister's shoulders. Then she put her arm around the younger girl and, together, they began to walk back to the inn.

'Why won't Annie let me see my father?' Flora asked when she had calmed down a little.

'I don't know. I really don't know. She just keeps saying that he mustn't be upset.'

'But why would seeing me upset him? I'm his daughter!'

'Annie is very worried about him.'

'Doesn't she think I'm worried? Especially when I'm not allowed to see him.'

'I suppose she wants to keep him calm.'

'Calm!' Flora stopped and tore herself away from Josie's protective grasp. 'The poor man is nothing but calm! Lying there all day in that miserable little cottage, seeing nobody but our dull little stepmother!'

'You shouldn't talk about Annie like that. She looked after us when we were children, and she's been a good wife to our father. And, besides, he does see other people. Dr Gilroy calls nearly every day, our cousin Philip comes once a week from Newcastle, and I . . .' Josie faltered when she saw the accusation in her sister's eyes.

'Oh, yes. *You* are allowed to visit Father, every day just about. That makes it all the worse.'

A gust of wind came down the bank towards them, bringing a swirl of smoke from the inn chimneys. Flora stared at Josie angrily and then she turned on her heel and began to walk back up the track. 'Goodbye then.'

'Flora . . . listen to me . . . I go because Annie needs help. Father is a big man – he has to be lifted . . . washed . . . fed.' Josie had to hurry to keep up with her sister.

'What about Margery's mother?' Flora glanced back and scowled. 'I thought Annie had engaged her to help?'

'She has. But Mrs Baxter can't be there all the time. She has her own family to look after. And, besides, some of the things that need doing are so . . . so personal.'

'Then why am I not allowed to help? I could wash him, shave him, comb his hair.'

'Perhaps Annie thinks you are too young for such tasks.'

'What has my age got to do with it?'

'Maybe she thinks it would distress you – or that Father would be embarrassed for you to see him like that.'

'You're not much older than I am and it seems it's all right for you to help in such a way.'

Josie shook her head perplexedly. There was nothing she could say.

'Well, then, I could read the newspapers to him,' Flora said. 'You said he likes it when you read the newspapers.'

'Oh, he does. Annie tried to stop me from reading the reports of the war in Afghanistan – no doubt she thought it too gloomy – but we both saw how frustrated he became. It's plain he doesn't want to be treated like a child.'

'He *is* getting better, isn't he?'

'I think so. Dr Gilroy says there's been a marked improvement but he doesn't want us to hope for too much. A stroke can leave people . . . different from before.'

'What do you mean?'

'The brain may not work in quite the same way.'

'That won't happen to our father. He's too strong. And too clever. He'll get completely better, I'm sure of it and – oh, don't you see – he'll want to know why I never went to see him? He must already be wondering where I am. He probably thinks I don't care about him!'

They had reached the inn yard and Flora stopped and faced Josie, a look of intense pleading in her eyes. 'Look, I'll tidy my hair and put on my coat and I'll come to the cottage with you. Surely Annie wouldn't turn me away at the door? All the village would see and there would be gossip. Oh, please let me come and see Father.'

'I'm sorry, Flora, Annie is quite determined that you should not come. And I really don't know why. And before you protest again, let me tell you that I believe you must agree to this.'

'Why?' All Flora's frustration was expressed in that one word.

'For Father's sake. If you were to come to the door and Annie barred your way into the cottage, Father might hear the commotion and be upset. Also – and I know you won't like what I'm going to say, but you have to hear it – Annie has been under great strain. She has worked endlessly to make him comfortable and give him every chance of recovery. We owe her much – and, therefore, we must respect her wishes.'

Flora stared mutely for a while and then she muttered, 'She needn't have taken that cottage. Grandma Hannah would have let them stay here at the inn and then she would have had us all to help, and Betty too.'

'I know that, but perhaps she wanted somewhere quiet. After all, there are no stairs in the cottage; everything can be arranged conveniently on one floor.'

Flora sighed. 'I suppose that's right. And I also suppose I shouldn't keep you here any longer.' With her hand on the latch of the kitchen door Flora paused and said, 'Well, at least will you tell Father that I love him?'

Josie nodded, then she forced a cheerful note in her voice as she said, 'Did you see there was a letter for you this morning?'

'A letter?'

'Mm. It's on the table next to your breakfast bowl.'

'I didn't stop for breakfast; I came straight after you.'

'Well, if I were you I would go in and apologize to Betty, who no doubt had your porridge ready, and then open your letter and read it while Betty warms the porridge up again.'

A change came over the younger girl; she smiled and seemed to shrug off her distress. 'The letter will be from Forbes,' she said, and she hurried into the inn without another word.

Josie almost followed her in. Flora had forgotten to return the scarf and the wind was cold. But she decided not to delay any further. Annie wanted to get the train to Hexham today and do some shopping.

As she was almost blown down the steep track to the village, she hoped Flora hadn't noticed that she had not promised to give their father her message that she loved him. She did not think she could risk that. As soon as everyone realized that Samuel Walton seemed to understand everything that was said to him Dr Gilroy had told them to talk to him and make him part of everyday conversations.

It wasn't long before Flora had asked Josie to deliver her first message and, when she did, she had taken her father's hand and, looking into his eyes, she had said clearly that Flora wanted him to know how much she loved him. His eyes had filled with tears. Josie had assumed that Samuel had been moved by the message. But, strangely, behind his chair Annie had looked not only distressed, but frightened too.

The second time she gave him such a message from Flora he had started to weep uncontrollably. This time Annie went white with some unexplained emotion – was it anger? Josie could not even begin to guess what was so disturbing her father and stepmother, but she had decided, even without Annie's urging, not to mention Flora again until she could discover what was upsetting her father so.

She thought that Annie had probably made the right decision about not staying at the inn. The cottage was an altogether more peaceful place to nurse Samuel back to health. And yet, she had been surprised that her grandmother had not even tried to dissuade Annie from going. And her grandmother had not been to visit Samuel, not once, although she sent Betty regularly with bowls of home-made broths and stews, apple pies and batches of scones.

'The poor lass has enough to do,' she would mutter. 'She won't be wanting to stop and gossip. Betty can simply leave the dishes and come away again. If there's anything Annie wants she can tell you, Josie.'

At the cottage Annie was dressed in her hat and coat and ready to go. Josie apologized for being late but her stepmother managed a wan smile. 'That's all right,' she said. 'If I leave now I'll be in good time for the train. Your father is asleep and Mrs Baxter is sitting with him. Would you like to keep me company as far as the station?'

'Of course.'

Josie was surprised to be asked. Since Samuel had been stricken down her stepmother had barely uttered a word that was not to do with his welfare or with housekeeping arrangements. But perhaps the prospect of a day out had encouraged her to relax a little.

When they reached the station there was still some time to spare so they went to sit by the fire in the waiting room. Annie took a list from her handbag and scrutinized it. 'These things are all necessary, you know,' she said when she saw that Josie was looking at her.

'Of course they are.' She wondered if Annie felt guilty about leaving Samuel and was worried that Josie thought the shopping trip frivolous. But before she could think of something reassuring or encouraging to say, Annie thrust the list into her hands.

'Do look at it and see if there's anything else you can think of.'

Josie studied the list in surprise. She supposed she had been expecting to see personal items, little luxuries that could not be found in the village store. Such things as perfumed soaps for Annie and superior hair dressings and shaving soap for her father. All those things were on the list but they only formed a small part of it.

Most of the items were household goods: a half dinner service and a half tea service, cushions, two footstools, a cinder guard, an occasional table, a hearthrug, curtain material and even pictures for the walls. Before Josie had finished reading she looked up at Annie in astonishment.

'I want to make the cottage more homely,' her stepmother said. 'We may be there for a while. Perhaps until . . .' Annie took the list from Josie, folded it and put it back into her handbag. 'I shall have everything delivered, of course.'

'Until when, Annie?' Josie's heart was thudding. Surely Annie wasn't trying to break it to her that her father was going to die?

Annie saw her expression and her eyes widened. She took hold of Josie's hands. 'I've frightened you. I'm so sorry. I can guess what you're thinking and I can assure you that your father is getting better and growing stronger day by day. No, I was simply trying to tell you that we may not be going back to the house on the quayside.'

'What? Never?'

'No, my dear. I can't see us ever going back. We shall stay here in the cottage until Samuel is strong enough to face a move. I can't say when that will be, so I have decided to make the cottage more homely for him – for both of us – until we can decide together where exactly we shall buy a house.'

They heard the whistle of the train as it approached the

station and the windowpanes of the waiting room began to rattle. Annie got to her feet. 'I wanted you to know this because . . .' Annie paused and shot Josie an anguished glance, 'because I . . . we . . . I mean . . .'

Suddenly Josie knew what her stepmother was going to say. 'You don't want Flora and me to live with you, do you?'

'Oh, Josie, don't look at me like that. There are reasons . . .'

'What reasons?' Josie felt a sudden flush of anger. She knew how hurt Flora had been to be shut out of their father's life, and now Annie wanted to shut her out too.

Annie shook her head. 'I can't explain. But it's for your father's sake. You'll have to trust me.'

Josie calmed down a little. 'Is it something to do with his health? With his recovery?'

Her stepmother seized on the last word gratefully. 'His recovery, yes. But here's the train.'

The train was indeed steaming into the station and Annie hurried out of the waiting room. Josie felt that everything was most unsatisfactory. She had been told half a tale – perhaps even less of the truth than that. 'But where shall we live?' she asked the retreating figure of her stepmother. 'Flora and I?'

'At home, of course.' Annie was already opening the carriage door.

'Home? The house on the quayside?'

'Yes. With your Aunt Charlotte. Philip must provide for you. He owes your father that much.'

Her stepmother climbed aboard and settled herself in her seat. A station porter interposed himself between Josie and the train, and shut the door.

'Does Aunt Charlotte know about this?' Josie asked, and she had to raise her voice to make herself heard above the guard's shrill whistle.

Annie, safe now, smiled and puckered her brow as if she hadn't heard. The train began to move and her stepmother waved and mouthed something like, '. . . talk later . . .'

Then, as the train pulled away, she sat back in her seat and was obscured by a puff of steam blown along the platform by the wind.

Of course Aunt Charlotte must know, Josie thought as she

made her way back to the one-storey cottage at the far end of the village green. Philip has been visiting my father and stepmother every week to discuss business. Annie wouldn't contemplate something like this without telling him. But what could Annie have meant by saying Philip must provide for us? Why should he? Surely it is my father's business that is providing for all of us?

Josie couldn't make sense of Annie's words. She decided that her stepmother must mean that Philip should not object if she and Flora went home to live. But, there again, that hardly made sense. The house on the quayside did not belong to Philip; it belonged to their father and it had always been their home.

By the time she got back she found that Betty had been with a pan of broth and Mrs Baxter had put it on the hob to keep warm.

'The young 'uns'll be coming back from school for their midday meal soon,' Mrs Baxter said. 'Is it all right if I slip home now?'

'Of course.'

This was what usually happened, but Josie had never been left completely alone with her father before. Mrs Baxter must have sensed her unease. 'I won't be long,' she said. 'And mebbes he won't wake until I get back. Mrs Walton said the wind kept them awake much of the night, rattling the tiles on the roof an' all.'

Josie watched through the window as Mrs Baxter pulled her shawl tightly round her thin shoulders and hurried across the green, then she tiptoed into the bedroom where her father was sleeping. The cottage had only one bedroom, and most of the space in it was taken up by the bed. The rickety chest of drawers and wardrobe had been moved into the passage to make room for a battered old chaise longue where Annie slept.

Suddenly Josie saw how intolerable Annie's life must be and she understood fully her need to try to make this bare little cottage more comfortable. She also saw that the house on the quayside, with all its stairs, would be quite impossible. Until he was walking again – if he ever did walk again – her father would be a prisoner in his bedroom and Annie would probably be up and down all day. But where would they go? And, when they did go, did Annie intend to allow Flora and herself to visit them?

She left her father sleeping and went to sit by the fire. She had brought a newspaper back from the station; she knew that even though her father could not speak he was still concerned with world events. This was obvious from the way his eyes would flare with life whenever she read something that particularly interested him.

She glanced through the newspaper and found a report of the new refrigerated stores that were being constructed in London in preparation for the arrival of the first cargoes of frozen meat from Australia. She would have to take care to read out the details and the facts correctly, for she knew her father would be interested in the concept of ships fitted with refrigeration machinery.

The report also mentioned that those involved in the British meat industry were, not unnaturally, becoming anxious about this new development. And then it ended with a flight of fancy as the writer expounded his ideas of how small the world was becoming when British housewives would soon be able to feed their families with beef from Australia and mutton from New Zealand.

Then laying the newspaper aside Josie sat quietly for a while, listening to the wind buffeting the solid stone walls of the cottage. She glanced across to the window and saw an old woman almost blown across the village green as she made her way to the post box. When she got there, the wind tried to snatch the letters from her hand but she managed to thrust them into the box and then turned, laughing, to talk to a friend who had just emerged from the village store.

Thinking of the letters that had nearly been lost made her remember the last letter her father had sent her. The letter she hadn't read until it was too late. In fact, she had forgotten all about it until days after her father had been stricken and, when she did read it, she wondered if the tragedy might have been prevented.

She had kept it with her ever since and now she drew it out of her pocket to read it yet again. In it her father had told her that Annie and he had enjoyed their holiday but he had been feeling a little tired of late and that Annie was convinced he ought to see a doctor. Nonsense, of course, but he wished to keep her happy so they were already packing up to come home. He said he would post the letter before they set off but that, in all probability, he and Annie might be home before the letter reached Moorburn.

If only Grandma Hannah had known that, she might never have allowed Ralph Lowther to come into the inn kitchen that day. And her father might not have had a stroke. For Josie was by now convinced that something Sir Ralph had said had affected her father deeply. Enough to precipitate what had happened.

When she and Flora had got back from their picnic in the cottage that day they had been shocked to find their father lying in the front parlour in a state near death. Their grandfather had got two of his customers to carry Samuel in there and Annie would allow no one to come near him. Except Josie.

Flora had been left weeping in the kitchen and, in the parlour, Josie tried to comfort Annie while they waited for Dr Gilroy. She'd thought Annie was going to lose her mind. She had rocked backwards and forwards repeating, 'Wicked man. Wicked, wicked man!' And then a jumble of words that sounded like, 'He loved her so . . . the poor man loved her so!'

Josie had known better than to question her stepmother. She'd hoped, instead, that Grandma Hannah would enlighten her. When Dr Gilroy arrived she'd returned to the kitchen to find Betty trying to comfort both Flora and Grandma Hannah. Grandpa Jack had left one of his village cronies in charge of the taproom and he was sitting at the table staring at the womenfolk helplessly. He shot Josie a despairing glance and shook his head. It was beyond him.

'What happened here?' Josie had asked.

But her grandmother shook her head, and all she would say was, 'I curse Ralph Lowther and I rue the day I ever let him walk across the threshold. I tell you this because you must never see him again.'

'But why?' Josie had asked.

'It's in the past. It should have been left there,' was all she got by way of explanation. 'Now heed me, both of you. If you love your father you will mark my words.'

Both weeping themselves by now, Josie and Flora had agreed. But nothing more had ever been said and they were left to ponder that it must have been an old quarrel between the two men that had sprung to life again. Although in the back of Josie's mind she couldn't quite forget that Ralph Lowther, although admitting that he knew who their father was, had said that he'd never met him.

Now, sitting peacefully by the fire in the cottage in the village, Josie looked at the letter once more. She read it over and over as if looking for an explanation. But, of course, there wouldn't be any. Whatever had happened had happened long ago, probably when her mother was still alive. Josie folded the letter carefully and, putting it back in its envelope, she returned it to her pocket. She would keep it for ever, just in case those were the last lucid words her father would ever write.

When Philip entered the kitchen of the house on the quayside Patience was deep in conversation with her aunt, the cook. The two women seemed to draw nearer together as they stopped talking and looked at him. He had the impression that they had been talking about him. Nevertheless, Patience smiled sweetly and Mrs Dobson rose to her feet and bustled over to the range where the kettle was steaming on the hob.

'Would you like a cup of tea, Master Philip? Here in the kitchen where it's cosy.'

Mrs Dobson had always been easy-going, but today Philip thought her smile was a little forced, as if she were trying extra hard to please him.

'I would like tea,' he said, 'but I'll take it with my mother and our guest. Patience, would you bring tea and cake to my mother's room. Violet can help you.'

'It's Violet's day off,' Patience said. 'And I don't feel like climbing all those stairs.'

Mrs Dobson stared at her niece and shook her head. Philip thought some unspoken message had passed between them. 'Patience is only joking, aren't you, my lass? Of course she'll do as you ask but she'd better have one of the lads from the store to help her.'

Patience didn't say anything but she got up, rather heavily, Philip thought, and went to the dresser to start collecting the cups and saucers that would be needed. Philip stared at her for a moment and then said, 'Very well, I'll ask Eric.' He waited for a response but neither woman spoke so he added, 'Ah . . . I'll, um . . . then I'll go straight up.'

His mother had hardly smiled for weeks. Not since Annie's letter had arrived telling them what had happened to Samuel. Each time Philip returned from visiting his uncle at Moorburn she would have a long list of questions for him and she desperately sought any crumb of comfort she could in Philip's assurances that Samuel seemed slowly to be making a recovery. The catechism was always the same.

'But can he speak?' she would ask.

'No, Mother.'

'Not at all?'

'Well, he opens his mouth and some sort of sounds come out but you would not recognize them as words.'

'And do you think his powers of speech will return?'

'His doctor says it's possible. But he may have to learn over again, just like a child.'

'And his mental faculties?'

Philip would pause at this point, torn between giving an honest answer, which he knew would give his mother hope, and the answer that would suit his purposes best.

'I'm not sure,' he would say. 'My Uncle Samuel seems to listen to what I have to say – and he even nods or shakes his head. But I'm not sure whether he fully understands or whether his poor brain has muddled everything up.' And this was true enough, Philip supposed.

'And Annie? She is looking after him properly?'

'What would you expect? She's devoted to him.'

'And she must be grateful to you, Philip.' His mother would always cheer up a little at this point, although her expression would remain anxious. 'And isn't it fortunate that Samuel had the foresight, before he went on holiday, to sign those papers giving you authority to run the business for him while he was away?'

'Very fortunate, Mother.' And Philip reflected every time

she mentioned this that his mother would never know exactly how much of the business he had already wrested from his uncle's control.

He paused on the landing outside his mother's room. His mother was actually laughing. Her visitor had managed to cheer her up. Astonished, he knocked and entered and had a feeling of *déjà vu*, but this time it was three people who stopped talking and looked up towards him as if he were interrupting an interesting conversation.

'I've asked Mrs Dobson to send up some tea and cake,' he said in the awkward silence that followed his entrance.

His mother smiled and her companion, Janet Rodgerson, rose to her feet. 'It's Violet's day off today. I'd best go down and help,' she said.

'That won't be necessary,' Philip said. 'It's all arranged.'

He knew it to be foolish but he was vexed that their visitor should see that this was such an informal household. No doubt Forbes Robson lived in such splendour that he would simply have to utter a wish and some nameless servant would carry out the task. He was quite sure that a servant having a day off would not present a problem. But he hid his irritation when he saw that Forbes was smiling.

'That's kind of you,' Forbes said. 'I'm partial to a bit of cake.'

Well, Philip thought, for all his vast wealth, he's certainly quite at ease with us more humble beings. And I can see that my mother has been charmed by him. The little group was sitting by the fire and, as Philip went to get the folding table and erect it in readiness, he found himself vexed again, that he, the master of the household, should be doing this.

He was all the more irritated when Forbes quite unselfconsciously rose to help him and, furthermore, he went to seek a chair for Philip from beside the bed. Philip wondered if his mother was at all embarrassed at having to receive such an important visitor in this room where she both lived and slept, and he glanced quickly at her but it seemed that she was completely at her ease.

As Philip settled himself Janet Rodgerson quietly went about the business of getting a clean tablecloth and some napkins from the chest of drawers.

'Philip,' his mother began, 'Mr Robson has offered to help us.'

'Really?' Philip was aware that he was flushing. 'I can't think why he should make such an offer. I wasn't aware that we need any help. We are managing very well. In fact, we have done since my uncle and his wife first left to go travelling.'

'Oh, no, of course not. You have made a fine job of running Samuel's business, and it's not that. Not at all. It's the girls . . . Josie and Flora . . .' She faltered when she saw Philip's frown. 'I mean, Mr Robson wants to make life a little happier for them and, now that I am to be responsible for them, easier for me.'

Philip made an effort to banish his frown. He managed an enquiring smile as he glanced at Forbes Robson. After all, this was not a man to make an enemy of.

'You already know from my letter that I came here today to make my intentions – my honourable intentions, as they say in the romantic novels – clear to you.' He grinned engagingly and then adopted a more serious air. 'With Captain Walton so gravely ill, I thought it proper to approach you. He has trusted you to be in charge of his business and I'm sure it is in order to regard you as head of the family while he is incapacitated.'

He's buttering me up, Philip thought. But, nevertheless, he couldn't help responding to the man's none-too-subtle flattery. 'You wish to marry Flora,' he said.

'That's correct. And I imagine that just like her father might have done, you will tell me I must wait until Flora is older. Quite rightly.'

'You will have to be patient. She's not sixteen yet.'

Forbes nodded as if that were the only agreement that was needed. 'But there is another matter. Your mother has told me that Captain Walton and his wife may not be returning to this house for some time – if ever – and that Josie and Flora will not be going to live with them.' He frowned. 'I understand that Mrs Walton wishes her stepdaughters to remain here with their aunt.'

Philip nodded. 'Of course. Where else should they go?'

Forbes looked down at the floor. It was clear that he didn't know how to continue. Charlotte glanced at him and took up the tale. 'Mr Robson has suggested it might not be easy for me to have the girls here. I mean . . . the way I am.'

Philip was genuinely hurt. 'You have everything you need. You know I would do anything for you!'

'Oh, Philip, my dear, you've been a wonderful son. And this is no criticism of you. It is this house, my dear. With my poor old legs refusing to carry me about I have become a prisoner in this room. Now I'm not complaining. You provide me with everything I need and I have Janet. But it's the girls I'm thinking of. What kind of life will it be here for two lively young women with their father and stepmother gone and only an old crippled woman to see over them?'

'So how exactly has Mr Robson offered to help?'

'He's offered us the use of a house in Gosforth. It's very pleasant – near the Town Moor. It's not too big but it's conveniently laid out and there is a conservatory and a garden. It would be very agreeable for me, dear.'

Philip shook his head. 'It wouldn't do to have Flora living in the house of a man she's not yet married to.'

'I realise that,' Forbes said quickly. 'But it's my mother's house, not mine. It was hers before she was married to my father. In fact, she grew up there.'

'Well . . .'

'And if you think it would be more seemly you could always pay some rent. But I've been writing to Flora, you know, and she really is quite distressed about what has happened. She is both grief-stricken over her father's condition and puzzled that her stepmother does not seem to want her.'

'I can't understand Annie,' Charlotte broke in. 'I know she has had a lot to bear but she is being positively cruel to poor Flora.'

'Now then, Mrs Bertram, hinny,' Janet Rodgerson took the older woman's hand and remonstrated with her, 'give the poor lass time. Mrs Walton, I mean. Grief can do funny things. She may have her reasons and perhaps she'll explain them one day. But meanwhile you want her to get on with the job of getting your brother better, don't you?'

'I suppose so,' Charlotte Bertram said.

Philip was mortified. What on earth would Forbes Robson

think of a household where servants butted into conversations and spoke to the mistress as if she were an equal? But Forbes seemed not to have noticed. Perhaps he thought Janet was a friend of the family rather than a paid companion. Philip thought that even worse and he scowled.

Forbes, however, went on eagerly. 'All I am concerned about is trying to make life happier for Flora – and her sister too, of course. I do hope you will agree to let Mrs Bertram set up a little household in Gosforth with the girls – and, of course, Mrs Rodgerson should come too.'

Patience and Eric had entered the room while they'd been talking and now Janet Rodgerson was directing them to set the tea and cake on the table. Patience had apparently shed her strange mood and was smiling as she set the table, whereas Eric seemed overawed to find himself in the domestic quarters of the building and in such exalted company.

When Patience and Eric had gone and shut the door behind themselves, Philip said, grudgingly, 'If my mother wishes to set up home in Gosforth I won't object. But I would remind you that as long as their father remains incapacitated and, indeed, if he should – I mean, if anything should happen to him – I am his daughters' legal guardian. This is stated in Captain Walton's will.'

His mother uttered a soft moan at his words and her companion was immediately at her side. 'There, there, Mrs Bertram, pet,' Janet Rodgerson said. 'Master Philip is only saying what he has to. And Captain Walton was quite right to make everything legal and proper. We all know the captain's going to get better but it could be years before he can take charge here again. He would want Master Philip to look after things.'

Forbes watched as Charlotte Bertram smiled waveringly at her companion, who then began to pour the tea. The expression on Philip Bertram's face was unreadable. Forbes was convinced that he'd made the right decision to offer Mrs Bertram and her nieces the use of his mother's house.

He'd made allowances for Flora's youth when she'd poured out her hurt feelings in her letters. He thought perhaps the stepmother had been a little unfeeling but maybe she had enough to cope with and Flora's intense emotions would just have been too much for her. There would be some such explanation for her not allowing Flora to visit but now was not the time to seek it.

After all, they all had the same aim: to help Captain Walton recover his strength and faculties. Or had they? Janet Rodgerson handed him a cup of tea and he took the opportunity to glance sideways at Philip Bertram, Flora's cousin. There was something about the man that Forbes didn't trust. He would not have made such a success of his own business affairs if he had not been a good judge of people. Forbes decided then and there that he would set some discreet investigations in motion.

And he would also set everything in motion for the move to Gosforth. Mrs Bertram would nominally be the head of the household there, but Mrs Rodgerson would be his ally. The woman was rough around the edges but she was intelligent, hard-working and, he guessed, trustworthy. He wondered who had had the good sense to employ her.

Forbes was not an overly imaginative man like his brother, Ambrose, but by the time he left the house on the quayside he was feeling depressed. There was an oppressive atmosphere about the place – an air of past grief and hopes that had come to nothing. He couldn't bear to think of his beautiful, free-spirited Flora living here. Thank God he had the means to provide an escape.

Patience came into the office behind the chandler's shop and, turning, locked the door behind her. Philip looked up from his accounts book and regarded her warily. She had been moody lately, and not nearly as biddable as she had been when they had first become lovers.

But now she was smiling flirtatiously. 'Don't you know what time it is?' she asked. 'It's nearly midnight, the shop is closed, and you're still working.'

Philip laid his pen aside and, carefully blotting the column of figures he had been entering, he closed the book and smiled up at her. 'There,' he said. 'No more tonight. Come here.'

He pushed his chair back from the desk and made room for her to sit on his knee. He held her close and, closing his eyes, he buried his face in her warm bosom. He heard her gasp with pleasure. He felt the stirrings of his desire but, after a moment, she pushed herself back from his embrace and said softly, 'Don't you want some supper?'

'Not yet.'

'My aunt has left a pan of barley broth simmering.'

'Good.'

'And there's a mutton pie keeping warm.'

'We'll share it . . . later . . . with a draught of port-wine.'

Philip clasped her close to his body again. She resisted at first and then she turned her face so that he could kiss her. The next time she pulled away from him she slipped off his knee on to the floor, pulling him down to join her. Although his need was urgent Philip took his time. Something about her tonight made him want to give her pleasure and instead of the hasty fumbled affair their lovemaking had become, this time he would not go ahead until they were both completely naked and Patience was frantic with longing.

Afterwards they lay on the hearthrug; Patience nestled up against him and his arm resting protectively across her body. When he felt the softness of her flesh and traced the curve of her belly downwards he felt desire stir again, but Patience suddenly sat up and crossed her arms and shivered a little as she hugged herself.

'I'm cold,' she said. 'Shall I build up the fire?' Without waiting for his reply she began to put on her clothes.

Philip sighed and sat up. 'No, I'll see to the fire,' he said. 'Time to bank it up for the night. You go ahead and set the table in the kitchen.'

When she had gone, Philip thought about what had just happened, and what he had decided to do about Patience. His mother probably still believed that, in order to make sure that he would inherit his uncle's business, he should marry Josie. She'd never said as much but he knew that's what she'd been hoping for.

And he had considered the idea but had known that Flora, when she was old enough, would have been the wife he would have preferred. Not for her character or her intelligence, but simply for her beauty – and that hint of wildness that, as she grew and matured, would drive a man frantic.

Surely she would be one of the most beautiful women of her generation. And, if Flora was the image of her mother, as his own mother had told him she was, then he could understand fully why a mature and sensible man like his uncle had fallen so completely under Effie's spell.

But it seemed that Forbes Robson had laid claim to Flora. Forbes Robson was one of the richest men in Britain; he had used the bounty that the coal mines had brought his family to create new businesses and garner even more wealth. And it was hinted that he had a mind to become involved in politics. He was certainly shrewd enough. And all in all he was probably the right sort of husband for Flora, Philip had to admit that.

Forbes would indulge the girl, shower her with luxuries, but he would not put up with waywardness. There was no question that he was besotted with her – and he would gentle her along – but he would keep her on a tight rein. He would control her. And that was something Philip was beginning to acknowledge would be too troublesome for him to attempt.

Philip knew that he wanted a more biddable woman. A quiet life, if you like. And that was why Josie wouldn't do either. She was far too intelligent. He had no idea whether she would respond to his courtship – she kept her feelings well hidden – but even if she agreed to marry him, it wouldn't be too long before she would begin to suspect what he had done. And what he had done meant that he had no need to marry her in any case.

But imagine never being able to relax. To have to keep your guard up at all times. There was only one woman whom he could trust with his secret. And that was because she already knew of his underhand dealings with various sea captains and shipping agents. She had seen these men enter and leave after the shop assistants had gone home at night and the household was in bed. She had served them drinks and refreshments.

He had never discussed it with her in detail but, although she wasn't as intelligent as his cousin Josie, Patience had an animal cunning so she had probably guessed a long time ago the scale of what he had done. And she had never criticized him. He'd had to warn her not to talk to anyone about his late-night business and he'd kept her sweet by making love to her. And that had been no hardship. Perhaps he had been foolish in letting her believe that they would be married one day. For a while that had worried him but he'd thought he would deal with that when the time came.

And now the time had come to deal with it. And he had surprised himself by the decision he had made almost without having to think about it. He'd guessed a short while ago what all the whispered conversations between Patience and her aunt were about. He'd seen the anxiety in her eyes and noted her efforts to keep him sweet. She was working up to telling him something.

Tonight, when he'd observed how her breasts were more full than before and seen how the curve of her belly had become more pronounced, he'd known he could not wait much longer. He wanted a wife who loved him – why not? But he didn't want an equal. Life would be much more comfortable with a woman who didn't question him – and would think herself lucky to be married to him.

Patience was a servant; furthermore, she was the kind of girl who would never have been accepted as a lady's maid. His mother would never let him forget that, just as she had never got over the fact that her brother had married a servant, even though she and Annie now had an uneasy friendship.

But, over the years, Annie had changed and she had grown into the position of the captain's wife. Patience also would surely be capable of learning how to speak and behave more like a lady.

Philip straightened up from seeing to the fire, closed his account book and locked it away. He would go through to the kitchen and ask Patience to marry him without giving her the chance to tell him what she was undoubtedly going to tell him – that she was with child.

It amused him to let her believe that he truly loved her and that he wanted to marry her even without knowing about the child. As she was the only person who knew about his wrong-doing, it would pay him to keep her sweet.

* * *

Vincent couldn't understand why his father was so determined to pursue his grievance with Captain Walton. 'The man's been struck down,' Vincent told Fox. 'He's lost both his strength and his faculties – that's what I've heard. Why not let it be? Whatever he did to annoy you happened a long time ago.'

'No one crosses Fox,' the old man muttered, and he shook his head.

Vincent wondered if his father was becoming feeble-minded. Many years ago there'd been an incident when Fox Telford had been badly injured. No one knew exactly what had happened. He'd gone off on some business on the day of the Christmas fair on the quayside and he hadn't come back for hours.

When he did, he'd frightened the wits out of Vincent's mother by staggering into their private room in the lodging house like a dead man – that's the way she'd put it. His face had been as white as paper and there was a great river of dried crusted blood starting at the top of his head and running down to his collar.

He'd never told anyone what had happened but, ever since then, his temper had been worse than ever and there had been moments when he didn't act rationally. They already had the house, a bolt hole up on the North York Moors, and Vincent's mother began to spend longer and longer spells there, especially after Vincent was sent away to school.

Now, sitting in his private room in the lodging house which had become filthier than ever since his wife had stopped coming here, Fox started muttering, 'It was the same lad, I'm sure of it.'

Vincent didn't know whether he was expected to respond. 'What lad?' he asked eventually.

'I got a glimpse of him, you know. Just a glimpse, when he ran off with the roast chicken.'

Vincent stared at his father in horror. Had he completely lost his mind? 'What lad was that, Father?' he asked, trying to humour him.

He was rewarded with a look as sharp and as evil as he had ever seen. 'You think I've lost my wits, don't you?'

Vincent recoiled from the sheer menace in the tone. 'No, of course not.'

'Well, I've thought about it over the years, you know.'

'Yes . . . I'm sure you have.'

'Divven't patronize me!'

'I wouldn't dream of it.'

'*I wouldn't dream of it! Nah, nah, nah!*' His father grinned and imitated Vincent's way of talking. 'Never forget you owe it all to me – the way you dress and the way you talk an' all.'

'I won't, really I won't.'

'And you'll do as I say?'

'Yes. But . . .'

'*But?*'

'I wish you would give me a good reason why.'

'It was the same lad. That's why.'

'The same lad who what?'

'I've had plenty of time to think about it – to go over it in my mind and I know it was the same lad as ran off with the chicken. And if high-and-mighty Captain Walton hadn't interfered, hadn't stopped me catching the thievin' varmint that night, he would never have survived to—' He broke off and his eyes widened as if he'd realized he'd said too much.

'Survived to what?' Vincent asked.

'Never you mind.' Fox was muttering again. 'Never you mind, my lad. But if the lad and the lass escaped me then Captain Walton won't. Understand?'

'Yes . . . no . . .' Vincent sighed. Now there was a lass as well as a lad involved in this crazy topsy-turvy tale.

Fox had fallen silent and Vincent risked looking directly at him. To his horror he saw that tears were sliding down his dirty face.

'I'll go, then,' Vincent said quietly. 'I'll do as you say. I'll find out all I can.'

His father didn't reply, he simply raised one hand and made shooing motions. He wanted Vincent to leave.

It was bitterly cold on the waterfront. The fog had rolled in from the sea and it was so thick that he could hardly see more than a step or two in front of him. He'd have to tread carefully. He didn't want to end up in the river. Furthermore, all sounds were muffled, which was even more disorientating. He could hear footsteps and the occasional shout of alarm, but he didn't know which direction they were coming from. The whole experience was ghostly, he decided, and he tried not to give way to the conviction that every time his foot struck the ground, another footstep echoed just behind him.

At one point the sensation was so strong that he stopped and turned quickly, expecting to see his pursuer, whether real or phantom. But there was no one there. Just a swirl of fog above the greasy cobbles.

By the time he reached the appointed meeting place, a cheap but cheerful drinking house favoured by apprentices, the lad was sitting staring despondently down at the sawdust-covered floor. He must have thought Vincent wasn't coming.

Vincent stopped for a moment and stared at the youth. He looked tired – after all, he must have been working all day – and he looked shabby and underfed. He'd probably have told Vincent all he needed to know in exchange for a hot pie and a tankard of ale. But it had pleased Vincent to slip the lad a coin or two over the past few weeks and, as he hadn't wanted to humiliate his informer and thus make an enemy of him, he'd always pretended the money was for some small sample purchase from the chandler's shop. Confectionery tonight, he guessed when he spied the brightly coloured tin on the rough wooden table.

'Sorry, I'm late.' Vincent smiled encouragingly as he approached the table. Eric Hopkins glanced towards him and scowled. 'No, stay there,' Vincent said, although the lad had made no attempt to rise. 'I'll get the ale in.'

Vincent went to the bar and ordered a jug of ale and two tankards. He frowned and backed away a little when a shabbily dressed fellow slipped up to the counter beside him and immediately buried his face in a foul-looking handkerchief. Vincent stared at the man's cheap coat, still glistening with damp, and wished he was anywhere but here amongst the poor and the hopeless. Then he remembered that he could have been on the continent by now, perhaps Italy, if it were not for Jacob Goodwright. And he began to understand why his father could be driven by a desire to get revenge.

The landlord followed him to the table with the jug of ale,

and Vincent sat down and prepared to do his father's bidding, yet again.

'I thought you weren't coming,' Eric said somewhat peevishly when he had taken a sup of his ale. A bubble of froth remained on the lad's upper lip where a few sprouting bristles announced his approaching manhood.

'It's the fog,' Vincent said. 'I had to go carefully. I suppose I should have set out sooner.' He reached for the tin. 'Almonds?' he asked as he picked it up. 'Sugared almonds?'

'Aye, from Sulmona. That's in Italy.' Then remembering to keep up the pretence, Eric said, 'They're silver-coated – edible sugar, of course. The Eyetalians hoy them about at weddings and the like. Mr Bertram thought he'd try them for a while, see if they take on.'

Vincent pushed some coins across the table. 'Well, I'll be pleased to sample them. Please tell Mr Bertram he will have my order if the goods suit.'

It was all nonsense, of course. Even from the first time he had followed Eric from work and struck up a conversation with him he doubted if the lad had believed he really was a merchant looking for new import stock. But Eric had been ready enough to go along with the charade and he'd brought sundry trifles along, supposedly with Philip Bertram's knowledge but probably stolen, for Vincent to 'sample'.

The fact that this had never resulted in an order was never mentioned. The lad knew that the real purpose of the meetings was for Vincent to glean information about the chandler's business, and family too, and it didn't seem to bother him in the slightest that he was revealing matters that were confidential.

Vincent guessed that it might have been different if Samuel Walton was still in charge. The good captain had a reputation for fair dealing in business matters and concern for those who worked for him. But the man's nephew was an altogether different proposition. This lad, for example, looked tired and hungry; Vincent guessed that would not have been the case if the captain were still at the helm.

He didn't even have to ask many questions tonight. Eric started, as he usually did, by giving an account of the day's trade and then, almost eagerly, telling him of his unexpected venture into the domestic quarters of the house on the quayside. Vincent could hardly believe his luck. Eric had kept his eyes and ears open and was almost bursting to tell of the visit of the great Forbes Robson, its purpose and even what had been decided.

Vincent knew his father would be pleased with him when he took this information home. Fox had long ago decided that the best way of wreaking revenge on Captain Walton was through the people he loved best: his daughters. Particularly the younger.

When Fox had learned the identity of the young woman Vincent had caught stealing in the Grainger Market he had been beside himself with glee. The idea of involving her in the jewel robbery had been only the start. No matter that Vincent had promised Flora that she would never see him again after he had got away with the jewels, he had known that his father would not have let the matter drop. And now, it seemed, the girl had much more than her reputation to lose.

Vincent sent Eric on his way and ordered himself a glass of rum – and then another. He would need it to keep out the cold, he reasoned. When finally he ventured out into the night again he had cheered up enough to notice that the shabby fellow with the head cold was sitting at the next table with an empty tankard. He tossed the poor chap a handful of small coins and laughed when they fell on the floor and the fellow had to scrabble amongst the filthy sawdust to find them.

The fog had lifted a little and Vincent could hear the shouts of the crews preparing their vessels to sail with the morning tide. No footsteps followed him home.

Jacob picked up the coins, small change he noticed, and slipped them into the pocket of the threadbare young clerk sitting on the bench next to him. It amused him that skills he had first learned in that long ago childhood and then perfected on the streets of New York could be put into reverse. Coins slipped into a pocket whereas once he would have taken them out – along with all manner of other goods. For that is how he had lived, as a thief, until Isaac had rescued him.

And before that blessed moment he had also learned how to become a master of disguise and, sometimes, to become almost invisible as he slipped through the festering alleys in pursuit of his prey – or, equally, to avoid capture. He had learned to become noticed and yet ignored. To be part of the passing crowd. And in that way he had listened and learned many things he needed to know.

Like tonight. He had been following Vincent Telford for some time and he could still remember his dismay when he'd discovered whose son he was. That was why he'd seemed familiar, of course. Everyone along the quayside knew Fox Telford. Jacob had caught sight of him more than once when he'd been out at night. He'd kept to the shadows, but not because he was afraid. His days of living rough had taught him ways to defend himself that the old thief would never dream of. But now it seemed he would have to deal with both the fox and his cub.

Then, when he'd begun to listen to Vincent's conversations with the lad Eric Hopkins, he'd soon come to realize that there was someone else who needed investigating, Philip Bertram. This had taken different skills and not a little money.

Now, Jacob stepped out into the night and, using the grubby handkerchief, he wiped his face of the dirt he had deliberately put there. He would go back to his room at the mission and bathe and try to sleep. And then, in the morning, he would go to Moorburn.

Chapter Sixteen

Early the next morning Jacob Goodwright alighted from the train at Moorburn and asked the stationmaster to direct him to the cottage where Captain and Mrs Walton had taken up residence. The man was pleasant and inclined to gossip. Jacob learned that not only did the villagers feel that poor Mrs Walton was being charged too much rent by the old miser who owned the cottage, but they didn't know how she managed with only Elspeth Baxter to help. Of course, Miss Josie went every day to help her stepmother and that was a blessing.

'Are the captain's daughters not living at the cottage?' Jacob asked.

'There wouldn't be room, bonny lad. No, the lasses are still with their grandparents at the inn. The Bluebell Inn – look up there.'

They were standing at the entrance of the station by now and the stationmaster raised his arm and pointed towards a tidy-looking building standing on the hillside and overlooking the village.

Jacob thanked the man and set off for the cottage. No matter that the news he brought was dismal, his heart lifted at the prospect of seeing Josie. But he would see Mrs Walton first. He wasn't looking forward to telling her what he had to but he was even more uncomfortable about the news he had to break to Josie. In fact he wasn't sure if he could. After what had happened to her father, how could he tell her that her sister had been in league with a common thief?

Annie herself opened the door to his knock. She was surprised to see him, and at first he thought she was not going to invite him in. But she quickly remembered her manners and he soon found himself sitting by the fire in the living room of the cottage while his hostess set about making a pot of tea. The kettle was already steaming on the hob and a tray on the table held everything that was necessary.

Jacob guessed that Josie could not have arrived at the cottage yet and for that he was grateful. Once he had talked to Mrs Walton he would decide what, if anything, he would say to the captain's elder daughter. Perhaps it would be better if he said nothing at all and, no matter how much he longed to see her, he simply returned to Newcastle once his business with Mrs Walton was done. He was glad that he had a little more time to decide.

While Annie was busy Jacob studied his surroundings. The room was clean and comfortable but hardly luxurious. A kindly-looking woman in a large white pinafore was dusting and tidying but Mrs Walton spoke to her quietly and the woman shot Jacob a curious glance before leaving the room and closing the door behind her.

'Please don't mind Mrs Baxter,' Annie said. 'We don't get many visitors; naturally she's curious.'

She gave a wan smile and Jacob realized how strained she looked. She had lost weight and there were dark circles under her eyes but, paradoxically, he had never seen her looking more attractive. It was the sort of tragic beauty brought on by suffering, he thought.

After giving him his tea she sat down at the other side of the hearth. She closed her eyes for a moment as if relishing the chance to rest and then she opened them, smiled at him and took a sip of her tea.

'Captain Walton is asleep,' she explained. 'But he will awaken soon so I've asked Mrs Baxter to sit with him. I can't see why you shouldn't go in to see him. I believe it's good for him to have visitors, but I warn you, he won't be able to talk to you. You realize that?'

'I do, and, although I would like to meet the captain, it is you I have come to see.'

'Meet him? Of course, you haven't met him yet, have you?'

'Each time I tried to there were unforeseen circumstances.' He smiled. 'But I've come here today because of my concern for you . . . and for the captain's daughters.'

Annie frowned. 'I don't understand. Why should you be concerned?'

'Out of friendship. You have been a great help at the mission, and we miss you.'

'Do you?' Annie looked surprised and pleased. It was hard to tell because of the warm glow of the fire, but Jacob imagined that she had flushed with pleasure.

'Yes we do. Particularly the mothers with young children. You seem to have a gift for dealing with the little ones.'

To his dismay Annie's expression changed to one of deep unhappiness. He realized immediately what he had said but did not know how to make amends.

'I never had children of my own,' she said. 'It has been a great sorrow for me.'

'I'm sorry.'

Captain Walton's wife shook her head and smiled sadly. 'I had Josie and Flora to care for, of course. I was their nursemaid, you know.'

Jacob nodded.

'When Captain Walton married me it was because he needed a mother for them. That was the only reason.'

Jacob was shocked that she should talk to him as candidly as this but he guessed she was speaking the truth and he could not contradict her.

'And I did my best for them.' She spoke as if she was trying to convince him – and herself – and then she sighed. 'But I fear my best was not good enough.'

She was seeking reassurance but Jacob couldn't give it to her. 'Why do you say that?'

'Poor Josie.' She shook her head. 'Poor, poor Josie.'

'Mrs Walton, you're upset and I'm not sure I know why.'

'She was such a good little soul,' Annie went on. 'Always biddable, always loving, but so undemanding that it was easy to ignore her and give all my attention to Flora. But I was not the only one at fault there.' Her voice suddenly became stronger. 'Her father too was completely taken up with the younger child. I believe that between us we have indulged and spoiled her. And now look what has happened!'

Jacob was puzzled. As far as he knew, Flora's family did not know of her involvement with the thief Vincent Telford. This was something else. He had no idea what could have happened.

'Forgive me,' Annie said. 'You have come here today to offer sympathy and I'm grateful.'

'Obviously if there's anything I can do to make your life easier, I will. You have only to ask.'

'That's kind of you but we have everything we need. Oh, this cottage is small and not as convenient as it might be, but we'll be moving as soon as my husband's health allows.'

'Back to Newcastle?'

'I'm not sure where we'll go. The coast, perhaps. A house with a view of the sea.'

'You won't be returning to the house on the quayside?'

'No. It wouldn't be suitable for an invalid, and it will be some time before Captain Walton will be well enough to work again. Frankly I don't think he ever will be. His nephew will continue to manage the business.'

'Ah, yes, Philip Bertram. He . . . he is . . .'

Jacob was perplexed. He had known it would not be easy to say what he had come to say. How do you tell someone that he suspected they had been cheated by a man they should have been able to trust?

'What is it?' Annie was alerted by his hesitation.

'I can't think of any easy way to say this, but I have reason to suspect your husband's nephew has . . .'

Annie put her cup and saucer down on a little table and suddenly looked very grave. 'Stolen Samuel's business from him? Is that what you're trying to say?'

'You know?' Jacob was astounded.

'Philip has already informed me.'

'He told you himself?'

'Oh, he didn't put it quite like that. He didn't tell me that he was a swindler and a cheat. He wrapped it up in fancy long words that he thought I might not understand. And he was so careful to blame Samuel – saying that my poor husband had not been fit to run the business for a long time and that

351

everything he, Philip, had done in gradually taking control was to protect all of us. And I'm sure most people would see it that way. Especially as Samuel has actually signed all the relevant papers. That's what Philip told me.'

'Do you think your husband knew what he was signing?'

'Who can say? He has been tired and overworked for some time. He may have been confused. Or simply too trusting.'

'I see. But what will you do?'

'Nothing. Philip made it plain that it would be very difficult to prove that he has not acted correctly and, as he has every intention of making sure that we do not suffer, of providing a house and a generous allowance, it would be wise for me to accept that it is better not to oppose him.'

'But—'

Annie held up a hand. 'No, Mr Goodwright. All I want is for my husband to recover, to be able to walk and to talk again and to return to a more normal life. Philip can have the business – so long as he keeps his word and looks after Samuel.'

'But what about Captain Walton's daughters?'

'Philip will not put them on the street.'

'I mean their inheritance.'

'That can't be helped. And in any case I'm told that Flora hopes to marry Forbes Robson. She will be well provided for.'

Jacob was puzzled by her choice of words. Why had she said 'I'm told' suggesting that she hadn't spoken directly to Flora about the matter? And he was surprised to see the bitter look that came over Annie's face when she talked about her younger stepdaughter. Whatever had happened to drive a wedge between them must have been serious.

'But what about Josie?' he asked.

Annie Walton stared at him bleakly. 'That can't be helped.'

'Poor Josie,' Jacob said softly, seeing that, once again, the elder of Captain Walton's daughters was to be passed over.

'My husband must not be told of this,' Annie said suddenly. 'Nothing must be said that would worry him or upset him and hinder his recovery.'

'Of course not,' Jacob assured her. 'But one day he might be well enough to want to return to his business. What will you do then?'

'I don't know.'

Annie stared miserably into the fire. Jacob saw that it would serve no purpose to continue the conversation. He had no doubt that what Philip had told Annie would be correct and that it would be very hard to prove he had done anything illegal. But that was only true of the captain's legitimate business concerns.

Jacob had discovered that there was another side to Philip Bertram's activities. For some years now he had been using Captain Walton's business as a cover for his own dealings with crooked agents and unscrupulous sea captains who cared nothing for the welfare of their crews and would cut the rations to the minimum while making sure the ship's owner paid for the full amount.

It was a dangerous game the captain's nephew had been playing, for the men he had been dealing with would stop at nothing to avoid detection. In all probability he had been sailing very close to the wind. Jacob would have to tread carefully, but he was determined that one day, in one way or another, Philip Bertram would account for what he had done.

All he could do now was assure Mrs Walton that he would help in any way he could. She seemed to make an effort to throw off all gloomy thoughts and she made him promise once more that he would not mention any of this to her husband before she suggested that he might like to go in and see the captain now.

'It will be good for Samuel to see someone new,' she said. 'Josie and I both try to stimulate him by talking about anything we think will interest him and, to give Philip his due, he is most respectful to his uncle when he visits. He talks about buying and selling and interesting new stock, always pretending that my husband is still the master.'

'Really?'

'I must admit I was surprised at first, but I have come to believe that, devious and greedy though he undoubtedly is, my husband's nephew is not a cruel man. I have always been aware of how much he cares for his mother, and she, in turn, has never let him forget how grateful they both should be to the captain for taking them in and providing them with a home when Philip's father left them penniless.' Annie sighed. 'And, after all, perhaps Philip really believes that what he has done is for the best.'

Then, not giving Jacob a chance to respond, she led the way out of the room and across a narrow passage to the bedroom. She asked him to wait at the door while she checked to see that everything was in order. A moment later Mrs Baxter came out carrying a towel and some shaving tackle on a tray. She smiled up at Jacob and said, 'You can go in now, sir.'

Jacob paused with his hand on the door and collected his thoughts. This would be the first time he would come face to face with Captain Walton since arriving in Newcastle to set up the mission. He had wanted to visit him before now – and in happier circumstances – but he had been nervous about the outcome.

'Are you there, Mr Goodwright?' he heard Annie call. 'Didn't Mrs Baxter tell you you could come in now?'

Jacob took a deep breath and pushed open the door.

Samuel Walton was sitting up in bed, propped amongst clean plump pillows. Jacob was shocked to see the dark hair streaked with grey and the strong lines of the good man's face weakened with pain.

Mrs Walton was fussing over the bed, straightening the sheets and blankets and placing her husband's hands to rest on top of the flower-patterned eiderdown. She did not turn to greet Jacob but took her husband's face tenderly in her hands and spoke directly to him.

'You have a visitor, Samuel,' she said. 'Mr Goodwright. Remember Mr Goodwright? He's the young American whose father founded the mission. I go there to help with the children. Remember?'

It brought a lump to Jacob's throat to see how intently the captain seemed to be listening to his wife's words; how he frowned and seemed to be straining to make sense of them.

The window of the room was small and only a weak ray of sunlight penetrated the lace curtains and fell across the bed.

'Come forward, Mr Goodwright,' Annie Walton said. 'Come forward so that my husband can see you.' She turned Samuel's face towards Jacob and then stepped back. 'Look, Samuel,' she said. 'Mr Goodwright has come to talk to you.'

Jacob stepped right up to the bed and the sunlight fell across his face. Samuel Walton stared at him blankly. Jacob felt the tension inside him easing and at the same time he was dismayed to think that such a man had been reduced to this.

And then he heard Annie gasp. He glanced at her to find she was staring at Samuel's hands. They had risen from the bed and were reaching towards Jacob.

'Give him your hands,' she whispered.

He did so and found them grasped firmly.

'Look,' Annie said softly, 'look at his face. He's smiling at you.'

And Captain Walton was indeed smiling, a funny lopsided but endearing smile. His lips began to move. He was trying to form a word and, having no success, he gave way to an expression of deepest frustration.

'What is it, Samuel?' Annie asked him. 'What are you trying to say?'

A sound halfway between a laugh and a sob escaped the captain's poor twisted lips but his eyes were smiling. Jacob felt his hands being squeezed more tightly.

'Don't worry,' he said. 'I'll come again. You'll be able to tell me another day.'

Captain Walton nodded. They both knew what it was he would say.

Josie collected her father's newspaper from the newsagent's and tobacconist's kiosk at the station. Betty, who had come with her, bought two magazines. Hannah's maid-cum-companion loved to read by the fire at night and she would pore over the fashion plates and devour the latest instalments of the serial stories. John Braithwaite, the young man who worked in the kiosk, knew her tastes and would alert her if a new story by a favourite author was about to begin.

This morning he had something else for her, a book. Josie watched fascinated as John managed to convey with a few gestures that it was a murder story: a hand across his throat as if it were being cut, looking through an imaginary magnifying glass (the tool of a great detective) and then dropping his head to one side while holding one hand above his head as if he were grasping the hangman's rope.

And then Betty held the book open, pretended to read, closed it and made as if she were handing it back. It was all quite clear. She would read it and return his book. Josie had watched the two of them converse in such a manner several times and, also, she had noticed that the young man was attempting to master the sign language that deaf people used. She wondered if perhaps more than a simple friendship was developing here at the newsstand.

Betty put the book and her magazines carefully on top of the cloth that covered the goods in her basket – Hannah's daily offerings to Annie and Samuel – and they left the station. The day had started brightly enough but in the time it had taken them to buy the newspaper and the magazines and for Betty to indulge in conversation with her friend, the sky had darkened. Heavy clouds were rolling down from the moor top to seep through the village streets and leave the rooftops and the pavements glistening with moisture. Lights gleamed from windows, and the smoke from coal fires, unable to rise, drifted with the mist, making it more dense and no doubt leaving trails of soot.

Josie and Betty glanced at each other and nodded. It had not taken words to decide that they would not walk across the green and no doubt get the hems of their skirts soaking wet. But, as they continued to walk round it, they noticed the figure of a man crossing the grass in their direction. From his position it looked as though he had come from one of the last few cottages, near Annie and Samuel's cottage, in fact, and Josie paused for a moment, peering through the murk and wondering whether it could be her cousin Philip. No, she decided, he was not tall enough.

She was just about to walk on when she realized that Betty was also staring at the advancing figure. Josie smiled and inclined her head in the direction they were going as a signal that they should begin walking again but Betty took no notice of her beyond a quick glance and a dismissive frown. She returned her gaze to the man walking towards them across the green and, as he drew nearer, her eyes widened. Josie tried to decide what emotion was gripping the young woman so fiercely that she appeared rooted to the spot. She decided it was shock.

Then, without warning, Betty suddenly thrust the basket

towards her roughly. Josie grasped hold of it just in time to prevent it falling. 'What . . .' she began, turning her face towards her companion so that she would be able to read her lips, but the girl had gone.

Josie watched in astonishment as her grandmother's maid, heedless of the wet grass, ran across the green. Just before she reached the approaching figure of the man they both stopped, and it seemed to Josie that they were staring at each other. She didn't know how long the moment lasted but the next thing that happened was even more incredible.

Betty flung herself into the stranger's arms and, even at this distance, Josie could hear the wild sobbing sounds the girl was making. Even in her state of astonishment Josie had the presence of mind to look about her and she was glad that the inclement weather had kept folk indoors. She knew that not all of the Bluebell Inn's customers approved of Betty, and this behaviour would only reinforce their prejudices. She decided she had better go and see what was happening.

Not knowing what she would discover, Josie began to walk towards them. By now Betty had fallen silent and had stepped back, and the way she was standing suggested that she was staring at the man's face intently. And he was talking to her in a low voice. He had taken hold of her arms and was speaking slowly. Josie could not see his face but she knew somehow that he was speaking clearly so that Betty could read his lips. Whoever he was, he knew that Betty was deaf.

They were so intent on what they were saying to each other that they did not seem to notice her walking towards him. It was only when he heard her startled gasp of surprise that he looked up and saw her.

'Jacob,' she said. 'Jacob Goodwright. But how. . . ?'

Betty, seeing Jacob glance up, turned a tear-stained face towards Josie and she took her arm and smiled through her tears. She touched Jacob's shoulder and her mouth worked as she tried to speak out loud. At first Josie had no idea what Betty was trying to say. She shook her head and looked from one to the other of them in bewilderment.

And then looked at him, *really* looked at him for the first time. And instead of a well-dressed gentleman she saw a ragged

357

boy; the boy who had saved her sister's doll and then saved Flora herself when she had jumped from the merry-go-round at the Christmas fair on the quayside.

She had the basket over one arm but with her other hand she caught Betty's hand and held it tightly. 'I know,' she said. 'I know what you're trying to tell me.'

Josie was aware that, just like Betty, she had begun to weep. But she was not crying with sorrow. She turned to Jacob – who was not Jacob – and, smiling through her tears, she said, 'You're Tom. Tom Sutton, aren't you? I never thought I'd see you again.'

Josie handed the basket to her stepmother and, remembering to take out Betty's book and magazines, she excused herself.

'Grandma Hannah sent these,' she said. 'A new-baked loaf and some teacakes, I think. But do you mind if I don't stay this morning?' she asked. 'I have . . . I have something I must do.'

Annie looked puzzled – she was probably wondering why Betty hadn't delivered Hannah's baked offerings, as she usually did – but she smiled good-naturedly. 'That's all right, dear,' she said. 'I'll read the newspaper to your father. I would like that.'

Josie turned to go but, suddenly on impulse, she turned back and hugged her stepmother. Annie looked surprised but, after a moment's hesitation, she returned the hug.

'Take care,' she called when Josie took off and ran across the green. 'You'll get your skirt soaking wet!'

Josie heard her but she didn't stop. She was clutching the magazines and book with one hand but she raised the other and waved without looking behind. She wanted to catch up with Betty and Jacob – Tom – who had already started to walk up the track that led away from the village and to her grandparents' inn.

Grandma Hannah said they could go and sit in the parlour. The old woman had been surprised when they walked into the kitchen. Josie had introduced Mr Goodwright as a friend of Annie's – it was all she could think of doing for the moment and, in any case, that was true – and she said that they needed to discuss something.

'I'll explain later,' Josie said. 'But would you mind if Betty sat with us? You see I think Mr Goodwright may be an old friend of hers.'

'An old friend of Betty's?' Grandma Hannah said. And then she surprised Josie by saying, 'Is this Tom, then?'

'Yes . . . but how do you know his name?'

'The morning she arrived here, a Christmas Day it was, she was grieving for someone. I heard your father tell her that someone called Tom would want her to be safe and happy and that she was not to worry about him.'

'I see,' Josie said, although she didn't really, at least not very clearly. But that was why they needed somewhere quiet to sit while everything could be explained.

How pleased she was that Flora had persuaded Margery Baxter to take the train into Hexham with her today. It was market day and as well as wandering round the stalls they intended to have a meal at a popular café in Beaumont Street, opposite the abbey. They would not be back for hours yet.

Now, although it was only mid-morning, the sky was darker than ever. The lamps were lit and the fire was blazing in the parlour. When Josie had finished talking to her grandmother she walked in to find Jacob looking at the framed paintings hanging on the walls. He turned to smile at her.

'Betty tells me these are your work,' he said.

Betty was by his side and she nodded and smiled. Josie had no idea how Betty had told him such a thing but she was already beginning to realize that these old friends must have worked out a way of communicating many years ago. Perhaps Betty had taught him the sign language.

'They're very good,' Jacob said. 'Have you ever thought of exhibiting your work?'

'No, never.'

'Well, you should. And if you have another view of the old keep, like this one, I'd like to buy it and send it to my father.'

'Your father?'

'Mr Goodwright.' He paused. 'It's time I explained, isn't it?'

'Yes.'

Jacob and Josie took the chairs at each side of the hearth and Betty drew up a padded stool and placed it so that she could sit and look up at Jacob's face and follow the movement of his lips while he talked.

'Where shall I begin?' he asked.

'First tell me what I should call you?' Josie said.

'Jacob. Jacob Goodwright. That's who I am and have been ever since Isaac and Martha Goodwright rescued me from the streets of New York and took me into their home and their hearts. They regard me as their son and I wouldn't have it any other way.'

'You stowed away, didn't you?'

'How do you know that?'

'One Christmas Eve, a long time ago, I was looking out of my bedroom window and I saw a small figure climbing up one of the mooring ropes of a vessel that was bound for America.'

'What made you think it was me?'

'I'm not sure. I probably didn't at the time. But then I never saw you again.'

'Yes, I stowed away.'

'How did you survive the journey?'

'I hid in—'

'A lifeboat!'

He laughed. 'Not very original.'

That was true. But Josie remembered her dreams . . . the rocking motion, the canvas above her, the salty tang of the spray and the bone-white decks in the moonlight.

'But to live in such confinement!' Josie said.

'I would slip out at night,' he said.

And, of course, Josie already knew this. It was almost as if she had been there with him. 'But what did you eat? Drink?'

'The only thing I had to steal was water. I had my rations, thanks to your father.'

'My father?'

'He knew I had to get away from Newcastle.'

'Why?'

For the first time Jacob faltered. He looked grave, and when he spoke he took Betty's hand and looked into her face. Josie saw how still the young woman had become.

'I . . . we . . . had angered someone very dangerous.'

'We? You mean you and Betty? What had you done?'

'Betty and I lived as we could. We were children of the streets. We begged, we stole, we had to in order to survive. It was not the way either of us would have chosen to live.'

'And this person you angered?'

'Was evil.'

'What did you do?'

Jacob shook his head. 'It's not for me to say. And, in any case, it should be left in the past.'

It seemed to Josie that Jacob was reassuring Betty when he said this. She noticed that he gripped her hands more tightly. After a moment Jacob released his hold a little and sat back in his chair. He smiled at Josie. 'Your father promised me that he would find somewhere safe for Betty, and I knew I could trust him. And, of course, I intended to ask him what had become of my old friend – as soon as I had met him and worked out how to tell him that his wife's friend Jacob Goodwright was once known as Tom Sutton.' Jacob smiled. 'But now I have found Betty and she has told me that she has been very happy here. She says your grandparents are good people.'

'But I cannot understand why my father did not find somewhere safe for *you*,' Josie said. 'Why did he let you become a stowaway? Of all people he would have known of the dangers! And yet you say he actually helped you by giving you rations!'

'And turning a blind eye!' Jacob laughed softly. 'You see, your father also knew that nothing he could have said would have stopped me. I was determined to go. To leave this country and start a new life. I used to watch the emigrants waiting on the quayside, I saw how determined they were, how full of hope that the New World would be a better place to live than the old.'

'And was it?'

'Not for everyone.' Jacob leaned forward again. The firelight played across his face. He looked troubled.

'What was it like?' Josie asked. 'What did you find when you arrived there?'

'It wasn't a bit as I imagined it would be. You know, people call America the New World so I expected everything to be clean and bright and new. When we docked I had to hide amongst the immigrants who were disembarking. I mingled with a large unruly family, whose children were nearly as ragged as I was. In fact I'd chosen them some time ago; the boys were badly behaved, their mother had a new baby and their father had to care for the younger ones. The older lads had been running wild.

'Well, I kept in the midst of them until we were safely ashore and then I slipped away. When I looked about me I thought for a moment that we hadn't gone to America at all, that we'd turned round and sailed right back home again – or at least to some other British port.'

'Why did you think that?'

'The buildings were old and tired – just like at home. When I left the docks I found the alleyways were narrow and reeking with decaying rubbish. The filthy windows of the dwellings were cracked or broken. I think I'd never experienced such despair. I thought if the New World is like this I might as well have stayed at home. I even contemplated stowing away and going back again – until I remembered what might be waiting for me.'

Josie saw the look that passed between Jacob and Betty at those words and she wondered if he would ever tell her the full story.

'So what did you do?' she asked.

'What could I do? I hadn't come all that way to curl up in the corner of some crumbling tenement and wait to die – or, worse, be murdered.'

'Murdered?'

'Oh, yes. Even the poor patched clothes I wore or my haversack would have been prize enough to tempt some poor soul – and probably a child.'

'A child? No, you can't mean that!'

'But I do. There are as many abandoned children living on the streets, if not more, as there are right here. They live how they can, again, just like here, but with one difference.'

'What was that?'

'Everyone carries a weapon of some sort. Usually a knife. I very soon learned to defend myself and, in a fury of despair and anger, I became an even more proficient thief than I had been before.'

'Was there nothing else you could do?'

'If there was I didn't discover it.' He sighed. 'I had no real

362

plan, you know. I'd heard that America was the land of opportunity so I suppose I thought I would be able to find work straight away – as an errand boy, perhaps, except I couldn't read or write. Or perhaps a street sweeper, a stable lad, anything to earn an honest crust. But there was nothing – at least if there was there were a hundred other lads all going after the same job.'

'New York must be a terrible place.'

'Oh, no, don't think that! It's not all like that. And just think of some of the cities in this country – there is just as much hardship. It's the same the world over. No, I've learned that America is a wonderful country, and there are good people working to ensure that things will improve for all the new-comers to its shore. People who are descended from folk who have already made the journey and prospered there – like Isaac and Martha Goodwright.'

'How did you meet them?'

'As you know, Isaac has a successful trading empire. They are wealthy and childless, and are driven by conscience to try to help their fellow men. And they do so in all kinds of ways. But Martha, particularly, works with the street children, orphans most of them – and I don't just mean she donates money – she spends part of nearly every day cooking and cleaning in one of the establishments they founded.'

'And you were living in one of the orphanages?'

'No. I was living in an abandoned brewery. The walls were crumbling, the beams rotten and the place was rat-infested. There were other children there. We drew together into a group like a family; we looked after each other. We would share what we had stolen or scavenged, make fires at night to keep the rats away – throw embers at them if they got too bold. Take turns to watch over the little ones.'

To Josie's dismay, as she listened to Jacob's description of his life in New York, she felt an ache of misery growing in her throat. She knew she was near to tears. Perhaps Jacob sensed this for his voice took on a more cheerful tone.

'We would tell each other stories – one of the girls, Molly, could read –' here Jacob took Betty's hand and smiled at her, 'just like you, Betty. I would steal books for her when I could.'

Betty nodded and smiled and made a soft sound in her throat midway between a laugh and a sob. Josie could see that this tale meant much to her.

'But the true stories were the ones that frightened us.' He grew solemn again. 'The older boys said that in the very building we were taking shelter in there had been many murders, one every night for three years. Those who believed in such things said the place was haunted by all the lost souls of the poor victims.'

'How dreadful.'

'The worst thing was that there was nothing for those children to do, no way forward except to become criminals themselves. Our little group, that had grown together to give us a sense of family, was becoming a gang of hardened criminals. I knew I had to move on again.'

Jacob was silent for a while. Neither Josie nor Betty stirred. Save for the crackling of the fire the room was quiet.

'I lived alone for a while,' he said eventually. His eyes were unfocused as he stared at the fire.

What was he seeing, Josie wondered.

'Then one day I saw a gang of big lads set upon a woman in the street. It was a respectable street in one of the slightly better parts of town, but the gangs were getting bolder. The woman had just come out of one of the big houses. They surrounded her, whooping like savages. I could see she was terrified. I wanted to shout to her and tell her to throw them her purse – they would have snatched it and gone without hurting her – but I knew she wouldn't be able to hear me and she clutched her purse tightly with both hands. I saw two of the lads had cudgels. It was getting serious.'

'What did you do?' Josie asked.

Jacob smiled. 'What makes you think I did anything?'

'I'm sure of it.'

'I acted instinctively. I was smaller than any of them and I was pretty sure I was fleeter. I dashed up, dodged in between them and yanked the purse right out of her hands and then I took off like the wind.'

'You what?'

Jacob's grin was wider than ever. He looked at Josie, whose

eyes were wide, and then down at Betty's upturned face. Betty was staring at him unbelievingly. Josie was reminded that Betty had been watching Jacob's lips closely and probably understood most of what he had been saying. And like Josie herself, she was shocked and disappointed.

Betty said something that sounded like, 'Noooo . . . nooo,' and dropped her face into her hands.

Jacob reached forward and prised her fingers away from her face. He looked into her eyes and said, 'I'm sorry. Don't cry. It's all right.'

'You mean you didn't take it?' Josie said. 'You were teasing us? That's cruel.'

'No, I wasn't teasing. I did take the purse – no, Betty, listen.' She had begun to shake her head again so Jacob said clearly and carefully, 'I wanted to draw the gang away from the poor woman. It worked, they all came after me. I ran for my life – literally! Then I went to ground.'

He paused and Josie realized she had been holding her breath. She let it out with a sigh. 'You'd better finish the story before you make us both very cross with you.'

'I knew the best places to hide. I laid low all day. I can't pretend I wasn't tempted to keep the purse. But I kept thinking about the lady. She had such a kind face. So that night I took the purse back to the orphanage.'

'The orphanage?'

'Yes, that was the building she'd just left.'

'And the purse belonged to Martha Goodwright?' Josie said.

'So I discovered the next day. I didn't dare go back on the streets; I thought the gang might have recognized me. I asked the matron to take me in – and furthermore would she please find a place for me in one of the other establishments, preferably as far away from New York as possible.'

'And your wish was granted?'

'In more ways than I could have hoped for. Mr Goodwright wanted to meet me and thank me. Mrs Goodwright was convinced I had saved her life.'

'You probably had! So did they send you to another orphanage?'

'They took me home with them, cleaned me up, bought me

clothes and sent me away to school. The school was another of their foundations and it was specifically for children like me – but we were encouraged to aspire for anything we were capable of; we were not just trained for apprenticeships or domestic service. There are lawyers, doctors, teachers living in America now who all started off in that school.

'In the vacations the pupils all went to stay with good, kind families. I went to stay with the Goodwrights.' He smiled. 'It's a long story, but Martha became attached to me and they adopted me. They are kind and loving parents. I have been very fortunate.

'Oh, and something else.' He smiled at Betty. 'I asked them to look for a friend of mine and they did. I have a sister. They adopted Molly too.'

Grandma Hannah insisted that Jacob should have his midday meal with them and she told him he was welcome to stay the night. But he told her that he had to get back to Newcastle. In truth, he could have stayed. He would have liked simply to be with Josie but he did not want to be at the inn when Flora returned.

He cursed himself for a coward but, now that he had spent these hours with Josie, he was further away than ever from being able to decide whether he should tell her about Flora's part in the jewel robbery. And with this lying between them he knew it was not the time to reveal how much he cared for her – and to ask her whether she felt the same way. These thoughts were troubling him when he took his leave and that was probably why he suddenly seemed cold and distant.

Later that day Josie realized that when they had met he had been on his way to the station. He had been to visit her parents and then it seemed he had been going to return to Newcastle without coming to see her. But, of course, there was no reason why he should. It was Tom Sutton who had been her friend, not Jacob Goodwright. None the less, she did feel more than a little disappointed.

Chapter Seventeen

December

'What are you doing sitting here by yourself, lass? I told Mrs Bertram we'd finished a while back, and she's waiting for you to come and have a cup of tea with her.'

Josie looked up from her bed to see Janet Rodgerson smiling at her from the doorway of the bedroom that she and Flora had shared since they were small children. 'I suppose I was just thinking . . . remembering . . .' Josie said. 'It's hard to believe that this may be the last night I spend here.'

Mrs Rodgerson looked troubled. 'Does that make you sad?'

'Of course. I don't want to leave this house. I've been happy here.'

'Have you?'

'You sound doubtful.'

'Mebbes I am. It seems to me . . . I shouldn't say this, but . . .' she shook her head. 'No, I divven't want to offend you.'

'Go on. I promise I won't be offended. I'm curious.'

'Well, perhaps you have been happy. You've wanted for nowt. Your father's a kind man but, well, I divven't want to criticize him, but it's not been hard to see that he's always favoured your sister.'

'No, I can't accept that. I've never been deprived of anything; I know he loves me. It's just that our mother died giving birth to Flora, and Flora, who looks so like her, became special to my father.'

'And you've never resented that?'

'Never. She's special to me too.'

'Yer a grand lass, Josie. A good sister. But after what you've just said, don't you think it's strange that yer stepmother won't let Flora anywhere near yer da now? I don't think she's been allowed to see him since he was struck down, has she?'

'I've thought about that and I think I know why. I think my father must have indicated somehow that he doesn't want Flora to see him.'

'But why would he do that?'

'Because he loves her so much. I think he doesn't want to distress her.'

'Distress her?'

'If she saw the change in him it might be too much for her.'

Janet shook her head. 'Well, I suppose you could be right, but somehow I divven't think so. Your sister may look like Dresden china but I believe she's tough as bell metal. Ee, I'm sorry, I shouldn't hev said that!'

'No, that's all right, and I too believe that Flora is quite strong enough to cope with the situation. Perhaps I will be able to convince my father of that as he improves.'

'And he is getting better, isn't he?'

'Yes, slowly but surely. And he seems to be happy in the rooms my stepmother chose for them at Tynemouth. He sits at the window and watches the ships coming in and out of the river mouth. Now that some movement has come back he's even beginning to keep a log – a sort of diary of shipping traffic.'

Janet suddenly crossed her arms over her body and shivered. 'Well, if you don't mind, Miss Josie, I think I'd like to go and sit by the fire in your aunt's room. Are you coming?'

'Yes, I suppose we're all done here.' Josie rose and turned to pick up two objects that had been lying on the bed beside her. 'But we must find room in one of the boxes for these two.'

'What've you got there?'

'I found them at the back of the cupboard. My old rag doll, Susan, and Flora's doll, Annabel.'

She held them up for Janet Rodgerson to see. The woman smiled. 'Give them to me. I'll wrap them carefully and find a safe place for them. Childhood memories, I suppose?'

'Yes,' Josie said. 'I wouldn't want to part with them.' And

she knew in her heart that, precious though the moppet Susan had been to her, it was Flora's doll, Annabel, that she treasured the most. Not because the doll had a porcelain face and real blonde curls, but because of the day she had been hurled from the window and ended up in the hands of a certain ragged boy . . .

On the way to her aunt's room Janet asked her if she would mind overseeing the return of any books to the subscription library and the registering of the new address. 'Poor little Violet's run off her feet and I can't trust that Patience to do it – or rather Mrs Bertram, as we hev to call her now.'

Josie smiled. 'She has other things to think of, I believe.'

'Uhum, yes, clever lass that she is. Your poor aunt hasn't come round to the idea yet. Not only does she hev a daughter-in-law she's not particularly fond of, but she's going to be a grandmother a lot sooner than is decent.'

'I'm sure my aunt will relent when she sees the baby.' Josie wondered if it was a mite improper to be talking about her cousin and his wife like this to someone who, after all, was a servant, but somehow she could never think of Janet Rodgerson as anything but a sensible friend.

'You're right, pet,' Janet said, 'bairns can work magic and melt the ice in many a heart. And at least your poor aunt won't hev to live here at young Mrs Bertram's mercy. Tomorrow we're off to the house in Gosforth.'

Aunt Charlotte was nodding in her armchair by the fire. But when she heard them enter, she stirred and smiled. 'There you are,' she said. 'All done?'

'Yes, Mrs Bertram,' Janet Rodgerson replied. 'Miss Josie and I have managed everything between us.'

'I suppose you are telling me that Flora has not helped you at all?' Aunt Charlotte sounded stern but Josie could see from her smile that she was amused.

'She wanted to go out,' Josie said. 'I told her it was all right.'

'But where was she going on such a cold day?'

'To school.'

'School? But I thought she'd decided not to go back?'

'That's right. But she wanted to talk to Miss Garrett about something . . . she said she wanted to apologize.'

'For being a handful while she was there, I suppose?' Aunt Charlotte laughed.

'Something like that.'

'Well, all I can say is that she must be growing up a little and it's about time. I'm very pleased with her.'

Josie was pleased too, although she wasn't quite sure exactly what it was Flora was going to apologize for. She had caused a lot of bother, it was true, and made a fuss about many things. But she had not been the first of Miss Garrett's pupils to be a 'handful' and she would not be the last. But if this visit to their old school today was a sign that she was maturing, then Josie could only be pleased. Even if it had meant that Flora had managed to avoid any hard work, as usual.

Miss Garrett asked Flora to sit down and then said, 'Would you mind if I just finished writing this report?'

The headmistress had not smiled and it was not a question. Flora felt that she was being deliberately put in her place. There was a small fire burning in the hearth but it wasn't sufficient to heat the high-ceilinged old room adequately and Flora shivered a little and drew the folds of her new winter cloak more tightly together. The cloak, a lovely cherry-red velvet, had a hood trimmed with silver fox fur and it had been a gift from Forbes's mother.

It had arrived at the house on the quayside along with an identical cloak for Josie and a charming letter saying that Mrs Agnes Robson hoped that Flora and Josie would enjoy wearing the cloaks and that she hoped to meet both of them when she returned from Egypt. Meanwhile she had left instructions that the house in Gosforth be ready for them at the beginning of December.

Scratch, scratch went Miss Garrett's pen over the paper and Flora watched as the headmistress went on writing as if she had forgotten all about her. She noticed that Miss Garrett was wearing fingerless gloves and that, every now and then, she had to stop writing to dab at her nose with a large white handkerchief.

Then, at last, she carefully wiped her pen and laid it aside.

Still without looking up, she blotted her work and finally sat back in her chair.

'Well, then, Flora,' she said. 'I must admit that I am surprised to see you. Do you wish to come back to school after all?'

'No, it's not that.'

'I was very sorry to hear about your father's illness, you know. I expect you want to be at home with him?'

Flora looked down. She had no idea how to respond. How could she tell this woman that she did indeed wish to be at home with her father but that her stepmother wouldn't hear of it? It would only confirm Miss Garrett's low opinion of her.

But the headmistress's voice took on a kinder tone when she said, 'I'm sorry, dear, I've upset you. Of course you are worried about your father and I should have realized that you must have something important to say if you can find the time to come here. Now what do you want to tell me?'

At that moment Flora felt like making an excuse and leaving. It had taken all her courage to come to her old school and now she didn't know if she could go through with it.

'Well?' the headmistress said.

'I . . . I've come to apologize . . . and, if possible, to put things right,' she said in a rush.

There was a small silence, then: 'Well, that was the last thing I was expecting to hear,' Miss Garrett said. Flora looked up to find the headmistress smiling. 'I admit you were not always an easy child, Flora, but there have been worse than you.'

'No! There couldn't have been!'

'My dear, please don't get so upset. I suppose it's because you've been having a difficult time at home – it's caused you to think about the past and—'

'That's right. I've been thinking and I've decided I had to tell you – it wasn't Muriel's fault at all.'

'I beg your pardon?'

'Muriel . . . Muriel Rowe . . .'

'Ah, the bottle of lavender water.'

'In Bainbridge's. Muriel said someone else must have put it in her pocket, you remember?'

'Indeed I do. Are you saying that Muriel was telling the

truth and that we should have believed her? Was it you who took the bottle of lavender water?'

'No – yes, in a way – oh, dear. It's not straightforward.'

'Flora, please try to explain.'

'Well . . . Muriel did take the lavender water and no one else put it in her pocket, but I don't think she would have taken it if I hadn't told her to.'

'Told her to take it? You told her to steal something?'

'Not directly – oh, please don't get cross. I dared her to do it. It was a kind of game. I . . . I found it thrilling. And when she got caught I just let her take all the blame – and you see she's a much nicer person than I am because she could have told the truth and you would have known it was my fault.'

'Oh dear, Flora, what a sad little story.' Miss Garrett shook her head. 'And why are you telling me about this now?'

'Because I feel guilty, I suppose. I mean it was wrong, wasn't it?'

'Most certainly. And I shall write to Muriel Rowe and tell her what you have said. But it still doesn't excuse her behaviour, you know.'

'But she kept quiet – she protected me. She could have said that I'd made her do it!'

'Flora, if you are telling the truth—'

'I am!'

'Then you didn't "make" Muriel take the bottle of lavender water, you dared her to do it.'

'That's right.'

'She could have refused to do it.'

'Yes, but—'

'And she lied when she said someone must have slipped it in her pocket – she was trying to lay the blame on someone else.'

'Yes . . .'

'And after that she was trapped by her own lies, I'm afraid. You know she has always stuck to that story. She has never owned up to what really happened.'

Flora groaned. 'I thought it would make me feel better – coming here today and telling you the truth. I thought it would clear things up but now you're going to write to Muriel and tell her that you know for a fact that she was telling lies! I feel worse than ever!'

'And so you should. I must say I find it hard to have any sympathy for you. It was brave of you to confess, Flora, and I shall tell Muriel that you have insisted it was all your fault. Will that help?'

'A little.'

'Poor Flora, caught in a tangled web and it's all your own making. Now go home, my dear, and I'm sure you won't do anything so silly again.'

Flora caught a tram most of the way home and she sat hunched and miserable on the top deck. She had gone up there to make sure she was alone – none of the other passengers were foolhardy enough to brave the biting wind except for one fellow bundled up in a caped overcoat. She pulled her hood well up over her head and forward. This was to protect her ears from the cold, she told herself, but in reality it was to hide the fact that she was crying.

It had taken every ounce of courage she possessed to confess to Miss Garrett and she had done so under the mistaken impression that it would put things right. She was truly sorry about the way she had led Muriel on to steal that silly bottle of lavender water. Why on earth had she thought that sort of thing was fun – a game – to take things from unsuspecting shop-keepers? Just look what it had led to. She had become truly sickened with herself when she had realized that she was not just a clever daring girl playing a game but a cheap little thief.

Well, at least Vincent had promised that the robbery at Angela's birthday celebrations would be the last time she would have to help him. She was glad that it had all gone wrong, no matter what Vincent had said about the insurance company making good the loss. It was still wrong to steal the jewellery in the first place. Now she would have to hope that Vincent would keep his promise.

Today was the only day she had ventured out since she and Josie had returned to Newcastle. Tomorrow they were moving to Forbes's mother's house in Gosforth. And, just to be safe, she wouldn't go anywhere. She would stay at home every day and write letters to Forbes and read to Aunt Charlotte or do anything

Josie wanted her to do to help. And once she was safely married to Forbes they would live in London and she would never be in danger of meeting Vincent again.

'So Captain Walton is living in a fine apartment overlooking the sea at Tynemouth?'

Fox Telford wiped the froth off his upper lip with the back of a dirty hand and set his tankard down on the table. He was in a good mood.

'Yes, but he's still far from well,' Vincent said.

'Makes no difference to me,' his father said. 'Here – help yourself.' He pushed a jug of ale and an empty glass across the table. 'Want some bread and cheese?'

'No. I've already eaten.'

Fox laughed. 'In some fine restaurant, no doubt. Just remember who pays for the way you live, that's all.'

'I do remember and I try to do as you say.'

'Aye, you've done well these last few weeks.'

Vincent was just about to pour himself some ale when his father got up and, seizing the jug, took it over to the fire and thrust the hot poker into it. Then he brought the jug back to the table and poured a generous measure of brandy into the steaming ale before filling Vincent's glass.

'Drink up,' he said. ' 'S cold, today. I divven't want you catching a chill.'

Vincent undid the buttons of his overcoat; it was a coach-man's coat with a generous cape falling from the shoulders, not his usual sort of apparel, but he hadn't wanted to be recognized. The hat he'd worn had been big enough to cover his distinctive red hair and a muffler had obscured most of his face. He was only just beginning to thaw out after another day's work finding information for his father.

'But he's capable of understanding what's going on, you say?' Fox returned to the subject of his old enemy like scratching a scab on an old wound.

'I've told you, his wife pushes him out in a Bath chair and they talk to each other. Nothing complicated, but it's clear he's not lost his wits.'

'And his daughters?'

'You know I've been keeping an eye on them ever since they moved back to the house on the quayside.'

Flora hadn't gone out much. In fact, Vincent could only remember her venturing forth on one occasion, all wrapped up in a bonny red velvet cloak and hood. Puzzlingly she had gone to her old school in Jesmond and then straight home again. She had never noticed him following her. But then she wouldn't have been expecting to see him dressed as a coachman.

'And now they've moved into the house by the moor?'

'Yes,' Vincent replied.

His father meant the house in Gosforth that overlooked the Town Moor. It had been more difficult for Vincent to hang about there. There were fewer people around; he'd had to buy a little dog from the market and pretend he was one of the regular dog walkers. It was a nice little beast who was thriving on the rich scraps from the kitchen in Fox's lodging house.

Vincent regarded it now as it lay curled up on the dirty floorboards near the fire. His father had taken to it, even letting it sit on his lap but, knowing the man's uncertain temper, Vincent had decided to take the dog to his mother's house in Yorkshire when there was no further need for it.

Fox cut himself a slice of bread and a hunk of cheese, and smiled expansively. 'Well, now,' he said. 'I'll tell you what we're going to do.'

Vincent listened to the plan, which involved the theft of a painting, and wasn't much different to what he'd expected, but he really couldn't understand why his father should be bothered to carry it out for such small rewards and said so. His father scowled. 'It's not your place to question me,' he said. 'Now hev I made myself clear? Hev you any questions?'

'How do you know about the picture?' he asked.

His father grinned. 'Daft question. Just think on it.'

And, of course, it was a daft question. Fox's lodging house was simply a cover for all sorts of criminal activities and Fox probably knew the contents of most of the houses of the wealthy for miles around.

'And it really is worth so much? A little drawing like that?'

'It might be little but it's Dutch. What they call an Old Master. It's more than a hundred years old, by someone called

Cornelis van Something-or-other. I know someone in Antwerp who'll pay a king's ransom for it. And I know a skipper who'll take me there.'

'You're going to the Netherlands?'

'Aye, and never coming back.'

'But this place . . . the lodging house . . . ?'

'It can fester as far as I'm concerned. It's served its purpose and I've saved my pile.'

'And what about me?'

'You'll gan to your mother's, and when the time's right, I'll send for you both. Divven't fret, I won't forget my son and heir! What are you scowling for?'

'The girl . . . Flora . . . do you really think she'll co-operate?'

'Well, that's up to you, isn't it?'

His father looked at him threateningly and Vincent hastily agreed that it was. 'And then you'll leave her alone?' he asked.

Fox laughed. 'Aye. I suppose I will. After she's served her purpose.'

And with that Vincent had to be satisfied.

'Hard life,' Samuel Walton said and, although his speech was still laboured, Annie understood his words and also why he'd said them.

She'd pushed the Bath chair along the headland towards Cullercoats Bay and they'd paused to look down at the fishermen guiding their cobles back through angry white-topped waters into the safety of the harbour.

'Much danger – little money – women work too.'

Annie looked at the fishwives, as they were called, waiting on the beach to help their menfolk haul the boats up and unload the catch.

'Good women,' Samuel said. 'Lucky men.' Suddenly he brought his hand out from under the blanket and reached for hers. He squeezed it tightly and smiled up at her. 'Lucky man,' he said, and she saw a tear brim over and trickle down his cheek. 'I am a lucky man.'

'Are you sure you want me to sell them?'

Ralph Lowther stood with his land agent in the portrait

gallery of Four Winds Hall. 'Quite sure,' he said. 'They can either go with the house, some *nouveau riche* industrialist can buy himself a family history as well as an ancestral home, or you can send them to the auction rooms in Newcastle.'

The agent looked doubtful.

'What's the matter?' Ralph asked.

'You won't get much for them. They're hardly masterpieces, if you don't mind my saying so.'

'I don't mind what you say about them. My wife doesn't want them cluttering up the London house and that's that.'

'But—'

'What now?'

'You said it yourself – the pictures represent your family history.'

'And what use is a history if there isn't going to be a future?'

'I don't understand.'

'I'm the last in the direct line; I have no children, nor are there likely to be any, and the only distant cousin I know of runs an inn right here in Moorburn. Hardly the right place to hang the family portraits. And before you ask if she has issue, she has granddaughters, but I can assure you she would not want them to inherit anything to do with the Lowthers. Now let's go. I have to get back to London.'

Sir Ralph tossed the bunch of keys to his agent and strode out of the room. The man lingered for a moment and looked at the portraits. If he'd had a fanciful turn of mind he would have said the faces of the long-dead Lowthers looked reproachful. Before he left to follow his master he noticed a mark on the wall that showed one portrait was missing – or rather there'd been a picture hanging there until recently. He was not to know that no matter what his employer had said, he had decided to keep one of the paintings and had already shipped it off to London.

It was the portrait of a young girl in a flowing high-waisted gown of green velvet. The neckline and the sleeves were trimmed with fur. One of her hands was resting on the head of a long-legged hound. A tiny circlet of white flowers and dark green leaves crowned her abundant fair hair, which cascaded down over her shoulders. The portrait had been painted so long ago that no one could remember the girl's name. But Ralph didn't care what her name might have been. To him this was a portrait of Flora.

'I have a letter from our stepmother, would you like to hear it?' Josie asked.

She was sitting with Aunt Charlotte, Flora and Mrs Rodgerson in the morning room of the house in Gosforth. Bright sunshine streamed in through the windows but the lawns were white with frost and the bare branches of the trees looked very black against the sky. Inside the pleasant room the fire burned brightly and Aunt Charlotte looked as if she were about to drop off to sleep.

She roused herself to say, 'Yes, please, Josie. I hope there's more good news.'

'There is indeed.'

Josie had already read the letter over her morning tea. It told of her father's continued improvement and how happy he and Annie were in their home by the sea. As she read it out to the others she noticed that Flora rose from her chair and wandered over to the window seat where she sat down and pressed her face to the pane as she looked out into the garden.

At one point Aunt Charlotte interrupted Josie and asked, 'Does my brother's wife not give any indication of when you may visit your father, you and Flora?'

'No, she doesn't.'

'I expect she wants to wait until Captain Walton's a bit stronger,' Janet Rodgerson said.

'Do you?' Aunt Charlotte said. 'Well, if that's what you think, you're a better woman than I am, Janet Rodgerson. Do you want to know my opinion? I think the woman is positively relishing holding the reins of power like this.'

'Why would she do that?' Mrs Rodgerson asked.

'Because she probably thinks we've never given her enough respect in the past.'

'And did you? Give the lass respect, I mean?'

Josie was constantly surprised to see how her aunt's companion spoke to her like an equal – and how her aunt didn't seem to mind. The friendship, or whatever it was that had developed between them, was obviously good for both of them.

'Perhaps we didn't,' Aunt Charlotte said grudgingly. 'So now she's making us pay for it.'

'Or perhaps Mrs Walton is enjoying the experience of having her man all to herself,' Janet Rodgerson said. 'Hev you thought of that?'

Aunt Charlotte smiled. 'You're probably right. But she should consider his daughters' feelings, shouldn't she? I mean, Josie was allowed to visit when they were up at Moorburn, but poor little Flora hasn't seen her father since the day he was struck down. And she hasn't spoken to him since he and Annie set off on holiday. Now that's downright cruel!'

'Shall I go on?' Josie asked. 'They have been for some interesting walks and explored the old priory and castle keep.'

'Yes, please, pet,' Janet Rodgerson said. 'You read so nicely it's a treat to listen to you.'

However nicely Josie read it was obviously enough to send Aunt Charlotte off to sleep. Mrs Rodgerson smiled at Josie as she gently removed her mistress's spectacles and laid them on a little table nearby.

'Poor lady,' Janet said quietly, 'she can't sleep at night without a sleeping draught, but she can drop off any time during the day.'

'You look after her well,' Josie said, also keeping her voice down. 'My cousin Philip must be very grateful to you.'

Mrs Rodgerson flushed and looked pleased. 'Well, that's as may be. But now would you like a cup of tea?' When Josie nodded she said, 'I'll go and see if Cook can spare a slice or two of that raisin cake. Oh, my goodness, where's Flora?'

Josie looked towards the window seat but her sister was no longer there.

'I didn't see her leave, did you?' Janet Rodgerson asked.

'No.' Josie started to get up.

'You stay there and keep an eye on your aunt. If her feet fall off the footstool it jolts her old bones. I'll go and see if Flora's all right.'

When Janet Rodgerson came back a little later she told Josie, 'Tea and cake on its way. And I caught up with Flora just as she was going out.'

'Out?'

'She's not going far. She said she needs some fresh air so she's going to walk in the grounds. Divven't fret – she's all wrapped up in that bonny new cloak. Ah, here's the tea.'

Flora couldn't resist leaving the path and walking across the frosted grass in order to hear the crunching sound her footsteps made. Then she stopped and breathed out several times just to see the way her breath misted in the cold air. She could feel her cheeks stinging and decided she wouldn't stay out long.

The gardens surrounding the house by the moor looked attractive, even in the winter. Flora had no knowledge of garden flowers or plants but she could see that the grounds surrounding the house had been arranged so that there was always something in flower, or a splash of colour, no matter what month of the year it was.

She stopped to admire some spidery yellow and orange flowers borne on bare branches; Josie had told her that she thought they were witch hazel and she intended to make some preliminary sketches and then, perhaps, paint some water-colours.

Flora wandered along the path towards the heather garden, which was near the boundary wall. She stopped and frowned when she realized that the gate that led out on to the Town Moor was ajar. She was pretty sure it was always kept closed, although in her few excursions into the grounds she had never been curious enough to try it to see whether it was locked.

Then, as she began to walk towards the gate in order to investigate, she heard a scuffling noise behind her. Fearing it was a hungry fox or some other wild creature, she stopped and spun round. The lower branches of a leafy shrub shook violently and a small, raggedy dog emerged. On seeing her it seemed as startled as she was. It yelped and then promptly sat, looked up at her through overhanging wisps of hair and raised one paw.

Flora smiled. 'Hello, doggy,' she said. 'Are you trespassing? And do you want me to shake a paw?'

Small though it was, the dog must have pushed open the

gate, she decided, and she crouched down, about to take the paw it offered. She hesitated. 'Are you tame?' she asked. 'Will you bite?'

'Rags won't hurt you,' a voice she recognized said. 'He wants to be friends.'

Flora almost fell over as she rose and spun round at the same time. 'How did you get here?' she gasped.

'Steady,' Vincent said, and he reached forward to stop her from falling. He held her arms for a moment and she stared into his eyes as if hypnotized. His smile was insolent.

'My, that's a bonny red cloak,' he said.

Flora leaped back, righted herself and faced him with eyes blazing. 'Go away,' she said. 'You promised I'd never see you again!'

'Yes, I'm sorry about that, but things didn't go quite to plan, did they?'

They stared at each other and the little dog, perhaps sensing the tension in the air, got up and ran to hide amongst the shrubs.

'I did everything you told me to. It wasn't my fault that things went wrong,' Flora said at last.

'Wasn't it? Are you sure you and the American didn't hatch a plan to stop me getting away?'

'Why would I do that?'

'Conscience. I could tell you had long stopped enjoying our game.'

'It wasn't a game! And I did want to stop. But you said that if I did you would . . . you would tell people what I'd done. You would expose me.'

'I did, didn't I? And there's even more reason now why you would want me to keep quiet, isn't there?'

Flora felt the ice forming inside her. 'What do you mean?'

'You hope to marry Forbes Robson. I don't suppose an important man like that would want a bride who was an accomplished little thief, would he? And your poor father – I hear he's getting better – I would hate to be the bearer of news that would cause him to relapse or even to . . .'

'Even to what?'

'Perhaps even to die.'

'Don't! Don't say that! Please, please go away and stop tormenting me!'

'I will. This won't take long. I'll tell you how you can end the torment once and for all. Listen very carefully.'

True to his word it took only a few minutes for Vincent to tell her what he wanted her to do, then he left her standing on the path near the shrubbery and exited the garden through the gate that led on to the moor. He closed the gate behind him and it was only then that Rags emerged from his hiding place under the shrubs and raced barking after his master. But the gate was firmly closed and there was nothing the dog could do.

Chapter Eighteen

Josie pulled on her cloak and hurried out into the garden. She thought Flora had been out rather a long time in the cold. She was worried that her sister had been upset by Aunt Charlotte's conversation earlier so she wanted to make sure that the younger girl was all right.

She had spotted a flash of red from the window of the morning room and realized that Flora was heading towards the heather garden. The quickest way would be to slip out through the conservatory. She was careful to close the door behind her to keep in the warmth needed by the profusion of exotic plants.

The first thing she heard was the barking of a dog. Well, it was more like an agonized yelping and there was also a desperate scrabbling sound. As she turned a corner in the shrubbery she saw two things: the figure of her sister standing completely still in the middle of the path and just a short way beyond her a little dog hurling itself at the gate that led out on to the moor.

Josie had no idea how the little creature had got into the grounds of the house but it obviously wanted to get out again and she couldn't understand why Flora wouldn't put it out of its misery.

'What's the matter, Flora?' she called as she came up behind her. 'Are you frightened of the dog? I'll open the gate and let it out, shall I?'

Flora remained silent. She didn't acknowledge Josie's presence in any way. In fact she held herself so still that Josie thought she must have gone into a state of shock. Before walking past her sister towards the gate she stopped and touched her arm. She could feel Flora trembling.

'You're cold,' Josie said. 'You've stayed out here too long. Go back to the house. I'll see to the dog.'

Alerted by a muffled cry of pain she turned to look at Flora's face – and was shocked by what she saw. Her sister was crying. Her eyes were red and the lids swollen as tears streamed down her face.

'What is it?' Josie breathed. 'What has happened?' A solution presented itself. 'Has the dog bitten you?'

Flora shook her head. She made no effort to move so Josie said, 'Right, stay there, I'll let the poor thing out, and then we'll go back to the house together.'

But before she could move the gate began to open and there was a moment of confusion. Flora gasped and covered her face with her hands. The dog, not waiting for the gate to open more fully, seemed to leap and swerve through the gap and its yelps changed to joyous barks as, no doubt, it took off across the moor. And then Jacob Goodwright walked into the garden.

'What are you doing here?' Josie asked.

She heard a gasp of surprise from Flora. 'Do you know him?' her sister whispered through spread fingers.

'Of course I do. Look. It's Jacob Goodwright. Who did you think it was?'

Flora stopped shaking. But she refused to take her hands away from her face. Jacob closed the gate and came towards them. 'Flora thought it was Vincent Telford coming back,' he said.

Josie stared at him. 'What are you talking about? No one called Vincent Telford has been here.'

Flora uttered a low groan. Jacob remained silent. Josie looked from one to the other. 'And what on earth are you doing in those clothes?' she couldn't help saying when she took in at last the shabby patched overcoat Jacob was wearing and the long knitted muffler wound round his neck.

Jacob smiled. 'The clothes I'll explain later but, as for the other questions, I think it's time Flora told you what has been happening.'

'Flora?' Josie asked wonderingly. 'What does this mean?'

Her sister shook her head violently. 'I can't! I can't!' she exclaimed.

'You must, Flora,' Jacob said. He sounded stern. 'If you don't then I won't be able to help you.'

'Help me?' At last Flora dropped her hands and looked up. 'No one can help me!'

Jacob's expression softened. 'Let's go inside,' he said. He began to unwind the greasy muffler and undo the buttons of his coat. He took it off and, folding it, placed it over his arm. Its ragged condition was no longer obvious. 'I don't want to embarrass you,' he explained to a bewildered Josie, 'but we really must go in and talk about what has just happened.'

Once inside the house they went into the library. A fire burned in the hearth and pale sunlight falling through the tall, mullioned windows revealed shelves full of leather-bound books decorated with gold trim. Aunt Charlotte had examined many of them when she had first arrived and announced that, in her opinion, the books had been bought by the yard simply to dress the room.

Nevertheless, she had opined, there was some good reading here and it would mean she would no longer be dependent on the vagaries of the library deliveries for some time.

The furnishings of the room strove to reflect an atmosphere of culture: there were paintings on the walls and the latest literary magazines were displayed on the table. Josie had wondered whether the magazines were changed regularly even when none of the family was in residence, or whether someone had thoughtfully ordered them when it was arranged that Aunt Charlotte, Flora and herself should move here.

They had met no one as they entered the house through the conservatory, and now Jacob laid his coat across one of the chairs and kneeled to build up the fire. Josie removed her own cloak and then went to assist Flora. Her sister was icy cold and trembling. Josie chafed her hands and made her sit by the fire.

When the fire was blazing satisfactorily Jacob rose and looked around. His eye fell on a small table where there was a tray bearing a cut-glass decanter and several small glasses. He took the stopper out of the decanter and sniffed. 'Brandy,' he said, and he smiled. 'And I think it's a good one. But good or not, it's what we all need.'

He filled three glasses and, kneeling before Flora, he placed one of them carefully in her trembling hands. He waited until her hands steadied round the bowl and then he rose and gave another glass to Josie. 'Sip it slowly,' he said.

Josie obeyed him and found that she welcomed the fiery taste. Flora looked up at her with big eyes as if seeking permission, and Josie nodded. Her sister hesitated before she took a sip from her glass and then she said 'Ugh!' Josie smiled. That was more like the girl she knew.

Jacob had arranged chairs for himself and Josie near the fire, and as soon as they were settled he said, 'Flora, it's time you told your sister about Vincent Telford.'

Flora sighed and it seemed her sigh came from the very depths of her despair. 'Do I have to?' she asked.

'Well, I could tell her what I have discovered. And I could guess what has been happening. But I don't know how you met him in the first place, do I?'

Flora bit her lip and looked down into her glass of brandy. In the silence that followed Josie noticed how the firelight gleamed on the glass and how it softened her sister's delicate features, making her look more beautiful than ever.

'Flora?' Jacob prompted after a while.

'Oh, very well, I suppose I must,' Flora said, and she took another sip of brandy, this time appearing to savour it, before she began to tell them how she had met Vincent in the Grainger Market one day and exactly what had happened next.

Josie listened and she was appalled. More than once, as Flora continued the miserable tale, she drew in her breath and opened her mouth, about to ask a question, but Jacob caught her eye and shook his head. Josie knew that he was warning her not to interrupt the flow, instructing her that it was better to let Flora tell it her own way, no matter how she stumbled over the details, and regardless of the fact that tears were streaming down her face.

'But I told him I didn't want to go on with it,' she said at one point, 'and he promised I would never see him again if I helped him steal the jewels at Angela's birthday party!'

Josie could restrain herself no longer. 'Why on earth didn't you tell me?' she asked.

'How could I? I was so ashamed – and I really thought that would be the end of it!'

'But to steal from our friends? Didn't you see how wrong that was?'

'Of course I did. But I was trapped. And, in any case, Vincent told me that no one would suffer. That the insurance company would "pay up", as he put it.'

'But some of that jewellery was of sentimental value to the girls who owned it. Didn't you think of that?'

'Yes . . . I did.'

'And is that why you didn't take my necklace and earrings?' Josie asked.

Flora couldn't meet her eye. 'Yes. Our father gave them to you.'

'You gave Vincent your own necklace and earrings.'

'Only because he said it would look suspicious if I didn't. He didn't know I hadn't taken yours.'

'And put them in your evening bag with the rest.'

'How did you know about the bag?'

'You dropped it in the garden. But don't worry. Nobody knows except a young gardener and me.'

Flora looked anguished. 'What could I do? Vincent threatened to expose me. To tell Father somehow exactly what I had done. To tell the world! Don't you see what that would have meant? Not only would I have gone to prison but it would have brought disgrace on all of us. Don't you see? I was trapped. I just couldn't think what else to do. Why don't you believe me?'

'Oh, Flora. I do believe you. What a tangle.'

Now that Flora had confessed Josie couldn't bring herself to add to her distress by telling her that Angela had suspected she was involved.

'Please don't look at me like that! I've been wicked, I know, but I didn't mean to be, and I never meant it to get this far.'

'Of course you didn't.' Jacob, who had been silent until now, spoke decisively. 'And you haven't been wicked, just young and foolish and extremely gullible. Of course it was wrong of you to take trinkets from the shops and the market stalls, there is no excusing that, but after that it was Vincent Telford who was the wicked one. He is an experienced thief and he exploited you. I've met many men like him.'

'Have you? Where?' Flora forgot her misery for a moment and regarded Jacob with startled interest.

Jacob smiled and shook his head. 'That's a long story. I haven't time to tell it now. What is important is that I believe you are truly sorry for what you have done.'

'I am! Even when Vincent started slipping money in my pocket – my share, he called it – I gave it all away to the children in the street – and I've tried to put other things right, believe me.'

'I do, and I'm sure your sister believes you too. The reason that she is sitting there so silently is because she is shocked. Isn't that right, Josie?'

Josie had been staring at Flora as if seeing a different person from the girl she had grown up with. When she heard Jacob's question she said, 'Yes, of course I believe her.' Then, 'Oh, poor, poor Flora. How could I let that happen to you?'

'No, Josie, it's not your fault.'

Flora rose from her chair and then sank on to the floor beside Josie. She rested her head against Josie's knee and Josie began to stroke her hair.

'I've always tried to look after you,' Josie said. 'And I'll always blame myself because I didn't see that you were troubled.'

Jacob got up and looked down at them. 'I'm sorry but we haven't time for this,' he said.

'What do you mean?' Josie asked.

'Flora has confessed and I think we agree that she is sorry for what she has done. But it isn't over yet, is it?'

Flora didn't look up. She shook her head and mumbled, 'No.'

'That's why Vincent came here today, isn't it?'

'Yes. He said I'd never see him again but he's broken his promise.'

'And no doubt threatened you again.'

'Yes.'

'He's blackmailing you. Probably he's even said that if you were exposed as a thief now, it would kill your father.'

'Yes.'

'What does he want you to do?'

'Wait a moment,' Josie said. 'I'm not sure how you know so much about what has been happening.'

'I've been following Vincent Telford ever since the night of the jewel robbery. That explains my strange manner of dressing, by the way,' he smiled. 'It's a disguise.' Then he continued, 'If Vincent had been a common thief trying his luck and failing I might have let it go. But, you see, I'd seen him with Flora. I was in the garden that night when they met by the Chinese pavilion.'

'You knew all along!' Flora said. Startled, she sat back and stared at him almost accusingly. 'Then why didn't you say anything?'

'I kept quiet at the time for obvious reasons.'

'Obvious?' Josie asked.

Jacob seemed to lose a little of his composure. 'Yes . . . my regard for . . . for your stepmother.'

'Oh.'

'And my respect for your father. You should understand that, Josie, after what I told you.'

'Yes, I do.'

Flora looked at them impatiently. 'I don't think I understand what you're talking about. But that doesn't matter. I'm grateful, of course, but even though you've been following the wretch, I still don't know what on earth we can do.'

'First you must tell me what it is he has asked you to steal.'

Both Josie and Flora flinched at his choice of words but Josie said gently, 'I think we must trust him, Flora.'

Flora sighed. 'A picture.'

Josie frowned. 'A picture from this house, you mean?'

'Yes.'

'Any picture?'

'No. It's a special one. He even told me where to find it. In the library.'

'In here?' Josie began to look around.

'Yes.'

'Where? Which one?'

'I don't know, I haven't really looked at the pictures in here, but I can describe it. Vincent said it's by some Dutchman. It's quite small and it's a drawing, not a painting, of an old woman and two children. She's telling them a story.'

'I know it,' Josie said. 'Look, over here.' She led the way to where the picture was hanging.

The three of them stood and looked at it. This was unmistakably the picture that Flora had described. An old woman in a pinafore sat on a wooden armchair and two small children sat at her feet. She was leaning forward, her eyes large and her expression intent. Her hands were raised slightly, one higher than the other, in a classic storyteller's pose. The children, a boy and a girl, sat with their arms wrapped around their legs as they listened, spellbound. There wasn't much background to the scene, just the hint of a hearth, a steaming cooking pot, and a sleeping cat.

'It's wonderful,' Josie said.

'Well, yes, it's very appealing,' her sister agreed. 'But surely it can't be worth as much as Vincent thinks it is?'

'I suppose some people – rich collectors – would pay a great deal of money for something like this,' Josie said. 'But I'm not sure why, if Vincent knew of its existence, he didn't just break in when the house was empty. Why is he involving you?'

'Pure spite!' Flora exclaimed. 'Probably because the jewel robbery went wrong. Now he wants to pay me back in some way. And to make me steal from my future husband's family is perfect for him.'

'And that was my fault,' Jacob said. His tone was light but he wasn't smiling. 'And childish though his motives seem to be, Flora may be right. I believe there's an element of revenge in it.'

'But what am I going to do?' Flora sounded desperate again. 'You said you could help me if I told you everything. All we've done is talk about it.'

'What exactly has he told you to do?' Josie asked.

'I'm to parcel the picture up as though it were a present,' Flora said.

'Present?'

'Christmas present. Then I'm to take it with me to the fair on the quayside on Christmas Eve.'

'And then?' Jacob asked.

'That's all he's told me. Oh, I'm to wear the red cloak I was wearing today so that he can spy me out easily.'

'Ah, and no doubt he'll use the cover of the crowd to steal your "present" from you,' Jacob said.

'Yes,' she said bleakly. 'So what shall I do?'

'You must go to the fair.'

Janet Rodgerson had been surprised but delighted when she'd knocked and entered the library to find Jacob there. She had come to tell the girls that their lunch was ready and she insisted that Jacob should join them. She bustled away to see to the extra place without giving him time to refuse.

Jacob reflected that Janet's appearance was convenient. There was no time for Flora to protest. He assured her that he had a plan but he was pleased when Janet reappeared to chivvy them along to the dining room, not only because he didn't want to say too much, but also because he would have much to do before his 'plan' was fit to be put into execution.

Mrs Bertram was pleased to have a guest and she asked him about his work at the mission as well as wanting to know more about his parents and life in America.

The two older ladies were so keen to engage his attention that they did not seem to notice how quiet Josie and Flora were. After the meal, coffee was served in a pleasant little drawing room, but Charlotte Bertram soon announced she was tired and she needed a nap.

'I keep telling you – if you sleep now, you won't sleep tonight,' Janet Rodgerson told her.

'Then I could just lie resting on the bed and you could read to me,' her employer said.

'Well, I could, I suppose, but I'm sick of the way you keep correcting me pronunciation. Yesterday when I read that love story to you, you said I quite spoiled the romance of it all!'

'Then Flora shall come and read to me.'

The younger girl looked surprised. 'Oh, but Josie usually does that. She is much better at reading aloud than I am.'

'That's true but I think you should take your turn. Josie does too much for us all, don't you think?'

Flora had no option but to agree, and Jacob and Josie were soon left alone. He was pretty sure from the knowing smile Mrs Bertram had sent his way that this had been contrived. Not because she had divined that he needed to talk to Josie, but because, he suspected, she was attempting a little matchmaking. After all, one of her nieces was spoken for. Why not help the other one along?

'So you really want Flora to take the picture to the Christmas fair?' Josie asked as soon as they were alone.

'Yes.'

'Is stealing from Forbes's family the only way out of her dilemma?'

'Don't worry. I've thought of something. But she will have to be brave.'

'Would she be safe?'

They were sitting at each end of a small sofa and Jacob reached for her hand. 'You'll have to trust me.'

Suddenly Josie found it hard to concentrate. Jacob's hand was cool but the sensation of skin on skin sent shivers of heat racing through her body. 'I do trust you,' she said when she had caught her breath. 'But it would help if you didn't look so worried.'

He tried to smile. 'I must admit there is something that is puzzling me.'

'What is it?'

'I believe the picture to be valuable. I can see why Vincent's father would want it.'

'Vincent's father?'

'Yes, his father is behind all this.'

'How do you know that?'

'I've been following Vincent for some time, remember. I've made it my business to find out – to discover what they might be planning. And, as I said, the picture is undoubtedly valuable, but I believe there's more to it than that.'

'Why?'

'I can't be sure, but I know the man of old. He's dangerous – and he bears grudges.'

'It's the same man who caused you to run away when you were a small boy, isn't it? The man you angered all those years ago.'

'Yes, and your father helped me. And it was not the first time Captain Walton had helped me evade his clutches.'

'So he bears a grudge against my father. He wants revenge?'

'Yes.'

'But why? What on earth had you done to anger him so?'

'This is Betty's story as much as mine, but I suppose you'd better know. One night she nearly killed him.'

When Jacob had finished his tale Josie found that she was weeping for the children Betty and Jacob had once been. 'How dreadful,' she said, 'to live like that.'

'And how fortunate we are now, both Betty and I. And because we owe so much to your father I am determined to help Flora. I must go now but I'll see you again soon.'

Jacob resisted the easy option of getting a cab back into town. When he left the house in Gosforth, he disguised himself in his old clothes again and set off across the Town Moor. He had not told Josie anything of his investigations into her cousin's activities; he did not want Captain Walton's daughters to know how their father might have been cheated out of his business. But Jacob knew enough now to pay Philip a visit, and that was something he'd have to do before dealing with the Telfords.

It was Christmas Eve and Janet Rodgerson couldn't resist walking around the downstairs rooms of the house and admiring the results of her efforts. There was a tall Christmas tree standing in a tub of sand in the hall, hung with gold and silver frosted-glass decorations and little nets full of sweetmeats. Janet had fixed a tinsel star on the top by the simple expedient of going up the curving staircase and leaning over.

She had been helped to dress the tree by two of the maids. She'd hoped Josie and Flora would help her but they had been moping around as if the Christmas season meant nothing to them. Janet supposed they were worried about their father and the fact that their stepmother had discouraged all visits since the move to the coast, so she forgave them.

Her finishing touch to the tree had been to fix dozens of tiny white candles on the branches. But she knew she would probably not dare to light them. She'd read in the newspapers that every Christmas season there were house fires caused by these candles. A blast of wind from an open door, a cat jumping to play with one of the baubles – that was all it might take. So the candles would remain unlit. But nevertheless they did look pretty in their little holders with golden bows.

Janet had never had a Christmas tree before. The most she had aspired to in her married home was to decorate the mantel with some evergreen branches. This year she had holly from the garden and artificial garlands from Bainbridge's to drape around the banister rails. Pine cones crackled in every hearth, adding their aroma to the scent of the fir tree.

The hall table was covered with neighbours' calling cards. Mrs Bertram had been delighted to discover that the folk who lived nearby wished to visit over the festive period and Janet was pleased for her. She would have little joy from either of her nieces with the moods they were in. But at least Philip had promised to call on Christmas Day. He had not indicated whether he would bring his wife, and Janet had persuaded Mrs Bertram to send the lass a nice letter inviting her.

'After all,' she'd said, 'you'd better make friends with her before her time comes or you'll not hev the joy of your grandbairn.'

But now she had the exciting job of hiding all the brightly wrapped boxes that had arrived only this morning. Forbes had sent them. She'd had a letter telling her to look out for them. Each box was labelled. There were large exciting-looking parcels – more than one – for all the family, including Janet, and even small gifts for the household staff.

Janet had found a little cloakroom where waterproof capes and boots were stored and she'd hidden the boxes in there. Tonight, when everyone was asleep, she intended to creep downstairs and arrange them around the tree.

It was time to go up now and wake Mrs Bertram. She'd been taking a nap again and that would probably mean she'd need a sleeping draught tonight. The doctor had assured Janet that the draughts were harmless but Janet argued that Mrs Bertram wouldn't need them if only she would stay awake during the day!

She walked upstairs slowly, savouring the look and the smell of the tree, and then, suddenly, she stopped as a name from the past flew into her mind to disturb her. *Douglas . . .*

She hadn't thought about her errant husband for months but now she found herself wondering whether he would be somewhere on the high seas on Christmas morn, or at home in a far country with his new little family. With the little lad who looked so like him and maybe another bairn by now.

'Douglas, Douglas, why did you hev to do that,' she whispered. 'Didn't yer realize you would break me poor heart?'

She waited for the familiar gloom to descend. And then realized that, not only did it not descend, but she hadn't felt gloomy for a long while now. She'd been too busy. And too happy. Yes, she realized with a lightening of spirit, she'd been happy. And she owed it all to Jacob Goodwright for finding her this position, and to Captain Walton for trusting her enough to take her into his home.

Jack had hung holly and mistletoe from the old beams in the kitchen and arranged evergreen branches along the polished shelves of the dresser. The scrubbed table was covered with food that was being prepared for the meal they would eat tomorrow, on Christmas Day. Hannah looked around and smiled, taking comfort from the age-old traditions.

There would be just the three of them: herself, Jack and Betty. Hannah wished her granddaughters were coming but they had promised to keep their Aunt Charlotte company in the grand house in Gosforth. However, the girls had promised they would visit Moorburn as soon as possible in the new year. Hannah would have to be content with that.

You would have thought from the amount of food on the table that she was going to feed an army but that was because from tonight onwards, there would be many visitors at the door, including the guisers with their play of St George and the Dragon. When St George had slain the dragon, and the floor was littered with the bodies of the men-at-arms, the man playing the doctor would bring everyone back to life and they would expect to be fed for their pains. Hence the preparations.

But the post had just been delivered and Hannah had given Betty the nod to clear a space at the end of the table and sit down with her letter. The lass sensed Hannah's eyes on her and she looked up and smiled.

'Is that from your friend Jacob?' Hannah mouthed clearly.

Betty nodded.

'He's well?'

Another nod and she went back to reading.

Hannah watched as the young woman smiled and frowned and smiled again, and she thought that the lass was giving every indication of a young woman in love. In fact, when she thought about it, and remembered how normally sensible Betty had been mooning about the place for some time now, she was pretty sure that her guess was right. And that worried her.

For she didn't know why, certainly nobody had told her anything, but she was almost certain that Josie favoured the young American too. And Hannah loved Josie with all her heart. She always had done, ever since the early days when she'd worried that Effie was not such a loving mother as she ought to be. Poor Josie, was she going to be overlooked again?

Suddenly she decided that she had to know. She went to stand beside Betty and put a hand on her shoulder. The lass looked up and smiled. Very clearly, so that Betty could read her lips, she asked, 'Do you love the man?'

Betty looked startled. She framed the word, 'Who?'

'Jacob, Jacob Goodwright.'

Betty reached for the notepad that she always kept in the pocket of her pinafore and wrote, 'Jacob is my friend.'

'I know that.' Hannah found herself getting agitated. 'But do you want to marry him?'

Betty shook her head. But she was smiling.

'What is it? What's so funny?' Hannah had never been vexed with the girl until this moment.

Betty saw Hannah's frown and she began to scribble furiously. 'I love you,' she wrote. 'You have been a mother to me. We were going to wait until he has a house but now I must tell you.'

'Tell me what?'

'John will be coming to see you,' she scribbled.

'John? Who's John? Oh . . . the lad who works at the kiosk in the station!'

Betty was nodding and smiling. She tried to write something else but her hands were shaking. Hannah reached for them to steady them and then she took Betty in her arms and hugged her. Then she drew back so that the lass could read her lips again.

'I'll miss you, but I won't stand in your way. And I'm right happy for you,' she said. 'Now let me have that notepad.'

Betty watched as Hannah began to write. 'Put your coat on,' Hannah said, pointing to where the coats hung on a rack by the door. Then speaking clearly she gave the lass the note. 'You can read it. It's an invitation. Run down to the station and give it to John. Jack and I will be pleased if he would join us at the inn on Christmas Day.'

Annie remembered all the years she had made every effort to make Christmas a happy time for Samuel's daughters in the house on the quayside, and relished the fact that tomorrow she and Samuel would spend the day alone together.

Samuel had told her that he was quite well enough to go to church in the morning – and he would walk along to St George's, if she didn't mind. And then they would take lunch at the Bay Hotel before returning to sit by their own fire in their comfortable ground-floor apartment in the old house over-looking the sea.

She had not bothered with a Christmas tree but had settled for a holly wreath or two and made sure that there was a sufficient supply of little luxuries. Philip had brought them a hamper containing among other things a fruit cake, shortbread biscuits, sugared almonds, gentleman's relish, port-wine and brandy. Conscience troubling him, she'd thought. She had felt like telling him to take it back again, but didn't know how she would have explained that to Samuel.

Her husband was so much better of late, and he had started talking of the day he would get back to work. So far both Annie and the doctor had convinced him that he would have to wait awhile yet, and that even when he did get back to work it must only be in an advisory capacity at first.

But now he spent his days reading, walking a little and resting when he needed to. And at night they slept in each other's arms as they had never done before. It was for comfort only, but Annie had begun to hope that their loving proximity would eventually lead to much more than that and that they would become the true lovers that they had never been before.

'Annie,' she heard him calling her from his seat near the window.

He had been reading the Bible, which lay open on his knee. She was alarmed to see that tears were streaming down his cheeks.

'What is it, Samuel?'

'I am strong now.'

'I know that. Almost every day there is an improvement.'

'You have looked after me, you have . . . protected . . . me.'

Annie was silent. What was he going to say? Was he going to tell her that now he was so much better he no longer needed her?

'You are happy?' he asked.

She saw that he was smiling that endearing lop-sided smile, and her fears died. 'Yes, oh, yes,' she said.

'And you make me happy. But . . .'

'What is it, Samuel?'

'When shall I see my daughters?'

'You mean you want Josie to come and visit us? I'll write to her straight away.'

'No.' He shook his head. 'Not just Josie, I want to see both my daughters.'

'Flora? But . . . ?'

'Look.' Samuel lifted the Bible and gave it to her, pointing to the passage he had been reading: 'The soul that sinneth, it shall die. The son shall not bear the iniquity of the father . . .'

Annie read no more. She looked up at him.

'Nor the daughter the iniquity of the mother,' Samuel said softly.

'But Flora . . . Flora is not . . .'

'She must never know,' he said. 'No one must know.' And then he grasped her hand and looked at her intently. 'I love Flora,' he said. 'I love both my daughters. We shall be a family again, Annie. Isn't that what you want?'

As Samuel looked searchingly into her eyes Annie knew

that whatever made this man happy would make her happy too. Too full of emotion to speak, she simply nodded.

'Good,' Samuel said. 'For, if I have that, I have everything.'

A group of mummers made up of high-spirited young men had crowded into the hall of the house in Gosforth and performed their little play for the benefit of the family and the servants. The performance was accompanied by much laughter and forgetting of lines – and falling over. Janet Rodgerson, charmed by the whole experience, had seen to it that they were well rewarded with mince pies and fruit punch. She closed her eyes to the fact that the young maidservants were all seized and kissed heartily underneath the mistletoe bough.

Mrs Bertram had also enjoyed herself, especially when the young men, as a parting gesture, sang her favourite carols for her. She had gone to bed early, happy and tired and declaring that there would be no need for a sleeping draught after all.

When she'd settled her, Janet came down again to find Josie and Flora sitting at each side of the hearth, not talking to each other. She wished she knew what on earth was the matter with the pair of them; they were as jumpy as a pair of cats.

Flora was reading a letter. From her beau, of course. Janet knew that Forbes Robson intended to visit soon because he'd written to Mrs Bertram to ask permission, and you'd have thought the lass would be overjoyed instead of pale-faced and nervy. Then she saw that Josie was trying to catch her eye.

As soon as Josie realized that Janet Rodgerson had come downstairs again she rose from her seat and hurried out into the hall. Janet understood her glance, thank goodness, and followed her out.

'Janet, I wonder if you could make us all a drink of hot chocolate. You know how Flora likes hot chocolate.'

'Why, of course I do. I'll ring for the lass, shall I?'

'No, I'd like you to make it yourself, if you don't mind.'

'No, I divven't mind. Are you not wanting to give anyone in the kitchen extra work on Christmas Eve, like?'

'No, it's not that. Oh dear . . .'

'What is it, pet? What's troubling you?'

Josie looked into the woman's kind face and realized that

the best thing to do would be to confide in her, at least partially. 'I was going to do this myself,' she said, 'I wasn't going to tell anyone, but I think it's best if you know.'

'Know what? You're beginning to alarm me!'

'No, don't be alarmed. Everything will be all right. But I want you to make the chocolate and put some of my aunt's sleeping draught in Flora's cup.'

'You what? But why?'

'I can't explain now. I don't know if I ever will be able to explain fully, but I'm asking you to trust me. Flora's tired, exhausted. She hasn't slept properly for days now. I'm sure the draught will work. I'll get her to her room, then I want you to stay with her and look after her. But most of all keep her there.'

'And what am I to say if she wakes up?'

Josie thought for a moment and then said, 'Tell her there's nothing to worry about – that it's all over.'

Janet looked at her long and hard. 'I'm going to do what you say,' she said at last. 'I divven't know why, but I trust you. But promise me one thing.'

'What's that?'

'That one day, if the time's right, you'll tell me what this is all about.'

'I can make that promise, but I don't know if the time will ever be right, Janet. That's all I can say.'

Janet's kindly face lit up with a rueful smile. 'Well, I suppose that'll hev to do. Now gan in and sit by the fire and I'll make the hot chocolate.'

Wrapped snugly in her red velvet cloak with the hood pulled well forward, Josie slipped out of the house and made her way to the High Street. The frost sparkled on the pavement and groups of revellers, some of them carol singers, hurried by, sometimes slipping and laughing as they caught on to each other for support.

Josie had decided to take the tram into town, remaining as anonymous as possible, and then alight at the Haymarket and take a cab down to the quayside. Plenty of people would be making their way to the fair and the cab driver, she hoped, would not make much of a lone young woman going there too.

The cab driver obviously wanted to get as many fares as possible on the night before Christmas Day and he bowled through town at a much faster pace than usual. Josie held on tightly during the final descent down the steep street that led to the quayside.

The fair was in full swing although it was much rowdier than it had been when Josie was a child. But then she had never been to the fair as late as this before. She remembered watching it from her bedroom window, though; the music and the laughter drifting upwards along with the odours of ale and fried food.

There was still quite a crowd enjoying the sideshows and buying trinkets from the stalls. She made her way to the children's roundabout. Vincent couldn't have known that the little wooden horses held such memories for her when he had arranged this as the meeting place. But, in any case, Vincent had told Flora to meet him there, not Josie.

She watched the ragged boys pushing the dobbies; saw the excitement on the faces of the few tired children who were left to ride them and the fond expressions of the watching parents. For a moment she almost forgot why she was there and then she felt a touch on her arm. Not just a casual touch: someone's thumb and fingers applied pressure. It was the sign. Then, a whisper. If she had not been expecting it she would never have heard it above the music of the merry-go-round.

'Have you brought it?'

She prayed that Jacob was watching as he'd said he would be. He hadn't told her what was going to happen next. Only that once Flora had handed over the picture she was to go home. She felt the pressure again and an impatient cough. She eased the small parcel out from the protective layers of her cloak and angled it sideways, expecting it to be snatched away from her. But instead the unseen hand seized her arm and began to drag her backwards.

'No!' she gasped with surprise and stumbled slightly.

As she did so her hood fell back and a voice said, 'You! Where's Flora?'

She looked up at the startled features of a young, well-dressed man – Vincent, she supposed. Before she could frame an answer he said, 'Never mind, I don't suppose it matters which sister it is,' and he began to drag her away.

'Where are we going?' she asked.

'Be quiet. My father wants you to hand the picture over to him in person. That's all.'

'Where is he?'

'Not far.'

He took her arm and guided her past the stalls and sideshows as if they were any couple enjoying the fair. But soon the crowds thinned and the lights and music faded. There was no sign that Jacob was following them. Josie was afraid.

The buildings they passed grew more ramshackle, the alleys darker, the gutters ranker. Eventually they stopped before an old warehouse, boarded up and obviously deserted.

'Who's this?' a voice whispered out from the shadows. 'You said she was a bonny blonde.'

'Her sister,' Vincent said. 'Does it matter?'

Silence. Then, 'You said he doted on her – the young 'un, I mean.'

'Well, she didn't come. I don't know why,' Vincent said, and there was a note of desperation in his voice. 'But this one's brought the picture. That's all you wanted, isn't it? Can't we get this over with?'

'Let me see it.'

Vincent took the parcel from Josie and tore off the wrapping. He held it out and, at last, the other man emerged from the shadows. Jacob had said that this was a dangerous man, an evil man, and Josie could well believe it. She had never seen such an expression of menace.

He took the picture from his son's hands and looked at it. 'Aye, that's it,' he said.

'And is it really worth a king's ransom?'

'Aye, well, mebbes it is, or mebbes I exaggerated. But the lass, now, whichever one it is, she's worth a ransom. A captain's ransom, if yer get my drift.'

'Kidnap! They'll hang you!'

'If they catch me. Which they won't. Not in this country. Come, then, little lass, are you ready to sail tonight? Take a trip with Fox Telford? Let's hev a proper look at you.'

The man stepped forward and grabbed Josie's arm. He pulled her so close that she could smell his foetid breath. She shrank back and managed to land a kick on his shins. But it wasn't that that made him loosen his grip. Someone had come up behind him and slipped an arm across his throat.

Fox Telford fell backwards but managed to squirm free. He turned to face his assailant and saw a stranger. And yet the face was familiar. An old memory stirred; an old hatred began to rise – then sank again into confusion when the man spoke with a Yankee drawl.

'Miss Walton isn't going anywhere, but you are,' Jacob said. 'And you're never coming back.'

The man laughed. 'And who are you to make me go anywhere?'

'It doesn't matter who I am. Look around you. Do you know these men?'

Fox frowned and then swung round as several figures stepped out of the shadows. Three, then four, but Josie noticed that another man hung back.

None of the men said anything but it was obvious that Fox Telford knew them – and that he was frightened.

'I can see that you do know them,' Jacob said. 'There are bigger fish than you in the sea, aren't there?'

'But why? Why should these fellers bother with me? I've never crossed them,' Fox muttered.

'It doesn't matter why. Just go – and take your son with you.'

The silent watchers had started closing in on Fox and he began to back away.

'Wait,' Jacob said. 'The picture.'

A look of pain crossed the man's face, then there was a moment of indecision before he turned and ran, still clutching the picture. One of the silent watchers took off after him but they didn't go far. Realizing that he would be outrun, Fox turned and raised the picture high above his head.

'If I can't hev it, nobody can!' he yelled and threw the picture in the river as far out as he could. But the effort to hurl it that far was his undoing. Unable to control his momentum he stumbled and fell from the quay into the filthy water.

'Father!' Vincent shouted and raced to the quay's edge. He

began to take off his coat as he peered desperately into the murky depths.

'Don't go in unless you can see him,' Jacob said as he came to his side.

'He's my father. I've got to.'

Josie noticed that the other men, save for the one who had not taken any part in what had happened, had melted away. Vincent would not be stopped. He plunged into the river and, to Josie's horror, Jacob also took off his coat and joined him in the water. To no avail. Eventually they had to give up and sat dripping on the quay.

'Don't worry, you won't hear from me again,' Vincent said as he got up to leave.

Jacob nodded an acknowledgement.

Vincent hesitated, then looked at Josie. 'Tell Flora that I wish her well,' he said. Then he left them. They heard his footsteps echoing away.

Only when silence had returned did the other man step out from the shadows. 'You'd better come home with me. I'll lend you some clean clothes,' Josie's cousin Philip said.

They sat by the fire in the kitchen of her old home and Jacob explained that it was Philip who had been able to call in some favours from the men who had helped them that night.

While Philip went to find clean clothes, Jacob explained, 'Your cousin knows how much he owes your father and it was not difficult to persuade him to help us.'

'But how does he know such people?' Josie asked.

'The trade he's in. They can't be avoided.'

And before she could question him further Jacob added, 'I've been talking to Philip lately, about your father. He's assured me that when Captain Walton wants to return to business, he'll find everything in order.'

Josie had the feeling that there was much that Jacob was not saying but at that point Philip returned and said, 'Patience has filled a bath for you.' Josie thought her cousin strangely subdued. 'I hope you'll find everything you need.'

Jacob thanked him, then smiled at Josie. 'I won't be long,' he said. 'And then I'll take you home.'

Later, in the hansom cab on the way back to the house in Gosforth, Josie said, 'Can we really be confident that Flora's troubles are over?'

'Yes,' Jacob said. 'Unless she concocts some more for herself.'

'She won't. Flora has learned her lesson. She's changed so much lately. Forbes will find a more thoughtful and considerate girl when he comes to claim her.'

'Let's hope that's what he wants,' Jacob said. 'And as for what she has done in the past, she will always have to live with that and wonder if Forbes would still have loved her if he'd known. Poor Flora. Oh no!'

'What is it?' Josie was alarmed.

'He will find out. The picture! My plan was to get it back before frightening Fox off. I never thought he'd throw it in the river. How can we explain away the missing picture?'

'We don't have to,' Josie said. 'The picture isn't missing. I made a copy. And I even found a similar frame. That's why I had to go to meet Vincent instead of Flora. If they'd realized it was a forgery they might have harmed her.'

Jacob shook his head. 'You must love your sister very much.'

'I do.'

'But for God's sake, Josie, what a risk you took!'

His voice was ragged and in the close confines of the cab she could sense the rawness of his emotion. Suddenly he took her hand and, placing it over his heart, he covered it with both of his.

'Can you feel my heart racing?' he asked, and he attempted a laugh. 'I don't believe it has quieted since the moment your hood fell back and I saw it was you instead of Flora. Thank God you came to no harm!'

'Thanks to you,' Josie whispered.

They stared at each other in the dimness, as if seeking in each other's eyes the words that might soon be said. Then Jacob smiled.

'Flora will be all right, you know,' he said, 'when she marries Forbes. He will take good care of her.'

'Why are you telling me this?'

'Because I'm worried that you will do something crazy like marrying Ambrose.'

'Why should I do that?'

'By marrying Forbes's brother you would be able to stay close to Flora, when that is the last thing you should do.'

'Why the last thing?'

Jacob sighed and drew her into his arms. The horse's hoofs clattered over the cobbles but Josie could hardly hear them over the beating of her own heart.

'I thought you would have realized by now,' he said. 'I love you. I think I have loved you since the day I first saw you when we were children. In all those years in America I never stopped hoping that I would see you again. And now I hope I can persuade you that there is only one possible future for you, and that is to marry me.'

Josie knew that no matter what the years might bring she would never again experience such a moment of astonishing happiness. Jacob loved her. She savoured the thought. In a moment she would tell him that she loved him, and always had. That he had been in her heart since the day, as a ragged boy, he had caught her sister's doll.

'Josie . . . ?' he murmured.

She turned her face towards him, ready to tell him what he wanted to hear. But before she could form the words he had covered her mouth with a kiss.